STOP ME
IF YOU'VE HEARD
THIS ONE BEFORE

DAVID YOO

HYPERION
NEW YORK

First Edition

1 3 5 7 9 10 8 6 4 2
This book is set in 11-point Sabon.
Designed by Alexander Garkusha
Printed in the United States of America
Library of Congress Cataloging-in-Publication Data on file.
Reinforced binding
ISBN 978-1-4231-0907-5
Visit www.hyperionteens.com

For Jessica

Acknowledgments

Thanks be to the following: my tireless editor, Donna Bray, along with the exhausted but indestructible Emily Schultz, the Atlas-like Jennifer Besser, and everyone else over at Hyperion; Steven "De Lovely" Malk and his ruthless boss, Lindsay "I forgive but I never forget" Davis, over at Writers House; my family and friends, who seem to only grow in number as I continue to slowly defang as the years go by; and most of all, mad ups be to multiplatinum, award-winning solo-recording artist Phil Collins, for graciously allowing us to reprint a portion of the lyrics to his painfully honest hit single, "A Groovy Kind of Love."

They say a baby's true baptism occurs
when he first falls out of bed.

—Lucia Berlin

Here It Is Saturday

The first time I met Mia we ended up in a hotel room by ourselves. I remember the room was blue because of the semiclosed shades. The jiggle of teacups on a room-service cart as it rolled past the door. An odor of stale cigarette smoke seeping out the pores of the yellowed, beige wallpaper. Despite the perpetual thrum of the air-conditioning that rattled the vanity mirror, the room felt windless, and in the bluish light I saw that she was staring at me, and I immediately looked away. This was the start of our story that I'm about to tell you—a traditional love story, in the sense that it ends badly.

It's like a rule that love stories have to end badly, and ours is no exception. *Romeo and Juliet*, the most famous love story of all time, ends tragically, and the hero and heroine's sad fate is precisely why it remains such an enduring love story, despite the fact that to the majority of people in today's high school society it's completely unreadable without an accompanying page-by-page Folger Shakespeare guide. But I digress.

Had the star-crossed lovers' plan actually succeeded, they would have lived past that initial honeymoon stage and eventually felt complacent, having to look at the same face for the rest of their lives. Romeo would have belatedly realized his true love for his fallen male buddy, Mercutio, and experimented with a sleazy local bard in an effort to quell the confusing mixture of disgust and numbness he felt lying stiff in bed with Juliet each night. Juliet, meanwhile, wouldn't even notice Romeo's emerging gaydom because she'd be pining for the same local hipster bard (think today's artsy-fartsy acoustic guitar–playing posers in the cafeteria, except with harps) as well, which means by that point what was left of their love story would have long since been extinguished.

But instead, it all ended badly for them, and that's why it's a classic love story. It's hard to believe their genius plan didn't work—she put herself into a medically induced coma in order to fake her own death, before being hidden in the family crypt. I mean, that's just gangbusters. But anyhow, this story that I'm about to tell you is just like theirs, except in my version Juliet screws over Romeo and doesn't off herself. Instead she ends up with another guy and lives happily ever after, while Romeo is crushed and goes a little crazy and ends up dying, completely alone, of a broken heart.

Maybe this isn't even a love story at all. You know that

famous question: If a tree falls in the woods and nobody is around to hear it, does it make a sound? Well, by that rationale, a similar question can be applied to my story: If a guy falls down in the woods and the girl he's deeply in love with doesn't hear it, did he make a sound—and more important, would she have given two shits if she *had* heard him? The point being, it's hard to classify a story as a love story once the actual "love" aspect of it no longer exists, and I know now that while my flame for her still burned Bunsen blue inside me, hers had long since been snuffed out. But ultimately, debating whether this is a valid love story is irrelevant, really, because all I know is that this is *my story*, and my story is of my love for Mia, and that's all that matters. Thousands of other things have happened to me in my lifetime, but they're, at this point, totally insignificant, because what other story is there to tell once you fall in love for the first time?

What can't be debated is that my story is definitely going to turn out to be a cautionary tale. Future mothers tucking their sons in at night will warn them, "You'd better not try to get what you want in high school, or else you'll get Albert Kimmed." My name will become a national catchphrase denoting abject failure. Pizza delivery guys who get stiffed on their tips will snap their fingers and mutter, "Rats, Albert Kimmed again." College co-eds on the beach in Daytona over spring break will frown up at the sunless sky for the second day in a row and plead, "Please, dear God, don't Albert Kim me up the (a parrot whistles) again."

While there's no question that this love story officially ended this morning in the field behind the school, the true beginnings of this story could be debated. If I were to start right in the thick of things, or what Greek statues (if they got struck by lightning and came alive) would refer to in bellowing voices as *in medias res*, I'd have to begin on the first day of school in the fall, when things got really crazy, when *he* entered the picture. But if I'm going to tell this story right— that is, if I'm going to treat myself fairly as the main character—I'm going to have to start on the first day Mia and I met, at the start of last summer. I need for you to see the whole picture, to understand who I was before the start of this sordid affair. Maybe then you'll come to understand and even sympathize with my actions. Regardless, I get to start this where I want to start it because, like I said, this is *my* story, and what is a story, really, but a narrator's defense?

PART 1

The Inn

In a rare moment of diplomacy last year, my parents actually gave me a choice regarding what to do for the summer. Usually each spring I would beg them to not follow through with the annual Korean-American tradition of overloading me with more activities than I'd had *during* the school year—like private sousaphone lessons and forced volunteer work at the local senior center. I wanted to just stay home like a normal kid so I could kill copious amounts of brain cells watching corny reruns of *The Cosby Show* (I'd developed a belated crush on Lisa Bonet after her wonderful turn in *Angel Heart*) and my all-time favorite TV show *Silver Spoons*. I wanted to spend lonely afternoons aimlessly shooting my BB gun off the back porch at rustling branches, accidentally setting fire to the tips of my bangs over the oven as I experimented with my mom's cigarettes, and enjoying all the other typical trappings of a lazy high school summer for a decidedly loserish teenager growing up in New England. But my parents never granted me this freedom, because, as I mentioned before, they're Asian.

Which is to say that, due to their heritage, my parents don't remotely understand the basic concept of relaxation—to the degree that if either of them ever falls asleep on the plastic-covered sofa downstairs, their mouth remains locked in a pursed expression, and their eyeballs do this freaky tennis match dance behind the lids that's kinda disturbing, yet at the same time utterly mesmerizing to watch. My hypothesis for this unnamed disease that turns them into human hamsters, running on the invisible treadmill of life until either a) exhaustion or b) heart failure greets them, is that their memory of their own childhoods is of constant toil and a complete absence of pleasure. As a result, they've been brainwashed since birth to be of the opinion that a summer spent enjoying life and relaxing is, and I quote my pops on this one, "a summer truly wasted . . . *forever.*"

They unfairly compare every aspect of my life to their own legitimately tragic childhoods, and as a result, everything I do is deemed slothful. Even when I do chores—the laundry, for instance—I can tell my mom's remembering her sorrowful long days as a nine-year-old peasant girl in a little village in South Korea, hunched over a boulder next to a stream, hitting her family's wet clothes with a stick all afternoon in the sun as human proxy for the dryer they could never afford. The expression on my mom's face as she watches me unload the washer and toss the damp bundles into the dryer and run it without cleaning the lint collector, can only translate into one thing: *You are such a lazy-ass.* I've pointed out to them on several occasions that they went through adolescence while the Korean War gripped their countryside, and that their families were both really poor. I constantly remind my mom that all she ever says about her own strict parents implies that they kinda sucked; in which case, my parents' desire to keep me busy and miserable isn't so much the result of their wanting the best for me, but rather their immaturely wanting me to experience what it was like to be them when they were my age so I can feel sorry for them. Anyway, the point is that all my lobbying for warm-weather freedom every year was done in vain . . . at least, until last summer.

My theory for their change of heart is purely visual; specifically, I'd turned sixteen and just endured a major growth spurt that torture-racked me into a gangly six feet tall, which to my parents surely seemed a more Manute Bol-like seven-foot-five, given their vertically challenged perspectives. As a result they couldn't deny that I was no longer a completely malleable little boy, and the thought of handing the adult-size me twenty-dollar bills and impatiently waiting outside of stores at the CambridgeSide Galleria while I "bought" Christmas presents for them seemed pitiful, especially considering that many of their Korean church friends owned liquor stores and wig stores and Laundromats in which their dutiful sons and daughters had been illegally working since like age nine. So my parents finally broke with tradition and gave me two options:

1) I could attend academic boarding camp again (to increase my odds of getting a full ride to a good college), or
2) I could get a job.

Given that my first summer at the camp was an unmitigated disaster, the answer seemed obvious. Boston's branch of the nationally renowned Symposium for Teenage Development is a ten-week boarding summer camp for, according to the brochures, "abnormally curious and advanced teenagers" to take academic courses in preparation for college. Despite having made the personal oath years earlier to stop trying socially at Bern High (I'll get to the "why" in a little while), I admit I'd secretly kinda figured—prior to arriving at this camp full of beautiful-only-on-the-inside teens—that I'd thrive in the lowered social standards of this bookish environment, or at least be considered normal among a bunch of unadulterated geeks. Alas, even at a nerdy academics camp for teens who actually want to study in stifling heat, I was branded a total loser, thanks to a rumor that I'd attempted to pleasure myself during a round table discussion in English class, that succeeded in outcasting me at this camp full of outcasts.

Me, the very fringe of the fringe.

Despite my checkered past at STD, I was still hesitant to choose a job instead. Up to that point in my life, the thought of getting a job hadn't ever crossed my mind. To be perfectly honest, I didn't really need one. As a sixteen-year-old mutant with no real friends (not even fellow mutants with whom to be mutanty together), I had no need for a car, which is traditionally the main impetus for desiring a steady summer paycheck. At first it seemed there weren't any alternative objects of desire in my mental queue. As I sat there contemplating the economic perks of hard labor, I thought, I mean, sure, I could always use a telescope or an authentic replica samurai sword from the back of *Soldier of Fortune* magazine, or a ham radio to talk to lonely truck drivers at night. Truth be told, if I *did* have the funds, I have to admit I feel like I would kinda like a bread maker and—okay fine, screw it.

I chose 2.

2

I live in a thoroughly plain, three-bedroom colonial with my parents on Columbus Avenue, out on the westerly outskirts of Bern. Behind our house is a big marshy field that stretches for over a mile, framed by an equally long line of trees that serves as nature's border between our town and neighboring Tappan. If you look through the trees behind our house, you can see the field, and farther in the distance, the slate gray roof of the Bern Inn, which is where I ended up getting a job for the summer.

The marsh used to be farmland back in the 1700s; now it's just this sunken field that runs parallel to Columbus. We live in a cul-de-sac, and between two of my neighbors' houses there's a path that leads through the marsh and woods all the way to the parking lot of the inn—my route to and from work. On my first day of work I took the path, and that's when I discovered the frogs.

The frogs were huge thick fat green ones that sat around the far edge of a little pond just off to the left of the path before you get to the trees. I didn't even see them at first. I heard the croaking and a strange echoing sound, and I followed the sound and almost fell down a steep, pebbly embankment. Luckily, I caught myself and stared down into the pond at the bottom of the steep grade. A huge cylindrical concrete culvert opened up into the pond, which is why there was an echo.

I'd never seen frogs like these before, they were that fat. They didn't look real. Their legs were thick and muscular; they looked like midgets' legs. It was a little muddy, and I was wearing new sneakers, but I crept closer to the edge and grabbed a handful of stones. I took a stone in my right hand, aimed—calmly exhaling like a sniper before throwing at the nearest frog . . . and missed. While I'm deadly with a slingshot from that distance, free-hand—not so much.

I spent five minutes chucking rocks at the frogs, and I couldn't hit one; the frogs sat unmoving as the rocks splashed harmlessly next to them. I don't know why I wanted to hit one so bad, but it became a mission. I finally launched two desperate handfuls of rocks all at once. That got the frogs to move. The sudden squall of pebbles made them dive into the water, and I stood still, waiting for them to come back up. They stayed under for about a minute before emerging on the other side.

Besides the frogs, the only other things in the pond were schools of tadpoles. The tadpoles darted around in the murky water after the frogs disappeared. They were small and quick, shooting around in every direction like spastics. I glanced at my watch and realized it was getting late for my first day of work, so I stirred up the tadpoles with a couple of pebbles before entering the thin wilderness.

My boss at the inn was a thirty-something guy named Gino Scarletti. He was the building's sole official maintenance man, but I later found out that this was purely a figurehead role, as he was universally considered the black-sheep son of the owner, whose three other sons were all wildly successful partners in a law firm called, naturally, Scarletti, Scarletti, and yet more Scarletti. The Scarletti family also owned the outdoor shopping complex Farragut Farms, and a squat brick building that my dentist's office was in; it was rumored that they had strong ties to the Boston Mob. Anyway, when a pipe burst or anything fairly significant needed fixing, the manager, Martino, didn't bother calling Gino to the scene, but instead direct-dialed professional contractors to come in and solve the problem. Gino was in charge of little projects, like replacing lightbulbs in high places that required his trusty stepladder, and repainting parking lot lines that didn't really need repainting.

All that you really need to know about Gino (in addition to the fact that he couldn't remember my name all summer long) is that he drove to work every morning in a fluorescent-green Toyota Celica with a hand-painted red racing stripe down the middle of the hood—you could actually see the sloppy brushstrokes. I sincerely believe there's a lot you can tell about a man by his hand-painted racing stripe. It made his car look like a Christmas present. Gino was skinny and had thinning blond hair, and he always peeled out of the parking lot, even when there wasn't anyone around to see or hear it. Depending on where he was working in the inn, he'd repark his Celica in either the handicapped spot out front or the handicapped spot outside the back entrance. Throughout the summer (even when it was ninety degrees and cloudless) he perpetually wore this light jacket, zippered up to his E.T.-ish neck—the kind of nondescript beige jacket you always see Islamic terrorists wearing in *Time* magazine photos.

When I arrived Martino smiled without showing his teeth and introduced me to Gino before rushing off to some meeting that probably didn't exist, and then Gino, mirroring Martino's demeanor, led me to his office, which was basically a stark, low-ceilinged storage closet with two restaurant barstools inside. I silently renamed the room his "cloffice." He pulled a string, and a low wattage bulb flickered on above us as he closed the door.

"So let me describe your position here at the inn," Gino said, then started coughing like crazy. "Hold on, I got something stuck in my throat."

Behind him on the wall were two covers of the same issue of *Seventeen* magazine featuring the supermodel Niki Taylor. I deduced that the reason he had two of the same cover was because one had a small rip on the bottom right corner, and that while he did find it necessary to buy a new, unmarred issue, apparently he didn't have the heart to throw the ripped one out. My mind started playing tricks on me, and for a flicker I swore I could see a small pile of human girl bones in the corner.

"Okay, so basically you're like my apprentice, and on any given day I might have a specific task for you, which I'll describe how to do and even demonstrate if you need it. For example, at some point we're going to have to re-mulch all the islands in the parking lot, and at the end of the summer my brother Carlo's getting married at the inn and I'm sure there'll be plenty for you to do for that, but aside from these side . . . tasks . . . for the most part you have one main job to do all summer, one task that we really need done and that you should focus on exclusively, and that's to vacuum every room in the inn."

"No problemo," I said.

"Actually, problemo," he retorted. "Problemo mucho. I don't mean just once-overing the floor; we have Mexican maids who do that every other day. No, you're going to have to move all the heavy furniture, including the bed, and vacuum under everything—which hasn't been done in years and years. Reason is, we'll be having important guests stay-ing with us for Carlo's wedding, and we want them to stay in a dust-free environment, so it's really important we vacuum every room thoroughly."

"Honestly, I think I can manage," I said quickly. I don't know why I felt so cocky and authoritative talking to this adult stranger—maybe I was thinking about that racing stripe.

"You will, but that's because you'll have a coworker

helping you move everything. The TV stand weighs a ton; I pulled my back last summer when—"

"I'm going to be working with somebody?"

Right at that moment there was a knock on the closet door.

"Like clockwork," Gino said, tapping the face of his Indiglo-ing Timex wristwatch and smiling at me. He grabbed hold of the string and hollered, "Hold on out there, we're coming out of the closet!"

He opened the door and I stepped out into the hall-way behind him, blinking as my eyes adjusted to the fluorescent lights, and when I saw who was standing there I couldn't help but take a step back, out of . . . fear? I don't know. The facade of confidence that I'd always affected in the hallways of Bern High crumbled in that instant, and I was left standing there helplessly with legs that felt cemented to the orange-carpeted hallway floor, a throbbing torso, and a closing throat, as if I was one of those people who are allergic to peanuts, and I'd accidentally just swallowed one.

"You must be Mia," Gino said.

"Hi," she said to him, looking at me.

Mia was wearing a faded yellow tank top and short, cutoff jeans that had little, frayed white strings that hung like tassels. I'd seen her in the halls at Bern High for two years and never noticed how strong her legs looked. Her thighs had a curve to them that looked powerful and atypical, compared to the anorexic and bulimic girls at our school whose thighs seem to curve inward in a way that reminds me of whittled wood. Her calves looked like they were perpetually flexed into an acorn shape. She wore no makeup. Her light brown hair was kind of flat and she parted it simply down the middle, like girls did back in the '70s; it was tucked behind her ears and came to a rest just below her shoulder blades. Her eyes were brown and so big they looked wet.

I was overcome with embarrassment that we were looking at each other, given that for basically two years I'd avoided eye contact with just about anyone, especially attractive females my age. I desperately needed a quick out to break the eye contact, and without thinking I suddenly slapped myself in the face as hard as I could, on the pretense that something had just attacked my left cheek. I glared up at the overhead fluorescent lights, as if searching for it. My eyes welled up with tears, that's how hard I whacked myself.

"Are you okay?" Mia asked, her teeth showing as she winced in sympathy for me.

"Wasp," was all I could get out as my throat was closing up and my cheek was stinging from the self-abuse. Gino instantly cowered with his hands held out in front of his face melodramatically, peeking through his fingers up at the ceiling, searching for the wasp in question.

Let's freeze this scene for a moment to consider a mind-set so deluded that it could actually provoke a human being to attempt to kick his own ass for the misbegotten purpose of saving face—as mine could, and did. I'd formed a succinct capsule description of Mia in my head, as I'd done with just about everyone who went to Bern High. The following profile flashed across my brain as I stood there in front of her:

Name: Mia Stone

Appearance: Around 5 foot 4, with light brown hair and pale, buttery soft skin, and overall blessed with the mousy good looks that girls with names like Mia are seemingly guaranteed in this world.

Social Standing: Everyone at BHS is either in love with her or hates her guts, as befitting someone with her universally desired/admired looks.

Academics: A book-smart, above-average student with "ridiculously shitty standardized test scores" (according to a conversation I overheard in the caf one day during sophomore year, between Mia and her best friend, Shauna Billingsley).

Music: She played the clarinet in the first section before quitting midway through sophomore year. She was proficient at it, but her brow was always furrowed when she played, so it was obvious it didn't come naturally to her the way the sousaphone comes to me.

Athletics: Track semi-star, specializing in the 100 and 4x100 relay, two-time defending conference champion in the 100 and fourth-place finish at States, multiple medal winner at the Bay State Games (according to the *Bern Ledger*).

It's hard to admit to myself that this capsule in my brain was actually highlighted in a fluorescent green font and encased in a red square with the word MATCH flashing across the bottom—along with an audible alarm sound—as if I were an Asian Terminator or something. She had an impressive resume, to be sure, but trumping any of these factoids about Mia was one defining detail that anyone within town lines immediately thought of when her name came up—and it wasn't her good looks, or her solid grades, or her newspaper-worthy athleticism. No. The single most important fact about Mia Stone was that she was precisely one half of the biggest power couple at Bern High. All of these other admirable, enviable details about Mia seemed merely surface in relation to the fact that she was the requisite arm candy of the king of the school.

Ryan Stackhouse.

Here's an evenhanded, abridged bio of the man of honor, circa last summer, *before* everything that happened: On the cusp of becoming a senior at BHS, Ryan (or "The House," as he was nicknamed by his lax teammates) was destined to earn a full ride to play D1 lacrosse in college, with the fratty good looks (that in daylight look senatorial and at night turn vaguely date-rapey) and chiseled physique of a guy who was seemingly created with the express purpose of running over other people his entire life. To boot, Ryan was unfairly blessed with brains as well as brawn, and was not only all-too-aware of his potential in life, but was fully committed to making his promising future a reality.

For a guy like me, The House was your typical nightmare—a cliché bully inexplicably perceived as a genial if charmingly fresh hero to all adults, a dark cloud approaching from the opposite end of the hall that would inspire me to duck into the nearest classroom until he and his mesomorphic (that is, twister-shaped) buds passed. He wasn't a very nice young man, to say the least, and I figured that was one reason why I was so nervous around Mia that morning, thereby explaining the rash of strange symptoms that hit me upon seeing her.

The other reason I was nervous around her was the fact that—at Bern High—Mia Stone was the embodiment of all-male fantasy, the perfect mix of madonna and "Lucky Star"–era Madonna, innocence and lust, plain M&M's and peanut, the duality that intrigued both boys and teen lesbos alike. At the same time, Mia was also the same girl who was in the one legitimately adult relationship at Bern High. Every school in America has one of these couples, a.k.a. the "class sweethearts," the most-likely-to-get-marrieds, the pair who amazes and frustrates us as we watch them sitting calmly next to each other in the caf, as if they simply know more about life than we do because of their time together. When The House would briefly put his hand on Mia's shoulder, you knew there were a thousand days of history being communicated through his hand to her shoulder, and it meant something to them, a secret language only they could understand. Whereas when a typical high school guy puts his hand on a girl's shoulder, he's in the process of turning her around to ask her a class-related question and probably pretending her shoulder's a breast.

This much I've learned, along with everything else that came to light this year: I may be a junior in high school, just as Mia is, but while she's more like a twenty-year-old, I might as well still be in kindergarten. I wilt at the comparison. I curl into an embryonic jumbo shrimp at the suggestion that we should exist on the same planet as each other.

Our story has taught me that.

* * *

So meanwhile, back at the ranch—er, actually, the inn—postslap I found myself so terrified of coming into such close contact with a girl like Mia that I ended up stupidly staring at her shoes. They were old Nike running shoes, smudged gray on the front, with a thin lime streak outlining the tongue. I was really examining her shoes at that moment, and I could feel the pulsating heat on my right cheek from my alien-hand-syndrome incident; my palm was also buzzing.

"Mia, this is—what's your name again?" Gino asked me.

"Albert," I said, surprised that it came out squeaky.

"Right, Mia, this is your coworker, um—"

Gino stared at me.

"Albert," I repeated.

"We already know each other," she said, smiling at me.

"That's just great. So let me describe your position here at the inn," Gino said. "Basically, it's like you're like my apprentice, and on any given day I might have a specific task for you, which I'll describe how to do and even demonstrate if you need it, but for the most part you have one main job to . . ."

I was momentarily distracted from my abject fear of Mia, and stared incredulously at Gino as he regurgitated word for word all that he'd told me a minute earlier, as if his larynx came prerecorded. He finished his spiel, there was an awkward silence, and then he said, "Well, let's get you two started."

Mia and I followed Gino to the maids' office, where he pulled out two industrial-size vacuums and a pair of dust masks. He hoisted the vacs onto an empty luggage cart, then handed me a clipboard with a pen attached to it by a fuzzy piece of green yarn.

"Keep track of which rooms you do on this piece of paper. It's called an occupancy sheet. What it is is a map with the entire layout of the inn on it. New ones are made every morning for the maid staff, with black boxes marking the occupied rooms so they know which rooms to clean first. Each morning you'll pick up a fresh occupancy sheet at the front desk. Make sure you only vacuum the empties. Start in the east wing. Go back later and do rooms you had to skip, when you get a chance. This should take you most of the summer, especially with all the minitasks you'll be doing here and there."

We left the vacs on the cart and he took us over to the east wing to show us the inside of a typical hotel room. The room was smaller than I'd imagined, and far less fancy; the bed was noticeably concave, and a poof of dust escaped when he pulled open the blinds.

"Okay, so doing a room is like figuring out a puzzle, like a Rubik's Snake. So what you do is you move the bed over, well, first you move this table and lamp against the front door, then push the bed into, um, vacuum under the—well, actually, it probably makes more sense to move the TV stand first, or wait, I—"

Thankfully, Gino's walkie-talkie squawked before his overworked brain exploded.

"Gino? Damnit, Gino, where are you?"

"I'm explaining to my new workers how to vacuum a room," he said.

"Get down to the restaurant right now, there's a leak in the men's bathroom."

He stared at the walkie-talkie for a few seconds.

"Okay guys, well, you get the picture, go back and get the vacuums and today's occupancy sheet and get started, I gotta run. . . ."

Gino took off, leaving the door open behind him. It hovered for a moment before shutting by itself, with an audible click. And that was it. We obviously knew how to use a household vacuum, and moving furniture around was self-explanatory, but since it was my first job I figured there'd have been a training video or something. There wasn't, and now we were left to our own devices.

And that's how I ended up alone in a locked hotel room with Mia Stone.

Okay, so we've reached the part where I'm about to start acting like a major weirdo, so it's important to take stock of my state of mind leading up to that day.

Fact of the matter is, before I met Mia, my life was playing out like a generic prison movie, minus the sodomy. You know the story: guy finds himself in the wrong place at the wrong time, and before he knows it he gets sent upstate for a crime he didn't commit. Nobody gives him a chance to survive, because he's little and isn't already jaded by a youth spent in and out of juvie. First week in the yard he gets marked for soap pickup by all the hardened cons who consider him fresh meat. He knows the only way a guy like him can avoid being made a sister is to do two things: refuse to ever shower in order to make himself funky, and second, wait for a choice opportunity to surprise the biggest guy in the cell block with a forearm to the back of the head. He has no chance of winning this one-sided brawl, but that's not the point. The objective here is to get publicly slaughtered, which he does, and a month later when he's released from the infirmary he finds out his plan has worked—his unprovoked scrappiness has bought him a smidgen of respect.

After months of resisting and trying to just keep to himself, he comes to terms with his less than perfect scenario and finally begrudgingly aligns himself with the white tank top–wearing skinheads. Under normal circumstances, this would indicate the end of the original human being and the true birth of the hardened con, but fortunately for him, he manages to stay on the fringes of that particularly sour social club. Instead he befriends a gray-bearded "old-timer," and they spend their afternoons together out by the bleachers, negotiating the sale of cartons of Parliament Menthols and lavender-scented hand soaps, under the unwatchful eye of their paid-off security guard.

He's finally succeeded in carving out a tiny little niche in this hellish microcosm of today's society. From our bird's-eye perspective we see that he's still living a life of utter peril and it's debatable how worthwhile his efforts to survive are in the grand scheme of things (he's in a maximum security prison for chrissakes), but it's a life he can somewhat stand, carving little chess pieces out of soapstone using a miniature claw hammer in his spare time, feeding tufts of stale bread to his pet rat, and helping the old-timer shelve the law books in the prison library instead of working in the steamy laundry room. This would qualify, with his and our immensely lowered standards, as a satisfactory conclusion to a dreadful situation.

But the movie never ends that way, does it? Just when he thinks he's found something akin to peace, what always happens in these prison movies?

The warden suddenly transfers him to a *new* prison.

As he's shuffled in cuffs through his new yard, he recognizes with dread the looks on the unfamiliar faces; the hardened cons are eyeballing the fresh meat. He realizes that his years of struggle in the old cell block to earn respect have disappeared in an instant; his hard-earned social cachet has slipped out through the bars of his new cell window. He's going to have to start all over again, and the reality of the situation hits him so squarely in the face, you can practically hear the smack.

Well, this is pretty much *exactly* what happened to me in real life.

You have to understand, I was *thriving* in my hometown back in Maryland, circa age twelve. I was in the midst of a cozy, electric-blanketed childhood, replete with morning bus-stop bottle rocket launches, blissful scratch'n'sniff sticker overdoses, and those giggly sleepovers on the weekends, where you're so happy you don't want to ever go to sleep, but at the same time you're thoroughly exhausted, and you end up quietly sobbing into your goose-down, mummy sleeping bag long after everyone else has conked out. I had plenty of friends whom I'd known since kindergarten. I was a toe-ball ringer in kickball and a two-time Campbell soups label contest winner; my preadolescence was clearly shaping me into a promising young man, when I was unceremoniously stuffed by my 'rents into the back of a rusted Oldsmobile Omega and found myself, three hours later, callously dumped in a new town in upstate New York, where everybody knew each other, and nobody knew me.

What the hell did I do to deserve the unjust fate of having an architect dad who got transferred right before I was to start middle school? I didn't deserve to be blindsided like this. I was a good kid. My only crime was shyness. That, and I must have picked up a misdemeanor for being born skinny, because in my new town, let's call it, say . . . Shitsville, I was swiftly and unmercifully bullied from day one. I knew my only chance to stop the incessant purple nurples, wet willies, and Bangkoks was to try to go wild on an eighth grader in the crowded main lobby in the morning before homeroom; and so I did, and got *totally* totaled. My mom was shocked, and I thought she made matters worse when she stomped into the administration office and reemed out the vice principal within earshot of half my grade, informing him (and them), "My son, Albert Kim, is such a fragile boy," and "How dare you allow this to happen to such a sensitive little child who still wets his bed all the time," blah blah blah, and my heart sank into my left sneaker. But to my shock, the next day I realized that my unsuccessful physical outburst worked, just like in those prison movies, and as a result . . . no more twisting of my nippleage from behind in the hallways between periods. No more sudsy wet willies while waiting in line at lunch.

Instead, everyone left me alone, just like that.

In time, I managed to align with a social group in school—the skate rats, who themselves resided on the periphery of the social circle, but at least they were officially recognized as living, breathing carbon-based life-forms, which was a big step up for me. By the end of middle school I had really long bangs and checkerboard-shaved sides and would ollie my Mike McGill deck almost two inches off the ground as we listened to Bad Brains and Black Flag all afternoon. This sort of mindless activity was the equivalent of prisoners carving chess pieces out of soapstone. While I didn't have as many friends as I'd had back in Bethesda, I was now officially a part of the scene, something I didn't think was possible that first week of school. I even acquired a schoolwide adopted nickname, "Preacherman," because I was the only eighth grader whose parents still made him go to church. All in all I was sorta happy again, and looking forward to entering high school armed with a life of some sort.

In retrospect, I should have recognized this feeling of happiness in my belly to be a harbinger of doom, because sure enough, one afternoon that July, my dad came home all sunny-faced with the news that we were moving once again, this time to a suburb just outside of Boston called Bern, which is where I live to this very day. It was a fitting name for the town I was being transferred to, having been torched by my 'rents for the second time in my life, without having even reached my fourteenth birthday.

Unfuckingbereavable.

So for a second time we relocated. All my hard work in Shitsville, down the drain. I'd scratched and clawed (literally) my way to the bottom of the social totem pole (prior to that I had been splayed out on the wood chip island surrounding the totem pole) and had been content hanging on for dear life, with an actual chance at having a decent high school experience, when my parents decided to shake my metaphorical snow globe once again. A law should be established to ban moving a kid to a new town right before ninth grade. It's downright unethical, the sort of thing that should provoke social services to file a 51A on my dad's ass. I had a few weeks to myself in my new home before school started, and I just lay there in bed all day long, staring up at the stucco ceiling, lamenting my predicament and feeling depressed as hell. Why did this happen to me? Why couldn't we have moved to Southern California, where I'd been told that almost everyone's Asian? Plus I was skinny, shy, and my hair was too stiff to feather properly like the Smith kids' across the street. Day after day I'd just lie there, listing in my head the various reasons why I was down in the dumps, and I nearly convinced myself I'd deserved it. But something in me decided to try to make a go of it once again. I promised myself the night before high school started, with my hands folded as if in prayer, that I'd pick up the pieces and rebuild once again.

But this time, things didn't work out quite as planned. In

fact, my future was decided for me in the first week of school, before I even had a chance to take a mental Geiger counter read on my surroundings. That's how it is for new students in high school. You have like, an instant, tops, to make headway socially. All can be lost before you even realize you were playing the goddamned game in the first place, which is exactly what happened to me that first week. Oh, I lost, all right—big-time and irrevocably. Specifically, my lowly position on the social totem pole was determined in fifth period gym class, in what quickly became known among the student body as the "Broom Incident."

That fateful day, there wasn't an even number of students in class, and we were learning to square dance in coed pairs, so Ms. Bender, the requisite lesbian gym teacher, forced me to partner up with the janitor's broom. All the girls with their new boobies stood next to their fidgety guy partners, who, unbeknownst to the girls, were considering the class second base, and everyone was giggling because they were nervous, and I could actually see the hormones flying around the room (incidentally, airborne hormones kinda look like miniature Sopwith Camels). And there I was, the new guy, stuck making small talk with a handle of wood.

After Bender taught us the basic moves, she turned on the boom box, which started blaring Sir Mix-a-Lot's "Square Dance Rap." To this day I don't know how my classmates coordinated it, but all the other couples somehow knew to freeze and let me prance around in an extended solo. After maybe ten seconds, I realized I was the only one dancing, and immediately stopped. Everyone was staring at me with their mouths open, and I could feel my cheeks turning red; and what happened next would curse me for the rest of freshman year, and longer, for that matter. I felt like I needed to improvise in order to salvage the embarrassing situation, so I leaned over and gave the top of the broom handle an epic kiss. At first I'd thought I'd turned what was a disastrous moment into a "nice one, Albie" moment, but shortly I realized how catastrophic my actions were that day. I now know that my classmates were subconsciously filing away what would become an unspoken law—that for the rest of my social life in Bern, Albert Kim was only allowed to hook up with inanimate objects.

After the Broom Incident, I think I kinda knew that I was screwed socially, but I still made a game effort of trying to fit in for the rest of the semester. But to no avail. Despite my efforts, I still got shoved into the lockers so often that I learned to wear my ski jacket with the hood up at all times, to cushion the blows to the back of my head.

I remember there was a night during Christmas break when I realized that I had no hope. Clearly, whoever was upstairs— God, or more likely a teenage alien with the Milky Way on a petri dish—had deemed that I wasn't meant to make it socially at Bern High. I pictured the alien, looking down and smiling at me through his three mouths because I was his favorite amoeba to fuck with. That's the only explanation I could come up with as to why I kept getting invisibly kicked in the ass like this. As far as I could tell, I didn't deserve this fate. I hadn't run through my allotted karma points the way other people my age had. For example: I had never killed an animal in my life (up till then, at least). I was courteous to the elderly, even in instances when it didn't matter. I felt bad for others, and I'd put on a smile in the face of adversity and had never whined for long. Yet there I was, alone and miserable at the start of my four-year sentence at Bern High.

Well, it was all over now.

No more stressing and lamenting my social status, because there was no point. Nothing was going to change. I was maturing, I realized. I finally understood my grandmother, who visited us once from Korea, and after a lifetime of misery was always so negative. One time we were sitting at the kitchen table and she tried to open a bag of Cape Cod potato chips, and after like eight seconds she couldn't get it to open, so she tossed the bag over her shoulder and muttered in Korean (my mom later translated it for me), "Life is too damn hard." I didn't get her then, but I understood her now. Life *was* too damn hard, and now that I knew this, all that was left for me to do was to free myself from this pathetic little life I'd been given.

I contemplated suicide that night for all of five minutes, but it didn't feel like me. Nor did the prospect of offing fellow students, the other du jour alternative to solving life's problems for depressed teens like myself. It just seems ironic to me that kids want to kill other kids out of frustration that they're universally hated in the present, when the very act guarantees they'd be hated forever. Instead, I came up with what turned out to be a radical solution, something never done before, to my knowledge at least, in the history of high school.

I was going to become an *intentional* loser.

5 Do you know what a dolphin is? Jesus—of course you do, but do you know about how mammals like dolphins shunt their blood in order to survive in really cold water?

What they do is they cut off circulation to the extremities and only allow the blood to flow into the necessary parts, like the brain and the heart, in order to survive in adverse conditions. We humans do it, too—that's why our fingers get cold first, long before the rest of our bodies. Anyhow, I decided to make like a dolphin and shunt all blood distribution away from my loins; and instead of going to high school dances hoping to make headway with a girl or strategizing how to sit at the right table at lunch or trying to be included in the all-important, pseudo-random picture-taking sessions in the hallways, I opted instead to mentally become a monk and just wait for the slate to get wiped clean when I finally left Bern for good. With regard to making friends, I declared to myself that I would stop caring and not only no longer try to make friends, but actively embrace isolation, as if it was a gift. I was going to spend my precious energy on things that I had a chance with. Namely, video games and foosball.

To tell you that I succeeded gloriously in becoming a major loser is a foregone conclusion. By the time I met Mia in the summer before junior year, I was by anyone's standards a typical loser: I'd never kissed a girl; I wasn't good at sports; I liked to spend hours drawing pictures of fighter jets attacking dinosaurs on the edge of cliffs. . . . Despite being sixteen years old, the closest thing I had to friends were the neighborhood kids, most of whom were in the sixth grade.

Oh, I was a loser all right; most of my wet dreams were in Japanimation.

The sixth graders that I hung out with after school revered me because I was so good at the things they loved to do—namely, video games and foosball. My persona made for a total loser in high school, but it made me really cool among sixth graders. And I liked hanging out with them. I realized in short order that a sixth grader is the perfect age friend for a guy like me. I had acquired an unearned leadership role due to my advanced age and size, and we shared the same asexual interests. While my true peers were hanging out at the mall not realizing how bored they were, I was free to dominate sundown rounds of Ghost in the Graveyard and Pepper (kinda like laser tag, except with BB guns) and marathon Ping-Pong matches. Billy Timmons, probably my best prepuberty-age neighborhood friend, worshipped the Cult of Albert and would often bring home new friends on the bus to meet me. Here's a telling exchange typical of these situations:

Billy: This is Albert, that guy I was telling you about.
Billy's friend stares at me as if I'm a Sasquatch.
Me: How's it goin', pal.
Billy's friend: Are . . . are you . . . retarded?

In retrospect, I suppose I did look kinda retarded—a much taller, older guy like me willingly hanging out with a bunch of little kids like that (we even had our own tree house).

Anyway, now that I'd taken myself out of the game with my peers, I became an observer at Bern High. It gave me a vision the other students didn't have. Not to sound sour-grapey, or like one of those sullen, pseudo-adultish high schoolers who try to seem above it all to mask the fact that they'd trade their left arm for a piece of the social pie, but I really started to see how ludicrous everything was. Now that I wasn't participating in anything remotely social, I could see how childish and lame even the "coolest" kids acted on, for example, Carnation Day. For weeks in the fall, students buy little cards to send anonymous love notes to other students in homeroom, and to see that the popular people's moods actually depended on the outcome of that homeroom amazed me. It made me feel really free and light not to be swept up in all the high school BS. Nobody realized how obsessed they were with their social status. And no student was immune to it. It wasn't just the jocks and preps who were consumed with social status—the nerds and outcasts, who on the surface didn't seem to care, were just as guilty of what was basically reverse snobbery. They thought it was cool not to be cool, and the fact that they looked down on people with lower GPAs was another form of snobbery. Every group at Bern High seems to do that—they take the one thing that defines them, even if it's a less than admirable quality, and consider it the sole aspect of a person by which true greatness is measured. There are art snobs, prototypical jocks, elitist rich kids who consider their parents' net worth *their* worth, and there are even some egotistical wood shop morons who consider you an ass if you don't know how to properly work the band saw in Industrial Arts class. It's insanity masked as sanity since everybody to a man does it. Except for me, and I was immune to it all, and it made for good live TV, to walk around watching my peers implode and rise up and fall and rise up again, day in, day out.

Maybe everything that happened this year with Mia could have been avoided. I'd cultivated this ability to analyze everyone else through careful observation, when the one person I didn't understand and needed to figure out the most was . . . *myself*.

I'm just messing with you. Anyhow, a strange thing happened to me as a result of becoming an intentional loser, something I hadn't anticipated at all: I quickly became an anomaly at Bern High. I became a loser that nobody picked on, ever. Nobody could understand me. Nobody could figure out how someone like me existed—a guy with seemingly no interest whatsoever in finding social acceptance? It befuddled everyone, and as a result I traversed the high school highways with full impunity. I've read stories in outdoors magazines about how bears leave mentally ill people alone because they can sense the chemical imbalance in their brains and it weirds the bears out—that's sorta like what happened to me in the hallways of Bern High. I was a social curiosity to everyone because my modus operandi was so unorthodox, and it gave me a strange form of respect in a way. I didn't get picked on, or even made fun of, at least not to my face. Maybe everyone in school was secretly terrified of me and worried I was perpetually on the verge of going berserk and bringing a gun to school or something. I didn't do anything to dissuade them from having that opinion of me, because it beat getting bullied on a regular basis.

And thus, I became so incomprehensible to the general public that I became a ghost in the hallways of Bern High.

I was able to disengage from high school society in part because my parents were so clueless. Or rather, they were typical Asian American parents, and so they were blind to recognizing that their son was totally alone and barely hanging on as a teenager, and therefore they naively did nothing to help me. The pressure to excel and meet the standards established by society of what "success" is are a thousand times more rigid and intense when you're raised by Korean parents. This is the result of the typical distorted immigrant perspective of how life really is in the States. I'm sure it applies not just to Asians but to any foreigner from any ethnicity who comes to this country. In the case of my parents, they aren't native English speakers, so they struggled socially upon first arriving in this country, and to this day they feel as if there's a subtle secret code that they'll never quite understand, and as a result they'll never feel comfortable, never quite feel truly American. More significantly, they don't believe it's possible for *any* Asian to ever fit in naturally in the States, including their son who was born in this country.

Asian parents feel that life is going to be hard because their sons and daughters don't resemble the pale-skinned Smith kids across the street, and they think the only way to compensate is to dominate and beat the white teenagers in every other respect. Asian parents would never admit this in public, but in truth they consider a mediocre Asian student the equivalent of a blind, deaf, and mute white kid with no arms or legs, and by that rationale they feel that if their Asian kids excel and get all the right accolades and become doctors or lawyers or engineers, then maybe, just maybe, they'll be able to barely survive.

There is, however, a silver lining to this oppressive life strategy that I had to subsist under, at least for me: I was able to live under the radar at school *and* at home. So long as I kept my grades up, my parents assumed things were hunky-dory with me and left me alone. By the time summer rolled around after sophomore year I was surprised to realize that I was midway through high school, and I was even more surprised to find that I was sorta happy. I mean, I was totally disengaged from life socially; I was a self-induced case of arrested development; I was completely alone—an undeniable loser who didn't engage in life in the slightest (and thereby wasn't really living). I was Maverick *after* Goose died but *before* he rebounded by downing a handful of commie MiGs over the Indian Ocean to save Ice Man at the end of *Top Gun*; I was, quite simply, a husk of a teenager, and yet in my own pathetic little way, I found that I was somewhat content with my life.

And so this was my mental state when I met Mia.

"Hi, finally," she said, breaking the silence.

I stared inquisitively at the wall just to the left of her face, unable to meet her gaze. I stared so intensely that she even turned around for a second and tried to figure out what I was looking at. I tensed my neck and tried in vain to turn my face a bit so I could make eye contact with her, but my neck wouldn't budge. This was surprising, to say the least. Eventually her smile faded—she puffed out the pocket above her top lip with air to make her look like a chipmunk and then fizzed the air out through the sides of her lips. It sounded like this: *squeeeed.* What was going on with me?

"What did you think of the final in English?" she asked. I nodded enthusiastically. "Don't you remember? We were in Mr. Gracie's class together."

I replied by tilting my head and scrunching up an eyebrow, with my mouth still gaping open, as if I were mimicking Munch's painting *The Scream.*

Mia looked kinda scared. "Are you okay?" she asked.

I forced out a sound—I went for words, but given my mystery condition I was clearly shooting too high. Instead, the following spilled out of my mouth:

"Rrrhennn," I—well, meowed. I tried again. "Mhhrrrrrinn?"

This is what it feels like to be in a locked hotel room with a girl like Mia, if you're a guy like me: You're rendered immobile because your feet have rooted to the floor. Your vision is tinted red from the blood intermittently spurting behind your eye sockets in disgusting rhythm with your heartbeat from your exploded pituitary gland. Your quads start shaking, the jiggly feeling rising slowly up your legs to your waist and then torso—it feels like you have a heart arrhythmia. Your senses heighten dramatically, and time seems to slow down; you can hear a fly buzzing behind a curtain, along with the sound of a backhoe digging a hole in the lot next to Dunkin' Donuts . . . *twenty-seven blocks away.* Your discomfort and panic quickly give way to an almost euphoric sensation, and you soon feel relaxed, despite still being immobile. To put it in more relatable terms, it feels like you've just finished running a marathon, downed a hypercaffeinated Starbucks grande latte at the finish line, whereupon a hidden sniper shoots you in the chest, and then runners behind you push you off the end of the pier (this is one of those marathons that end on a pier) into freezing cold water with cement blocks tied to your ankles.

That . . . and you suddenly have a wicked boner.

"Um, okay, so why don't you go get the vacs, and I'll go pick up the new sheet from the front desk, and we'll meet in the east wing, okay?" Mia finally said.

She didn't even wait for a reply, correctly assuming by this point that I wasn't going to give her one. I did, however, manage some sort of response—in the form of pursing my lips in disapproval, which made her frown back as she left the room. The sound of her steps quickly faded into the carpeted hallway outside. I looked at my reflection in the mirror. I felt my lungs fill up with air, and eventually my lips parted and I belatedly said to my reflection, "Hi, Mia, yes I remember the . . . goddamnit."

I walked back to the maids' station. The big vacuums were on the floor by the door, but the luggage cart was gone. I picked up the vacs and carried them to the east wing. They weren't that heavy—plus I had an abnormally strong right

37

arm from carrying my sousaphone home from school every Friday, so I could practice over the weekend.

Mia was chatting with Martino, the manager, by the entrance to the east wing. My symptoms, which had somewhat dissipated in the privacy of the maids' station, now returned full force, and I felt my cheeks hot plate and sizzle, and the full body calcification returned. I could tell, of course, that the heat on my cheeks meant that I was blushing, which in turn made me blush harder, so I made exaggerated straining sounds so she'd think my cheeks were red from the effort. She heard my grunts and looked up.

"Hey!" she said, and waved me over. Now that I had her attention, my confident gait devolved and I had no choice but to waddle over to her like a goddamned penguin without making eye contact, my chin pressed against my neck. When I saw her feet, I knew to stop and set the vacuum down. Saying some sort of greeting in return was totally out of the question, but I managed with great mental effort to at least raise my right hand this time, palm out. She looked at my hand and then my face and then back to my hand and then finally mimicked me, lifting her own right hand, palm out, and looked at me sternly.

"How," she said in a deep voice.

"How," I said back to her, slowly.

A minor victory (I'd said a single word!), but then we stared at each other for a couple more seconds. Say something else, I pleaded with myself in my head. She was starting to make that expression I'd seen girls make a thousand times with me—their eyes widen and they look away from me with pursed lips—an expression I referred to as the "Oookay, psycho" look. Nothing came to me.

"How," I repeated.

She stared at me.

"These vacuums are superheavy. My arms feel like they're going to fall off," I said. My throat had opened up! "And I'm not actually an Indian."

"Me neither," she said, and then she *touched* me. Well, we shook hands. She had a really strong grip. I'd gone in with the dead-fish grip because I wanted to seem sensitive, plus the fact that I just think it's funny, but she squeezed my hand so hard she actually made one of my knuckles pop. I yelped.

"Oh God, I'm sorry!" she said through clenched teeth, immediately letting go.

"It's fine, I let that happen on purpose," I said, then put my hands together and tried to crack my knuckles even though I'd never been able to do it. "Sorry to use you like that. It's a terrible habit. I already have arthritis. Sometimes it gets so bad I can barely get any sleep and—"

"Why don't you get a luggage cart," Martino suggested. "It's only going to get heavier as you go from room to room, and the maids use one when they do rounds."

"Good idea," I said, and walked away.

I turned and started jogging away, but I was hyperconscious that she was watching me, and it felt like I was walking on the moon—each step slow and Neil Armstrong-y—and I knew it looked ridiculous, so I stopped "jogging" when I got to the end of the hallway and walked instead. I stole a glance back at Mia and Martino with my peripheral vision. She bent her body, grasped the vacuums with both hands, took a deep breath, then exploded upward as if she was doing a clean and jerk; she hoisted them so powerfully they banged against her thighs, and she almost launched them over her head like a keg toss. She was so stunned at how light they were that she emitted a little, "Ooh!" in surprise. That, coupled with my dead-fish handshake, and I could tell she was puzzled by how much of a pathetic Wussy McMuffin I was.

"Fudge," I whispered softly as I turned the corner.

Vacuuming hotel rooms turned out to be simple work, if time consuming. To be honest, at first we weren't that good at it, despite the ages-eight-and-up instructions. That first day we ended up denting just about every wall we encountered, as if we'd both lost loved ones to walls in the past and were carrying out long simmering vendettas against them, and in one room we accidentally tipped over a TV and broke it, which we nonverbally agreed to not report to Gino.

Mia and I vacuumed two rooms that morning. It took a little while to figure out the order of furniture to vacuum under. Since there was a thick blanket of dust under the furniture, you'd have to be careful because by moving the furniture it would spread some dust on the carpet that wasn't under furniture, and so you'd have to vacuum that part up as well, etc. We quickly realized the most efficient order was to start by the windows and work our way to the door, like washing a car from the roof down. If we worked steadily, it took about fifteen minutes to vacuum a room. I found that focusing on the work helped dissipate my semiparalysis a bit, because it gave me something to do besides focus on the fact that I was alone in a hotel room with Mia Stone.

In time I learned to adapt to my newly debilitated self. For example, while holding a conversation with Mia was out of the question, I found that I could speak in clipped, rudimentary phrases, so long as they were simplistic directives aimed in her general direction. "Move here," I'd say, pointing at an open space. Another favorite phrase of mine was, "Pull back," followed by a series of caveman grunts of approval upon completion. *Mmmm. Hmmm.*

At around noon Gino dropped by to tell us our lunch options. We could either order something from the restaurant and have it docked from our paychecks, or we could bring our own lunch or go out for lunch. I hadn't brought anything to eat, so I opted to check out the restaurant.

Mia said, "I'm going to get something to eat," and abruptly left the room. Gino and I looked out the window and watched her walk through the rear parking lot to her car, a rusted yellow Corolla with an empty bike rack on the roof.

"She is F-I-N-E fine," Gino said, standing by the window. He turned to me. "But I bet she's a total tease, am I right or am I right?"

A surge of anger coursed through me; I felt protective of Mia. I felt like he didn't have a right to talk about her like that. Of course, he was creepy as hell, so rather than chide him for it, I instead said: "Yeah, totally."

"I don't doubt that, brother," he said, peeking through the blinds. "Baby got back. Tell me something, Andy, why do jailbait teases have the nicest asses?"

"Uh, I don't know, why?"

"Because God likes to screw with the elderly," he muttered, shaking his head.

I didn't say anything. He looked over at me.

"Don't you agree?" he asked.

"Honestly, I don't have the slightest clue what you're talking about," I replied.

"You will, someday," he said, turning back to the window. "Now go get some lunch."

I left the room, glancing back as the door closed behind me—Gino had his left cheek pressed against the glass, staring out the window as Mia drove off in her Corolla.

I walked over to the inn's restaurant, The Three Ferns, located just off the front lobby. There was a tall lady in a business suit reading the *Boston Herald* at a table in the corner by herself, mindlessly eating cubes of honeydew melon with a spoon. I passed through the double kitchen doors as Gino had instructed, so I could order lunch from the chef. There were a couple of prep cooks dicing onions, and when they saw me they nodded over at the wall, which had a menu tacked onto it. I scanned the lunch menu—everything was expensive; we're talking double figures for even the appetizers. The chef approached me, and I said to him, "I suddenly have to urinate, I'll be right back." I tend to use big words like "urinate" when I talk to adult strangers, even though I know they say "pee," too, and anyway that was the first and last time I ever went into the kitchen.

Instead, I spent the lunch hour flexing my stomach, battling the hunger knot growing inside me. I tried to drink as many gulps from the water fountain as possible to at least give myself the illusion of feeling full, which made me have to hit the bathroom a half dozen times, and when I exited the bathroom for the sixth time, Mia was walking through the back entrance. She smiled at me.

"Nice lunch?" she asked.

My throat felt weird again, and I was oddly confused by her question.

"Really?" I asked. "What was it?"

She stared at me.

"Okay, dudes and dudettes, back to work," Gino said from behind, mock-aggressively, then laughed awkwardly. "Where'd ya eat yer grub, Mia?"

"I went home and ate," she replied.

"And where exactly is your home at?" he asked.

"Bern," she said flatly.

"No, I mean—" Gino started, but she was leaned over, away from him, fiddling with the vacuum cord. He glanced at me with his eyes all lit up, as if he was pissed off at her, and he mouthed the words, *See what I mean?* and shook his head at me for approval; I looked away.

"If you need anything, call the front desk and they'll page me," he said, then entered his cloffice and shut the door behind him. The crack under the door didn't light up, and Mia smiled at me. I think we were both pretending we had X-ray vision and could see Gino sitting on a stool in the dark, waiting for us to leave. We stood there for a couple extra seconds, because it felt like we were in control.

The symptoms returned full force that afternoon, and we

vacuumed three rooms without saying a word to each other. Most of the time the vacuum was running so we couldn't talk anyway, but when we'd move furniture she'd sometimes try to engage me in conversation. To mask my paralysis I employed various pitiful tactics, like I'd pretend I didn't hear her, or I'd rub my ear and say, "Hello? Well that's weird," to myself, as if I was newly deaf. She stopped trying after a while.

I breathed in the recycled cold air from the air conditioners all afternoon, and by the end of the day I had a slight headache. We returned the vacuums to the maids' station. There was a fenced-in room with a lock where the maids kept all the heavy equipment. Mia used the master key to unlock it, and she pulled the vacuums in and pushed them into a corner. The door swung closed behind her, and before she opened it she grabbed hold of the fence and shook it and shouted, "Help me!" and it made me laugh out loud; it was the first natural, honest sound I'd made all afternoon, and I blushed. She followed me out to the parking lot.

"So, do you need a lift home or anything?" she asked, probably encouraged by my involuntary laugh.

"I'm walking," I said, looking at my feet, as if to confirm it.

"Okay, well, see you tomorrow," she said semibrightly.

I nodded, and it wasn't nearly enough. I needed to say something this time, anything, so she wouldn't think I was a complete imbecile, so I gritted my brain and forced the following improvised sentence out: "Hopefully I'll see you tomorrow, Mia, unless, of course, you get totaled on your drive home and die," I said, fake giggling.

"Oh my God," she said, gaping at me.

"Later, 'gator," I squeaked before walking off. My quads were throbbing again as I cut through the thin line of trees and out of sight, whereupon I hit myself in the forehead and winced behind a big oak tree for a few minutes. I was a prisoner in my own body. I listened for the sound of her car starting up, leaving the parking lot. What the heck was going on with me?

I stepped out into the field and all of a sudden remembered the frogs from the morning. The morning felt like a lifetime ago. I walked over to the spot and looked over the edge. The frogs were right where I'd last seen them, croaking along the edge of the pond. The sky was overcast, and the air tasted slightly salty. I picked up a couple of rocks and tried to hit one for fun. I failed, but as I was midway through a second handful it occurred to me that my breathing had returned to normal, and that my legs were no longer shaking—they felt downright spry. I dropped the stones and started running in ever-widening, self-made crop circles in the field for a couple of minutes, reveling in having full motion again. "CAMEL! MONKEY! EDDIE VEDDER! SPEED WALKING! DIPSHIT!" I shouted as I ran around and around, testing out my throat with random words, until it felt back to normal.

7

I walked into the house and found my parents sitting sullenly at the kitchen table in total silence—which is how they prefer to communicate with each other, and when I shut the garage door they looked up with typically stunned expressions, as if they'd forgotten they even had a son. I've always attributed this puzzled expression to the fact that they work so immigrantly hard and are simply disoriented ninety-nine percent of the time they're home, resting for the next day's work. I like to think that, because otherwise the only logical answer is that they're a pair of highly functioning idiot savants.

"There's the working man," my dad said in a booming voice, smiling at me from the kitchen table. He dramatically looked at his watch. "My goodness, do they have you working overtime already, son?"

It clearly wasn't funny to anyone, and yet my mom started laughing on cue, like a creepy psycho. I walked over to them and sat down at the kitchen table. I picked up my fork and stared disappointedly at my plate of warm spaghetti and meatballs.

"How was it, working for the man?" my mom asked. "And by that I mean *the* man, not *my* man!"

"Oh, honey, quit razzing the boy," my dad said, pinching her on the butt. He giggled and reached over and clapped me on the back. "You done good, kiddo."

Seriously, my folks are like this—they act so phony around me it's disturbing. I wouldn't be surprised if they actually were North Korean spies, which kids in my grade sometimes accused them of being during dodgeball. It's not that they're phony in a malicious way; rather, it's that they talk phonily because they're thoroughly clueless and think it's how they're supposed to talk in this country. In keeping with the fifties feel to everything in our house, they unknowingly model themselves after Ward and June Cleaver from *Leave it to Beaver*. What's even weirder is that it's so hard for them to talk this enthusiastically about life that our dinner conversations last all of thirty seconds before they get exhausted and return to whatever it was they had been silently lamenting.

A minute passed, and it occurred to me that I hadn't said a word since stepping through the door, and yet my parents didn't press further, relieved I wasn't trying to extend the formalities. The three of us sat there in silence, my dad gazing inquisitively at the busted ice maker on the refrigerator, my mom staring into her mug of cooling coffee, and me quietly picking at my food, replaying meeting Mia in my head.

That night Billy invited me to play Ghost in the Graveyard with the fellas.

"I'm going to have to pass," I told him. "I feel kinda weird."

I theorized that I felt older because of the summer job and from being forced to interact with a girl from my grade, so it was embarrassing to think about running around with eleven-year-olds in the dark, sweating profusely as I hid for over an hour in a neighbor's hedge, staying hidden even when it was obvious that not only was the game over but everyone else had gone home for the night (I play these games with gusto). Instead, I just listened from my bedroom and casually spied on the game with the lights off. I couldn't see anything, but every now and then I heard someone run through the backyard, softly giggling to himself. I felt a pang of jealousy that I wasn't out there extending my streak of twenty-one rounds of Ghost in the Graveyard played without anyone ever being able to find me, or relishing my advanced stalking skills and hunting them all down with ease. But I still didn't feel in control of myself. The throbbing was still there, a dull ache in the backs of my legs, and it only got more intense lying in bed in the dark. I felt like I was one big vein.

I realized the sagelike calm that I'd had around my classmates during the school year was a total sham. It was based on the fact that I didn't actually interact or come into close contact with other people, ever, aside from my sixth-grade neighborhood buds. I mean, I'd always known that my strategy as an intentional loser was simply to shut everyone out, but I'd had no idea that it stunted, or maybe even regressed my social development to the point that now I couldn't interact with someone my age without going into semicatatonia. The main problem with being in this state at work was that it produced a lot of . . . quiet. Which is to say that there was no escaping the fact that Mia and I were alone in a hotel room for the bulk of our workday; we were constantly surrounded by dead air, and that silence was my nemesis. How was I going to deal with this? I brainstormed all night, but the only solution I could come up with was to continue to drown out the dead silence between us with the sound of the vacuum, which meant my solution to dealing with my debilitating disease was to just constantly work really hard, as if I were really passionate about vacuuming hotel rooms all day.

* * *

When I got to work the next day Mia was waiting for me outside the maids' station. She smiled at me, as if she'd forgotten how bizarre I'd acted around her the day before. It made me feel sad, because I knew I was going to act like a fricking weirdo around her today too. Mia raised her right hand, palm out, as I approached.

"How," she said, giggling briefly. She frowned. "I'm sorry, that was probably offensive, wasn't it?"

"Whatever," I said, sighing to myself as if I were offended, even though I thought it was actually really funny. And so a new tactic had emerged: the other way I dealt with being around her was by being mean to her, or at least dismissive.

Here's a primer on how to act around an attractive, popular girl in close quarters, if you're a guy like me. First and foremost, the main principle you have to adopt is the aforementioned strategy of constant motion. If I kept moving my feet at all times, I could distract myself enough that the throbbing would go away, or I'd be focused on something else at least.

Anytime she made eye contact with me, I'd either look away in seeming disgust, or I'd glare at her until she looked away first, as if we were desperate male elks having a stare down during the tail end of mating season. If she accidentally brushed up against me while we moved furniture together, I'd flinch as if I were Linda Blair in *The Exorcist* getting stung with holy water, or I'd snap, "Watch it!"

As for combating the paralyzing dead silence, I started snapping at her for being weaker, or slower than I was— which of course meant I had to bust ass and work as fast as possible. When we'd finish a room I'd leave immediately, and she'd have to hurry to follow me.

Basically I acted like a major asshole, but I had no choice.

Anytime Mia asked me a personal question—that is, anything not pertaining specifically to work, I responded with only one sentence: "I don't know." Granted, it's a serviceable answer to some questions, but the more Mia tried talking to me the weirder my response sounded.

"Where did you live before you moved to Bern?" she asked me one morning.

"I don't know," I replied.

Another time she asked me:

"Do you have any brothers or sisters?"

"I don't know."

If Mia asked me for any sort of advice regarding the work at hand, I adopted a well-known retort: "I could tell you, but then I'd have to kill you."

"How did you clean the vacuum brush, Albert?"

"I could tell you, but then I'd have to kill you."

"No, seriously."

"Seriously, I could tell you, but then I'd have to kill you."

"We need to get this done, Albert, so stop fooling around."

"Yes, but if we did, I'd have to kill you."

"Come on, Albert."

"Kill you."

Basically it's like there were all these synapses misfiring in my brain, and soon enough I started developing all sorts of weird tics from being in such close proximity to her, like my right eye started involuntarily twitching whenever I was around her. Another one was that I started pressing my nostrils together like twenty times a minute whenever she'd look at me. The worst tic by far, however, was that I started swearing a lot.

"Albert, do you mind helping me move that table again, I think I missed a spot," Mia said.

"No fucking problem, just wait a goddamned second while I put my stupid-ass dust mask back on. There, now the cheap-ass mask is back on my face; now where the hell is this rat bastard table you need me to move, goddamnit?"

"Um, never mind," Mia said.

I knew she didn't think it was cool that I was cursing like a sailor; it didn't sound remotely cool coming out of my mouth, but I couldn't help myself. I wanted to stop desperately. I went to the bathroom and braced my palms against the emerald countertop and stared in the mirror and tried to plead with myself to stop swearing.

"Goddamn shit nuts poopity poop balls," I said instead, then sighed.

As a result, within a day or two Mia stopped trying to talk to me, despite the boredom of vacuuming rooms all day in silence. Apparently ignoring a girl, snapping at her for touching you, and swearing profusely is a bit of a turnoff for the ladies. It was kinda depressing, but I took solace in the fact that while she seemed annoyed by me and ignored me, she outright despised Gino. He was constantly hitting on her, under the guise of badgering her about work, asking her personal questions that he figured didn't seem personal (e.g.

"Huh, yeah, it is, the pool's really shallow—say, have you ever gone skinny-dipping?").

Sometimes I'd sit down at the edge of the mattress and take a break, and she'd silently do the same, sitting down at the desk. She'd stare at the ceiling for a few minutes, blinking slowly, as if deep in thought. Occasionally she'd look over at me and touch her throat, as if she were an elderly woman and had forgotten I was sitting there.

Despite my social disease, the fact remains that Mia and I still managed to work well as a team from the start. Without using words we were able to work efficiently, moving the furniture around and navigating around the occupied rooms and accomplishing all the other aspects of the job. I could read subtle nuances in her body language—her eyes, the nods—and she could do the same with me. In retrospect, it seems clear to me that there was a connection that allowed us to communicate with so little. There was definitely something between us.

8 "There you are, Arnie," said Gino. "I was just telling your coworker that today you guys are going to help me re-mulch the islands in the parking lot."

Gino and Mia had been waiting for me right outside the cloffice. The door was slightly ajar, and I deduced that Gino had suggested they wait in his cloffice and she had refused. I knew why Mia was smiling to herself. It was our first side job. We'd been vacuuming rooms for two weeks by this point, and were dying of boredom. It'd felt like we were in prison—all day it was sunny outside, and there we were, wearing dust masks, vacuuming in the blue, over-air-conditioned rooms all day. Anyway, to spend a day outside sounded like a reward.

We followed him outside. There was a huge pile of mulch with a couple of shovels and pitchforks stuck into it on the back of a flatbed truck, along with two wheelbarrows leaned up against the side. There were six little islands in the parking lot that had tiny shrubs that were just starting to sprout, because they'd recently been planted in the old mulch, which was almost gone at this point. What was left were little pieces of wood that were completely gray.

Gino proceeded to give a ten-minute speech on how to re-mulch the islands. It was a simple task—basically you just add mulch to the mulch and that's it. But Gino had a very specific OCD when it came to describing how we had to use the shovels to make what he referred to as "little levees" along the edge of each island, which he theorized would keep the new mulch from spilling over.

"So what you do is dig up a little levee like this—"

"We know, Gino, you've told us ten times already," I cut him off.

"Yeah, Alvin, but it's really important to—"

"Oh my God, his name's Albert," Mia said.

"Right—Albert, why do I have such a hard time remembering?"

"Do you really want me to answer that?" I muttered, looking over at Mia for a corroborating smirk, but she ignored me and stared at the mulch.

Our joy to be outside lasted all of thirty seconds once we started actually working, as we realized this was hard labor—we're talking orange-vest-wearing, on-the-side-of-the-highway-type hard labor. Within minutes our hands and arms and eyebrows were dirty with fresh mulch because we'd made the grievous error of wiping the sweat with our dirty hands. It was hot out, the last week in June, and neither of us was wearing hats or sunscreen. My shirt was soaked through, and soon I was developing a wicked headache. It got so hot that a stifling haze spread out over the parking lot, the kind where if you try to look through the air, it looks blurred, like shower glass. At one point I even saw a mirage by the side entrance.

"Do you see that purple lion, or is it just me?" I asked Mia, pointing in the lion's direction. He was ominously staring at me, his purple tail lazily flapping on the pavement, making a discernible slapping sound.

"Maybe you should drink some water," Mia suggested.

Gino sat on the pile of fresh mulch on the bed of the truck and blatantly stared at Mia. I realized that he was sitting on the truck intentionally for a better vantage point to look down her tank top while she shoveled. Mia realized it, too, and turned away from Gino at that point. Gino didn't put two and two together and hopped off the truck, put on his pair of aviator sunglasses, and started talking to us as we worked.

"Do you need help with that rock?" Gino asked, as Mia struggled to lift a big rock that was jutting out of the ground.

"No thanks," Mia said, and I watched Gino glare at her.

A couple of minutes later: "Let me help you with that levee," Gino said, reaching for her shovel.

"I got it," she said.

Gino eerily stared at the back of her neck, as if at any moment he would lean over and bite into it.

And a couple of minutes after that: "I'll handle the wheelbarrow, you take a minibreak," Gino said, trying to take over the wheelbarrow.

"Gino, stop it, let me do my job," she said.

"Fine, I was just offering to help. If you don't need my help, that's kosher, I have plenty of important work to do inside, maybe I'll even get a refreshing glass of iced tea. You children keep at it, this should take all day."

And as Gino stomped off, he added softly, but not too softly, under his breath, "You worthless skank."

Mia's eyes grew wide and I felt a surge of rage in my chest. I picked up my shovel and saw that my knuckles gripping it were white. I stood there for a moment, glowering at Gino as he disappeared into the inn. I looked over at Mia. She was visibly shaking. She realized I was watching her and she glared at me. I quickly turned my back and started futzing around with the pile of mulch in my wheelbarrow, listening carefully to hear when she started working again.

"I hate Gino," she said quietly.

I turned around.

"He's a jerk," I said.

"I hate this job," Mia added.

This hurt me because I felt the job included me, not just Gino.

"Why don't you quit, then?" I asked.

"Because I can't!" she snapped, then picked up her wheelbarrow and heaved it over to the truck. I watched her refill it, and when she came back toward the island she didn't look up at me.

Mia got this hard look on her face after the incident with Gino, and she just shoveled and shoveled, barely looking up. The smell of the mulch became awful as the day wore on, and grew in pungency the deeper into the fresh pile we dug—the smell was a combination of seltzer and smushed prunes. My entire body was sore, especially my back, but so long as Mia was shoveling hard, I kept up with her.

Gino didn't come back outside for the rest of the day. Looking over at the inn now and then, I got the distinct feeling he was watching us from a window, but they were all golden with the glare of the sun.

At the end of the day we finished mulching the final island, and it definitely felt like we'd been through something together, Mia and I, and I could tell we both wanted to acknowledge it. For a moment we stood back and looked at the islands, newly mulched, the truck empty. It looked really good, actually, and I felt a sense of pride at our accomplishment. I could tell Mia was thinking the same thing, because for a millisecond a smile started to cross her lips as she scanned our collective work. Then it was gone.

"That's it, then?" Mia asked.

"I think we're done," I agreed.

And that was it. She walked directly to her car, got in, and left.

The next day Mia seemed a different person. Or rather, she stayed the same person she was at the end of the previous workday. Instead of resetting overnight and greeting me cheerfully like she always had, she barely nodded at me, and we vacuumed in complete silence. At noon she promptly put down her vacuum and muttered, "Have a nice lunch," and left. It was obvious that she now lumped me in with Gino and the job itself and hated all three of us. I went to Gino's cloffice, where I'd been leaving a bagged lunch to eat, and I started chewing on a soggy, warm, bologna-and-cheese sandwich in the dark. I didn't have time to lament Mia's new attitude, because Gino showed up a few minutes later.

"Let me ask you something important, and make sure you keep this on the down low," he said, carefully peeking out into the hallway before closing the door behind him. "Do you think you could work more efficiently if you were working with a guy instead of Mia?"

"I don't think it would make a difference," I said quickly.

"Well, I do," he replied. "The only thing is I can't just can her without a legitimate reason. I had to fire a worthless girl last summer and it turned into a mess—apparently you can't fire someone for merely being totally useless. Anyway, I have to have a reason because Martino likes her, so do me a favor and keep an eye on her for me? Let me know if she does anything stupid, and I'll get you a real coworker pronto."

"Okay," I said.

Gino stared at the Niki Taylor cover for a second.

"Another generation of bitches. Like she could hold a candle to . . ." His voice trailed off, and then he was gone.

9 "Never mind Gino, you're going to be working exclusively for me the rest of this week," Martino said, leading Mia and me down the west wing. It was the Thursday before Fourth of July weekend. He stopped in front of a door at the end of the hall that I hadn't noticed before, past the business conference rooms. It was marked ROOM 224. "Here we are. Albert, give me your master key."

I handed it to him.

"Carlo, one of Mr. Scarletti's sons, is getting married at the inn this Saturday, and we need you two to fix up the inn real nice for the reception."

"I thought we were vacuuming the rooms for the wedding and that it wasn't till the end of summer," I said.

Martino rolled his eyes.

"Is that what Gino told you? He doesn't know what's what. It's just something that has to be done this summer because it hasn't been done in a while, that's all. Figures that Gino wouldn't even know when his brother's wedding is. You'll focus on three main tasks: cleaning all the storm windows in the restaurant, which is where the reception will take place, and wiping down all the brass fixtures in the hallways on the first floor."

"That's only two things," Mia said.

Martino giggled.

"And number three lies beyond this door right here," he said, turning the key and pushing the door open. "Lady and gentleman, welcome to . . . the Honeymoon Suite."

Mia gave a low whistle behind me as I pulled the vacuum

cart through the door. The Honeymoon Suite was unlike any other room in the hotel. For one thing, instead of beige wallpaper, the walls were a soft pink with a white-and-gold border along the top. The first room you walked into was a living room area with a huge-ass TV and a leather bar fully stocked with bottles of liquor and silver cocktail shakers and glass steins. Beyond it was a fully furnished kitchenette. There was a single window behind the kitchen table with its two antiquey wooden chairs, and along the windowsill were a number of leafy potted plants that looked like they got watered regularly, as opposed to the wilting, browned rubber plants in the regular hotel rooms.

Past the kitchenette were two doors: one was for a bathroom with a Jacuzzi, and the other was for the master bedroom. The master wasn't huge, but the bed was king-size and the sheets were really silky and pinstriped, unlike the starchy off-white cotton sheets in the regular singles. Instead of paint-by-numbers paintings of farm scenes that filled every other hotel room in the inn, this one featured silver-framed, black-and-white photos of the Boston skyline.

"Nobody ever uses it. Gino must have locked it by accident. So . . . what do you think?" Martino asked me.

"It's beautiful," I said, in an unintentionally effeminate, singsongy voice.

Mia started to laugh, but quickly caught herself, remembering that she hated all of us.

"No, I mean, do you think you can handle moving the furniture around in here on your own? Most of it is much bigger in this suite, and of nicer quality, which means heavier in most cases."

"We'll manage," I said, in a deep voice.

"Mia, since you probably know about housecleaning better than Albert, why don't you take the lead on the fixtures and storm windows."

"Sure," she said.

"It's Thursday, so you have two days to get these three tasks done," Martino said.

Vacuuming the Honeymoon Suite turned out to be the only task we did right. It took all morning because there was so much furniture everywhere. The TV cabinet was twice as big, because it housed a pair of four-foot-tall Infinity speakers inside it, and so moving that took twenty minutes alone. I liked vacuuming the suite, though. I daydreamed the whole time about staying in the suite someday as an adult. I think Mia must have been lost in a similar daydream, but I couldn't tell for sure, because she was still in no-speak mode with me.

That afternoon we went to the maids' station and Mia grabbed two big bottles of Formula 409 Cleaner and a dozen washcloths. The head maid, a really nice Mexican lady with horsey teeth, showed us where the stepladders were, and then Mia instructed me to work one side of the hall while she did the other. It turned out to be a bigger task than we thought—there was brass lettering outside of every conference room, the big sign on the wall outside the restaurant was brass, and most time-consuming were the brass light fixtures that were every five feet down the length of *every* hall. It took us the rest of the afternoon to get the job done. I was freezing because my shirt was damp with sweat, and had perpetual goose bumps all afternoon.

"Tomorrow we'll tackle the storm windows," I told Martino and Gino when we clocked out. Gino patted me on the back, getting between me and Mia, facing away from her.

"Thanks, Andy," Gino said loudly. "You really housed today."

Even though he was being an ass by intentionally not thanking Mia, and once again had gotten my name wrong, it kinda made me feel good. I guess I just like positive reinforcement in general, even if it's phony. Anyway, it only lasted that brief moment, because the next morning I arrived at work and I could immediately tell Mia and I were in some sort of trouble. For one thing, Martino was standing with Gino outside the cloffice, waiting for us. They both had their arms crossed, and it looked symbolic.

"What the hell did you use to clean the brass fixtures?" Martino lit into me. "You've really done a number on us, Albert."

The door opened behind me and Mia entered the hallway. Her pace slowed when she saw Gino and Martino.

"They're all ruined!" Gino shouted at us. "You used cleaner on it, right?"

"Yeah, 409, I swear to God," I said.

"You morons, you don't use cleaner on brass fixtures! You're just supposed to wipe the dust off with a damp cloth."

"Whoa—that kinda felt like entrapment," I said.

Mia stood stiffly next to me.

"I don't know what—" Martino started. "We might have to postpone the wedding."

"I'll figure it out, Martino," Gino said. "At least get the storm windows done this morning, then get back to vacuuming in the afternoon; I'll deal with you children later."

Gino and Martino stalked off. I turned to Mia but she was already heading for the maids' station. As we walked down the hall past the restaurant we saw what we'd done. The 409 had eaten away at the brass fixtures, and so now everything was rusted-looking instead of shiny. Some of the fixtures even had an aquamarinish tint to them, as if they were antiques retrieved from a sunken ship.

"The reception could have a pirate theme," I suggested, but she ignored me.

I felt guilty getting the Windex from the maids' station— for all I knew Windex only *sounded* like it was meant for windows, and we'd find out later that we'd made them un-see-through or something. But the storm windows seemed the easiest task, which is why we'd saved it for last. We spent a good hour carefully taking the storm windows down and carrying them out onto the lawn behind the restaurant. The restaurant was circular, with thirty of these six-foot-tall storm windows lining the walls, providing a view of the back lawn that led to the woods. They'd replaced the entire back lawn with fresh, dark green, fake-looking sod, in preparation for the outdoor ceremony that weekend.

The storm windows were really heavy, an inch thick, and to clean them, one of us would stand a window up while the other sprayed the opposite side and wiped it down with a cloth. Then that person would hold it up while the other did the same. Despite the fact that we weren't communicating at all, at one point I did press my hands against my sides as she cleaned her side and pretended to be General Zod trapped in a Phantom Zone mirror, and she smiled for a flicker, before catching herself.

"Hold it steady," she barked, and I stopped miming.

The waitstaff, having shut The Three Ferns down for the day, were busy cleaning the inside of the restaurant, so we weren't able to put the storm windows back in until early afternoon. So once we were finished cleaning, we laid them out in a long row on the grass and took lunch.

Things were still hectic at the restaurant an hour later, so we decided to vacuum a couple of rooms before reinstalling the storm windows. It was a nice day, and I felt gloomier than usual vacuuming in the dark, bluish room while outside it was bright and warm. We had just started the second room when the phone rang!

"Hello?" I asked.

"Get your asses down to the restaurant, pronto!" Martino screamed into the phone.

"How did you know we were in this room?" I asked.

Martino slammed the receiver down. I took a deep breath.

"What's happened?" Mia asked.

"Nothing, they're probably just going to bitch at us for not putting the windows back up yet."

"They told us to come back later," Mia reminded me.

"Dude, I know."

Gino was sitting in the restaurant by the entrance, and he

kinda resembled that statue *The Thinker*, except with a ratty beige jacket. The chef looked at us with equal parts sugar and urine. We followed his eyes out into the yard. Martino was standing in the middle of the lawn, scratching the back of his neck as he glared down at the grass, and my stomach fell. We slowly went out to join him, and when I saw what he was looking at, I groaned.

The sun, magnified by the inch-thick grass, had scorched thirty yellow rectangles into the new sod. Behind me Mia gasped.

"We're going to have to replace this with new sod this afternoon. It's gonna cost an absolute fortune," Martino said. "I can only pray that the sod's still fresh enough that it's at least close to the same color."

"I am so sorry," Mia said. "It didn't even occur to me that the window would act like a magnifying glass."

"Mia, I don't see how you can keep working here," Gino interjected, appearing at Martino's side.

"What?" Her face instantly paled.

"We need Albert, because we need those rooms vacuumed, but you have too many strikes against you."

"But it was an accident."

"But it was your decision to use the 409 on the brass fixtures. We can't have this incompetence. You're fired. You can leave now."

Martino was slightly gentler.

"We'll mail you your last check," he said.

Mia didn't move. She was on the verge of tears. I looked at Gino. He was making a tremendous effort to appear as if he was frowning, but he couldn't fully hide his satisfaction.

"It's my fault," I blurted out. All three turned to me. "I'm the reason everything got ruined, so you should fire me."

"No," Gino said, his eyes widening at me. "What are you talking about?"

My hands were shaking, and I was feeling simultaneously heroic and terrified. It occurred to me that if I got fired, I wouldn't be able to hang out with Mia anymore. I shook the thought out of my head.

"I was the one who demanded we use 409. I took charge; I laid out these windows, it was my decision, so you can't fire her for my mistakes. I'll go."

"But she can't move the furniture herself," Gino retorted.

"She's not getting fired because of my poor decisions," I said. Gino turned to Martino.

"We can't keep them both if they screwed up this bad," Gino said. "But we need Albert. He's stronger."

"Enough!" Martino shouted. "This is all on you, Gino. You're responsible for your employees' actions. Just find a solution."

Martino stomped off, muttering to himself. I could make out the word "Gino" a couple of times in his ramblings as he turned the corner and disappeared.

"Fine. Personally, I think you're covering for her, Albert, but I have to let it go this time." Gino gave it one last shot, trying a different tactic with me. His eyes softened, in the way that I imagine serial killers look when they're trying to convince a neighbor's cat to let them pet it. "Seriously, bud, you don't have to do this. You're not getting fired, but this will hurt you in the future; you can still come clean with me."

I shook my head.

"But I'm not lying," I said, not blinking. "It was all me."

10

I got to work Monday morning and Mia was already in one of the rooms, moving the small furniture around. I opened the door and knocked on the front until she looked up at me. "Hi," I said softly.

She walked over to me and held out her right hand. I shook it.

Mia said, "Listen, I wanted to say thanks for Friday. You didn't have to. I really need this job, I can't afford to get fired, so anyway, thanks, Al."

"Don't worry about it," I said.

We stood facing each other for a few seconds. It was really awkward for both of us, so I looked to my left and she followed my gaze, and now we were both staring at each other through the vanity mirror.

"Oh, hi," I said to her reflection.

She giggled.

"You are so strange," she said.

Things changed after that. Our wall of silence was officially broken with that handshake, and I realized that I'd finally gotten used to being around her, and because of my chivalrous act she now saw that I was a good guy and not merely the weirdo, cursing-like-a-sailor bastard I'd portrayed myself to be up till that point. The rest of that morning we joked about how badly we'd screwed up the wedding, and how much we hated Gino.

"I had no idea the 409 would do that to the brass," Mia said. "I swear I use that stuff on everything in our bathroom at home, and I'm pretty sure the towel rack is made of brass, and it doesn't change color like that."

"We really are the worst maintenance workers ever," I said.

"The all-time worst!" she amended.

"In the history of mankind!"

At noon we lugged the vacuums into a new room and decided to break for lunch. It was sort of an awkward parting, but it's worth noting that we said good-bye to each other this time, which felt like progress.

"I have a theory," Mia said after lunch as we gripped opposite ends of the TV stand. "One, two, three . . . lift!"

We hoisted the TV stand over to the space between the bed and the door, unearthing a rectangular-shaped felt blanket of dust where the TV stand used to be.

"I don't know if I'd call that a theory," I said between breaths. "That just sounded like you were counting out loud a few numbers in sequence."

"I haven't told you it yet," she said. "Wow, you're so like 'on' all the time, aren't you?"

I made a mental note to stop failing to be funny.

"So anyhow, listen, this is important," Mia continued. "Let's review the facts, like detectives. Fact number one: Gino for some reason hates my guts and wants to fire me, right?"

I nodded.

"But he can't until we're done vacuuming all the rooms, right?"

I nodded again.

"So that means the one thing that's providing us, or at least me, with job security is the fact that we still have rooms to vacuum."

"How long did you spend thinking about this?" I asked.

"Don't joke, I'm being serious. Here's the interesting part—look at this."

She handed me the master occupancy sheet.

"What am I looking for?"

"How many rooms do we have left?" she asked.

I realized what she was getting at.

"That's only a few days of work," I noted.

"Precisely, and how much longer is summer?" she asked.

"Well, it's almost mid-July, so that means we have a month left or so."

"Albert, I can't have this job end in a few days. I need this to last all summer."

"But we're almost done with the rooms. Maybe Gino will find extra work for us."

"You know he won't. At least for me."

She was right.

"So what do we do?" I asked, and Mia grinned.

"And now we get to the part that makes me a genius," she said, stroking her chin. "There's just two things we need to do. First, we have to go back to the east wing, the first hallway we started at, and pretend to vacuum the last few rooms in that wing."

"I don't get it, we already did them."

"Because we need Gino to think that's where we're at."

"But he's heard us in these rooms. I've even heard his voice outside this room this morning."

"We can say it was the maids," she said.

"I don't know about that, but go on, I'm listening," I said. "What then?"

"Then we just pretend to vacuum the rest of the rooms, but slower this time."

"I'm sorry, but I'm not following."

"Come with me," she said.

We hoisted the TV stand back into place and then dragged the vacuum cart back to the east wing and picked a room near the end of the hall. I followed her into the room and she shut the door behind us.

"Get it?" she asked.

"We now have to revacuum these rooms all over again? That would be so frustrating."

"No, silly! We don't have to do anything now! All we have to do is whenever we move into a new room, we move a piece of furniture, say the TV stand, and occasionally we just run the vacuum in the corner, and if Gino ever comes by and knocks on the door, we just open it and he'll see that we're about to vacuum under the TV stand! Do you get it?"

A fluorescent lightbulb went off in my head; that is, it flickered at first, while making an audible buzzing sound.

"That. Is. Genius."

"I know! That way we can stretch this job out through the rest of summer, but the perk is we've unknowingly set it up so that we get a minivacation now, for the rest of summer, really, until maybe the last week, because we've already vacuumed these rooms!"

"How long do we stay in each room?" I asked.

"I figure it took us around twenty minutes to do a room, but we worked so fast and hard. I think we can slow it down to maybe forty-five minutes a room. That way we keep moving in case Gino's keeping note of what room we're in."

"But what do we do for forty-five minutes?" I asked.

She beamed at me.

"Anything we want!"

We were both thrilled with the plan, but that morning we found ourselves unable to enjoy our newfound freedom. Her big idea was to watch soap operas on TV, but we were too nervous to play it too loud because Gino might be able to hear. We tried to watch it on mute, but TV on mute kinda sucks, especially repeats of *Wings*, which is the boringest show of all time to begin with, so instead we just sat there, not really doing anything, which was a little boring, but it beat working. We'd talk quietly, and she described her family to me. She had an older sister, a junior at Bates, who was spending the summer in Costa Rica, which is why Mia got to use her Corolla for the summer. She described her dog that died when she was eleven. She witnessed it getting hit by a car, and then the dog ran in a panic into the woods, and they never saw it again, but there was blood on the road and so she was positive it had died. I told her details about Shitsville and my life in Maryland. The unfiltered cool artificial air and the tiny enclosed space must have done something to our heads, because Mia started asking me really bizarro questions:

"In fifty years are we going to find out that Coca-Cola gives us cancer?"

"Do you think taking antibiotics slows down a body's ability to fight a cold?"

"Is it true that the thirteen colonies are listed on the side of a quarter?"

One time we were watching an African savanna scene on *Mutual of Omaha's Wild Kingdom* and Mia turned to me and said, "Can zebras smell metal?"

On the screen the camera guys were in a jeep and the zebras were ignoring them, paying attention instead to a pair of glowing, amber lion eyes spying on them from the brush. Mia and I looked at each other for a moment, and then we started laughing like crazy. I had to double over and hold my insides, that's how hard I was laughing.

"It's a legitimate question!" she said.

"You think like a little kid."

"Shut up."

"No, it's cool, you think anything's possible. That's nice, in this day and age."

"In this day and age," she mimicked me in a deep voice.

"Hey, look at me, I'm a zebra," I said, leaning against the metal frame of the mirror and inhaling deep. I frowned. "Nope, nuthin'."

"Maybe that's why we get along, because you ARE a child," she replied.

"Oh go fuck yourself!" I shouted, my swearing-around-Mia problem reemerging unexpectedly, but this time it made her laugh.

"Do your parents let you curse like that in the house?" she asked.

"No, they don't," I said. "So I have to whisper all the time when I'm home."

She stared at me for a second, then broke out in laughter again, and I joined her because it felt good to laugh together, and as we laughed I don't know how much time passed, but at some point we realized someone was knocking on the door, hard, and we froze. Even though our plan was solid, we froze. Mia went over to the door and opened it. Gino charged into the room.

"What are you two doing in here?" Gino asked, surveying the room. Despite the slight wrinkles in the bed from where we'd been sitting, the room looked pulled apart, as if we were about to vacuum. "Didn't you vacuum this room already?"

"What? No, we didn't," I said.

"But I heard you down in this section a month ago," Gino said, clearly puzzled.

"That must have been the maids," Mia said.

He glared at her.

"What rooms have you done so far? Let me see the sheet."

I ran a finger down the east wing.

"That's it? What else have you done?"

"Gino, it takes almost an hour to do a room; we're actually way ahead of schedule," I said.

I ignored Mia, who was giving me a hearty thumbs-up behind Gino's back.

"How long will it take to finish?" he asked, staring at the sheet.

"We'll be done before school starts, I can guarantee it," I said. Gino frowned. "I've never started a job I couldn't finish."

Mia giggled. Gino looked at her.

"Sorry, Gino, I have to deal with this all day," she said. "He talks like a drill sergeant, trying to push me."

"Well that's actually good, Mia," Gino said. "It's not funny at all. If you were more like Albert you'd be further along I bet. Okay, well, get back to work. No more laughing, either."

He left. I crept over to the door and peeked through the peephole. I couldn't see him, but I had a feeling he was nearby, so we ran the vacuum for a couple of minutes.

Because of this scare, we developed a simple set of rules to protect against a roaming Gino. First and foremost, we learned to lock the goddamned hotel room door. Second, we were always on alert for movement outside. But we got lax. Gino would walk by and instead of turning on the vac or even getting up off the bed, I'd say loudly, "No, let's move it here, that way we can vacuum it without having to move it again." We always knew it was Gino because there'd be a pause in the footsteps, and then they'd resume a moment later, as if he had been leaning up against the door.

At first I was too nervous and actually vacuumed under the furniture, and when Mia stopped me I continued to stand there, running the vac back and forth over the same spot, as if that would be better than simply leaving it on. My nervousness only lasted an hour or so, before we settled back into hanging out in the room, bored out of our gourds.

"Do you ever think your fingernails look like people?" she asked me at one point that afternoon, and we ended up for what felt like hours and hours staring at our hands. I looked over at the clock by the bed and was stunned it was only three o'clock.

"Jesus," I said. "Tomorrow I'm bringing a pack of cards."

We played Gin Rummy to 1,000 the next morning, and then in the afternoon we actually played an entire game of War. Neither of us had ever finished it before. She won. Seeing the game to the end was something I'd always wanted to do, but alas, it turns out War sucks. We played cards for two or three days before we got sick of every game. A part of me kinda felt like revacuuming the rooms we'd already done, just so we'd have something to do. In fact, I suggested it.

"Are you insane?" she asked. "That would be the worst thing we could possibly do. This is pitiful. We have to be able to figure out ways to entertain ourselves."

I took out the hunter green Bern Inn stationery in the faux leather folder resting on top of the bureau.

"We could have a drawing contest?" I suggested.

"Oh my God, no!" She looked horrified. "Okay, right now, think of a cool game for us to play."

"Like what?"

"Right this second, make up a game on the spot," she said, her hands on her hips.

"That's impossible, I can't just think up—"

"Entertain me, monkey!"

I thought about it for a minute and she stared at me the

whole time. I left the room and ran down the hall to the ice machine and grabbed two ice buckets. I returned and handed one to her, and we sat at opposite ends of the room, each with an ice bucket between our legs. The objective was to flick cards into each other's ice buckets. After a while we got pretty good at it, actually.

"Your job is to think up games for us to play," she said at the end of the day. "Tomorrow I want you to have something planned for the morning."

And so the next morning we lugged the vacuums into a room and I sat her down in the chair by the window.

"Remember those hearing tests we had in elementary school?" I asked her.

"Oh yeah—I do!"

Her excitement rightfully lasted all of three seconds.

I said, "Well, it's time for another hearing test. Now go lie down on the bed and close your eyes."

"Why?"

She was apprehensive, and I got the sudden, distinct feeling that she was worried I was going to try to parlay the game into us kissing or something. It made me blush.

"Just trust me," I said.

"What are you going to do?"

"Just close your eyes and listen," I said, drifting backward to the bathroom. "Tell me if you can hear when I turn the water on."

I waited twenty seconds, then slowly turned on the tap. Ten seconds after that: "I hear it!"

I went out into the main room.

"I think you might have major hearing loss. Do you go to a lot of concerts at like the Worcester Centrum or something?" I asked.

"Shut up!" She threw a pillow at me. "Again."

"Go 'beep' when you hear it," I said, and she nodded, her eyes already closed.

This time I didn't even bother turning on the faucet. A few seconds later when she shouted, "Beep!" I shouted back, "Good job, now reset." And I'd just stand there with my hands in my pockets. We did this a dozen times, and it made her so happy to get it right, and each time I'd exaggerate my compliments:

"Wow, I really turned it slowly that time, but you still heard it."

"You must have really clean ears."

"Are you sure you're not cheating?"

"Is your mom a bat? Because I swear you must be using sonar."

"Wait a minute," Mia said. "Am I really hearing it that well? Seriously."

"Honestly, Mia, I haven't turned on the faucet in like ten minutes," I admitted.

At first she was furious, and hit me in the head a dozen times with the pillow, then she started laughing like crazy, till her face turned red. It sounds corny in retrospect, but it was as if the room was filled with nitrous oxide, because we just laughed and laughed. We stopped eventually because it literally hurt to laugh any longer.

"That was the best game I've played in a long time," she said.

And so that became our shtick. Every morning I'd come in with a new idea for a game, explain it to her once we'd set up camp in one of the rooms, and then that's what we'd do for the entire day, just talk and play my silly games. They were beyond stupid, but that was the point. The stupider the funnier, according to Mia. Like one morning we played hide-and-go-seek—the stupid part being the fact that we were in a tiny hotel room. Mia would stand in the corner and count to fifty, and while she counted I'd very quietly lie down on the carpet a few feet behind her with the comforter covering me, and she'd shout, "Ready or not, here I come," and turn around and see me lying there like a slug, and she'd burst out in laughter.

"Nuts," I'd say, peeking out from under the comforter. "I really thought this was a killer hiding spot this time."

Our favorite game that we played regularly was called the Damnit Game. Its origins: One afternoon we were staring out the window and below us was a rare sight—a group of kids. Two of the maids had brought their children to work that day, and these four Hispanic kids were facing each other in a circle in the parking lot below us, each with their right hand held out in the middle, as if on top of the butt of an invisible baseball bat. They wouldn't say anything, or even look at each other, they just stared down at the clump of hands, and every thirty seconds or so one of them would mutter, "Damnit!" and they'd all giggle and release their hands from the pile and take deep breaths. Then a moment later, they'd rejoin to play another round of whatever the hell they were playing.

After about five minutes, Mia started laughing really hard and fell back on the bed. "What the heck is going on?" she shouted.

"I have no idea. Maybe that's our game this morning, we have to figure out how to play it!"

We stood facing each other. We put our right hands in, hers resting a millimeter above mine. We stared at our hands. What could the objective possibly be? I wracked my brain, but nothing came to me.

"Damnit," Mia said, and pulled her hand back.

"Huh? What happened?" I asked. "You get it? Explain it to me."

"Yeah, don't you?" she asked. "I lost."

I was puzzled, but then her smile betrayed her.

"Oh . . . right," I said.

"Nice one," she said, nodding.

"It was luck," I said.

"You're so modest. Again." She put her hand in. I settled mine just above hers.

Five seconds later, I surprised her.

"Damnit," I muttered, and pulled my hand away as if she'd won. "You're getting better at this. That was really quick."

"This game's amazing!" she said.

I know it sounds ridiculous, but at the time it really felt like the greatest game ever. In quiet moments between rounds I'd marvel at the fact that a week earlier we hadn't even been on speaking terms and the job sucked, and now it felt like we were starting to become friends.

It rained really hard the first week of August. Every day at five, when our workday ended, the rain would abruptly stop—as if on a predetermined schedule—just in time for my walk home. The parking lot would remain strangely steamy, and before heading into the woods I'd spend a good ten minutes circling the parking lot, checking out all the pavement rainbows (which I have to admit aren't as cool looking to me as they were when I was little, but if I see one I still feel obligated to at least try to marvel at it). But at the end of the day on Thursday it was still pouring when Mia and I exited the inn. She tugged on the back of my shirt and pulled me under the awning.

"Let me give you a ride home," she said, pointing at her Corolla.

"No thanks," I said, feeling like I was pressuring her into giving me a ride even though that feeling was wholly unwarranted.

"I won't take no for an answer, so you might as well give up, because I'm physically stronger than you," she said.

"That is true, I have to admit. When people ask me to describe my coworker in one word, I always say, 'powerful.'"

"Shut up!" she said, shoving me in the back. Next thing I knew she was sprinting for her car, and so I gave chase. She shouted, "Go ahead, the passenger side's unlocked."

Sitting next to her in her car felt so mature, compared to the rest of my life. The dashboard smelled rubbery and the vanilla pine tree hanging from her rearview mirror looked brand new, and the thought of Mia buying the pine tree herself seemed so adult to me. It felt like I was jumping from sixth grade to midway through high school just by sitting in a car seat. I didn't know where to put my right hand—whether to keep it by my side or place it somewhere on the door or rest it above the glove compartment.

Mia fiddled with the radio dial.

"Do you like music?" she asked me.

I stared at her. "I'm not retarded."

"Well then find something good," she said, returning her hand to the wheel as she alarmingly started steering like she was driving a hay wagon on the TV show *Hee Haw*. I braced myself with one hand against the dash, and with my free hand started searching the radio stations as she veered into the opposing lane, making a left turn out of the parking lot.

"Where do you live?" she asked.

"Columbus Ave," I said.

She stopped the car with a jolt. Luckily there weren't any cars behind us.

"Are you joking?" she asked.

"You got me," I said. "I thought it would be really funny to screw myself over on a rainy day and have you drop me off nowhere near where I actually—"

Thankfully she cut me off because I didn't know where I was going with that.

"I live on Columbus, too," she said.

Columbus was a long road, but it shocked me I didn't know this already.

"What number are you?"

"In the cul-de-sac," I replied. "1269."

"I can't believe we live on the same street. I'm on the other end, by Belknap."

"Still, that's crazy we live on the same street and didn't know it," I said. "I've never seen you on the bus."

I realized the reason she was never on the bus was because she probably got rides with The House every day, in addition to the fact that the bus was universally reserved for freshmen and losers. She didn't say anything, and in retrospect, I wonder if she felt embarrassed for me for a flicker. Anyway, with the main roads busy with commuters coming home from work, plus the driving rain, the trip ended up taking almost fifteen minutes. Maybe the lack of visibility due to the rain was making her a crappy driver, but I winced and braced myself as she repeatedly edged out into intersections so far that passing cars had to swerve to avoid clipping her front end; for right-hand turns she'd take baby steps, constantly tapping on the brakes, as if she was trying to trick the driver behind us to slam into her back bumper, etc. As she finally drove through a four-way intersection without looking, I shouted in a panic, "Cars on all sides!" even though there weren't, and she slammed on her brakes so hard my forehead hit the windshield.

"That wasn't funny," she said, gripping the wheel.

We had to come to a full stop in dead traffic for over a minute just to turn on to Columbus. Seal's "Kiss From a Rose" was playing on the radio, and without realizing it she started mindlessly humming along. She was incredibly, shockingly out of tune, and I smiled at her, wondering if she was kidding or if she really was that tone-deaf. She noticed me watching her and stopped.

"What?" she asked.

"Uh, does your commute always take this long?"

She nodded.

"It takes me only five minutes to walk to work," I said. "And I even usually stop on my way, so it's probably less than that."

"Five minutes?" she asked. "That's impossible!"

"It's just a straight shot behind my house," I said.

"I want to see for myself. What time do you leave?"

"Seven fifty," I squeaked—my throat tightening for the first time in weeks.

"I'll be there, wait for me," she said. She pulled in front of my house. "Okay?"

I opened the door and stepped out into the rain.

"I'll wait by my mailbox," I said. "But if you're not here by seven fifty-five, I'm gone. I'm outy. Seriously."

"Deal," she said, and beeped twice as she drove off.

I didn't feel like going inside yet so I stood out in the middle of the yard, under a canopy of green leaves that served as a broken umbrella. It was no longer a heavy downpour but a steady, drenching rain. The grass was so tall the blades bent over and looked like hair. I could barely make out the lines from mowing it two days earlier. My shirt was so soaked that my shoulders resembled artificial limbs, an orangish plastic. A crow floated by overhead; raindrops pelted its navy blue feathers, knocking it down a few inches before it rose again. A potentially rabid (because I swear it seemed to be smiling at me) deer, without warning, ran through the yard and into the woods, dangerously close, but I didn't feel nervous in the slightest for some reason. The neighbor's orange cat soon followed in wild pursuit. I'd never seen a cat run around in the rain before, let alone chase a deer. It looked almost prehistoric, with the lush grass and the mist. The cat's striped tail disappeared through a thicket. The rain was warm and I felt happy now that Mia and I were getting along so famously, but at the same time the fact that we were kinda friends at this point felt so unrealistic I couldn't quite appreciate it the way I should.

The next morning I went out to my mailbox at 7:15 to wait for her. I felt crickets in my stomach, and the pessimist in me felt certain Mia wasn't going to show up at all, but then at seven forty she appeared down the street. It was such a long straightaway that we could see each other for a full minute, and I felt embarrassed for both of us, so I pretended to not see her and turned away, opened the mailbox, and dramatically peeked inside it. Then I put the red flag up. Then down, then back up, as she neared.

"Mom, make up your mind, you schizo, do you want the flag up or down?" I hollered at the empty house (both my parents had gone to work already). I jumped back a little too dramatically when I pretended to see her for the first time. "Oh hey, Mia."

"Albert, I thought about it last night and I'm pretty sure it's impossible your route takes five minutes, there's just no way!"

"Wanna make it interesting?" I asked.

"You mean put money on it?"

"Yeah, it'll be fun."

"Okay, sure," she said. "How much?"

I thought about it for a minute.

"How about a thousand dollars?"

She started to laugh, but then realized I was all business.

"Why don't we just make it an honor bet," she said.

"Technically, wimps don't have any honor, but I'll let it slide this time. Here, I'll time it," I said, pressing buttons on my Ironman watch.

She followed me onto the path and under some branches, into the field, and gasped. It was like I was showing her Narnia for the first time.

"I haven't been in this field since I was little. There's a hill down that way that we tried to go skiing on once," she said, pointing.

"That's the inn right there," I said, pointing straight ahead at the sliver of visible gray roof.

She looked stunned.

"You were right . . . I can't believe it's this close."

As we neared the drainage pipe I turned left off the path.

"Where are we going?" Mia asked, as I led her to the edge. It was so muggy it felt like it was going to rain soon. I was sweating so much my shirt was sticking to me.

"You'll see," I replied.

Even though we were pals-y around each other, it was only within the confines of the inn, and I could tell she suddenly felt a little nervous. I'd noticed the day before on the car ride home how uncomfortable it was to interact with her outside of work. I pictured the frogs, sitting at the edge of the pond. I wanted to finally hit one this time, for her. I wondered if she'd even find the frogs half as interesting as I did, but I quickly blocked the thought out.

"What is it?" she asked, pulling on my shirtsleeve. "Tell me."

She stopped when we got to the spot.

"Why are we here?"

"Look over the ledge. Or edge, I'm not sure."

She gasped when she saw the frogs.

"They're huge," she said quietly, almost reverently. "You never told me."

"It's a surprise."

I didn't even have to mention the rocks before she bent over and picked one up.

"Let's try to hit one," she whispered, and she leaned in when she said this. Her breath smelled like a combination of ketchup and spearmint gum—her favorite gum flavor; she was always chewing a piece.

We headed over to the spot where I always stood, and I laid out a row of perfectly round, smooth stones. She threw first, and missed terribly. I was glad for that. It made my throws look a lot better. We got through the pile, and like I figured, neither of us could hit one. I could feel her losing interest, so I grabbed a fresh handful, but Mia shook her head.

"It's impossible," she said. "That's probably why they never bother to move. It's like they know we can't hit them."

I didn't say anything.

"You know what?" she went on, halfheartedly flicking a

stone at the frogs, the stone barely making it down the embankment. "I was thinking last night, you don't even know what's going on with me these days, I should probably explain it."

"What do you mean?"

"You know how when you saved my butt I told you that I really needed the job?"

I nodded.

"Well, I never explained why I needed the job so badly."

"I assumed after the water faucet test that you're saving up for an ear operation, right?" I said.

She didn't laugh.

"I'm being serious," she said. "The reason is Ryan and I broke up at the beginning of summer."

My chest tightened.

"Really?" I asked, trying to stretch my torso by extending my arms as far apart as I could. I looked like I was impersonating Jesus.

"Yeah, it's a long story, but the point is we went out for three years, and all his friends are my close friends, and I wanted a clean break, and so I needed to focus on something this summer that had nothing to do with him, where I wouldn't run into him or his friends every other day, so I got this job."

"Oh."

She threw another rock.

"I was a wreck when it happened, and so I really needed the distraction, but it's been way more than that, and I have you to thank."

"Me?"

"Yeah, you've totally made me feel better. Even this, the frogs. These games. It's just what I needed. You have no idea."

We didn't say anything for a minute or two. She stared down at the frogs, seemingly deep in thought. I felt confused by the news that she wasn't dating The House. I couldn't process it. I felt good that she said I was helping her, but it also felt weird to me, like I was a nurse or something.

"We should have a rule about this place," she said.

"Like what?"

"We can only throw five rocks apiece, otherwise it would just seem like mindless murder if we threw till we eventually hit one. We're trying to hit them, not stone them to death," she said.

"I just want to be able to do it. I've been trying to hit them longer than you. Trust me, it gets frustrating as hell."

"But this place is sacred, kinda. It's pristine. So we have to respect the frogs, and the place, you know? Five throws apiece."

"Okay, but only if we do one more round right now, just this once," I offered. "It's not that big of a compromise."

We shook hands. I finished throwing my handful before she even started with hers. If I had siblings, I'd be the first to open my Christmas presents, every single year. She measured her rocks as if she were an archer, and they landed harmlessly on the gravel next to the pond, a good ten feet past the frogs. She stared at the tadpoles for a minute, swimming around in the pond, occasionally bumping into each other.

"Someday I'll hit one," I said. "I'll hit one for you."

I know it sounds corny as Care Bears, but I meant it, and in retrospect, I think she knew I was being serious, because her eyebrows furrowed momentarily.

"Let's go," she said.

"Wait a sec, aren't you going to acknowledge that I won the bet?" I asked. "Have you no honor?"

She smiled at me.

"And precisely how much time has elapsed, according to your watch?"

My stopwatch read just over twelve minutes had elapsed.

"Well, we stopped here for a while so I could show you the frogs, but you know the walk would've taken around five minutes."

"Sorry, I only go by what your stopwatch says. Which means you lost!"

"But that's bullshit."

"Come on," she said, rolling her eyes. "It looks like it's going to start pouring any minute, and besides, we're getting late."

12

The rain finally let up a few days later, but it felt like an invisible dark cloud had come to rest above us. Even when it was sunny outside I felt gloomy, and she acted abnormally serious around me, and we didn't laugh like we normally did in our private hotel playground. I realized our friendship was changing, and I wasn't sure how I liked it. I mean, it seemed that we were getting closer because she was talking more personally now. Once she explained that she'd broken up with The House, it's like a floodgate had opened in her head, and now that was all she ever talked about. She'd just rattle on and on about all the things that were wrong with The House—his disinterest in ever trying anything new, his fear of showing a sensitive side, etc.—some of which she'd known all along, and some of which she was only realizing now that they were broken up. She'd felt like a beauty pageant winner: ceaselessly waving from The House's Bronco II at the cheering masses at Burger King on Friday nights. Making appearances at The House's lax games and sports banquets, his all-afternoon "quid fests" with the lax guys where they sat in the woods squirting dip spit into empty Snapple bottles and talking about pro sports. It seemed at first that the main reason they'd broken up was because she didn't feel she had a life of her own.

"Have you seen him since you broke up?" I asked.

"No," she replied. "It's really weird, I don't think a week, let alone a few days, ever went by the last three years when we didn't see each other, and now I haven't seen him all summer."

I was casually recoiling the cord to the vacuum because I'd seen the light break under the crack of the door, and my Gino radar, or what Mia had coined "Gino-dar," had gone off.

"Is that weird for you?" I asked.

"Yes and no," she replied. "I mean, of course it's weird, and kinda sad, too, but at the same time I'm surprisingly okay about it."

"Did it end amicably?" I asked.

"He was mad at me when I told him, but the weird part is

I bet he's doing better than I am at this point. I mean, the only thing in his life that changed is that I'm no longer in it. But since I spent all my time with his family and friends, it's like I just voluntarily marooned myself on an island."

"I thought you just said you felt 'surprisingly okay about it,'" I countered.

"Well, I'm surviving. Maybe we have different definitions of the word 'okay.'"

"I think 'okay' means 'awesome,'" I said. "I guess I have lower standards than you."

"What does 'awesome' mean to you?" she asked.

"That someone's lying," I said.

"Oooh, you sound so cool," she said, shoving me.

"That did sound cool, didn't it?" I said. She had a distant look in her eyes all of a sudden. "Anyway, I wouldn't sell yourself short. I'm sure you not being in his life is a huge gap."

"Thanks. I don't know what I mean anymore. I know it's hard for both of us, and I'm glad I broke up with him, but it's just, well, quiet these days."

"I'M SORRY TO HEAR THAT," I shouted, leaning in. She pushed me away.

"I'm glad for it," she said. "I needed the quiet."

I frowned.

"Well, when you're ready to reengage with real life, just be sure to say good-bye to me, okay?" I said.

"Why would you say that?"

"I'm just kidding," I added quickly, but I wasn't smiling.

"Oh," she said.

At the end of the day we walked through the woods into the field. We made our customary stop at the ledge overlooking the frogs, and we each threw a handful of rocks. As usual, we weren't able to hit a goddamned thing. We'd been throwing rocks at the frogs every day, and as a result it was now hard to find rocks—we'd take several minutes just to collect a handful.

"What do you do after work?" Mia asked me.

I tensed, as if she'd just accused me of something.

"Nothing," I said quickly.

"Seriously, tell me."

"Um, I eat, then I watch TV. Sometimes I look out my window at stuff."

"You sound like a cat," she said. "Or like you're in prison."

"That second analogy's crossed my mind before," I admitted.

"I don't feel like going home yet. My parents love Ryan, and they keep badgering me about getting back together with him. It's like their favorite topic. I hate it."

"Sounds like an arranged marriage."

"Practically. But at the same time they were actually really strict with him back when we were dating—especially my mom. She was always policing us, so we spent most of our time at his house. Anyhow, it's so hypocritical that now that we broke up she keeps asking about him—she urges me to invite him up to our summer house on the Cape to spend the weekend! He'd come over and she literally sat between us on the sofa whenever we watched TV. A sleepover back then would have been considered sacrilegious! I can't figure out why they're acting like this."

"Parents aren't meant to be understood," I said, and she nodded.

We got to my driveway and she stopped.

"So what are we doing now?" she asked.

It felt strange that we were about to hang out outside of the inn, outside of our route from my house through the field to the parking lot. Usually we'd say bye and I'd walk into the garage and then hide behind the wheelbarrow and watch her walk away until she disappeared from view. I didn't know why; it just felt like the natural thing to do, I guess.

What were we going to do? An idea formed in my head.

"You like games, right?" I asked. She nodded. "Well, we can go see these little kids I sometimes watch, they play all kinds of games."

She frowned.

"I don't know," she said. "Maybe we should watch TV?"

"Trust me, you'll have fun," I said, leaning in conspiratorially. "But here's the thing. These kids can get obnoxious. They're all in the sixth grade. My mom makes me hang out with them whenever I can stand it, because none of them have any siblings, so I'm like a big brother to them. I make them feel like we're all best buds."

"That's so nice of you."

"It's a huge sacrifice of my free time, but it makes me feel good," I lied.

"You're full of surprises, Albert Kim," she said, patting me on the shoulder.

She followed me up to Billy's loft. It was a big room above the garage where we played video games and foosball.

"Hey, fellas," I said in a goofy voice. They looked at me funny. "I brought a guest with me today. Boys, meet my coworker, Mia."

Billy and the guys stared disinterestedly up at her. They were lounging in the beanbags, playing Mortal Kombat III. Billy halfheartedly offered Mia a beanbag, and she sat down in front of the TV.

"Where have you been all summer?" Billy asked me.

"Working for the man," I replied.

He nodded and sort of chuckled knowingly to himself, as if he'd ever worked a day in his life. I turned to Mia.

"Do you wanna try fighting?" I asked her.

"I'll watch for now," she said. She turned to me. "When I was in middle school I used to love playing Zelda."

"Albert is the best at every game, probably the best in all of the commonwealth. He's finished Castle Wolfenstein ten times," Billy bragged to Mia. He leaned over and high-fived me. "You're the king! Boom-shaka-laka."

Jeffrey, the littlest sixth grader, had a wild look in his eyes. I mentally tensed.

"Oh my goodness, my throat is so tickly," Jeffrey said, covering his mouth. I glared at him, but he ignored me. He started fake coughing while secretly inserting phrases into the coughs, which of course were plain as day to understand. The fellas started laughing.

Cough . . . cough . . . touch her titties . . . *cough . . .* do her, Albert . . . *cough . . .*

"Oh man," he said, looking up at Mia. "I don't know what's wrong with me."

Mia giggled.

I turned off the Sega Genesis and plugged in the old school NES. RC Pro-Am was wedged into the slot, along with a tape cassette case because the machine was semibroken. "Here, try racing, Mia," I said, shoving a controller into her hands. I showed her what buttons to use, and she was really terrible at it, but she liked it.

"The rain clouds are good, they slow me down so I feel more in control."

Billy and the fellas laughed.

"You want to avoid them!" Billy shouted. "The point is it's a race!"

Cough . . . cough . . . man, she's really stupid . . . cough . . . cough . . . kiss her, Albert . . . cough . . . .cough . . . show us your butt!

"Easy, Jeffrey," I said, and then I silently mouthed, I am so going to kill you later.

He snickered and still had that wild look in his eyes, but he stopped cough-talking.

We took turns racing for twenty minutes, and then they switched back to the Sega and were playing Mortal Kombat III again, ignoring Mia and me. I was surprised that they weren't embarrassed at all in her presence, as I'd been at the start of summer; apparently, they were still asexual robots. She patted me on the shoulder.

"I'm all gamed out," she said, discreetly slashing her throat with her right index finger.

"Okay, guys," I said in a deep adult voice, enunciating really slowly as I stood up. "What do we say to guests when they leave?"

They stared at me.

"Good-bye, Mia," I said in a singsongy voice. "Come on, guys, let's give Mia a really nice 'loft send-off.'"

"What the hell are you talking about?" Billy asked.

"Never mind," I said, and led Mia to the door. I whispered in her ear. "Jesus, they're so shy around you."

We walked out to the road. She stuffed her hands in her pockets and stood on her tippy toes for a second. I felt a cozy sensation in my belly when she did this.

"Ryan never played games," she said. "He was so dull in that sense."

"What? Doesn't he play, like, every sport imaginable?"

"Sports, yeah, but not games. Nothing's for fun with him. It's just competition and advancing and beating everyone. He would never make up a game like you do."

I didn't say anything. I was feeling that weird tightness in my chest again.

"That's a good thing," she added. "You're so creative."

"Thanks," I said. "You too."

She smiled.

"I'll see you tomorrow morning, okay?"

"You got it," I said.

We high-fived and then she turned and started walking toward her car. I immediately began walking away, wanting to turn around, but I couldn't. I rubbed my torso—it felt like I was in the grip of a boa constrictor. I started pounding on my chest while I walked, and focused on my breathing. The heart-attacky feeling eventually went away, but the sad feeling lingered throughout a typically silent dinner with the 'rents, and hours playing Doom on my outdated Tandy computer in my bedroom. I felt sad, but also confused and uncomfortable—all in one. I wasn't tired, but at eleven I turned out the lights and lay in bed. I pictured Mia. Specifically, I was thinking of that moment in the maids' station at the end of the first day of work, when she shook the fence and pretended to be trapped behind it. Next thing I knew, I was imagining we were husband and wife, torn apart by war in some Eastern Bloc country. Mia had gotten arrested one night for not having the proper papers on her and was now a refugee stuck in an internment camp. I daydreamed a softly lit montage of scenes from before the war: the two of us slurping watery cabbage soup together in a tiny apartment; Mia looking really precious in a tattered, purple shawl as she handpicked slightly rotting fruit from a wooden cart down in the center of the village; Mia clapping and giggling as she watched me dance on our hard-packed dirt floor at night— that Russiany dance where you're kinda break dancing on the floor to a polka with your arms crossed over your chest; and lastly, I pictured myself sitting alone in the squat, gray apartment on a bright morning, holding a newspaper, and the headline read WAR OVER! but I wasn't smiling at all because Mia had died a day earlier in the internment camp, from untreated chronic bronchitis. The soldiers had let me into the camp to see her because they knew she was close to death, and she just lay crumpled in my arms with her eyes closed, barely breathing for a few minutes. But then with a heroic final surge of energy, she raised her right hand, palm out, and with the last bit of breath in her body she whispered, "How," to me and smiled as she sputtered up disturbingly phlegmy blood before finally keeling over.

I jerked up in bed, rubbed my eyes, and realized they were moist. I didn't know how long I'd been lying there, daydreaming like this. My entire body was throbbing—that familiar ache for the first time in almost a month, but it didn't feel scary this time, or confusing; it suddenly made perfect sense to me. I now understood what those bizarre physiological symptoms that had tormented me at the start of the summer meant. My inability to talk in Mia's presence, to walk normally, that perpetual heat on my cheeks, and that serious feeling I'd had the last few days around her. It wasn't merely the result of not being used to interacting so closely with someone, let alone a girl—it was way more than that. It was *Mia herself*; she'd made me feel so strange all summer. I realized now that the throbbing I was feeling was literally my blood redirecting to the shunted parts; specifically, my loins. For two years I'd redirected blood away from my crotch, but now it flowed back with a vengeance. I could feel it now, coursing through me stronger than ever as I pictured her, which meant only one thing.

I'd fallen in love with Mia.

13

Realizing my feelings for Mia was like a switch turning in my brain, and overnight I transformed into a sixteen-year-old hopeless romantic, with my sights pointed center-mass at Mia. I felt like I was seeing her for the first time that summer, I mean *really* seeing her, as if I'd had a mental guard up until then, even as we'd hung out and played games together, and only now was I truly seeing just how lovely she was in person. Her hair was slightly wavy in a way I hadn't noticed before, and her glassy, brown eyes were much brighter than I'd remembered. Despite her athletic quads, she was otherwise a tiny wisp of a girl; she stood barely five feet tall, and I'd guestimate she weighed at most a hundred pounds soaking wet, ninety-eight pounds completely dry. My fantasy dream girl was an animated mouse at the time, Mrs. Brisby from *The Secret of NIMH*, so it actually worked in Mia's favor that she was so adorably mousy looking.

Everything about her suddenly seemed so adorable to me, things I hadn't noticed before. Like every now and then she would very softly chuckle to herself, under her breath, and she was obviously thinking about something else while talking to me, and I loved catching her doing that. One time she had a headache, and I watched her fill up a paper cone full of water and take out some Advil from her purse, and I thought it was so cute that she took ibuprofen like an eight-year-old, gulping some water *before* sliding the Advil in her mouth ultracarefully so she didn't spill any water out of her lips. But the thing about her that I found most adorable was that she had this habit of omitting the word "the" from things that started with "the," and she also had this other habit, where she added a "the" to the beginning of phrases and titles that clearly—at least to ninety-nine percent of the rest of the English-speaking world—had no "the" at the beginning of them. Some examples:

Now that I've finally read the book, I'm dying to see the Tom Cruise movie, *Firm*.

I swear I spent all of tenth grade listening solely to Pink Floyd's *Wall*.

Oh my God, I feel soooo bad for what happened to the Magic Johnson.

I've since realized that what passed for "cute" coming out of Mia's mouth last summer I'd diagnose as potentially mild retardation in anyone else, but I was absolutely floored by her. And it wasn't just her looks, or her soft voice—I liked that she was different from the other popular girls. Most of the pretty girls at Bern High are incredibly mean girls. Deep down, they just aren't good people. Everyone seems to be well aware of this but doesn't really care, because the girls are pretty and popular and so the masses willingly let themselves get enslaved to them. Whereas with Mia—in addition to being a keeper looks-wise—she was a truly sweet person on the inside as well. Not to sound creepy, but I could *smell* it. Okay, that did come out creepy. Anyhow, the fact that she was an unmistakably nice person raised the stakes of my crush, and I wanted so badly to tell her how I felt, but didn't. The thought of her actually feeling the same way about me was so unrealistic, and of course the feeling that developed immediately following the epiphany of my love for Mia, which was followed by the realization that I had no chance with her, was a deep-seated depression. From the outside, I appeared the same—but on the inside I was crumbling.

The next couple of weeks flew by, and my depression got

really bad when we finally hit the last week in August. We had only one week left at work, our holiday together was coming to a fast end, and I was running out of time—once school started again she'd hang out with her friends, and I'd go back to my life as the wandering intentional loser. Or would we hang out? I had no idea, but there was no disputing the fact that our summer together was definitely ending, and I think we were both feeling sad about it, because we were both quiet on Monday morning.

Further exacerbating our gloominess was the fact that our "genius" strategy had caught up to us. For weeks we'd hung out and skipped out on the work, not realizing that the last week we'd have to work like crazy to get all the rooms done. By ten-thirty that morning, we'd vacuumed seven rooms and my muscles felt achy. I massaged my back. Mia turned the love seat around so it faced the window. She perched on one of its armrests and stared out at the parking lot with her chin in her hands.

I sat at the edge of the unmade bed. On a tray in front of the vanity mirror was a leftover, barely touched breakfast of steak and eggs, a pot of cold, sludgy coffee, and a chewy square of hashed potato. I pretended to watch TV on mute, staring peripherally at Mia's butt.

"Are you okay?" I asked finally.

"I'm so hungry," Mia said, holding her belly.

My belly growled at that moment, as if she'd given my stomach permission to whine.

"Me too," I said, groaning.

She slid off the armrest and sat down next to me.

"I mean, I'm really, really hungry, Albert," she said, slowly, staring at me.

We looked over at the room-service tray.

"Should we?" I asked.

"That's disgusting," Mia said, but she kept staring at the cold food.

"And besides," I added, "we could get sick from bacteria."

"I almost feel out of breath when my stomach rumbles," she said.

"I don't think potatoes develop bacteria. Maybe we could try the hash browns."

"At least the burned parts have to be safe, right?"

We raced to the tray and pounced on the hash brown square and pulled it apart like it was a wishbone. My piece had a cartoonish, perfect half circle of a bite in the middle, with little indentations of the previous owner's teeth, even. I took a knife and cut around it.

"Are we really doing this?" she asked.

"Yes," I said, and I pretended to put it in my mouth. Mia stuffed half of hers in her mouth and started chewing. I took my hash browns out, wet but unbitten. "I can't believe you did that, that's really gross."

Mia punched me in the shoulder.

"Eat it!" she said, guarding her open mouth with her hand. "I'll kill you if you don't."

I didn't need convincing. I bit into it. The meaty insides of the potato were cold and mushy, but the outside was chewy and salty. It was unbelievably delicious.

"This is so good," she said, closing her eyes and smiling as she chewed. When she opened her eyes I had the uneaten end of the steak hanging from my mouth and she burst out laughing.

"Don't! That's so dangerous, you could get salmonella."

"You only get that with chicken and salmon," I corrected her. "Look, I'll cut around the bites."

"Don't do it," she said, leaning in.

I cut the steak into an untouched square. It was fatty and tough. I cut it into little pieces. Mia uncapped the minibottle of A.1. and doused the meat. I handed her a fork.

"You first," she said, pressing the fork into my hand.

I stabbed a piece and swallowed it immediately.

"Wow, I didn't really have to twist your arm, huh?" she noted.

I gave her the thumbs-up.

"I can't," she said, giggling.

"It's just cold, but trust me, it's scrumptious."

"God, the word scrumptious makes my mouth water!"

"Scrumptious," I repeated.

"Stop it," she giggled.

"Moofasa!" I shouted. "Er, I mean, scrumptious."

"Okay already," she said, pushing me away.

She forked a piece dripping with A.1., shut her eyes, and very methodically inserted the piece into her mouth and started chewing carefully. I felt like we were those rugby players in the Andes after their plane crashed, trying strips of man-flesh for the first time, but I wisely opted not to tell Mia this.

"Is good, no?" I asked, involuntarily grunting with pleasure.

She swallowed, wincing as she forced it down. She opened her eyes. Her face looked a little green, actually.

"I can't believe I just did that. Wait, you're eating another one?"

I looked up at her with a big gob of meat in my mouth and shrugged.

"If you slash someone's tire, why would you feel guilty slashing the rest of them?" I reasoned.

She sighed and had another bite, handed me the fork, and I ate a second piece. Less than a minute later the steak was gone. I went ahead and scooped up the untouched over-easy egg and swallowed it like an oyster without chewing.

"Yuck!" she cried. "God, you must have a death wish."

Mia snuck out to the ice machine down the hall and returned with some ice to make iced coffee. But apparently there's more to it than that, because according to her it "absolutely tasted like shit." She downed the whole pot anyway.

"Ryan would be so disgusted with me if he saw what we did," Mia said. "He'd probably kick your ass."

It jarred me any time she said his name. I looked at my shoes. She went on.

"He never could relax. He doesn't like to do crazy things like this. Everyone thinks he's such a brave guy because he's big and athletic and tough on the lacrosse field, but in every other aspect of life he's the most cautious person ever."

I nodded. She went on.

"The whole family's like that. The Stackhouses are all

about appearances, and they're this perfect family on the outside, but on the inside they're just as messed up as any other family. He has two brothers and a sister, and they were even more successful than Ryan—both his brothers played lacrosse at Princeton, and his older sister, Porter, was an all-American squash player at Penn, and all three now work on Wall Street and live in huge apartments on the Upper West Side. They're like the Kennedys, well, except for all the tragedy."

"Maybe because he has such a bright future the stakes are just higher for him than everyone else our age," I said—I don't know why I was suddenly defending him.

"No, it's a weakness, trust me. He doesn't even like to go into the city because he won't ride the T. I mean, I'm not used to the T myself, but I'm not going to not visit the pier because I won't ride the T." She paused for a second, then blurted, "He's a germ freak! He is, he washes his hands like fifty times a day! The irony is that he shakes hands all the time, and he hates it so much."

"Is that why you broke up?" I asked. "Because he's so narrow-minded?"

She stared at me.

"Sorry, none of my business," I said quickly.

"No, it's okay," she said. "That's not why we broke up, but I can't get used to the fact that I went out with him for so long and never realized these things. It makes me feel . . . weak, for not noticing sooner. I am so naïve it's not even funny."

"Or maybe you've changed," I suggested.

"Neither of us changed, I just didn't notice these things until . . . the spring."

She sat down on the bed.

"You don't have to tell me."

"No, I want to," she said.

I wanted to sit down next to her but instead leaned up against the vanity.

"We broke up because I wouldn't have sex with him," she said.

I blushed. Even though I'd assumed they'd had sex a million times, like all high school couples, she still seemed so innocent I couldn't get around hearing her say the word. My stomach ached, but it wasn't from the food—which, in retrospect, probably was loaded with all kinds of bacteria.

"He always wanted to from the beginning. We started dating when I was just starting eighth grade; he was a freshman. It was easy to say no back then, but he really started putting pressure on me once I got to Bern High."

"You didn't want to?"

"I don't know. Sometimes I did, but something in me didn't want to, and now that he broke up with me, it's like I'm seeing his true colors, and I know that must be why I didn't do it with him. I think I knew deep down that he wasn't the right guy for me. The first time you have sex with someone should be special. I mean, it rarely happens that way in real life, but that doesn't mean I don't deserve not to rush."

"You were too good for him," I said.

"Thanks," she said, but she seemed miserable.

"Don't sweat it, Mia, you do know that everyone thinks Ryan's a jerk, right?"

She glared at me.

"What?"

"I mean, he's the king of the high school, but everyone hates him. He's more like a dictator, ruling with an iron fist."

"That's not true."

"Everyone fears him. He's popular the way Mussolini was popular and, like, Pol Pot and stuff."

"Help me put this bed together," she said, pointing at the other side of the bed.

"What—are you mad at me?"

"No, it's just time to finish this room. Come on."

We pulled the sheets up, the fleece underblanket, and the blanket on top. She tucked the blanket over the pillows and wedged it between the mattress and headboard. It dawned on me that she was talking to me like I was her confidante, like I was a girlfriend. I sighed.

"Now the bed's made," she said, and sat back down on the edge of the mattress. After maybe thirty seconds of what appeared to be deep thought, she patted the space next to her. "Sit here."

My hands started shaking, so I hid them by leaning back on them.

"Let's nap," she said, smiling at me. "I don't want to talk anymore, and I'm too zonked to play games; I feel that food coma after eating."

"It's risky," I said.

"I don't care anymore," she said. "Summer's almost over;

they could fire me and it wouldn't matter. The door's locked, anyway. I doubt we'll even fall asleep."

I stared at her.

"Just for half an hour or something."

"Okay," she said.

We lay back on the bed. No parts of our bodies were touching, but I felt static.

"Good night, Albert," she said.

For a few minutes we lay there with our eyes closed. Outside, an electrician's truck was parked at the entrance, and the song "A Groovy Kind of Love," by Phil Collins, was filtering out the open windows.

When I kiss your lips,
Ooh I start to shiver
Can't control the quivering inside
Wouldn't you agree,
Baby, you and me . . . got a groovy kind of love

I hated the song with a passion, and felt really embarrassed by the lyrics because I was lying next to Mia as it played. I worried that she might think I thought Phil was talking about us, not to mention the fact that I'd never really listened to the lyrics before, and it vaguely sounded like Phil was describing getting an erection; but soon I got the feeling we were both just pleasantly listening to it. I started picturing a little scene: Mia and me playing miniature golf, me holding her from behind, my fingers laced over her fingers gripping the putter. "Oh, so you hit it *that* way," Mia cooed admiringly as I taught her how to putt.

The song ended, and I realized I wasn't remotely tired. I felt so intense, I could almost see with my eyes closed.

"Wake up," Mia said, shaking me.

"Hold on, we're cleaning up this mess," I shouted, trying to sit up but almost falling over. I whispered to Mia, "Is it Gino?"

She laughed.

"He's not out there," she said. "We both fell asleep."

"How long were we out?"

"Almost an hour," she said. "I had a nightmare."

"What was it?"

"That I woke up and Gino was standing at the edge of the bed, smiling down at us."

"That's horrifying."

"Let's take our lunch break."

"I don't think we should eat room service again."

"My belly hurts," she said.

"Mine too," I admitted. "Hopefully it's just mental."

Everything, even being mildly poisoned together, felt romantic to me. At the end of the day I felt drowsy (probably still the poison) with love for her, and it felt like a new form of paralysis to stand next to her and resist the urge to bear hug her and kiss her on the forehead. She put the vacs away and shook the fence again, pretending she was trapped behind it.

"Get used to those bars, kid," I said.

She beamed.

"I know that line! The *Back to the Future* is like my favorite movie ever!"

I suddenly felt intensely jealous of Michael J. Fox, of any guy, really, that Mia thought of or mentioned in passing.

"Michael J. Fox is under five feet tall," I blurted. I couldn't help but continue lying. "He has to wear a red hat wherever he goes, even if he's not in the woods."

"What are you talking about?"

"I don't know."

Tuesday and Wednesday we followed the same routine. We'd vacuum a half dozen rooms in the morning, then in the afternoon we'd take naps. We barely talked. This is what it was like to nap with Mia:

She'd place an arm on my chest after a minute or so. Her arm was warm, and I'd flinch a little each time because my chest is flat and there's an unidentified bone that sticks out in the middle. I'd picture The House, who had body-builder pecs that probably didn't disappear completely when he lay on his back. Her left cheek would glance my right cheek. I could feel her face; it was warm and her skin felt like silk. After ten minutes my hand would finally come to a rest on top of her hand that was on my chest. I'd gently rub my thumb across her knuckles. She'd turn her head so she was half an inch from my face. My lips, though facing up at the ceiling, would be less than an inch from her lips. Tiny breaths from her nose on my cheek. I'd keep my eyes closed and pretend to sleep, and with eyes closed I'd be able to freely observe her movements and expressions by analyzing the sounds, her breaths. After a little while she'd turn her back to me. At this point I'd open my eyes. One time I noticed an old spiderweb dangling from the ceiling above us. It swayed a bit to the right, then back again. I stared at the stucco ceiling and tried not to breathe, and I don't know when I fell asleep.

When we woke up we'd be real quiet, and things would feel awkward for a few minutes as we fumbled around the room, trying to get back into the flow of things. Because we were disoriented we'd accidentally bump into each other in passing, and we'd say "Sorry" to each other a couple of times and automatically back away like bumper cars.

14 On Thursday we vacuumed like crazy in the morning to give us a little cushion for Friday—that way we'd have to vacuum only a couple of rooms on our last day of work. At lunchtime Mia surprised me with lunch. She'd whipped together two kinda sloppy-looking peanut butter and marmalade sandwiches, a Ziploc baggy full of pre-cut celery for us to share, and two cans of warm Coke. It was impressive—I'd never known a nonmother to be able to make lunch like that before. I have this weird mental block where if I'm home alone and want a sandwich, I can't do it—even if the pantry and fridge have everything I need to make a delicious turkey and cheese sandwich with lettuce, tomato, onion, mayo, and mustard, I can't for the life of me do it. I get slothful and the best I can do is roll a slice of turkey into a cigar shape and dip it in a jar of mayo (which tastes really gross, by the way).

We were sweating profusely, so our picnic wasn't that

good, because we were so uncomfortable, and the celery, because of the humidity, was all bendy, plus it turns out that marmalade is as disgusting as it looks, but it was fun to sit cross-legged on the bed and eat messily. The afternoon passed by too quickly; I didn't want our job to end. The fact that school was starting next Wednesday made it feel like life wasn't real, as if this was all just an exceptionally vivid dream. I tried to work up the nerve to ask her about us, but I couldn't. The possibility that she'd have no idea what I was talking about, or blush and frown, mortified me. I didn't want to ruin what we had. I didn't want to call to the surface some ugly truths, if the case were that she was going to go back to her old life next week, and I'd resume being a loser nobody saw after school or on the weekends. As a result of holding my questions in, I felt increasingly surly, negative, and the irony is that I didn't really talk to her that afternoon and ended up wasting one of our last days together. It felt good in a sick way to be so negative, and I started focusing on things, like how we never hung out on the weekends; and I grew convinced she was using me, that this was a parasitic relationship, just so she could stand going to work each day while she took a step back from real life.

"Are you okay?" she asked several times.

"I'm fine," I said, quicker each time.

At the end of the day I walked past her and the frogs, not stopping.

"What are you doing?" she asked, holding up her rocks.

"I have to help my parents clean the house, they're having guests over," I lied.

She looked out at the frogs, then dropped her rocks and jogged to catch up to me.

"I don't feel lucky today anyways," she said.

"Me neither," I said.

My parents were in the kitchen when I got home from work. Mom was standing next to the round kitchen table, drinking coffee. It was a usual sight: my dad eating Korean food with my mom seemingly standing guard over him, drinking coffee. I've never seen her eat at the kitchen table in sixteen years—like the mom in *A Christmas Story*, one of my favorite movies—never heard her eat or scrape at a plate while I was in my bedroom upstairs, and yet she's perpetually finished with her meal, having coffee. Some kids try to catch Santa putting presents under the Christmas tree; my mission when I was little was to try to catch my mom eating a meal.

"I'm preparing your favorite for dinner," Mom said, holding up a big Ziploc bag full of chicken. "Shake and bake!"

It wasn't even my favorite, but I just nodded and smiled wanly at her.

"Thanks, Mom, I'll be down in a minute," I said, and went upstairs and collapsed face-first on my bed and promptly fell asleep due to a combination of fatigue and depression. Next thing I knew it was dark out, and the phone was ringing. I never got calls from anyone, really, except sometimes from Billy when I was late for an after-dinner round of Ghost in the Graveyard, but I picked it up on the first ring, somehow expecting it to be Mia, and it was.

"I have a surprise for tomorrow," she whispered, then hung up.

Of course I spent hours lying in the dark, analyzing that one sentence, trying to figure out what the surprise was, and when I finally fell asleep the sky was that annoying-as-hell bluish color, and birds were chirping. When the alarm woke me up I was exhausted, but remembered immediately the phone call, and pushed myself to get ready for work.

She met me out by the mailbox at seven thirty, and we walked for the last time to the inn. It was a nice morning— sunny, but not scorching, some dirty white clouds in the sky. The field smelled like chlorine for no particular reason.

"So what's the surprise?" I asked.

"You'll see," she said.

The screaming frogs were echoing in the drainpipe as we approached them.

"Let's not throw rocks this morning, okay?" she asked. "I think I'd feel sad if we finally hit one on the last day."

"We wouldn't be able to anyways," I said, dropping my stones.

"It's like there's a force field around them, protecting them," she said.

"That's one way to look at it," I said. "Another is to admit that you're fast, but you're just not that good at hand-eye activities."

"I'm serious!" she said. "We've now thrown so many this summer that there has to be divine intervention going on, or something else. It's like they've earned the right to exist."

We vacuumed two rooms in the morning, then for lunch

we shared a boring leafy salad with spongy croutons and a chemical-tasting diet Italian dressing that she'd brought in a big Tupperware bowl. And then in the afternoon we did the final two rooms in reverse order, so we could hang out for the last hour and a half in the second-to-last room. Which makes no sense to me now, but at the time it felt like a genius solution. We heard Gino peel out of the handicapped spot in the back parking lot. He'd been taking long lunches in the afternoons, we'd noticed, the last few weeks. Maybe he'd been taking them all summer.

"So are you ready for your surprise?" she asked.

I nodded.

"Close your eyes," she said. "And hold out your hands."

I did. She placed something in them. It felt like a toy, plastic hockey puck.

"Okay, you can open your eyes."

It was a tin of Skoal mint long-cut chewing tobacco.

"Ryan taught me how to dip last year. I only do it on special occasions. Have you ever dipped?"

"No," I said, feeling embarrassed for being such a straight arrow. The desire to lie overtook me, and I muttered under my breath, "But I am a recreational crackhead."

"What's that?" she asked, not quite hearing me.

I sighed.

"Nothing."

"Anyway, Ryan dips so much he actually gets these little white splotches on the inside of his gums. It's gnarly, and he always tasted like dip."

I winced.

"But it's good if you do it only occasionally."

I opened it up. It was three quarters full.

"I can't pack it the way Ryan does, because my hands are too little, so I do this," she said, closing the tin and flicking the top a dozen times. When she reopened it the tobacco was packed tighter, with a small crescent space in one end. She pinched a dab and took it out. "Do as I do."

She then pulled her bottom lip open with her free hand and placed the pinch of Skoal inside it, then closed her mouth.

"Use your tongue to move any little flecks of it, and in a minute it'll start really producing tobacco juice, which you can spit into this cup," she said, handing me a plastic hotel cup. "It gives you a nice buzz."

I didn't want to dip at all, but of course I did. It smelled terrible, I couldn't place what it reminded me of at first. Mia lay back on the bed with her dip cup resting on her stomach.

"Now lie back, like this," she said, patting the space next to her.

I lay beside her.

"I feel more of a buzz if I lie back," she said, then pitched her head forward to dribble brown spit into her cup. She leaned back. "I don't really like to drink, I don't have a taste for it, and I'll never smoke because of track, but I like to dip every once in a while. It feels . . . relaxing."

My head was waving already. I wasn't so much having a nice buzz as I was on the verge of freaking out. Loose flecks of tobacco kept finding their way to my tongue, and I swallowed a couple by accident. My tongue was perpetually cringing because of the tobacco spit feel, and my stomach was starting to feel funny—strangely full, as if I'd just eaten a loaf of bread or something. A loaf of bread filled with chewing tobacco.

Mia turned toward me, onto her side.

"I know this is going to sound lame, but I kinda feel sad that this job is ending," she said.

"Me too."

"I hated the job itself, but I liked our walks to work in the morning, and I liked playing games with you all day."

"Thanks," I barely whispered.

"I needed this, Albert," she said. "I dated Ryan for a long time and didn't think I could handle breaking up, but you saved me. If I didn't have this job I'd be curled up in bed, miserable."

"Can I ask you a question?"

"Anything."

"Are we going to hang out once school starts?" I asked.

"Of course!" she said quickly.

This actually depressed me, because it sounded so buddy-buddy to me, squashing any hope for a romantic speech on her part, which I was kinda banking on, if anything was ever going to happen between us.

"Let's not think about it right now. Just enjoy the buzz," she said, and closed her eyes but didn't turn away. Instead she snuggled up to me and I could feel her tiny hands against my belly. It felt amazing and it felt like we were about to kiss, and I could tell she wasn't sleeping, but within seconds I finally realized what the smell of the dip reminded me of: the mulch we had to shovel onto the islands in the parking lot earlier in the summer. A second wave of nausea hit me, and I abruptly said, "I'll be right back, I have to get something," barely able to get the words out. I saw her open her eyes, surprised, and I leaped off the bed and out of the room and ran down the hall to the bathroom and ferociously threw up in the sink. It was so intense—the kind of booting session when afterward it feels like you have a piece of corn stuck in your throat, even though you don't really.

I passed Gino in the hall and he grabbed my shoulders.

"You look pale," he noted. "You feeling okay . . . Aldo?"

"Yes, my name is Aldo," I said, feeling less wavy. "Aldo Nova."

"Albert!" he shouted, getting it right for the first time all summer.

"The irony," I said.

"So you're done today," he said.

"Yup."

"If you ever want to hang, don't forget us here, okay?"

"Take it sleazy, Gino," I said, patting him on the back as I took off down the hall. I had to find a mint or something to clean my breath. I was happy now because I felt so much better without the disgusting dip in my mouth, and it really settled my stomach to throw up, but we were about to kiss and I needed clean breath. I had no change so I went to the maids' station and rummaged for some quarters on the office desk, then I went all the way over to the opposite wing of the inn to the vending machines and bought a can of Sprite and a pack of Wrigley's spearmint gum, her favorite. I gargled the Sprite and chomped on two pieces as I jogged all the way back to the room.

I moaned. The room was empty and dark. The vacuums

were gone. The TV stand was pushed back in place. The marked-up occupancy sheet was gone. And Mia was nowhere in sight.

I ran to the back entrance. She wasn't there, either. I did a full circuit of the hotel and couldn't find her anywhere, so I tore out the back entrance. It was raining lightly, and I booked through the tree line and into the field, and up ahead to the right I saw her, standing on the ledge overlooking the frogs. I walked over to her.

"Why'd you bolt?" I asked.

"You're the one who took off first. I thought you'd left for the day, you were gone so long," she said, staring down at the frogs, watching the rain bounce off their shiny green backs.

"Thanks for the dip," I said. "It was great."

"No it wasn't," she said.

We stood there for a long while, not saying anything. Finally, "It's raining, Mia."

"I know it is."

"So . . . are we going to just stand here?"

"Nobody's keeping you here," she said. "You can go home if you want."

"I don't want to go home yet."

She looked at me.

"Me, neither."

Our shirts were soaked through, and I could clearly see her brown bra. Her hair was streaming, and strands of it stuck to her neck sideways. Maybe my imagination has distorted what happened next, because it doesn't seem possible that it could play out like a movie like this, but it did—it happened *exactly* like this: we rushed into each other and started kissing really hard, almost violently. It felt too professional for my first kiss, and I felt out of control, but didn't stop. She had her arms around me and I put my arms around her waist. With my eyes closed it surprised me how long it took for my arms to settle there. Her lips were cold and bumpy at first, but then turned warm and smooth, like when you suck on Swedish Fish, and she opened her mouth and I opened mine and she made a soft sound and I squeezed her against me. We stopped kissing after a few minutes, and the rain was splashing off our noses and we didn't say a goddamned word; we just stood there smiling at each other, looking deep into each other's eyes, and then we burst out laughing, both of us at the same time, a shaky, uncontrollable trainlike laughter, as if we'd just heard the funniest joke in the world. And we stood there like that in the rain, overlooking the pond with our frogs, for a long while, hugging and kissing and laughing and staring at each other.

It was the happiest I'd ever felt in my entire life, and the first time I'd felt truly happy since age twelve back in Maryland, before my parents moved me to Shitsville and then Bern, before the Broom Incident and my devolution into intentional loserdom. Before I met Mia I'd thought I'd finally figured out how to survive, how to live, but now I knew I was only faking it. I was merely hibernating, not because I needed to survive, but because it was easier than trying. I realized I had been taking a forced nap for two whole years, and now I'd finally woken up; it was the Sleeping Beauty effect—except that the beauty kissed me, waking *me* up. Now I was alive. I felt so fucking happy that I began crying as we stared at each other; I started bawling, but she didn't even seem to notice at all, because it was still raining, and I guess to her I just looked shivery.

"I'm so glad I got this job," she said.

"Me too," I half shouted, because of the rain, which was now fittingly torrential. I looked into her eyes. "Are we something?"

She giggled and kissed me with her lips slightly spread apart so our teeth clinked together like bottles.

"Yes, we are definitely something," she replied.

I was cold and when I laughed with joy and replied, "Good," it sounded like I was making fun of stutterers. We leaned in and kissed again.

The summer was ending.

Mia and I had fallen in love with each other.

We were really happy.

And this is when everything went to hell, because of what happened next.

PART 2

People We Know and Like

The first day of school is always so pro forma. Perfunctory announcements are made over the PA system by the administration, as if school's been in session for months, but no one pays attention, because the sole point of the first day of school is for the student body to conduct an unofficial teenage fashion show. The hallways are converted into impromptu runways as the majority of students wear their just-purchased-latest-favorite outfit to school, premiering the "new and improved" tan version of themselves, as if it's even feasible to undergo a radical transformation in only seven and a half weeks. As if that week slumming it at the robotics camp in Orlando, or the weekend you got felt up for the first time in a parentless cabin on Lake Winnipesaukee, or the lesson you learned placing out of contention in the national equestrian trials in Lake Placid has transformed you into something new. As a result, the first day of school is a day intended exclusively for self-involved public preening, a massive showing of feathers, and for once, to my surprise, I was going to be an active participant.

I hadn't realized that my summer with Mia was going to change my life so dramatically; in fact, I only realized it in a sudden panic on Tuesday night, right before classes started. I'd been sitting on my bed for hours in a vaguely meditative state, recalling various pleasant episodes from our summer together at the inn (e.g.: playing the Damnit game, eating cold steak doused in A.1. etc.) when it dawned on me that I was officially no longer an intentional loser.

The fact was I'd relinquished that mantle the moment I kissed Mia for the first time. I shut my eyes and pictured the ledge, the frogs down below, and there I was, holding Mia in my arms in the rain, and I clearly remembered asking her verbatim, "Are we something?" and recalling her response, "Yeah, we're something."

Yeah, we're *something*.

Mia and I were something.

Something.

I went over to my desk and hoisted my unabridged dictionary (that I'd received from my parents as my *main* Christmas present when I was twelve) and looked up Webster's definition of the word:

some·thing [səm•thing] *pronoun*
  1. some thing; a certain undetermined or unspecified thing:
  e.g.: *Something's happening.*
  2. Informal. a person or thing of some value or consequence

However vague the definition of "something," it was clear that at that point Mia had made an enthusiastic oral agreement, a verbal contract with me that we were now dating. I was clearly—according to the dictionary, "a person or thing of some value or consequence," which in loose translation meant we were an item, boyfriend and girlfriend, something greater than friends; at the very least it couldn't be debated that this term indicated that I meant more to Mia than any other male meant to her. Thus, it was the official start of stage two, right? And if this were true, if technically I was now dating Mia Stone, arguably the most desirable girl in all of Bern High, then one could also reasonably infer that I was no longer an intentional loser. I was now *something*. Which, more significantly, meant that I was no longer *nothing*. Which would mean that high school now represented something new for me.

I'd always scoffed at how my classmates would actually plan their outfits; it all felt so materialistic and shallow (the philosophy behind my intentional loserdom is strikingly similar to that of Communism), and now here I was, frantically tossing button-downs onto my bed, trying to pick a winner. My wardrobe wasn't nearly outdated enough to qualify as retro, and I quickly realized I needed to visit a clothing store ASAP. Alas, it was late, and all of the stores were closed. I vigorously shook my head to convey displeasure (I'm cartoonish like that), and then I started feeling embarrassed with just how quickly I'd dropped my apparently pseudo disinterest in all things high school. Approximately 2.4 seconds had elapsed, to be exact. Did this mean I'd been a full-of-myself poser for two years, merely pretending to be disinterested in having a social life, but actually secretly (if unconsciously) praying for a major role reversal? Well, in any case, the answer was moot, because now, all of a sudden, I'd been reborn during the summer as a guy with a role, a place in society, and the first day of school was going to be my reemergence at Bern High.

Which meant, most pressingly, that I really needed to figure out what the hell to wear the next day.

As expected, the fall fashion show was in full effect when I arrived at BHS. The overwhelming new-shirt scent made the school smell like a department store. I'd worried the entire bus ride that my outfit would seem more second-week-of-school appropriate, but it turned out I was one of the lucky few, because every other guy was wearing the same exact pattern Gap rugby shirt, and there were at least a dozen girls wearing the same off-white linen shirt and capris khakis, as if they were in their late thirties and attending a chichi clambake on the Vineyard or something. The theme was preppy overall this year (after two years of grunge—with untucked flannel shirts and baggy jeans de rigueur for the girls at BHS). These students were on edge because of the presence of so many of their same-outfit-twins (or SOTs, as I'd secretly coined them), and I felt relieved that I hadn't rushed out to the mall and picked up one of these popular shirts. To combat the fact that there were a dozen other people dressed exactly like them, these SOTs kept tucking and untucking their shirts as they passed their respective clothing twins, trying desperately to appear at least remotely different from one another.

I hadn't talked to Mia since our hot kiss, because her parents had whisked her away to the Cape for the weekend, and I was starving to see her. With Mia nowhere in sight, I felt a nervous tightness in my chest due to lack of experience looking my classmates in the eye (it was the equivalent of my more socially well-adjusted peers being forced to stare down mountain lions), but at the same time I felt deeply excited to be finally reintroducing myself to high school society. I took what felt like a ceremonial deep breath and began my first pass down the main wing. I said hello to a handful of other upperclassmen, and they all seemed deeply confused by my extrovertism. In all fairness, it was to be expected, given the previous me's ambivalence toward them, but it still rattled me when I'd hear remarks behind my back as I'd continue on my first foray down the social catwalk:

I didn't know he spoke English.
Did he just call you "Homeslice"?
I liked him better when he was that creepy mute guy.
I'm pretty sure that guy's a narc.

I opted to head downstairs to the freshman/sophomore wing, where I instantly felt much more comfortable. Like a hungry old bear, I could smell the cumulative fear around me, and it soothed my frayed nerves. The high school environment was just as unfamiliar to the frosh as it was for me. I stopped at the desk that was set up at the end of the hall, where students signed in and received their locker number and combo lock for the year. A little freshman guy was struggling to get his combo lock open.

"Do you want me to show you how to use that thing?" I asked him.

"Get the hell away from me," he replied.

A group of frosh girls walked by. One of the girls smiled at me, and I opened my mouth to say hello, but no words came out, and instead I gave her an affectionate left hook to her shoulder. I got all bone, and she oofed. "Sorry, that was a little harder than I intended, just saying hi, that's all."

"Did that guy just punch you in the shoulder?" one of her friends asked her.

"I think he did," another girl said.

I hate it when people refer to me in the third person when I'm standing right next to them, because it creeps me out and makes me feel like I'm a ghost or something.

"Gee, he must really like you," the third friend said.

"Okeydokey. Sounds like you guys are analyzing his platonic tap a little too intensely; I think he's going to continue down the hallway now and let you get settled in," I said quickly, socking the other three in the shoulder, albeit softer this time, *pop! pop! pop!* as I walked by. They stared wide-eyed at their shoulders where I'd punched them, as if I'd left welts.

The homeroom bell rang, and everyone dispersed in a mad rush, giggling as they booked it for their respective classrooms.

A new, young teacher standing in a doorway was staring at me. I waved at her. She frowned and went inside her classroom and shut the door behind her. Within seconds I found myself walking alone down the empty hallway; the only sound was my shoes clicking on the cement floor.

"Well, that went well," I muttered to myself.

After homeroom I walked into my first class, AP chemistry, feeling kinda bummed that I hadn't seen Mia yet that morning, and instead of sitting in the middle of the room in order to force myself to interact with everyone, I chose a corner desk by the windows. The silver lining to this first day of school was that I could tell my classes were going to be ridiculously easy, because I recognized just about every item on the syllabus, thanks to my intensive two-month stay at STD the previous summer.

The chemistry teacher didn't have anything planned for us besides handing out the syllabus, and so for the last twenty minutes of class we just sat there in little clumps of conversation. Though I'd engaged in less than ten minutes of socializing thus far that morning, I was already exhausted (my endurance for maintaining eye contact with people had dropped to dangerously low levels), and I felt like I needed to take myself out of the game and mindlessly stare out the window until I caught my second wind. The new me, however, was shouting at me to engage my classmates, to ensure that I got off on the right foot with everyone.

Across the street there was construction going on—a garden nursery being added to a nature food store. A *kerplunk* sound as a backhoe drove a metal pole into the ground. It sounded vaguely fartlike, so I muttered, "Oh, excuse me," and winced, as if I was embarrassed that I'd ripped one in class.

The only student who kinda reacted positively to my joke was Billy Timmons's older brother, Brett, a senior. Okay, so maybe he wasn't exactly laughing, but was sort of gaping at me and making a coughy laughing sound that I interpreted as appreciation. Otherwise everyone else looked over at me with glazed eyes, which I probably should have interpreted as a distinct lack of interest. But every time this backhoe pushed this piece of metal into the earth it really did sound like a fart, so I kept trying to make people laugh.

Kerplunk.

"Ooh, excuse me."

Kerplunk.

"Ugh, this is the price I pay for eating that breakfast burrito."

Students groaned, but I was now really committed to my little gassy joke and doggedly stared out the window at the backhoe, waiting for the sound.

Kerplunk.

"What I'd give to be silent and deadly. People think it's enviable to be scentless, but unless you're wearing headphones, you always know when I let one go!" I said, unable to conceal a tiny, self-satisfied giggle afterward.

"What the hell is wrong with you?" Cindy Durante shouted suddenly from across the room. I looked over and realized that everyone was glaring at me.

"Did I just hear the H-word?" the teacher asked, not looking up from his Monday *New York Times* crossword.

Between classes I'd sashay down the hall (I'm not exactly sure what "sashay" means, but that's what it felt like) and greet all the people I'd ignored for the first two years of high school, and the response was always the same—nobody knew what the hell to make of it. My strategy was essentially to emulate a dog in heat and desperately try to shin-hump everyone into liking me. But as the morning progressed I felt increasingly tired of dealing with the surprised reactions and the back-handed comments, and eventually my sole mission between periods was just to find Mia.

One of the downsides of not having any real friends was that at lunch I was faced with the less than thrilling prospect of having to sit at the unofficially designated "abject loser" table by the entrance. In years past I hadn't minded sitting with the exchange students and students with gland problems, because frankly I didn't give two damns, and rarely bothered to look up from my overbreaded chicken nuggets to even notice people not noticing me, but this time it was sheer torture to sit there with Something Sanchez, the new Mexican exchange student (who according to the chatter I'd picked up in the hallways between classes, had already gotten nicknamed "Speedy"); two faceless losers adrift in a sea of people who mattered. I scanned the lax tables for Mia, but she was nowhere in sight. It's lame to admit, but I felt kinda humiliated sitting there at that table, even though it had been my regular post, and after a few minutes I decided to go back to the kitchen and stand in the lunch line again, just to kill time.

The House and Jonesey (his best friend and lax cocaptain), were in line ahead of me. It was my first time seeing him in school that day, and I have to admit I felt a slight jolt, as if my body was anticipating a sudden beatdown or something. But when we made brief eye contact, I could tell he knew nothing about me and Mia and my stomach stopped bubbling. There was a pause in the assembly line because the lunch ladies were bringing out a new batch of square slices of pizza. The House drummed his fingers on the metal countertop, occasionally muttering, "Any day now," until finally he lost patience and picked up a slice from a passing student who had just paid for his meal. The House chomped down and took a third of the slice in one bite.

"What the hell? You're going to buy me a new slice," the frosh guy stammered, realizing that the asshole that had chomped into his pizza was none other than The House, who dropped a meaty hand over the kid's shaking shoulders.

"Actually, you're going to want to eat that one. See, my DNA's in my saliva, so if you eat it maybe it'll make you bigger," he said, patting the kid forward.

Jonesey clapped The House on the back and said, "Good one, bro," as the line resumed. I freely glared at their backs, wondering how the hell Mia had ever associated herself with these meatheads.

"Hey, wake up!" a lunch lady shouted at me. "Are you going to take a slice or not?"

"No thanks, I already ate," I said, letting myself out of the line.

"Weirdo," a freshman muttered at me as I headed back into the caf.

My search for Mia continued.

I actually saw her from a distance a number of times that afternoon. She was perpetually in a state of hurrying just out of view. At the end of one hall, I'd struggle against the current to reach her, but she'd disappear inside a classroom just as the bell rang, and I'd have to run in the opposite direction to find my own class. Later I'd see her leaving the art room and rushing to the library, and I'd carve a shortcut through the administration wing to cut her off at the library, but the library would be empty. I'd search each carrel for her and as I stepped back out of the stacks I'd see the back of her head through the window as she exited the library and turned down the hallway back to the art room. It was like Mia was a ghost, and it wasn't until the break after seventh period that I finally talked to her.

"Albie!" a voice cried out behind me, and my heart sank to my shoes and rose back up to its rightful place immediately; I don't know how astronauts deal with that shit. I wheeled around and Mia charged into me, shoulder first. I gritted my teeth and pretended it didn't sting.

She looked different, as if I hadn't seen her in years. Her clothes were nicer: bell-bottom jeans and a new, ribbed T-shirt that hugged her curves, as opposed to her daily summer uniform of denim cutoff shorts and her baggy red Bay State Games T-shirt with the number twelve stenciled on the back.

"What's with you?" I asked.

"First day, I'm spazzing out!" she said. "I haven't seen anyone since the spring."

"You saw me all summer," I reminded her, deeply hurt.

"Oh, right," she said, slapping her forehead. "I totally forgot."

"Anyway, where the shizat have you been all morning?" I asked. "I've been looking for you."

"All over. It's the first day of school, what do you expect?"

"Do you want to hang out after school?" I asked.

"Can't, I've got an SGA meeting," she said. "And then I'll have to rush home, eat dinner, then meet up with Shauna and a few others to work on homework. I'm going to be ready to crash by then; maybe I'll call you if I'm still awake when I get home."

"How about this weekend?" I asked earnestly.

She laughed, as if I was being obnoxious.

"Don't be melodramatic. Today's crazy but we can hang out tomorrow morning, okay? Meet me in the caf; Shauna and I always have doughnuts and coffee with everyone," she said.

"Sounds like a plan."

"Great—I gotta run, so I'll see you tomorrow morning," she said, and she reached in and awkwardly hugged me and, frankly, it felt forced. But I broke what felt like public protocol and squeezed her, and for a split second, I could feel it, her body sighed; I could feel the breath leave her lungs, and the rest of her gave in and momentarily collapsed into me, as if her body was wordlessly reaffirming to me that we were something special, because there's no way she'd hug any other guy this way; this was *more* than a normal hug, and I closed my eyes and turned my nose into her hair and breathed in deep, but then she pulled away and I caught a millisecond of a serious look on her face before it perked up again. "Now get to class!"

I watched her run down the hall. "Look back at me," I softly pleaded with her, but she entered a classroom without looking back. I didn't mind her not looking back at me, though, because her hug had said more than enough, whether she'd wanted it to or not.

Before the door to her classroom closed, I heard her classmates simultaneously shout "Mia!" as if she were a regular entering a dive bar for the nine thousandth time.

Or maybe that's just how people greet people they already know and like.

16

School finally ended, and I stepped out into the sun a semidefeated man. All day I'd tried my hardest to engage high school society and—while I hadn't been outright rejected—I felt I was going about things completely wrong, and had no clue what to do differently. On top of this I'd developed a brain-rattling headache and was showing symptoms of early-onset hypochondria: I kept staring at both sides of my hands for visible germs, repeatedly wiping phantom itchy spots on my cheeks with the back of my left sleeve.

I got on the bus and sat down in the back among a group of freshman guys. They were staring out the windows, watching The House and his buddies do Supermans on the flagpole.

A Superman is this thing the sportos do—they take turns grabbing the flagpole really tightly, around waist high, then they hoist their bodies up and extend their legs out and hold themselves up parallel to the ground, using sheer brute strength. He looked bigger than I remembered, and he had a little bit of scruff on his cheeks. He looked older with the facial hair, and I bet college students probably didn't peg him as a prospective student when he visited their campuses. I scanned the parking lot for Mia, but didn't see her. The House hoisted himself in the air doing a Superman and, while he was large for a seventeen-year-old, and incredibly buff, I noticed that he had a gut. After five seconds he gracefully dropped to his feet. Jonesey shoved him and Ryan held his side with one hand while punching Jonesey stiffly in the chest with his other. I could actually hear the punch through the semi-open window, and it made me wince.

"That shit's crazy," one of the freshman guys said, watching Jonesey take his turn grabbing the flagpole. "Jonesey is so jacked."

"Actually, that's just upper-body strength," a voice said. "Look, he has chicken legs by comparison to his torso. Proportionally, he just doesn't make any sense."

I turned around. It was a guy that I recognized from the year before.

"That's true, actually," I added. "Plus, it's also a bit of a visual trick involving leverage that allows them to even do it."

"Really?" the freshmen asked in unison.

"Smoke and mirrors," the sophomore said. "That's all it is."

"Well, he still looks pretty badass," one of the freshmen

mused, staring back out the window.

The sophomore rolled his eyes at me, and I laughed. I realized it was the first time I had felt a legitimate connection with another classmate all day, so I asked him, "What stop do you get off at?"

"My stop's after yours," he said. "Why?"

"Well, I was thinking, if you aren't busy, maybe you could get off at my stop."

"Why?"

He just stared stupidly at me with his head cocked sideways, as if he were a dog and I was hopelessly trying to teach him how to speak English. Right then I should have realized that he wasn't interested in becoming friends and that our little banter together wasn't a bonding moment, a stepping-stone toward a fruitful relationship, but I was desperate for a mini social victory, and figured we could play video games at my house or something, only my mind must have been frazzled because I felt like I needed to say a specific game, and I was suddenly drawing a blank, so instead I merely said, "I was thinking if you weren't busy you could come over and . . . play."

The entire bus gasped.

"Did you just ask that guy to come over and play?" a freshman asked, incredulous.

Even the nerdy girl (wearing an oversize T-shirt with an unsarcastic painting of a puma on the front) turned around with a big grin on her face.

"I meant play Final Fantasy or something," I added quickly. "I don't know what RPGs he's into."

"Bullshit," someone shouted. "You asked him to come

over and play! What are you, in sixth grade?"

That jarred me. Like those twist endings in thriller movies, I suddenly saw an extended montage of me that day fumbling to socialize in school: punching those freshman girls in the shoulder, making those stupid fart jokes, and now I'd asked a guy to come over and "play?" Jesus . . . I *was* a sixth grader, after all.

My headache returned, and I closed my eyes and leaned my head against the window. Normally I love doing this. The vibrations of the bus as it rumbles over cracked pavement repeatedly bounce my head off the window in a soothing fashion that makes my teeth rattle, but I could hear everyone making fun of me. I pretended to be asleep, thinking maybe they'd quit heckling me, but they were relentless.

"I can't believe he asked you if you wanted to play."

"Where's his hands? I think he's playing with . . . himself."

"Is he really sleeping all of a sudden? I bet he's faking. Poke him."

"No, leave him alone. Maybe he'll have a nocturnal emission."

Everyone roared.

Needless to say, it felt like the longest ride of my life. The bus finally deposited me at my stop, then made a series of pathetic revving sounds as if it were halfway up a hill, even though Columbus is completely flat. I kicked a stone down the road, not really thinking about anything. As I walked up my driveway I heard laughter coming from the Timmons's backyard. I stood there for a minute, not making a sound, realizing I was at a crossroads of sorts. Despite feeling like I'd graduated from hanging out with sixth graders, clearly the first day of school had proven that I was wielding a fake diploma, and I kinda needed the nurturing confidence boost of hanging out with twelve-year-olds so I could feel whole again. I was about to head inside my house when I veered left, walking with hands outstretched as I bulldozed through the thin line of trees separating our yards. I walked quickly so I wouldn't have time to take a deep breath and reconsider this act of regression. As I entered the backyard I snapped an impossibly loud fallen branch (it sounded like Joe Theismann's final play of his NFL career), and everyone in the backyard looked over at me.

"Hey, neighbor," Brett said.

It dawned on me that Billy was in middle school and wouldn't be home for another hour. Instead I'd interrupted his older brother, Brett, sitting on the steps to the loft with three of his senior friends—two guys and a girl. The girl was an artsy chick with pink streaks in her hair, which she wore in a nestlike bun held up by a pencil. She was wearing what looked like a gypsy's dress—a long dark skirt with a couple of scarves wrapped around her waist—and there was a big, fake, blue pendant or brooch hanging around her neck. Over this ensemble she wore a red poofy down jacket.

"Hola," she said to me.

"Oh, you speak French?" I asked.

She looked appalled. "That was Spanish," she replied.

"I know . . . I was making a joke."

"Oh," she said, glancing at Brett. "That was funny."

I sighed.

The other guys both looked like that guitarist in Radiohead who looks exactly like the guitarist in Weezer, with their shaggy brown mops of greasy hair covering their dark eyes, accompanied by a greenish tint to their skin that kinda worked. They were both wearing youth small T-shirts to accentuate how thin their Q-Tip arms were—one of the shirts had BERN YOUTH SOCCER written across the chest while the other one read MILL CREEK SUMMER CAMP.

"This is Nate and Mark, and you just met my Parisian friend, Kelly," Brett said.

"What's going on?" I asked one of the indie guitarists—I think Mark.

"Nothing. Why?" he asked.

"Um, no reason?" I replied.

He just kind of grimaced at me, then looked at the girl with an annoying smirk. My blood boiled. I craned my neck as if listening for an imaginary phone ringing in my house so I could get the hell out of there, but Brett started talking again.

"So what's the story with you, Al?" he asked. "I've been hearing about you all day. People claim you've been going around saying hello to everyone. And then that farting thing in history class? That's unlike you, man. What happened, did you get hit in the back of the head or something?"

"No," I mumbled. "And that's not something to joke about—there are all kinds of nerve endings in the back of your head, which is why it's illegal to hit there in boxing matches."

"Uh . . . okay. So, have you seen my brother recently?"

"Huh—Billy? No."

"My brother and his friends worship Albert," Brett

138

explained to his friends. He turned back to me. "Anyway, you should stick around, you gotta see Billy when he gets home. He grew a mullet this summer. It looks ridiculous."

Brett's friends stared at me.

"Maybe next time, I was merely saying hi on my way in, I gotta help my mom move a . . . grandfather clock . . . down to the basement," I lied, backing away.

"Adios, Albert," the girl said unsmiling, waving slowly at me.

My mom was home early from work. When I came in she was standing over the oven with her back to me, stirring a pot with one hand and sipping a mug of coffee with the other. I leaned against the garage door and exhaled.

"Goddamnit," I muttered to myself. My mom's head perked up.

"Oh—hi dear, how was your day?" she asked brightly without turning around.

"Exhausting," I admitted. "Ultimately demoralizing."

"Well, keep picking 'em up and layin' 'em down, eventually you'll have a railroad."

"I have no idea what that means."

"That's great to hear. Now why don't you pour yourself a tall glass of SunnyD and tell me more about your day?" she asked, as she raised the mug to her mouth and took a long sip. She stared at the mug. "Ooh, hot."

"No thanks, I'm not thirsty. Now if you'll excuse me I'm going to go up to my room and pray for a sudden brain aneurism."

"Okay, honey, but remember, dinner's at five sharp, so no snacking!"

17

That night I kept reminding myself that Mia had said she probably *wouldn't* call, and that we'd set a date to hang out the next morning anyway, not so much to assuage the growing sadness that I felt from missing her, but rather because I was trying to trick God into getting Mia to call me through reverse psychology. Of course I knew it wouldn't work, but I kept saying out loud with a pained expression on my face, "No way she's going to call tonight," in hopes that God, or whoever you think is upstairs, would get tricked into thinking he/she/it was burning me by having Mia call unexpectedly. Truth be told, I have a deep lack of respect for God, and it shows in these stupid mind games I keep playing.

I understood that she had a social life already in place—that she was seeing her friends for the first time all summer and all that, but we had just kissed in the rain, damnit! It already felt like years ago that we'd kissed. For the rest of the night, as I lay in bed in the dark, I reimagined the scene, not so much to cheer me up, but rather because I was genuinely afraid of forgetting.

The next morning I woke up with heartburn, I presume in dread of having to face the high school masses for a second day in a row. I headed straight for the caf when I got to school and breathed a sigh of *phew* when I saw that Mia was sitting at a round table with only Shauna. The House and his buddies were nowhere in sight. Mia saw me and waved. I bounded up to them like a giddy golden retriever puppy; my sneakers even slid on a patch of shiny floor and I sorta spun a perplexed three-sixty and crashed into them.

"So this is the hangout spot in the morning," I said, craning around. "Not bad. I like what you've done with the place."

Shauna fake giggled. I could tell it wasn't sincere because otherwise she looked kinda pissed off at me.

"You guys have met, right?" Mia asked.

I nodded.

"Not officially," Shauna said.

"That's not true," I interjected. "Second week of first semester, freshman year. We were teammates in trig for that stupid game where you race up to the blackboard—we shook hands and introduced ourselves afterward, remember?"

"You have a really good memory," she said.

"Thanks," I said.

We stared at each other.

"So I promised you doughnuts," Mia said, interrupting our staredown. "What kind do you want?"

"Jelly's me favorite," I said (with the Lucky Charms accent for no apparent reason).

"Jelly and a coffee, coming up," Mia said.

"Whoa, hold up, if they have tea I'll have that instead," I amended.

"Tea?" Shauna asked, frowning.

"Yes, I'm a tea drinker," I said softly.

"I don't think they have tea here," she said.

"Let's go see," Mia said, and I followed her into the kitchen.

On the metal à la carte table there were three huge boxes of Dunkin' Donuts, a stack of Styrofoam cups, and two Mr. Coffees, bubbling with pots full of medium roast.

I tapped on the table.

"Excuse me, ma'am?" I asked. A lunch lady turned around. "Do you have any tea bags back there, and some hot water?"

"Tea? Really? Uh, maybe, I'll go check," she said.

She went into the lunch-lady office and after noisily fumbling around for a minute returned with a Styrofoam cup full of hot water. She handed me a Lipton tea bag.

"Do you have other kinds of tea?" I asked.

The lunch lady glowered at me, as if I'd just made a disparaging comment about her lunch lady mother.

I jest.

"Just walk away slowly . . . keep smiling," Mia whispered behind me.

We sat back down at the table. Like an unnamed new virus under a microscope, the crowd had already multiplied threefold in the time we'd been gone. Several tables were filled up with sleepy-eyed upperclassmen, with a steady stream forming a line into the kitchen. I was facing away from the entrance, and when The House and his cronies showed up I swear I could sense it in the hairs on the back of my neck.

"Ladies," The House said, putting his calloused paws on Mia's shoulders and squeezing them hard enough that she winced. He smiled at me. "And what have we here?"

I held out my hand and he shook it. I gripped it hard, and it felt like squeezing a new bar of soap. "Albert Kim," I said, in an unintentionally deep voice. Mia glanced at me.

"That's great," he said.

"Al and I worked at the Bern Inn together this summer," Mia said.

The House turned away from me.

"I have to tell you about my trip out West, Stoner," he said.

"Definitely!" she replied.

"Stoner?" I said, but nobody seemed to hear me.

"Come on, dude, before you bore her to death let's get some bear claws," Jonesey growled, and the entire pack moved as one into the kitchen, cutting the line. When they were gone, Mia leaned in and said, "Ryan and Jonesey like to pretend they're cops, drinking coffee out of Styrofoam cups and eating doughnuts every morning."

I earnestly fake laughed. Mia seemed to appreciate it.

The guys returned a minute later and filled up the seats around us.

"Pass me a frickin' bear claw," Jonesey said, taking a loud sip from his coffee. He stared angrily into the Styrofoam cup. "Tastes like watered-down piss, but I can't start the day without it."

The House was about to say something when he noticed my cup of tea.

"What the hell is that?" he asked.

"It's a cup. Or are you asking about my hand?" I raised it. "My hand?"

"Did you pour like half a cup of milk in there?"

"Oh, that. It's tea, not coffee."

"You drink tea?" he asked, seemingly astounded. "What are you, like, eighty?"

Apparently it was a big deal that I was drinking tea; you would have thought I'd just admitted I have a tail. Which I don't, for the record.

"Lots of people drink tea, Ryan," Mia said.

"No, it's okay," I said, touching her right knuckles. The House stared at our hands. "I'm just a tea drinker. It's more common over in England and stuff."

"Would you like a spot of tea and some crumpets?" he asked Mia with what had to be the lamest British accent I'd ever heard in my life, but she giggled out loud.

"Stop it!" she said.

Now The House wouldn't stop talking in his awful British accent.

"Albert," he said, pointing at the crumbs in front of me. "You're making an awful row with your chewing. Bloody hell, look at the mess you've made!"

I realized everyone else had laid out napkins as makeshift plates, whereas I'd made a mess in my area. Apparently my arrested development extended past mere social cues into basic table manners as well. To save face, I nodded at Mia.

"Tremendously observant bloke," I said to her in a fairly crappy but by comparison spot-on British accent. "A bit dodgy, but I believe Scotland Yard would be proud to have him, if only he'd switch over to Earl Grey."

Mia laughed.

"Wait a second," The House said, pointing at her.

Everyone at the table immediately stopped laughing, and I tensed. Mia did, too, I think.

"What's going on here?" he asked, wiggling his index finger back and forth between us. "Why are you even talking to this guy?"

Mia blushed. The House gasped, then laughed out loud. His meathead friends joined in, clearly having no idea why they were laughing but content in doing so, regardless.

"This has to be a joke," he said, and Jonesey started jabbing him in the shoulder.

"What am I missing?" he asked The House.

"I think you're looking at a new couple, Jonesey," he said.

"We're not a couple," Mia said quickly.

My stomach dropped, but nobody saw it because it was under the table. If anything, they might have heard a soft, unidentifiable poofing sound.

"You're not?" he asked. "So you're just holding hands as study buddies or something?"

We slipped our hands away from each other.

"We haven't really defined anything yet," she said, her voice trailing off.

"Ho. Lee. Shit." Jonesey said, really enunciating the periods between his words.

All the guys were staring at me incredulously. Except for The House. He was staring at me with his eyes narrowed. His body seemed slightly more sculpted, and I realized he was flexing all his muscles.

"Coup of the century," one of the lax guys muttered, shaking his head. He held out his hand and we high-fived awkwardly. "Gotta give the freak his props."

"This is like that movie *Can't Buy Me Love*," The House mused. "Did you pay her, Albert?"

"No!" I said.

"Seriously, level with me, Teabag. Did you postpone

buying a telescope to have the right to sit here this morning? How many hundreds of dollars did you pay Mia to hold your hand this morning?"

I blushed, picturing the telescope I'd planned on buying in a couple of months.

"Okay, you're being an ass, so we're going for a walk," Mia said, standing up, pulling on my shirtsleeve. "Shauna, I'll meet you in the art room second period so we can work on our posters."

"Whoa, easy, Mia, I'm just joking," The House said, pushing down on my opposite shoulder. "It's cool, Albert, I'm stoked for you guys. For real."

"Shauna," Mia said forcefully. "I'm going to get those markers."

Mia pulled me away from the table. The House raised his right hand and waved with his fingertips, smiling at me with what looked like flames twinkling in his eyes. I waved back and everyone at the table laughed, and when one of them muttered, "What a douche bag," Mia noticeably recoiled, but pretended not to hear it.

"I think they really liked me," I said.

She shook her head, then forced out a giggle.

"Sorry about that. Ryan's way cooler when he's not with those clowns."

"I'm sure he is," I said.

"Seriously," she said.

She seemed upset with me now, so I nodded fervently and changed the subject.

"So what are those posters for?" I asked.

"The pep rally," she replied.

"Oh, they're having it again this year?" I asked. She stared at me as if I was messing with her. "What did I say?"

"Albert, look around you," she said.

Practically every inch of the hallway was covered with posters and streamers. There were green posters that read, GO FROSH! and blue posters that read, JUNIORS RULE! and red posters that read SENIORS #1! and yellow posters that read, SUPERSOPHS! Several of the posters had been vandalized—big rips had been retaped, which meant the posters had been hanging on the walls yesterday, and I hadn't even noticed.

"How did you not know about this?" Mia asked. "The pep rally's in like, two hours."

Despite being universally ignored on Day One of his year at an American high school, Speedy Sanchez instinctively knew to feel superior to me when I sat with him that first lunch, and for that reason alone I felt a tinge of happiness to sit with him again, because who the hell was he to feel above me? I could sense him glaring at me from a distance as I stood in the lunch line, as if trying to mentally coerce me into not sitting down with him. I surveyed the à la carte options. Even though my stomach was rumbling, I wasn't in the mood for the lunch ladies' reimagining of chicken cordon bleu (replacing the ham with bologna), so I skipped the entrée altogether and merely grabbed the least alive–looking bowl of green Jell-O. I licked the dollop of budget whipped cream off the top and paid the cashier before making a beeline for a clearly revolted Speedy, figuring the sooner I got there the sooner lunch could be over.

"Afternoon, Sanchez," I said, sliding up right next to him. "I saw you nodding me over while I was in line."

"No, no, I wasn't," he pleaded, waving his hands in front of him over his tray, desperately trying to suggest this was an emergency. "I'm busy, please, no."

"Look, I'm not thrilled with the seating arrangements, either," I explained to him. "If there was a place for—"

"Albert!"

I looked up dumbly, not quite believing someone was calling my name.

"Albert Kim—over here!" the voice repeated.

I turned around. Brett was waving me over. I did the ol' look behind me to see if he was shouting for someone else, looked back, pointed at my chest, and mouthed, "Who, me?" to him, and to my utter surprise, he nodded and mouthed an emphatic "yes." I got up and ambled over to his table. He was sitting with those same two guys and that girl I'd seen hanging out with him in his backyard the day before.

"Hola," I said to her. She just stared at me.

"Why are you sitting with the exchange student? Are you friends with Speedy?" Brett asked.

"Actually, the guy hates my guts," I said.

"He hates everyone, so everyone hates him, it's a vicious cycle that's been going on for centuries," he said, rolling his eyes. "If that's the case, then, why torture yourself? Just grab your Jell-O and come sit with us."

I tried to feign disinterest to make it seem like a big decision, but I could barely contain my excitement for more than two seconds. "Okay, be right back," I said quickly, and went back to my table and grabbed my bowl of Jell-O. Speedy glared up at me. "HeySpeedyI'mgoingtositwithBrettandhisfriendsdoyouwanttocomealongofcourseyoudon'tokaygofuckyourself," I said, and headed back to Brett's table.

"Where's the rest of your meal?" Mark asked.

I shrugged.

"I wasn't feeling that adventurous," I replied.

"What, don't you like Mexican food?" Kelly asked.

"Chicken cordon bleu's French," I said.

"I know, I was making your joke," she replied.

I laughed.

"Well I guess that means either I don't get my own jokes or you're getting funnier," I said.

"I'll go with the first choice," she said, but a moment later she couldn't hide a little smile.

At first, part of me was worried this was an elaborate prank that was about to blow up in my face, but as I sat there not really talking to Brett and his friends, it slowly dawned on me that they didn't think there was anything strange about my sitting with them. Pitiful, I know, but their lack of revulsion with my presence seemed like tangible proof that my efforts to reincorporate myself into high school society were actually . . . working?

It felt like a subtle reprieve from my social hardships, and for the first time that morning my stomach felt slightly relaxed, and I began to eat. The only downside to having people willingly sitting with me at lunch was that I now had to eat my Jell-O like a normal human being rather than my usual, far more enjoyable modus operandi—alternating between sucking and blowing the Jell-O through the spaces between my front teeth for several seconds until it blends into a bubbly, viscous liquid, at which point I pitch my head back and gargle the sugary stew for a few seconds before swallowing.

Honestly, it sounds way grosser than it actually is.

After lunch I headed down to the gym locker room to take my preafternoon pee. I do this every day after lunch for purely academic reasons: so I don't have to deal with the pressure of trying to race to pee between classes or, God forbid, have to get a bathroom pass during AP English and miss out on a minute or two of the teacher's lecture.

I exited the locker room and almost ran into The House, who was leaning up against the brick wall. I was startled because his face was painted red for the pep rally, making his eyes buggy, and I actually yelped. He was wearing sponge devil horns that hot girls usually wear on Halloween to look sexy, but on him they looked terrifyingly realistic. He smiled at me, showing his teeth.

"Oh, hey, House," I said, blushing a little since it was my first time calling him by his nickname, and despite it being a well-known nickname it felt like I had to earn the right to say it, not to mention the fact that having never said it, I wasn't sure how to say it—was it "Oh, hey, House," or "Oh, hey, The House?" Anyway, right or wrong, it sounded like I was pretending to be close pals with him, and I was about to call him by his real first name when he said, "You got balls, bro. Big ones."

"Um, thanks?" I said, glancing down to make sure I was all zipped up.

"What do you think you're doing with Stoner?"

"What—nothing," I said instinctively, and I felt a glaze of revulsion at myself for my cowardice. I forced myself to stare The House in the eye. "I mean, we're hanging out. Why, is that against the law?"

"You know she's just hanging out with you to mess with me, right?" he asked mock-earnestly—that is, as if he wasn't insulting me. "She's playing you, man."

"Okay, nice talking to you," I said, starting to walk past him.

He poked me hard in the chest.

"Don't you even think of walking away from me when I'm talking to you, boy, I'll knock your ass out, I don't care if Mia told me to take it easy on you." I didn't say anything. "So like I was saying, I admit it takes a certain amount of sheer cajones to try to scam my ex right in front of my face, and not that I give a crap, since we broke up a long time ago, but just trying to get her practically gives me the right to go to town on you." The House casually flexed his biceps and they bulged out of his already tight T-shirt.

"I appreciate the intel, can I go now?" I asked.

"Do you really think you and Mia have something going?"

"You don't know the full story," I said, forcing myself to maintain eye contact.

"Really, and what's the story?" he asked, again mock-earnestly. "Clearly I'm in the dark, here, because the way I see it she's my recent ex-girlfriend and you're trying to hook up with her."

I didn't say anything.

"Dude, you're shaking," The House said, laughing. He clapped me on the back. "Relax, Albert, I'm just saying it might not be the wisest choice in terms of longevity to be trying to get close with my ex, that's all. I'm liable to get my feelings hurt."

Coach Turncliff, the gym teacher, showed up at this point. One look and he could assess the situation, and all he said was, "Leave it alone, Ryan."

I assumed I was the "it" in question, because The House raised his hands and backed away from me slowly. He walked into the locker room, and the door swung shut behind him. Coach Turncliff stared at me—he looked as if he'd told The House to back off merely because he was legally obligated to not allow him to kill another student on his watch, but that deep down he wished he'd showed up a minute later.

"What do you want, a hug?" he asked me. "Get to class, Kim."

I walked off, feeling rickety.

19

I soon forgot about my run-in with The House (although my fingertips were still shaking slightly twenty minutes later, because my fingertips tend to stay frightened longer than the rest of me) until the bell rang midway through sixth period and everyone cheered and dropped what they were doing and broke into a mad dash to the gym for the pep rally. Every year there's this schoolwide pep rally in the gym in the afternoon sometime during the first week of school. It's a really stupid tradition, and the reason I'd forgotten about it, despite its being the biggest event of the fall, is that I'd skipped it sophomore year. The rally isn't associated with any sports team or big game whatsoever, like more traditional pep rallies; it's a rally devised solely to build pep "in general." That alone is ridiculous, because the first week of school is pretty much the only week out of the school year in which students already have a modicum of school spirit already instilled in them.

The main currency of this pep rally is that each grade is given a color that they're supposed to "be" for the day, and whichever grade is most homogenously dressed in its allotted color wins the distinction of having the most school spirit. The students get really rabid about it, similar to the way they get ballistic about acquiring carnations on the aforementioned, conveniently titled "Carnation Day." This gets misinterpreted by the administration as genuine school spirit, when in fact what they're fostering with these pep rallies is quite the opposite: sheer animosity among the classes. If you ever saw one of Bern High's pep rallies you'd be convinced the inspiration was the L.A. County Jail scene in the movie *Colors*.

There are all kinds of hokey events throughout the afternoon, including the annual 2v2 volleyball match between two senior jocks versus the principal and vice principal (which the principal long ago set up himself so he could showcase his admittedly wicked cool topspin-reverse serve with his back to the net, and it's the one minute of the school year during which he's considered remotely likable). More appalling is the wheelbarrow ride for the "Campus Cuties." The students fill out ballots during homeroom that morning to deem who is the cutest couple at Bern High. Mia and Ryan had won it two years in a row, and would have been a prohibitive lock to win it a third straight year had they not broken up in the spring. Remembering this Campus Cuties thing made me smile—I figured Mia and I could maybe spend it holding hands or something, and it would offer a sort of closure on her long-term relationship ("Someone tell The House that there's a new cutie in town. . . ."). Maybe we could even win it ourselves senior year, I'd daydreamed. Anyway, the reward is that the winning couple gets toted via wheelbarrow around the border of the basketball court by the burlier freshman cheerleaders, and everyone in the stands cheers wildly, because for some reason this gets everyone's rocks off, don't ask me why.

The activities last about an hour, and then for the final hour before the day ends the four grades take turns shouting, "We got spirit—how 'bout you?" at each other until everyone's in a frenzy and instead of shouting, "We got spirit—how 'bout you?" students just blatantly throw unaffiliated gang signs and aggressive middle fingers and shout things like, "You're dead, frosh!" and it's all so hypocritical; but again, the majority of students, even the goth kids and other fringe students, seem to really get into it.

This was the first time since the beginning of freshman year that I felt excited to attend it; the only problem was that since I'd somehow missed that it was coming up, I hadn't worn anything blue that day. The matter was quickly resolved because Mia had brought extra blue clothes for emergency situations just like this. She had changed into bright blue nylon Adidas sweatpants and a blue long-sleeve shirt; her hair was in a tight ponytail and she had the word JUNIOR written across her face, her nose separating the N and the I.

That afternoon I stood in the center of the bleachers among my fellow blue brethren, screaming and cheering as if I'd been forced to wear a metal collar that would explode if I stopped cheering. It was fun for a while—despite the fact that nobody was really interacting with me, the fact that we were all cheering at the same time felt like we were unified and made me feel like I was part of something bigger. I liked the feeling of shouting at the top of my lungs and not being able to hear myself because it was already so noisy. And I have to admit, the junior class had school spirit to spare; our grade was a well-oiled machine. Every single junior had worn blue, and we made sure only people who had worn blue jeans and blue dresses could stand in the very front row. It was really impressive. I imagine it was kinda like watching the Blue Angels perform their balletic Mach 2 dance at air shows (well, except on the days when one of them dies).

I stood there for an hour, exuding crazy mad spirit, and right before the end of the rally the Spanish teacher, Miss Oliveri, walked into the center of the basketball court and—not realizing the point of a megaphone—screeched into it, "NOW WHO WANTS TO FIND OUT WHO THE CAMPUS CUTIES ARE THIS YEAR?" and everyone screamed. Chants of "House-House-House" started in the back row of the bleachers as two cheerleaders emerged from the double doors of the small gym dragging a Radio Flyer wagon behind them. Miss Oliveri took out a piece of paper, unfolded it, and said, "BIG SURPRISE, PEOPLE . . . THIS YEAR'S CAMPUS CUTIES ARE ONCE AGAIN, SENOR RYAN STACKHOUSE AND SENORITA MIA STONE!" and the entire gym erupted.

I cried foul, but nobody heard me. Mia and The House were already wearing cardboard crowns, and the cheerleaders pointed at the empty wagon with a flourish, as if they were hostesses on *The Price Is Right*. Ryan smushed himself into the tiny wagon. Mia laughed at the sight, as did everyone else. There wasn't any space for Mia to sit, and I was about to point this out when Mia went ahead and sat down on top of Ryan! He winced for a moment and she repositioned herself to one side, and he smiled up at her and—this sounds like a lie but it really happened—Ryan made eye contact with me and shot me a personal thumbs-up. Everyone stomped so hard that it felt like the bleachers would collapse any minute.

It was my first time having a girlfriend (sort of), and seeing her sit on another guy, another guy who was smiling and shooting me a thumbs-up as two cheerleaders labored to pull them around the perimeter of the gym, the wagon occasionally bumping over electrical cords and crooks in the wood, making Mia slightly bounce up and down. Less than two turns into the lap I found that I could no longer bear to watch.

Stupid pep rally, I thought. Stupid Campus Cuties. "They're not even dating anymore, for chrissakes!" I shouted, knowing nobody could hear me. I looked down at my blue sweatshirt. What the hell was I doing? This was all so phony, and I felt sick having to watch Mia ride around with The House in a tiny-ass wagon, and next thing I knew I'd taken off the sweatshirt and stuffed it through the crack beneath my seat and stood there in my orange T-shirt. The juniors behind me gasped.

As if they could sense a change in the air or something, the field hockey girls in my grade standing in the second row turned around and saw that I was blemishing their otherwise perfect blue bleacher, and they pulled me off and corralled me into the practice gym.

One of the girls pulled out the blue wool fire blanket from the metal first-aid kit on the wall, and they both tried in vain to get me to wear it like some kind of heavy shawl. I easily eluded the blanket like an insane reverse bull, with these psychotic field hockey matadors chasing after me. At first the girls were kinda giggling, because playing tag is fun no matter how old or popular you are, but they quickly got livid. I felt kinda bad for them, they seemed so helpless, unable to contain me. There was a huge roar from the entire student body standing on the bleachers in the big gym, and the field hockey girls groaned.

"Albert, please, the rally's almost over and the teachers are going to vote on school spirit," Shauna said.

Miss Oliveri poked her head through the double doors. "Ladies and Albert, I want you out here NOW," she said, glaring at me before heading back out into the gym.

They finally stopped chasing me. They were panting deeply. Since Mia's best friend, Shauna, was there, I couldn't admit why I refused to wear blue, but I still tried to be diplomatic.

"Look, I'm allergic to certain types of wool. This is maybe Shetland wool. If it was another kind I'd gladly—"

"Just put on the stupid blanket, you asshole!" Shauna screamed, and it stunned me, given that she'd been forced to make nice with me earlier, and I didn't resist when she then reached over and snatched the blanket from the other girl and shoved it into my chest, forcing me to take it. Then she grabbed me by the wrist, squeezing it really hard to show that she meant business. "Let's go."

We exited the small gym as if I were a prize or mascot, as if this were all part of a plan, and they led me to the third row of the bleachers.

Despite my near-sabotage, our grade won the pep rally. After the announcement, there were still ten minutes left in the school day. All the students were mindlessly shouting and running around the basketball court waving banners and signs, probably overexhausted, and I realized I could steal away without being seen. The teachers lining the far side of the gym looked busy policing the unruly seniors, and so I made my way off the bleachers and over to the nearest exit;

and I was shocked at how easily I slipped away.

I let the fire blanket drop to my feet, and I instantly started sprinting down the empty hallway toward the academic wing. I went down the stairs to the lower level and into the darkened hallway and jumped up and down like a spastic. For some reason doing this made me feel calmer, and after a while I felt slightly settled down. I went into an empty classroom and sat down at a teacher's desk. My hands were still shaking. I pictured Mia and Ryan riding around in the wagon. Everyone cheering for them. Everyone cheering as if they were still together. I couldn't remember if Mia looked happy.

I didn't know what to think.

The bell finally rang and I left the room and headed for the main entrance. The double doors to the gym exploded open and I was instantly engulfed by hundreds of screaming students bathed in red, blue, green, and yellow. The throng was so compressed that at one point I was moving, but I swear my goddamned feet weren't even touching the ground. We all spilled out of the entrance and moved as one huge mass toward the buses, and it made me feel like I was a surly leprechaun being forced to ride down a human rainbow.

20

It was around ten thirty and I was sitting on my bed, thinking. Why I tend to do most of my thinking in bed and most of my napping at my desk is a question for another day. Anyhow, I was sitting there thinking about how I didn't share a single class with Mia, and how I didn't see Mia nearly enough during the day, and I was debating whether or not it was possible to switch sections of classes so I could see her more when there was a dull thud against the window.

I looked up and saw a bunch of wet leaves smashed against the inner screen, a clump of mud splatting on the windowsill. I reached over and pulled the shades apart and looked out the window and saw a dark shape in the center of the yard.

It was Mia.

I unlocked the window and raised it.

"Come down here," she said.

"Shhh," I whispered.

I crept downstairs. My parents were snoring inside their master bedroom. Truth be told, I wasn't so much fearing getting caught, because I know how deeply my parents sleep; rather I was just a straight arrow up till then and sneaking out felt, well, illegal? Mia waved at me through the front-door window. I slowly turned the knob and started pulling the door open as slowly as possible, so it wouldn't squeak.

"Jesus, just open it already," she said in a normal voice, and I winced.

A minute later I got the door open and edged sideways out onto the landing.

"Follow me," I whispered, and led her by hand to the side of the house, away from my parents' open windows. We stood in the yard without saying anything for a minute, staring at each other. The moon was full and her eyes looked black. Now she was just wearing regular old jeans and a plain gray sweatshirt, even though her cheeks still had JUNIOR written on them with felt-tip marker.

"You used permanent marker, didn't you," I said, patting her on the shoulder sympathetically. "I did that once when I was little. You're just going to have to wait for it to wear off. It takes a couple of weeks."

She laughed.

"No I didn't! I just haven't washed it off yet."

"Don't you have a curfew?" I asked.

"I snuck out too," she said. "I was missing you."

My stomach fell, in a good way, like on a roller coaster, as opposed to in a bad way, like when you think you're having a dream where you fall out of a window, and then a second before you hit the pavement you realize, "Oh my God, this is no dream, this is real!"

"Me too," I said, my voice almost cracking.

We didn't say anything for a minute or so, but it was clear we were thinking about the same thing, because the first thing she finally said was, "That wheelbarrow ride was so fricking stupid." She looked down at her sneakers. They were dewy, with blades of freshly cut grass stuck to the tips. "It wasn't even a wheelbarrow this time, it was a stupid wagon, which defeats the purpose of calling it a 'wheelbarrow ride.'"

"You looked like you were having a good time."

"Well, hey, free ride," she said, smiling. It quickly faded. "Ryan hated it. Afterward he was joking with me that I'd broken his ribs, but then a minute later I saw him actually digging into his ribs a little. Maybe I should weigh myself!"

Again, her feeble attempt at a joke failed miserably with me; I remained stone-faced.

"Anyway, it was stupid, but I felt bad that you had to see it," she added softly.

"Why?"

"It just felt so weird, as if the school was trying to make it seem like Ryan and I had gotten back together or something."

"The public seems to think so."

"Well, not many people know about us yet, is what I'm getting at."

I ulped, which is not quite as demonstrative a swallow as gulping.

"But we're something, right?" I asked.

"Look, Albert, this isn't coming out right. What I mean to say is just that, look, we just kissed for the first time last weekend. Yes, we're something, but even we don't know exactly what it is, yet."

Not true, I thought. We're many things:

—Boyfriend and girlfriend.

—Lovers.

—A new couple.

Instead of reciting my mental list, I merely said, "You're right, it's only the beginning."

"Right, but then school started, and there's all these politics to deal with, and so anyway I don't want what we have to be rushed into some definition just so we have an explanation for our classmates or whatever—do you know what I mean?"

"Not really."

She bit her bottom lip for a moment.

"I know my friends have been a little . . . cold. I was hoping they'd be more welcoming, but in their defense they had no idea about us, so it was a shock, not to mention some of them aren't exactly thrilled that me and Ryan are no longer dating. Plus, you have to understand, Shauna's really protective of me—she was like this when I first started dating Ryan, too. I think she's jealous of you."

"Really?"

"But she's also been, I don't know, different. Or I'm different now—it's confusing. I haven't been exactly thrilled with her this week," she said, staring down at her shoes. "It's like she's still so into talking solely about the lax boys, and I feel like she fell asleep for years and years while I kept getting older."

"People change. It's not fair to expect to remain buddies with a girl just because you liked each other when you were nine," I said.

"Yes, but the fact is, we've all been best friends with each other since age nine, you know? You can't erase history."

"You can't be tied to them because of it, though."

"Okay, can we stop talking about my best friends for a minute?" she asked, and I mentally winced. "That's not why I came here. Listen, I just don't like our relationship being dictated or defined by society, not to sound melodramatic."

"So you're saying it is a relationship," I pounced.

She rolled her eyes.

"You're missing the point. I liked the pace of this summer. We hung out. We got to really know each other. Don't you feel like we're being rushed into becoming something just to satisfy people?"

I nodded, declining to point out that I liked the notion of being rushed into a relationship at that point.

"We don't have to rush," I said.

"That's all I'm saying. And don't worry about stuff like the wagon ride, it seemed weird but it's nothing, just remnants of my former life."

"I know."

"But at the same time, it's important to understand that we're not at the inn anymore. We're not alone all the time, with just creepy Gino spying on us," she said. "Things are different, and I don't want, you know, life, to ruin what we had this summer."

"But you're also saying what we had this summer isn't over, right? Maybe you didn't mean to use the word 'relationship,' but you did say this was 'something' less than a minute ago."

I knew I was sounding desperate, but I couldn't help it. If I'd had my way I would have had Mia sign a written contract about our relationship, or gotten a tattoo of her initials on my shoulder.

"Yes, Albert!" She sighed. "Okay, I admit it, you psycho, that's what this is, a relationship, okay? God."

I could tell she was only pretending to be upset, because a second later she leaned in and kissed me. I put my arms around her and squeezed as hard as I could, which admittedly wasn't very hard, but I figured she couldn't tell I was putting in max effort. And she gave me a hundred little kisses, tiny pecks all over my face, and each time she kissed me it felt like I was being born again. She made a sad little sound, and I opened my eyes.

"I have an idea," she said, rubbing noses with me. "An olive branch I'll extend to you. How about this weekend it's just you and me? I have to hang out with Shauna tomorrow night, but otherwise the rest of the weekend you have me to yourself, okay?"

"Thank you," I said, and I must have said it funny because she burst out laughing.

"You're crazy," she said.

"It's been a hard two days for me," I admitted.

"I know it has, Albert," she said, lightly pecking the tip of my nose, which tickled, but I forced myself not to rub it. "But you have to understand, the first week is weird for everybody. School doesn't feel normal the first week. We're going to have an amazing weekend together, and then I swear, everything will be different real soon. You'll see."

21

That weekend it was as if Mia and I were an old couple renewing our vows. I'd barely seen Mia at school because I hated being around her friends, not to mention the fact that they weren't exactly making a concerted effort to group-hug me all the time, either. After an at times tumultuous, abbreviated first week of school, things once again felt the way they had felt during the summer at the Bern Inn. Even the weather was warmer than usual. I soaked up being with Mia like a really high-quality paper towel, and I noticed it actually made me feel physically nourished to spend time with her. She even taught me things, improving me as a human being—like how to turn off the water when I brushed my teeth to help the environment, or how to make homemade Rice Krispies Treats in the microwave—both equally important bits of education. Even my senses seemed to be sharpening by simply being with her. Usually I didn't even remember to smell my surroundings, and just got by using only four of my senses, whereas now I couldn't help but identify and appreciate the scent of distant barbecues, future rain, the wet fur of golden retrievers.

My favorite parts about being with Mia that weekend were the parts I'd least expected to prefer. What I liked best about our dates was everything *around* them. That is, I liked the traveling to and from the destinations best. On Saturday morning we rode the T into the city to visit the Boston Aquarium. It amazed us that nobody ever looks out the windows when the train comes out of the tunnel and you get to see all the boats on the Charles River right before the Charles/MGH stop on the Red Line. Mia and I watched incredulously as a tall blond woman in a business suit sat there reading the *Metro*, not even bothering to glance up at the beautiful Boston skyline shimmering in the reflected sunlight. For her it was just another workday on a Saturday in her slow, inexorable march toward death, whereas for us witnessing the view that morning instantly made it our all-time best moment together so far.

Mia had mentioned that she distinctly remembered loving the aquarium as a little kid but couldn't recall any specific details. ("Do you know about the fish?" I asked, and she punched me in the shoulder.) It turned out the aquarium was closed that weekend for renovations, but it didn't matter because instead we stared with our hands pressed against the thick glass of the outer tank just past the ticket booth, watching the seals swim the length of their artificial habitat. It was better than any movie—you stare through the hazy green water, and at twenty feet away you can make out the silver missile of the upside-down seal coming at you, and he's staring at you with his unblinking black eyes, and he comes right at you, and it's 3-D and at the very last second he curls down, dives, and gracefully floats back to the other end. Mia giggled each time the seal made a pass. It started drizzling lightly and the breeze coming into the harbor was chilly, but we stayed outside watching the seals for over an hour.

Afterward, we walked along the pier and stared down at a hundred jellyfish floating (I think dead) in the green water. At the Grand Marriott overlooking the harbor, there was a wedding party hanging out on a deck twenty stories up—these little ants wearing black tuxes and cocktail dresses, smoking cigarettes, the girls giggling and waving down at us while the guys exuberantly gave us the finger. We walked over to Faneuil Hall, where we each had bread baskets of clam chowder at Quincy Market. The soup was a little watery, but hot, and afterward we kissed on the Red Line, and our soupy breaths canceled each other out and the creaminess made me want to bite down hard on her lip and draw chowder.

By the time we got back to her car in Davis Square it was late afternoon. Mia didn't feel like dropping me off yet, so we went to Good Times to play games. I impressed her when we joined a foursome in the laser tag room. She got killed off early in the game, and then watched me proceed to expertly hunt down the other team, as well as all the members of my own team, because I got cocky and bored and simply wanted to show off in front of Mia. It actually led to a scary moment: my teammates were members of one of the various Mexican gangs that used Good Times as an informal social headquarters, and after we returned our laser tag gear we briskly walked to the exits with the gang members ominously following us through the place, past the oblivious old men smoking cigars as they played Keno at the daytime bar, next to the outdated kiddy rides. Luckily the gangbangers pursuing us were greeted by a rival gang and Mia and I were able to slip out without even getting marked.

"That was terrifying," Mia said when we reached the parking lot, and I felt bad that I'd put her in that situation, but then she squeezed my left forearm. "But you really wasted them in there, didn't you?"

"I'd make a sick gangbanger," I bragged, and Mia rolled her eyes at me. "*Orales*! Seriously, *vatos*!"

"What does that mean?"

"I'm not sure. But seriously."

"Why don't you join a gang, then?" she asked.

"The hitch is you have to get beaten up as the final initiation into the gang, and it just doesn't seem worth it. Plus, my parents would have, like, three cows apiece."

"You're an idiot."

On Sunday I bet Mia a dollar that I could provide her a delicious meal for free. I picked her up and we drove to the Burlington Mall, where we did seven laps around the food court taking multiple samples of the food items until we were full. She wore nylon BHS sweatpants that made a swishing sound as we walked in circles. I made her laugh when I turned my Stanford baseball cap around as a pitiful disguise the second time we passed by Quiznos, so the guy holding the sample tray wouldn't recognize me. On the third pass I untucked my button-down and Mia laughed her head off. The Japanese guy advertising a tray of bourbon chicken glared at me as I reached for my fourth toothpick's worth of delicious, grade-D meat.

"I don't know," I said, overacting with all kinds of hand motions. "I like this bourbon chicken, but I'm torn with the pepperoni pizza over at Sbarro's."

"Well then," Mia said in a deep voice (overacting as well), "why don't we take a look at the menu at Sbarro's again, then make our decision?"

We giggled as we marched back to the Sbarro's, where we continued the act: "I know I definitely want this," I said to the balding manager at Sbarro's, nibbling on a sample cube-size bite of a chicken parm sub. "But I first want to get a water at Ginsu Cafe, because the water's cheaper there. Sir, we'll be right back, this is definitely what I want for lunch."

"We're going to get busted," she whispered out the side of her mouth, pulling on my shirtsleeve.

"For what, accepting free food samples?" I replied.

We tried to look casual as we headed back to the Japanese take-out place, and at the last second she wimped out and yanked me away, and we scrambled almost out of control for the mall exit, as if we were being chased, laughing breathlessly.

"We just ate an entire meal for free," Mia marveled.

"And we walked the whole time we ate, so we canceled out the calories," I added.

"Actually, I think I have a cramp," she said, digging a hand into her rib cage.

I was so happy that it felt like my veins were suddenly coursing with Coffee-mate creamer. In fact, I swear to God there was a cartoon deer standing behind Mia right then, nibbling on a discarded napkin, and some animated bluebirds fluttering by the sign for The Gap. A cartoon bunny hopped by and shrugged its shoulders at me, and I just waved at it gaily.

"What are you waving at?" Mia asked.

"Nothing," I blurted. "There is no rabbit."

She tilted her head at me and said, "I forgot how weird you are."

After eating our fill for free, we got free massages at The Sharper Image, pretending we were actually considering buying one for her parents for Christmas. Before we knew it, dinnertime had rolled around, and I drove her back to her house. It had been a perfect weekend, our time together just like back in the summer—as if we had the world to ourselves, and in my head I was thinking about giving her a little thank-you speech in the driveway, about how much the weekend meant to me or something corny to that effect, and the two times I lovingly glanced over at her she seemed deep in thought as well. But the speech never happened, because when I pulled into the driveway we were both depressed, which in turn made us both feel crabby, and we ended up muttering good-bye without even looking at each other.

I got to school on Monday feeling reenergized from our weekend together, but almost immediately something felt off. It wasn't until lunchtime when I realized what it was.

The House was missing.

That's how it is with people like Ryan Stackhouse. Love him or hate him, his absence is palpable, and school life doesn't feel right anymore. You could almost taste it, the fact that he wasn't there that day. Incidentally, his absence tasted like popcorn chicken. I lie.

When the news was disclosed that afternoon, nobody quite believed it. Ryan was the very embodiment of Ford-tough power, and the answer as to why he wasn't in school seemed—and still seems—impossible, even now. All morning, rumors flew around the hallways, snaking their way into the smoky teachers' lounge between periods, suggesting reasons of varying plausibility as to why The House wasn't in school, why he would possibly miss a single day of his senior year, which was set up to resemble not so much a fourth year of high school as a nine-month-long victory parade. Most of the rumors floating around were of a graphic or scandalous nature, which is typical in high school. A bit less scandalous was the rumor that, with his sparkling transcript and stellar SAT results and professionally produced, fifteen-minute video demonstrating his athletic prowess, he'd been offered a full ride to Dartmouth over the weekend and was already playing preseason beer games in some frat house basement.

I hadn't the faintest idea what the particulars were regarding his absence; all I knew was that whatever it was, it probably would take up Mia's attention, just as we were starting to reestablish what we'd had that summer.

Little did I know.

I was sitting alone at a round table in the caf during study hall that afternoon when it suddenly occurred to me that, not only was Ryan missing from school, but Mia had never shown up either. It sounds hard to believe that I wouldn't notice this, but for the first few days of school I'd rarely seen her—she was always with her friends and off working on posters for the pep rally, and I'd already kinda grown accustomed to not really seeing her in school.

The cafeteria was mostly empty, save for a handful of freshman girls experiencing their first laid-back high school study hall. I watched them with relish (and mayo) as they at first pretended to study, stealing glances at the comatose study-hall monitor before realizing their utter freedom, and after a few minutes they began gossiping loudly and brazenly chewing their gum with their mouths open. Occasionally they'd look over at me and frown. I recognized them, they were two of the girls I'd punched in the shoulder on the first day of school. It was clear now that they were of the soon-to-be-slutty variety of freshman mice that devolve into the popular crowd by sophomore year, and they'd arrived at BHS in full social-climbing mode, starting at the bottom of the hill—well, a row above the freshman boys—and they were looking to establish themselves ASAP.

Their social radar had semirightfully assessed that I wasn't worth smiling at. Their brief look and subsequent dismissal of me probably speaks volumes about my outward physical appearance that no personal description could ever capture. Had I cared about my social status I would have at least glared back at them or something, but a serious food coma was setting in from my greasy slice of square pizza, and I could feel my eyelashes turning into dead garter snakes, and as I put my head down on my forearms I heard one of the mice say, "I heard he got caught with his ex."

I perked up.

"What did you just say?" I asked.

"Oh, hi there, so sorry, but we weren't talking to you!" she said cheerfully, in that intentionally fake-sounding rising tone of happiness that infuriates me. I forced myself to take a deep breath.

"You're talking about Ryan Stackhouse, right?"

The mice rolled their eyes at me but couldn't resist bragging about their source.

"Jonesey said," and the mouse couldn't quite hide the millisecond of sheer pleasure she felt referencing one of the school's gods, "Jonesey said that Ryan and Mia got caught in a motel room in Gloucester. She's preggers, you know."

"Mouse," I said. "If you really want to make an impression, you need to get your facts straight. A, Mia broke up with Ryan, back when you were sleeping through short cartoons about lead poisoning in middle school, because she wasn't interested in making babies with The House, and B, Mia's actually my girlfriend, which you'll learn soon enough and realize that your naïve dismissal of me is the reason why you won't be invited to any parties this weekend, and C, it's not Jonesey, it's Mister Jonesey."

I was being stupid and didn't know why I felt so defensive, but I felt a glimmer of satisfaction as I left the caf, because I could hear the girl muttering softly, as if practicing, "Mista Jonesey. Mister Jonesey." The other mouse made a cat-hissing sound at me that in my imagination surely was accompanied by an aggressive swipe of a clawed hand, but I couldn't confirm it because by this time I was running in the opposite direction. I literally had to grab hold of the pay phone to keep from flying past it, and then I dialed Mia's house. Her mom picked up midway through the first ring. This set off a red flag, since I knew that Mia's mom worked five days a week as a saleslady at Voerg Farms.

"Aloha, Mrs. Stone, it's Albert; I'm trying to track down your daughter."

"Who is this?"

"Albert, I worked with Mia this summer, and—"

"I don't know who this is, but she's in the yard, please don't call again, we're trying to keep the phone line free," she said quickly.

"Oh, right, you don't have total phone, sorry. Does this have anything to do with—"

She hung up.

The school day couldn't end soon enough. I fidgeted through my final two classes and then relocated to my bus, where I resumed my fidgeting, watching in horror as the bus driver refused to shift past second gear the entire ride home.

When I got let off I broke into a sprint for Mia's house. A minute later I dug some fingers deep into my ribs to staunch the cramps I was getting and slowed to a walk midway down Columbus. When I saw her old, two-story colonial in the distance I caught a second wind and started running again. I ran onto the grass and loped past the house to the open garage door, whereupon I saw a flash of green whiz by the window of the garage, and I stopped.

Mia was doing wind sprints back and forth across the backyard. There was a light half-moon of sweat on her violet shirt. Her hair was in a ponytail, and a clump of it had stuck sideways to her glistening neck. For a moment I silently admired her, watching her run. She's legitimately fast, and had already received brochures advertising the nationally renowned track team at Villanova University, etc. I watched Mia do at least a half dozen wind sprints, and all the while she hadn't noticed me standing there, ogling her; I know because when she looked up and saw me she yelped.

"Sorry, you startled me," she said, breathing heavily. "How long have you been standing there?"

"Not long."

"Give me a minute."

I was going to attempt to engage her in some sort of witty banter, because we were still in that honeymoon stage of the relationship, and my initial urge anytime I saw her was to rub noses and make embarrassing cooing sounds, but her eyes unnerved me. Usually the picture of calm (because she's an old soul), they looked wild and darting, like a deranged squirrel's. She started running wind sprints again, but she wasn't taking breaks between sprints, so it looked not so much like she was running around the fancy track at BHS, but as if she were running away from an ax murderer in the woods or something. It was clear that she wasn't running for training purposes, but to exhaust herself. She ran two more sprints before pulling up again. She crossed her legs, bent over, and touched her toes.

"I need to know what's going on, Mia. Your mom was short with me on the phone," I said. "And at school, I overheard some freshmen mice saying that you were pregnant in a motel with Ryan, who was a no-show today, by the way, and—"

She was still leaned over, swaying slightly, touching her toes, when I saw two distinct tears fall and disappear into the dark green grass. A moment later she stood up, and her face was bright pink and wet. I rushed forward and hugged her, and she was instantly heavy in my arms. I looked down and saw that the bottoms of her running shoes weren't even touching the grass. When I looked up at the house I saw Mrs. Stone staring at us through the kitchen window. The phone rang inside, and she walked away, at which point I had to let go of Mia because she was really heavy and I'd been holding my breath, and the sight of Mrs. Stone staring at us made me lose my focus for a second. Mia fell to the grass in an awkward shambles. "Jesus," she muttered.

She then looked up at me and yelped, for the second time that afternoon.

"Take it easy," I soothed Mia.

A whiff of freshly cut grass passed through the backyard, and in the distance I could hear a dog barking.

"Ryan's sick," she said. "He has cancer."

"What?" I was stunned.

"He has something called Hodgkin's disease," she continued. Her voice was shaky, and when I put a hand on her shoulder it felt like she was shivering. Through the open kitchen window we heard the phone ring again.

"Is he at the hospital?" I asked.

She nodded.

"They're taking his spleen out as we speak," Mia explained, staring at the open window. "It's apparently a routine procedure, but that just might have been my mom trying to calm me down."

"I appreciate you spleening this to me," I said, but my stupid pun didn't make her laugh. Luckily she didn't even seem to hear me. Instead, Mia stared straight ahead through the trees, as if she had a headache and was focusing on the horizon. A few moments later she touched her bottom lip and started nodding to herself.

"He must have had it this past spring," she went on. "Because he was slower on the field. I remember him always complaining about it. I even noticed when we'd race each other. It makes sense his spleen's so enlarged with it—he always had the biggest belly, I mean, from the side he looked pregnant, but straight on he had a total six-pack over the potbelly. Me and Jonesey used to tease him about it."

Mia laughed out loud for a moment, remembering it. Then she caught herself.

"I can't believe he has cancer," she said, and buried her nose in my chest. Her hands scraped my back.

I pictured Ryan doing Supermans the other day.

"Don't say that, he'll be fine. That he's the ultimate athlete gives him the best shot, I bet," I said, wincing. She was really digging.

"Really?" she asked.

"Of course! His athleticism is like armor, okay?"

"Uh-huh," she replied.

"Okay, um, and so it's like the cancer's trying to eat through his armor, but he has a ton of it, way more than regular people; it's twice as thick since he's a superjock, so that buys him more time."

In hindsight, I probably could have come up with a better analogy, because I could tell Mia was now picturing something like out of the movie *Alien*, a piece of armor fizzing and smoking as a yellowish acid burned through it, and she was about to break down into tears again, but luckily her mom burst through the screen door to the porch.

"Ryan just got out of surgery," Mrs. Stone said.

"I'm going to ask Mrs. Stackhouse if I can visit," Mia said, heading inside.

"I think they'd appreciate that," her mom said.

"Okay, I'm down with that. When, tomorrow?" I asked.

"Hopefully now. His parents haven't told any of his

guy friends the news yet, because they don't want too many visitors," Mia said. "I hate to think that, besides his parents, Ryan's all alone right now dealing with this."

24

There's something phony about a candlelight vigil. I don't mean phony for the obvious reasons—that it's an antiquated ritual in this golden age of glow sticks, or the indisguisable fact that nobody who attends believes it'll do any good. No war has ever been cut short as a result of a candlelight vigil, no beloved dead person has—to my knowledge at least—ever been reanimated by one. Truth is, the majority of people who attend candlelight vigils do it merely to make themselves feel good. It's a swallowable act of altruism that even the most selfish person can handle. It's simple. All you have to do is stand in a fixed position for a few hours, hold a candle in a crowd, and sing along to a handful of protest-era songs that have already been conveniently queued together for you in disc one of the *Forrest Gump* movie soundtrack, and voilà, you're now a good person, at least for the rest of that particular month, or, in many cases (let's be honest) until the next candlelight vigil.

It's a far cry from digging a latrine in some third-world country and developing an immunity to elephant pee out of sheer stubbornness over the course of a two-year stint in the Peace Corps, but attending a candlelight vigil in a Podunk town like Bern, Massachusetts, carries with it a surprising karmic heft in the minds of those who attend, the younger me included. I have to admit I felt like I was healing a nation (and thereby securing my place in heaven) the night I was video-taped by the local NBC affiliate back in my similarly Podunk town in Maryland, as I stood in the thick of a candlelight vigil for the space shuttle *Challenger* disaster, vigorously singing along to Elton John's "Rocket Man." But I was seeing things differently that night, because for the first time in my life I wasn't a participant in a candlelight vigil, but rather—an observer.

There I was, looking out the window of hospital room 327 at Brigham and Women's Hospital in Boston, standing next to Mia as we watched a candlelight vigil form down in West Lot C of the parking lot in honor of the patient lying asleep in the room: The House.

Aforementioned überathlete supreme and sure-to-be-Brown-bound son, who also happened to be Mia's former long-term boyfriend—*that* guy, was lying unconscious or asleep in the metal bed while I focused on the burgeoning candlelight vigil below. From my popelike vantage point I came to a huge revelation that night: that candlelight vigils are phony, given the fact that everyone down there was clearly having so much *fun*.

Call me a conservative stickler, but I'm of the opinion that people at candlelight vigils should be silent, dour, prayerful, as they Voltron together into a single beacon of healing light. It didn't look like a vigil down there so much as it resembled the trash-strewn grounds on the third and final night of a fire-men's carnival; I could practically smell the fried dough.

That said, it made sense that everyone was enjoying themselves, since when you got down to brass tacks, there weren't that many people in the crowd who truly liked Ryan, because The House was considered a world-class prick, as is often the case with entitled, mesomorphic, superheroicly lantern-jawed teenagers unfairly blessed with 130-plus IQs. *Why be anything else when you're already everything?* is the eternal question pricks from sea to shining sea struggle with, and Ryan Stackhouse was no exception.

Let's pan around the parking lot for a moment:

There was Paul Waverly, a classmate of ours, who, only six hours previous, was spreading the rumor in the caf that Ryan was missing from school because he'd gotten retroactively busted for smoking weed on his last day of Outward Bound that summer—a youth camping trip (where normally you learn life lessons from burying your own poo) gone awry. Now he was jawing away with somebody's mother, nodding and shaking his head in order to physically express his shock and disbelief that this was all happening.

Behind Paul were a trio of hunched-over goth kids, specifically NIИ worshippers dressed from mascara'd head to Doc Marten'd toe in black; the type of scrawny students who Ryan, the previous two years, enjoyed routinely shoving into lockers in order to give his tri-headed triceps a minipump between classes. Boys who after school passed the time filling notebooks with blueprints for taking down jocks like The House, earnestly debating the ethics of filling an evil person's fruit-cocktail-juice box with ethylene glycol during lunch, had now positioned themselves in the third row, white-knuckling their matching Virgin of Guadalupe candles and probably taking turns trading stories from Ryan's past, as if they stood as proof of Ryan's impending sainthood. That's what happens when someone you barely know (especially a VIP like Ryan) gets seriously ill—how you actually felt about him up to that point becomes moot.

Scattered among what appeared to be the entire student body of BHS were students' parents, teachers, and in one corner a dozen or so "old-timers" who hang out at Bassey's Barbershop on Main Street every Sunday morning. The old-timers had been in the parking lot since the very start of the candlelight vigil; they were probably yet to even mention the name of the vigil's subject and didn't even bother to take one of the votives that a little girl was passing out from a torn paper bag. Instead, they were animatedly arguing, probably about BHS's chances to capture the state championship in football this season (it's a cliché, but that's pretty much the only thing your standard issue old-timer likes to talk about), and chain-smoking their el cheapo Kent cigarettes, which I suppose they considered a worthy proxy for an actual candle.

Young mothers beamed with pride as they watched their littlest ones hold lit candles in public for the first time, practically a rite of passage in a small town like Bern, while the wives of the old-timers set up a makeshift beverage station in an empty handicapped spot—the three white-haired ladies formed an efficient assembly line as one poured decaf, another arranged the steaming Styrofoam cups, and the third unwrapped an assortment of glass casserole dishes filled with powdery brownie-ish concoctions.

I guess the scent of fried dough wasn't my imagination, after all.

What a bunch of hypocrites—these candlelight vigils bring out the fair-weather sympathizers the same way deep playoff runs bring out pseudo Fenway faithfuls who all of a sudden, in late September, start wearing Red Sox hats with stiff brims. Cindy Durante made her way up to the front—the same Cindy, mind you, who the previous spring introduced negative advertising to the SGA presidential campaign for the first time, which she subsequently lost in a landslide to The House. It was a protracted, bitter public feud, and upon losing she was seen spitting on the hood of Ryan's Bronco II before bending his radio antenna into an upside-down L. Apparently those days were but a distant memory, as Cindy reached the front row finally and lifted up the first hand-painted sign of the night, duct-taped to a yardstick. It read in thick, red permanent marker:

RE-LAX, RYAN, WE'RE CRADLING YOU FROM BEHIND!

A downright bizarre and unintentionally homoerotic sentiment that was clearly the product of a nonathlete attempting to speak in the language of a jock. Incredibly, a handful of Ryan's lax teammates thought the sign was clever and nodded approvingly at Cindy, and with their bare hands pretended to cradle lax sticks, and soon everyone in the front row was looking up in the general direction of room 327, holding imaginary lacrosse sticks, having adopted this motion as the universal sign of love for an ailing lacrosse player. Jonesey stood in front and faced the crowd like a conductor, waving his imaginary lacrosse stick like a baton.

I even saw Billy and Brett Timmons's parents standing there, holding votives. At this point there were enough people down in West Lot C to warrant security, as two Boston Police squad cars parked fender to fender at the far end of the lot. I could tell the fuzz's presence excited the crowd of well-wishers, for they knew that when the police show up, the news crews can't be that far behind. I looked to the sky for helicopters, but there weren't any in the vicinity, not yet. All this in support of Bern's brightest star, Ryan Chase Stackhouse II.

I turned away from the window to steal a glance at Ryan. His parents were standing motionless next to his bed, and I felt guilty taking more than a few seconds to look at him, so I snuck a peek and then pretended to seek out a box of Kleenexes. The whir and sighs of various machines added audio testament that Ryan was still alive following his routine-but-still-terrifying surgery. The doctor had informed us that Ryan wouldn't wake up, in all likelihood, until the next morning, but I still felt uncomfortable as hell sitting so close to him, instead of Jonesey, or any number of other actual friends of his from BHS. I was there because Mia had asked me to come with her, because she couldn't do it by herself, and to say I felt out of place is an understatement of the grandest scale, given that it was obvious I wasn't exactly waiting in line to blow the guy like everybody else.

So let's recap the scenario: The House didn't show up to school on Monday, and it turned out that he had cancer, and the next thing I knew I was standing next to his hospital bed, looking down on a thousand people holding candles.

Fucking A.

Ryan's parents looked exhausted. They were sharing the one puffy olive-colored chair in the tiny hospital room. Mr. Stackhouse, a bear of a man, filled up the entire seat, while his wife sat perched, with perfect posture, on one of the arms. Mrs. Stackhouse was like a little bird, very pretty and thin and elegantly dressed. I suppose the bird analogy was in part a reference to her fragile bone structure, but there was also something severe about her expression that made her look hard, like a hawk. Her hair was in a too-tight bun that made the skin around her hairline white. Mr. Stackhouse was absentmindedly stroking his wife's back a little too hard, but for some reason she didn't complain, and instead just sat there, rigid—taking the unintentional spousal abuse, occasionally flinching, like a cat's ear.

Ryan's siblings were temporarily MIA. His older sister, Porter, was en route from Manhattan with her fiancé, while Ryan's brothers were planning to visit on the weekend. Every few minutes the phone in the room would ring—one of Ryan's siblings calling to get an update.

"Ryan told me to get in touch with you," Mrs. Stackhouse said. Mia blushed at first, but I could tell a part of her was wondering, as I was, if she was trying to make Mia feel needed by Ryan or make it clear that she didn't herself choose to corral her son's ex.

"What can we do to help?" Mia asked, undeterred.

"Well, let's see," Mr. Stackhouse said, putting his hand on Mia's shoulder and squeezing it till she tensed. "We haven't eaten yet; maybe you could watch Ryan for a bit while we take a break?"

"I'm sure you have plenty of friends down in the parking lot who want to say hi to you," Mia said. "There's an Au Bon Pain in the lobby."

"You kids will be fine, just call the nurse if you need anything," he replied.

Mr. Stackhouse drifted over to the window and peeked through the curtains. I was surprised to find that the sight of the candlelight vigil didn't make Ryan's dad smile. It was officially dark outside, now that it was past nine, and the streetlamps and lights in opposing office buildings cast a glow through the thin curtains. It seemed dangerous to me—not to be morbid but I really worried that Ryan could come to and think he was staring at the light at the end of the tunnel, and it might compel him to jump out of the bed and run to it or something.

"Every now and then check his forehead," Mrs. Stackhouse said. "If it feels hot, put a cold washcloth on it. He has a slight fever, so I've been putting one on his head every now and then."

"No problemo," I said, and it jarred Mrs. Stackhouse. I glanced over at the mirror to make sure I had a reflection. She then nodded at me without smiling, then looked back at her sleeping son and just stood there in the doorway. Mr. Stackhouse pulled her away, and when I looked over at Mia, her eyes were starting to well up.

The Stackhouses left the room. Mia and I stood at the foot of the bed and finally let ourselves stare at Ryan. He was propped up in bed, so it looked like he was half-sitting. According to Mrs. Stackhouse, there was a thick layer of wrapped gauze covering up a fresh scar that extended from below his belly button all the way up to the breastbone, from where the doctors took out his spleen. Mrs. Stackhouse had explained to us when we arrived that, prior to the surgery that afternoon, one of the surgeons had sat down next to Ryan and asked him to try a visualizing technique that might help Ryan's chances for a successful surgery. The doctor told Ryan to visualize his insides, and to pretend that his blood was scared of knives. The image that came to my mind was of the windshield of my dad's Oldsmobile after he sprays it with Rain-X; you don't have to use your wipers because the rain immediately races off the sides. Anyhow, after the surgery, the same doctor told Mrs. Stackhouse that, given the severity and depth of the incision, there was a remarkably small amount of blood loss. The hairs on my neck stiffened when she disclosed this little anecdote. Mia smiled because she was proud of Ryan, but then the reality of the situation dawned on her and her expression hardened again.

I realized I had been staring at Ryan's toes for some reason. They were sticking out from under the untucked sheets at the base of the bed, and they looked discolored, but I figured it was the fluorescent lights. I then looked back up at Ryan and gasped—his face was completely drenched.

"Did that just happen, or was his face always like that?" I asked Mia.

Mia gasped too. "I don't know," she said, and reached

over and touched his forehead. "Oh my God, he's burning up!"

She rushed over to the cabinet under the sink and rummaged noisily through the drawers. We'd been so quiet for so long the crashing sounds made me wince.

"Come here," Mia whispered to me, and tossed me a white washcloth. "Like an assembly line, you keep refreshing these washcloths with cold water, and I'll keep changing them."

I turned the cold faucet on and stuck two fingers under it. It seemed to stay lukewarm forever. When it finally felt cold enough I held the washcloth under the water until it got soaked through, then I wrung it out and lobbed it back to Mia. She carefully folded it into a square and then placed it on his huge forehead. I could practically hear the hiss and see steam rise out from under the cloth.

"Get the second one ready," Mia instructed me.

I hurled her a cold washcloth and she tossed me back the used one, and I was shocked at how warm it was—Ryan was literally burning up; it had only been on his forehead for twenty seconds, tops. Ryan's cheeks were bright red and shiny. There was a huge vein on his forehead that ran diagonally from one corner of his hairline to the opposite eyebrow. It was whitish, while the rest of his forehead was bright red, and it reminded me of the cover to the Van Halen album, *Diver Down*, and I could actually see the blood pulsing through it. It was gnarly, but I couldn't look away; the vein had me under its spell.

"Keep 'em coming," Mia said, and we kept at it like this,

for almost ten minutes, until Ryan's face was no longer flushed, and the used washcloths coming back to me were still somewhat cold, and it was during this time when I started to realize how much of a schmuck I was for thinking I was having a revelation about candlelight vigils, when truth was, I was missing the entire point.

There were two, actually.

As we tossed washcloths to each other I thought back to everything that had happened since that afternoon. I pictured Mia running wind sprints in her backyard; Mia waiting at the Davis Square T-stop for a train, staring unblinking at the billboards, as if she were studying for an exam; and then I pictured her there, in room 327, so focused on replacing cold washcloths on Ryan's forehead long after he no longer even needed them, and it dawned on me that she did all these things merely to distract herself from having to face the scary reality of the situation. The moment she stopped sprinting that afternoon, I realized, her mind was allowed to think, and she broke down in tears. That's one reason why people went to these candlelight vigils—to distract themselves from having to deal with the tragedy alone. And the second reason was that even though it might be phony, people attended these candlelight vigils to make themselves feel like they were doing something to help.

Ryan's cheeks had lost their color at this point, and my right hand was an arthritic granny's claw from squeezing the soaked washcloths a hundred times, and Mia was exhausted as well, but I didn't want to stop because— goddamnit—we were *saving his life.*

"I think that's enough for now," she finally said. "I'm zonked. Do you mind if I sit outside for a minute?"

"Of course not."

I could tell she didn't feel comfortable dealing with just sitting there in the room with Ryan, because she wasn't looking at him at all anymore. Neither could I. He was this huge monster; his nickname was "The House," for chrissakes, and there he was, making these cute mewling sounds that reminded me of Gizmo from *Gremlins*, and if I were to have given Ryan my finger he wouldn't have been able to even squeeze it.

Mia went out into the hall. A moment later I could hear another chair scraping along the floor—I pictured her pushing two together to create a makeshift cot. I looked over at Ryan and suddenly realized I was alone in the room with him. It felt wrong again, despite my actions in the last hour. I didn't want him to wake up and catch me staring at him. I felt awkward, so I went over to the window and pulled the curtains apart.

The crowd below was already beginning a mass, disorganized exodus, and the ensuing chaos looked absolutely insane to me. I turned around, whisper-shouting, "Mia, come here, you have to see this!" But Mia was already fast asleep, I could hear her snoring. Instead it was just me and Ryan, and I looked over at the bed and saw that he was awake, for the first time all night. His eyes were big and brown and not quite lucid, and we, for almost a minute, regarded each other, and I didn't know what to say, but it felt like we were sharing a touching moment, and I just sort of smiled at the guy and nodded slightly over at the washcloths, thinking he might put two and two together; and I had no intention of breaking the silence, but then Ryan's eyes narrowed, his chapped mouth cracked open a little, and he said to me: "What the fuck are you doing here?"

PART 3

Afterschool Special

26 The next day at school everyone was walking around like zombies, still reeling from the news. Students drifted into classes late and the teachers didn't even seem to mind because they were feeling discombobulated too. It felt weird to walk Mia to class that morning; classmates were constantly approaching and giving her deep-felt hugs. Mia would close her eyes in their embrace and softly say, "Thank you," each time. There was an absence of laughter in the air, and as a result, the school felt deathly silent. In sharp contrast to teenage fashion week, this week all the students somehow knew not to wear bright colors to school; in fact, most everyone, including the principal, was dressed in dark colors, as if we were indeed in a state of mourning.

Students treated Mia with kid gloves, but it was nothing compared to how everyone acted around the lax guys. Already the kings of the school, the varsity lacrosse players were now granted a sort of "martyr-by-association" status, as teachers fondly patted them on the shoulders in the hallways, and clumps of freshmen practically . . . bowed? whenever a lax guy walked by. The lax guys, of course, soaked in this newfound status and seemed to have changed into different people, at least temporarily. No longer shoving frosh into lockers, or slamming their lockers and marveling at the decibel level, or one-inch-punching closed lockers to prove their manliness (lax guys seem to have an abusive love affair with metal lockers in general), these holier-than-thou meatheads now walked around more slowly than usual, like musclebound monks, speaking in deep, patronizing voices, and nodding at just about anyone who would make eye contact with them, as if to say, "Go in peace." At one point I witnessed a frosh guy bump into a lax guy, and he cringed, and the lax guy, rather than wheel the frosh around and put him in a half nelson, instead squeezed the kid's shoulders and said in an earnest voice, "It's okay, little friend. Just slow it up a bit and you'll be fine."

"Thank you, sir."

At lunch I sat with Brett and his pals, not listening to the conversation as I scanned the lax tables for her. She was nowhere in sight. The fact that Brett et al. didn't even know I was dating her made me feel unfairly mad at them, as if they weren't supporting me or something. Granted, I hadn't told them that Mia and I were something, because it felt even less realistic to say it out loud; I almost didn't believe it myself. So I just sat there sullenly next to them, looking for Mia.

I didn't see Mia the rest of the afternoon, and my desperate search for her proved to be futile when she explained on the phone that night that she'd skipped lunch altogether to call Ryan at the pay phone by the music room, and after school went directly back to the hospital to sit with Ryan in his room through dinner. She watched fuzzy reception noncable TV with Ryan for hours and sporadically had to wait out in the hallway as the doctors ran further tests to see if the cancer had spread.

The nurse explained to Mia that, "If you're going to get cancer, Hodgkin's is the kind to get, because it's the most treatable and has a ninety-five percent recovery rate." Therefore, Mia explained to me, the prognosis for Ryan was optimistic.

"That's great news," I said. "When does he get to go home?"

"A week from Thursday," she replied.

"Do you want me to go with you to the hospital tomorrow?"

"No, it's boring, and Ryan mostly sleeps, and I think he wants privacy."

"Well, if you ever need company . . ."

"Thanks, Al, you're sweet," Mia said, yawning. "But I'm really tired. I'm not even going to do my homework. I have to go to sleep, okay?"

"I'll see you tomorrow at school," I said, and Mia said something that sounded like "Mmm" before hanging up.

The next day, however, I didn't see her in school *again*. At lunchtime I jogged over to the pay phone by the band room, but Mia wasn't there. Between periods I raced up and down the hallways, looking for her, but (forgive the pun) Mia was MIA. That afternoon when I got home I called her house. I knew she was already at the hospital, but I left a message with Mrs. Stone, the gist of it being something along the lines of, "Please tell your daughter I said hi and that she totally doesn't have to call or anything." To my utter dismay, both Mia and her mother thought I meant that last part, and as a result she didn't call me back that night. I waited by the phone until midnight before finally giving up and turning out the light.

Two days. For two whole days I hadn't seen her. It felt like two years. That great weekend we'd spent together, right before Ryan ended up in the hospital, felt like a lifetime ago. And now she was spending all her free time after school sitting next to a guy she didn't even really like that much. . . . I found that my hands were clenched into useless fists as I stared up at the ceiling. I started picturing myself in Ryan's shoes, and it sobered me up. I tried to imagine what it must feel like to be told you have cancer. I tried to pretend I'd been told I might die young, and my guilt literally gave me the shivers. Thinking about Ryan's situation for ten seconds gave me a coal-size lump in my throat, and I prayed for forgiveness for thinking whiny thoughts simply because I wanted Mia all to myself. I prayed that he got better soon, and I asked the Lord for forgiveness for my selfishness for even thinking about Mia hanging out with me instead of him.

I lay there with my eyes closed and tried to see God. After the blackness, and a few seconds before those red and green amoeba start squiggling around, I reached this brief state where I could see the universe. I could feel the coldness of space and infinity, and it was as close as I've ever come to being alone with God. I asked God why he gave Ryan cancer, because it terrified me that Ryan stood as proof that everything in this life is random, and that anyone can get cut down at any moment, no matter how you live your life or where you put yourself. You don't decide your future. I could tell it was one of those nights when I shouldn't even bother trying to fall asleep, so I just lay there, wide-eyed, staring at the ceiling for hours.

27 The next morning I finally found Mia. She was surrounded at her locker by Jonesey, whose ponderously heavy arm was draped over Shauna's shoulders, along with a couple other peaking-at-age-seventeen lax cronies. From across the hallway I watched them for a minute, unnoticed. I desperately wanted to approach Mia, and—despite feeling guilty the night before, staring wide-eyed at the ceiling and all that—ream her out a little for neglecting me, but I felt frozen by the presence of the lax crowd, particularly Jonesey. The guy hated me to begin with, but I had a vague premonition that he'd feel inclined to savagely beat me for talking to Mia now that Ryan was sick. My body clearly didn't agree at all with what I was about to do, but I ignored the internal bells and whistles of self-preservation going off

inside me, took a deep breath, and made my way over to them.

"Albert," Mia said, and I was pleasantly surprised to see her smiling at me. For a split second I wondered whether she'd be embarrassed to see me with all her friends around. I then considered the possibility that perhaps my keen understanding of sociopolitical cues based solely from the oeuvre of John Hughes films was misleading; of course she wouldn't diss me in public—this was Mia Stone, after all, the nicest girl in school despite her social pedigree, the girl who had kissed me and labeled us (multiple times) as something.

Something.

Jonesey and Shauna frowned at me, as expected, but without saying a word they drifted out of earshot (I assumed I was being paranoid, but I got the distinct feeling they were kinda waiting for me to leave), and the swarm of lax guys dutifully followed them off, reconvening their powwow approximately four feet away from Mia and me.

"Let's see if there's any leftover doughnuts in the kitchen," Mia suggested, and we started walking toward the caf, even though homeroom was in less than five minutes.

"Can I ask you something, Mia?"

"Anything," she said.

"Are we still something?"

Although I'm really nonconfrontational (to the point of, for example, offering money to vagrants *before* they even ask for it), I have moments like this where I suddenly cut to the chase.

"Of course we are," she replied. "Are you going to be asking me that every day?"

"This is only the third time I've ever asked you that in my entire life."

"Well, it feels like it's going to be a regular checkup."

"A lot has happened the last few days."

We sat down at an empty table in the caf. She sighed.

"No, you're right, I'm just out of it right now," she said. "I still haven't caught up on sleep since the vigil Monday night. Look, we're cool, but you're right, things are kinda complicated right now. I need you for some different reasons all of a sudden, you know?"

Actually, I didn't—I'd asked the question so she could shower me with soothing assurances that everything was gravy, but I nodded without really understanding. Apparently I looked exactly how I felt.

"What I mean is nothing between you and me has changed because of this, but it's a really surreal time, and right now I need you as a friend as well as, you know, something more."

"Okay."

Shauna and Jonesey strolled in, and, in retrospect, I'm ninety-eight percent positive they *were* spying on us, because otherwise they never "strolled" anywhere.

"Stoner," Jonesey barked, purposely not making eye contact with me, as if I weren't there. "You wanna snack? I'm going to work my magic on the hairnets for some freebie Nutty Buddies."

"I'm good," Mia replied.

"Don't go anywhere," Shauna said to Mia. "I have to talk to you."

The evil bastards disappeared into the kitchen. The

homeroom bell rang—this was my first time missing home-room . . . *in my entire life.* Wide-eyed, I looked over at Mia.

"We'll just stop by the office after homeroom and sign in late," she said.

A couple of seconds later Shauna came over and sat down next to Mia.

"Remember last spring when that frosh lax guy sent me a carnation?" she whispered to Mia, looking over at the kitchen to make sure Jonesey wasn't coming back.

"Yeah," Mia said.

"I think he totally likes me still," Shauna continued. "He keeps saying hi to me in a really friendly way. Kinda like how Jamie would be all friendly with you in the halls freshman year, thinking he wasn't being obvious that he liked you?"

"Right," Mia said, smiling.

I quickly deduced that Shauna was quite possibly the boringest person in the history of mankind. Jonesey soon walked over, inserting an entire Nutty Buddy ice-cream cone into his mouth with one decisive shove as he sat down across from Shauna.

"You're an absolute Neanderthal," Mia said, laughing.

"Damnit, brain freeze!" he shouted, wincing and hitting himself in the forehead.

"You shouldn't have shoved the whole thing into your mouth," Shauna said.

"You would know," he replied, and she punched him in the shoulder.

"Press your tongue against the roof of your mouth," I instructed him. "It'll get rid of the headachey feeling."

"Huh?" Jonesey glared at me.

"You have nerve endings in the roof of your mouth that—"

"It's gone already, Poindexter," he said, turning his seat so he faced Mia and Shauna. "Anyway, remember when Ry tried to write on Jamie's cheek when he was asleep in study hall with a pencil and accidentally stabbed Jamie, and then when we pulled the stub of lead out of his cheek it started gushing blood?"

Aghast that Mia would actually date a guy who found it the height of entertainment to write on peoples' cheeks, I looked to Mia for a conciliatory expression, but she didn't seem remotely embarrassed by the lame-ass story; instead, she just made a funny face at Shauna.

"That was so gross," Shauna said. "Eek!"

She actually said "eek," like an annoying cartoon come to life.

"I can't believe Jamie didn't go crazy on Ryan when that happened," Mia said.

"Jamie can't lift shit," Jonesey said. "Remember when Shauna sat on his back in science class and he tried to do a push-up but couldn't? It proved he's just thick, that's all. Otherwise the guy's a puss."

Then all three of them got real quiet, as if the memory had suddenly reminded them that Ryan had cancer. Jonesey started picking a piece of sugar cone out of his back teeth, and Shauna sort of gazed over at me and then looked back at Jonesey.

"I actually have to hit the library before first period," I said, clearly lying, but Mia didn't question me.

"You know we won't see each other all day, so why don't

you come over after school," she suggested. "I'm not going to the hospital today, so meet me at my house and we can continue our talk."

"Will do," I replied. "Maybe we'll go visit the frogs or something."

"Are you serious?" she said, not really paying attention to me because more popular people were flooding the caf and coming by and tapping her on the shoulder. I'd never noticed before how much people petted each other in school. I'd led, up till then, a relatively "pet-free" life. The Scrooge in me felt it was all so invasive, and I wanted to scold Mia for giving in to this touchy-feely culture, while another part of me—specifically my stressed-out shoulders—felt really lonely at that moment. She turned to me (and I swear, for a flicker she looked surprised to see me) and repeated, "Meet me at my house after school, okay?"

I nodded, and walked off. About halfway down the hallway I looked back to see if Mia was watching me. She wasn't. But Jonesey and Shauna were.

When I arrived at Mia's house after school she was already waiting for me in her car. I hopped in and we headed west on Route 2. She wouldn't tell me where we were headed. She seemed to be in a serious mood; in fact, we didn't talk for the bulk of the drive. Instead, she turned on the radio. Usually the acoustics in her Corolla were annoyingly tinny, but Boyz II Men's "It's So Hard to Say Goodbye to Yesterday" filled the interior with an almost angelic echo. At first Mia sang along with it, but her eyes got wet, and it was obvious she was thinking about Ryan. She hastily hit the SEEK button and the station changed. I stared straight ahead, pretending not to notice her teary-eyed like that. "Since You're Gone," by the Cars started playing, and we listened for a few seconds before she hit the button again. Now Madonna's "This Used to Be My Playground" kicked in, and Mia pressed the button again and "Tears in Heaven" by Eric Clapton came on. Mia groaned and pressed the button one more time and "Everybody Hurts" by R.E.M. started playing, at which point she just turned the damned radio off. Mia looked like she was going to break down any second, so I tried to distract her.

"Where are we going?" I asked. "Pennsylvania?"

"I just wanted to get out of Bern," she explained.

A few minutes later she pulled into the parking lot of a fairly nondescript motel. A dozen single-occupancy units in a long row; the rooms were probably lined with wood paneling. There was a silver ice chest with the word ICE printed in blocky, blue letters. We stepped out of the car and waited for a semi to pass before crossing the road—we walked through a wake of metal heat. The grass on the other side was tall and damp. We walked down some wooden steps with broken railings to the edge of a pond.

"Is this Walden Pond?" she asked.

"I don't think so," I replied. "Is that lame that we don't know?"

She didn't seem to hear me. I could tell she was all discombobulated—a bird sang in the trees to our left, and she jerked her head to the right, searching for it. I smiled goofily at her for a moment, then leaned in and kissed her. Her lips felt cold, and my heart sank like a metal paperweight in the ocean. I leaned back slowly, almost fearful of her expression.

"Are you okay?" I asked.

"It just feels kinda sacrilegious to kiss like this. . . . Do you have any idea what I mean by that?"

I pictured Ryan lying in a hospital bed at that moment, staring at the closed shades. My throat caught, and I shook the image out of my head. Literally—I shook my head a couple of times with my eyes shut. "Yes, but I haven't seen you in a while."

"But that's not going to change anytime soon," Mia said. "Ryan needs my support—in fact, he specifically requested it. He's coming home from the hospital a week from today, and I'm going to try to visit him at the hospital as much as possible until then, because he's so bored sitting there by himself, and then the week after that he might return to school, and I've offered to help him bring his books home, because he can't carry heavy things while he has those stitches from his spleen surgery, and the point is I'm probably going to be spending a lot of time with him. I need you to support me on this."

"Of course," I said quickly.

"And that means I won't see you whenever you want for a little while, sometimes I won't feel like kissing, and other times I might need you to hug me, or give me some space, or just listen to me vent for an hour."

"I'd like to listen to you vent for an hour."

"I know this is frustrating timing—we're just starting to date, but Ryan's sick, and even though he's going to be okay soon, I want to help as much as I can until he gets back on his feet, okay?"

"When do you think that will be, out of curiosity?"

"Let's see . . . if all goes well he'll be back in school in about a week, then I figure a few weeks I'll have to help him with his books and stuff, and then . . . my best guess is it'll be like this until the end of October."

"Why can't Jonesey carry his books for him?" I asked.

"It's lacrosse season," she explained. "So Jonesey has practice every day after school."

I exhaled.

"But this doesn't change us, right?" I asked.

She nodded.

"Think of it as a time-out," she said, "while we focus on helping Ryan through this."

"Okay," I said. "I'll do whatever you want. Whatever Ryan needs."

And in the back of my head I thought, End of October?

That night I lay in bed, staring out the back window, feeling wide awake. The moon was bright, and at one point I noticed that there was something shiny hovering above the tree line in the distance. For a second I thought it might be a UFO, but then I realized that it was the roof of the inn through the trees out my back window. I wracked my brain, trying to remember if I'd ever noticed the roof of the inn through the trees out the back window before. I thought and thought, but for the life of me I couldn't remember.

By the following Monday the outpouring of support for Ryan hadn't dissipated in the slightest—in fact, it had only grown even bigger. Supporting Ryan in his time of sickness was becoming the cause célèbre, not just among the student body at Bern High, but the entire *town*. Riding to school on the bus Monday morning we passed Ryan's house and I saw a handful of his neighbors raking the Stackhouses' front yard. All the other houses on the street were layered with foot-deep piles of leaves, but everyone focused on keeping the Stackhouses' lawn unblemished.

I realized that things were getting a little out of hand during homeroom, when Mr. Stacy disclosed to us that the annual turkey drive at Bern Middle School had been officially reconfigured and renamed over the weekend, so that it was now going to be called Ryan's Turkey Drive, with all proceeds going to help defray Ryan's medical bills rather than to the struggling soup kitchen in Dorchester that the drive had been affiliated with for over ten years. Word on the street was that people from Bern had already started to turn out in droves to the middle school, record numbers for this usually piddling turkey drive, shelling out dough to pay for turkeys a month earlier than usual. According to Mr. Stacy, people had been showing up since seven thirty to sign up for second and third turkeys. In previous years, none of these newbies had bothered to buy turkeys, but the twisted logic behind why they were participating now was something to the effect of, *This time, it's one of our own.*

Brett slid into the seat next to me.

"What are you doing here, Brett?" Mr. Stacy asked.

"Ms. Duprey's stuck in traffic," he replied.

Mr. Stacy was drawing lines down the chalkboard.

"Well, every homeroom's doing this, so I guess it's okay for you to stay," he said to Brett. "We're going to have an extra ten minutes in homeroom this morning to do a little brainstorming. I'm making some columns and we're going to come up with a list of ideas about what we can do to support Ryan Stackhouse in his time of need."

Brett and I exchanged glances.

"Bern Middle School has set the standard with their turkey drive. They've thrown down the gauntlet, so to speak, and it's time for us to meet the call to duty and one up them— we don't want to be shown up by the middle schoolers, do we, people?"

"We could draft a letter that we could give to all of our parents," Cindy Durante suggested, "asking for, say, a donation of twenty dollars. I bet if everyone's parents donated, we'd make more than the turkey drive."

"Not the most subtle idea ever, but I like where your head is at," Mr. Stacy said, writing her stupid idea down on the chalkboard:

—Write letter asking parents outright for money.

"What else could we do?" Mr. Stacy asked. "Come on people, let's put our heads together!"

"We could buy all the turkeys, then resell them at double the price," I suggested.

Mr. Stacy frowned at me.

"If you're not going to take this seriously, Mr. Kim, perhaps you'd prefer to spend the rest of homeroom in the vice principal's office?"

"But they shouldn't change the turkey drive in the first place," Brett said.

A universal gasp.

"So what you're saying is you don't care about Ryan's well-being," one of the goth kids said.

"No, I'm not saying that. I'm saying we've been donating the proceeds to that soup kitchen in Dorchester for over a decade. They depend on that money."

"But they're not our classmates. This is different. When one of us gets hit, you circle the wagons," another student said.

"But Ryan's got health insurance; he doesn't even need the money," Brett countered. "So I don't even get why we'd be raising money for him."

"I can't believe you're saying this, Brett," the goth kid said. "I would've never guessed the traitor would be you."

"What does that even mean?" Brett asked.

Everyone looked disappointed in Brett—some actually shook their heads sadly. In a moment that I feel shows some character growth, I resisted the urge to not say anything and let everyone direct their hatred solely at Brett the Traitor, and spoke up. "But it's true," I said. "Besides, the Stackhouses are loaded. This is literally taking from the poor and giving to the rich."

"Ryan shouldn't have to pay a dime!" someone shouted.

"Didn't you hear what Albert said?" Brett asked. "The money wouldn't even go to pay his health bills."

Nobody was listening to us by that point.

"You guys should picket outside with signs that say, 'We oppose supporting Ryan,'" Cindy suggested.

"Yeah," a few others shouted. "And then you should key Stackhouse's Bronco, so we can have a reason to jump you."

"Okay, people, let's try now to redirect our energy toward filling up this list of ideas," Mr. Stacy said, pointing at the chalkboard.

"How 'bout we expel Brett, and hell, maybe even Albert too?" someone suggested. "That's one way we can support Ryan—by weeding out the haters."

"Yeah!" everyone shouted.

"You bastards," Paul Waverly muttered to us, grimacing.

"Jesus, I was just trying to back you up," I whispered to Brett as he got out of his seat. "I'll see you at lunch."

"Stop talking to me," he whispered back. "I still have a chance to get out of here alive."

In lieu of the fact that nobody in any homeroom was able to come up with a killer idea to trump the middle school's turkey drive, at lunchtime on Tuesday the SGA announced a mammoth bake sale (or, as Cindy Durante cockily put it, "The bake sale to end all bake sales") to take place ASAP in the practice gym.

During study hall on Wednesday afternoon I went with Brett to check out the bake sale. Mia was working the register with Shauna in the corner by the gymnastics mats. Brett headed for a tray of doughnuts while I made my way over to Mia.

"How's business?" I asked.

"Brisk," she replied in a flat voice, staring at the cash register. "I think we've sold maybe seventy percent of our inventory and earned forty-six bucks."

"You seem out of it."

"I'm just trying to think of something to do for Ryan," she said. "Something big, because this bake sale positively sucks."

"Have you considered a nude car wash?" I asked.

"I'm being serious."

"You're being hard on yourself, if you ask me," I replied. "I think visiting him every day at the hospital's pretty big. Are you going to visit him this afternoon?"

"No, they're doing a bunch of little tests and stuff before he comes home tomorrow, so I'm taking the afternoon off," she said. "Yesterday this meditation teacher came to visit Ryan; it was really interesting."

"Oh yeah? I've always wanted to levitate."

Mia stared at me.

"I said 'meditate.' "

I sighed.

"Nobody ever seems to get that joke," I said.

"Maybe that should tell you something," she replied.

"Shut up."

"So anyway, the meditation teacher started out by asking us, 'What do you do when you get a headache?' "

"And what did you reply?" I asked.

"First, *you* try answering it," Mia said.

"I don't know, I guess take a nap. Or cry? Um, take a couple aspirin . . . drink a lot of water?" I suggested.

"Right—that's pretty much what we came up with, too, but the point she was making was that most people tend to not try to simply BE with the headache and experience it. Everyone's first instinct is to try to get rid of the headache, when the best answer is the exact opposite."

"That is absolutely ridiculous," I said.

Mia frowned.

"You just don't—"

"Unbelievable," Shauna said, tapping heavily on Mia's shoulder. "The nerve of that little bitch."

"Hi, Shauna," I said.

Shauna ignored me. She was staring at a group of freshman girls hovering by the brownie plates. I recognized the two mice from study hall in the caf. They were mingling with Jonesey and a couple other lax guys. Shauna glared at the mice.

"Look at that little slut, she's all over Jonesey," she said.

"Relax, Shauna," Mia soothed.

"I AM relaxed," Shauna said, proceeding to do that not-so-subtle move where you talk in a chillingly quiet voice but then practically shout certain words in a menacing manner. "I just don't get why those FRESHMAN STARFUCKERS would think to hit on MY BOYFRIEND in plain sight like that and not think they would ever have to face REPERCUSSIONS. I mean, there's a—Mia? Mia, are you even listening to me?"

Mia snapped out of her daze.

"Huh? Sorry, no, yeah, I am, starfuckers . . . and you were saying?"

"Come on, let's go say hi to Jonesey," Shauna said, pulling Mia away from the register.

"We can't leave our post," Mia said, exchanging looks with me.

"Just for a second, I just want to say hello. . . . I'd help *you*, Mia, come on," Shauna replied, dragging her away.

Mia shrugged at me. I watched Shauna, clearly pissed off, go up to Jonesey and say hello, and he was totally oblivious to how enraged she was. Poor Mia had to stand there as Shauna's wingwoman, until the freshman mice caught the drift and skulked away. Shauna then took Jonesey by the hand and they left the gym, leaving Mia by herself under the basketball hoop. I went over to her.

"So . . ." I said.

"I have to get Shauna back in here, come with me," she said, and we went out the exit looking for her. Shauna and Jonesey were nowhere in sight; the side parking lot was completly empty. The door shut behind us. I pulled on it, but it had automatically locked. I started pounding on it.

"That's it," Mia said. "I think I just figured out what we can do."

I turned around. Mia was staring down at the track.

"I did a Walk for Cancer once, when I was a little kid," she went on. "My grandma died of breast cancer and a year later we all went to East Longmeadow, that's where she'd lived, and we participated in this overnight walk. What it is is you're part of a team, and you have to constantly have a member of the team walking around the track nonstop for twenty-four straight hours. Before the walk you get people to pledge money, they promise to pay like ten cents for every lap you complete, and all the proceeds go to cancer research."

"That sounds great."

She started pointing at various spots around the track.

"We could set up all these tents here, in the middle of the track, so people could nap or whatever, and the entire town would join in, do shifts, and we could have booths by the bleachers with information about cancer research, and we could have cotton candy for the kids and then . . ."

And that's how Mia came up with the idea for the Bern Walk for Cancer, the first walk of its kind in the history of our town, to honor Ryan's fight with Hodgkin's, which, in hindsight, I now realize was the official beginning of the end.

29 My parents were having dinner out that Thursday evening—I think it was their first time going to a restaurant without me since I was born. The night before I'd sat in the living room with them watching half of some crappy cable movie in which one of the subplots was that the main couple was having marital problems, and per their marriage counselor's suggestion they started having "Date Night" once a month, and their first official date was going out to dinner all dressed up, as if it was a special occasion. Basically, anytime I think about my parents I get really sad; but that's not the point—the point is that when Mia called me at around six in a semipanic I was home by myself.

"Albert, my parents are over at the Stackhouses right now, helping decorate, and I'm supposed to pick Ryan up, but the car's out of gas. Can you drive?"

It was the first time she'd called me since establishing our little time-out, and for a flicker I felt like pointing this out to her, but I didn't, because I was just so damn happy to hear from her, in addition to the fact that she sounded kinda frantic.

"My parents are out to dinner in Boston, and my mom takes her keys with her even when she's not driving, in case they both need house keys," I explained.

"That's okay." Mia sighed. "I'll just call my dad and tell him to find another—"

"No, Mia, I'll figure something out," I said. "Just wait at your house, I'll pick you up in ten minutes."

I hung up the phone and felt a weird guilt wash over me, as if I'd just told a lie, which, in fact, I had, because I had no plan whatsoever. But I'd promised to help with anything she asked, and besides, all week I'd barely hung out with her. In school, Ryan's friends were always hovering around her, as if she needed constant care (or rather, as if *they* did), and on the rare occasions I got her away from them to talk, the topic always drifted back to Ryan: how he was coming home soon; how excited her parents were for him; how he'd try going to school at least part-time again next week. And that was just in school—trying to see her after school was all but impossible, because most days she went straight from school to the hospital to visit him.

Off the top of my head, I contemplated calling a taxi, but I didn't have any money on me, and besides, a cab ride from Bern to Boston would cost a minifortune each way. I looked out the window. The lights were on in Billy and Brett's house.

The room directly facing mine had a string of white Christmas lights hung across the edge of the ceiling, giving off a soft white light. It was Brett's room. I could see the back of his head—he was sitting at his desk. A moment later I heard a ding sound and realized it had come from me.

I'd been pacing my room in tighty-whities and an old T-shirt (fashion-wise I'm like a fifty-year-old man when it comes to relaxing at home), so I quickly pulled my jeans back on, put on a Maryland Terrapins sweatshirt, and spent five minutes frantically searching for my wallet, which threw me into a panic that I was running late. And right before I clawed my eyes out as self-punishment, I found it lying in plain sight on the desk. I then went into the bathroom, squirted an inch of toothpaste onto my right index finger, and brushed my teeth that way, because for some reason it felt faster than using my toothbrush. Finally I ran next door and rang the bell. A few seconds later Brett opened the door.

"I know this is really late notice, but I need a favor from you," I said.

"I'm listening," he replied.

"It's no biggy, but I need to borrow your car, dude," I said in as casual a voice as I could muster. It came out sounding like I was pretending to be a drunk, stoned surfer waking up from a nap.

"You're joking, right?"

"That wouldn't be a very funny joke, would it?"

"What do you need my car for?"

"I have to pick up Ryan Stackhouse from the hospital. Mia needs me to drive."

"Why would she ask you for a ride?" Brett asked. "Does she even know you?"

I glared at him.

"Actually, we're dating," I said, and I couldn't fully hide the self-satisfied shit-eating grin forming on my mouth.

"Seriously?" he asked.

I nodded, trying to get rid of my involuntary smile by picturing something gruesome—in this case a shark chomping down on a swimmer's leg. The smile lingered, so I then pictured the same swimmer making it to shore and getting attacked by a grizzly.

"Is The House cool with it?" Brett asked, scratching his head. Apparently some humans really do scratch their heads when they're confused.

"Yeah, he's thrilled," I replied. "At the official changing of the guard ceremony he was just beaming at me so brightly I blushed."

"What are you talking about?"

"Never mind," I said. "So can you do me this favor or what? Time is of the essence."

He stared at me for a moment.

"Wait outside, I'll go get my keys," he said, and ran back upstairs.

I was stunned that he so readily agreed to this, then I jogged around the front of the house and waited impatiently by his car. It was a used, four-door blue Acura Legend sedan, semirusted. A minute later Brett appeared around the corner and tossed me the keys. I almost caught them, and let out an excited whoop (if you were to watch a montage of me throughout my life trying to catch things that were thrown to me you'd know how big a deal this was). Brett smiled knowingly at me—he didn't look like he could catch for shit either.

"So what's the deal?" I asked, holding up his keys. "It feels like a prank that I'm meeting no resistance, here. Do we have to make out later or something?"

"It's your deal, so you drive," he explained. "I'm doing you a favor, but you're doing Mia a favor. Can you drive stick?"

I hmphed.

"Automatic's for wusses. I've driven stick in video games almost exclusively since like, age eight."

This meaningless factoid actually seemed to satisfy him, and he let me get behind the wheel of his three thousand pound car. Maybe some people are just decent, I thought. I made a mental note to write Brett a thank-you card or something after all of this was over and leave it tucked between one of his windshield wipers, and then got in the front seat. I didn't notice Brett hopping into the passenger side at the same time, and when I turned and saw him sitting there I yelped.

"You make a lot of sounds," he said.

"What do you think you're doing here?" I asked.

"You think I'm letting you take my car without me in it?" he said. "I'll sit in the back when you pick up Mia, don't worry."

I frowned at him. I knew it was probably selfish of me to think this, but I couldn't help but suddenly pray for Brett to have a serious-enough nonlethal heart attack that would incapacitate him for a couple of hours. I pictured Brett clutching his chest and collapsing onto the yard; I'd honk for Mrs.

Timmons to come out and assist her gasping son, and then I'd be free to take off solo for Mia's house. I spent a minute or so seriously considering the logistics of pulling a maneuver like in those action movies—where the driver reaches over and in one motion, manages to pull the latch and open the passenger side door, and shove out the undesirable passenger with his right hand—but then I noticed that Brett was wearing his seat belt already, which would add a third task. I would then have to also manage to reach out and pull the door shut, lock it, and then deal with the extreme guilt of starting up the car and callously pulling out of the driveway as Brett knocked on the glass and glared at me directly through the windshield. I sighed, realizing that I just didn't think I could look someone in the face while pulling a dick maneuver like that.

I looked at the dashboard clock and moaned. Since getting off the phone with Mia, all this had taken approximately twenty minutes.

"Fine, whatever, let's just go," I said, and turned the ignition.

Mia was waiting for us on the curb outside her house. I could see her shaking her head, staring out at the house across the street. I flashed the high beams at her and she waved. I skidded to a stop at her mailbox. Brett opened the door and got out.

"Mia, you sit in the front, I'll go in the back," Brett said.

She waved him off and let herself in the back.

"No time, we're late, Ryan's called a dozen times, let's just go."

Brett jumped back in the car and both he and Mia groaned

for thirty seconds as I turned what started out as a regular K-turn into a pathetic twelve-point Koosh ball turn or something, and then we were off.

Mia had scrawled directions onto the back of a used envelope and, to her horror, realized she couldn't interpret them at all, but it turned out Brett had gotten a lot of work done on his hernia at Brigham and Women's a few years ago, and he knew exactly how to get there. The sole hiccup was when we hit a rotary in Somerville early on in the drive. I've never understood how rotaries work, and it feels like they're designed solely to try to get you into an accident, and I've always kinda feared them—they're the true bane of my driving existence. Anyway, because I err on the side of caution when it comes to these roundabouts from hell, I ended up pulling a Griswold and made six revolutions in the packed rotary as cars on all sides honked at me.

"Look kids, Big Ben, Parliament," Mia said each time, not smiling, staring forlornly out the window. "Dear Lord."

By the time we reached the hospital we were no longer on speaking terms. Mia was so flustered with my inability to navigate a rotary that she muttered directives to me without making eye contact ("You know where his room is, meet me up there") and just hopped out of the backseat before I'd even come to a complete stop. She booked it toward the revolving glass doors without shutting the car door, and a moment later she was gone. Brett turned to me and placed what felt like a consolatory hand on my shoulder.

"Honestly, Albert, have you ever driven a car before?" he asked.

Brett agreed to wait in the car while I went up to Ryan's wing. I entered room 327 and gasped. Ryan was hunched over on the bed, his hospital gown wide open in the back as the doctor swabbed his butt with a medical Handi Wipe. I backed out of the room slowly. Mia was sitting in an orange chair outside the room. She was staring at her feet; clearly she'd just seen what I'd seen. I sat down next to her. I held out my hand, she didn't even notice it for twenty seconds before she squeezed it and didn't let go. We just sat there for a few minutes, listening to the occasional beeps of outdated-looking squarish machines passing us by and the idle chatter of nurses gossiping about how incompetent their rival, enemy nurses were. Finally, the doctor stepped out of the room. He could tell we were rattled, and said, "It's just a routine test, I have to get some equipment if you want to say hi for a minute."

Ryan's room at the hospital looked lived in, as if he'd been residing there for years. There was a display of get-well cards on the windowsill next to his perpetually nodding Ben Coates Patriot bobblehead. A frayed Bruins poster was taped to the bathroom door featuring a tender, softly lit portrait of Ray Bourque encapsulated in a cartoon hockey puck. A small air force poster of a stealth bomber hung on the far wall. The room looked decorated for the long haul.

Ryan stared straight ahead at the TV, which was off.

"Do you want us to take the posters down for you?" Mia asked.

Ryan nodded.

The doctor reentered the room, pulling a cart full of scary metal instruments.

"Whoa, aren't you supposed to start with the rack, first?" I asked, picturing the end of the movie *Braveheart*. Fortunately, no one got the reference, and my improvised burst of poor taste went unnoticed.

"Mia, Ryan would like you in here for the procedure."

Mia looked alarmed. She looked at me, then the doctor.

"Um, okay," she said.

"I'll be right in the hall," I said, patting her on the shoulder. I went outside and sat down in the orange chair. The door remained open, and there was a full-length mirror on it, so I could see into the room anyway. Here's what I saw:

Ryan, in a pair of red-striped boxers, curled in a fetal position on his side on the sea-green cushioned bed, with Mia sitting in a chair behind his butt. His boxers were pulled down, and I could see his butt crack in the reflection. Mia was staring right at it, wide-eyed. The doctor must have noticed this, too, because shortly after he said, "Do you want to come up here and face his head?"

Mia scraped her seat back and sat down in the chair facing Ryan, just out of view. The doctor inserted a needle attached to a tube to the base of his spine. I winced, but didn't look away from the mirror. My heart started beating wildly, and a part of me wanted to rush into the room, pull out the needle, and carry Ryan off to safety or something. He was staring right at me through the mirror, and I tried to make it look like I was staring off into space, as if I were looking *through him*. He kept staring at me, and I wondered if he was even focusing, himself. I waved at his reflection to see if his expression would change, but he didn't react. He then moved his head a little and stopped looking at the mirror; he seemed to be staring at where Mia was sitting.

"Albert?" Mia's voice called out to me a moment later.

I poked my head around the door. I couldn't help but grimace at the tube sticking into Ryan's butt. Clear fluid started filling it, and after a few seconds it turned cloudy, like cigarette smoke underwater. I felt light-headed, but I couldn't look away.

"Do you mind closing the door? Ryan doesn't like staring at his reflection."

I unwedged the rubber doorjamb with my foot and pulled the door shut behind me. A few minutes later the door opened and Mia pushed Ryan out in a wheelchair. She wore his purple backpack on one shoulder. Ryan nodded at me.

"Thanks for the lift, bud," he said.

"No worries, Ry," I said. "I'm just glad to be able to—"

"Put the story down on paper, okay?" Ryan pleaded with me. "Let's get out of here, I'm sick of being in this place."

We went down to the car. Brett got out and opened the rear door and helped us get Ryan in the car. Mia looked worried and sad, and I knew she was holding back tears, because her mouth looked so tense. Mia motioned for me to drive (that is, she made her raised fists look like she was turning an imaginary steering wheel left and right really fast), and I pulled the car out of the parking lot. Brett turned around and said to Mia and Ryan, "Ladies and gentlemen, the captain has asked that you please put your tray tables up and your seat backs in their full and upright positions!"

Mia and Ryan both looked stunned.

"Okay, okay, tough crowd," Brett said, turning back around and giving me a conspiratorial look. I shook my head at him.

Ryan was basically lying in Mia's lap, staring up at her. As we drove I occasionally looked in the rearview mirror at them. At one point Ryan asked Mia, "So what did you think of my butt?" and it probably wasn't anything major, really, but Mia definitely looked . . . embarrassed. My initial reaction was that her being embarrassed was probably a good thing, as opposed to, say, Mia responding enthusiastically, "It looked really awesome, have you been working out?" So Mia blushed, and then she rolled her eyes at him and resumed staring out the window, but there was maybe—at least in my opinion based on a shaky glance in the rearview mirror as I drove down a major road pushing fifty—a trace of a smile on her lips.

We drove in silence and the trip seemed to be passing smoothly until . . . I reached the rotary again.

Goddamnit.

I felt extra nervous about dealing with it because Ryan was in the car now, and I could tell he was probably a master at navigating rotaries, the way he was a master at doing just about everything else in life. I took a deep breath, said a silent, nondenominational prayer, and then veered into the right lane of the rotary without even checking the rearview or my blind spot, and a black Explorer leaned on the horn. Mia gasped. A maroon Escort wagon cut me off, and I reacted by blindly weaving back into the inside lane. This was of course not good; I needed to get back into the outer lane in order to turn out of the rotary, but the Explorer that had honked at me was now tailing the car that had cut me off, and by the time he turned out of the rotary we were now past my turn. The rotary was full. I knew I wasn't going to be able to cut over during this third pass, so I looked in the rearview mirror and calmly said, "Okay, folks, looks like I'll be getting it on the next try."

"You can do it, Albert!" Mia said.

I noticed in my millisecond glance that she was laughing, and I was grateful that my utter idiocy navigating rotaries seemed to be cheering her up. I made it into the outer lane and triumphantly was pulling around to our turnoff again with an undeserved cocky grin on my face, but at that moment I let rip an ill-timed brain fart, and for a fourth time missed the turn, this time through no fault of any other drivers; I simply spaced out and forgot to get out of the rotary this time. Mia groaned. Stupidly, I thought—even though in my head I knew it didn't make sense—that's okay, Albert, just take the next turn and turn around, and that's exactly what I did. So I got off the rotary, but onto Route 16, a different main road.

"What the hell are you doing?" Ryan said, wincing as he sat up in his seat.

"Chill, Ryan," I said. "Just dealing with some rookies on the road; you relax now, we'll be out of this in no time."

"What's with this guy?" Ryan asked Mia.

I bristled.

"Ryan, you didn't know this about me so I'm not mad at you, but just so you know, I really don't like it when people talk in third person about me," I said, white-knuckling the steering wheel. "I'm tense as it is."

"I just want to go home," Brett said sadly, pressing his right hand against the passenger side window.

I turned around on a private road and nearly pulled into a Mack truck (more gasps from the backseat), as if I were casually committing suicide, and then zipped back to the rotary. It was really busy, so I stopped at the entrance to the rotary and just sat there waiting for an opening. The Mack truck and two cars behind it started honking at me for past transgressions, but I ignored them, pretending for all appearances to feel placid. When an opening to enter the rotary finally presented itself a minute later (the cars behind me would probably argue I could have gone at any time), I gunned it, not bothering to switch out of first gear, even though I was going thirty-five mph and the engine was whining really loudly. Somehow I managed to weave my way into the inner lane, and everyone in the car started screaming at me, which in my defense only flustered me more and actually contributed to making me continue to drive in circles.

"Get us out of here!" Mia screamed.

"I swear to God I'm gonna—"

"Will you please go into second gear?" Brett pleaded with me.

And then just as quickly as everyone had flown into a rage about my driving, the mood changed inside the car. I think by the tenth or twelfth revolution everyone started to feel a new desperation to get out of the rotary, and rather than feel hatred toward me it was as if it was no longer my fault and that the rotary was now considered a rip in the space-time continuum or something, and everyone seemed to be really pulling for me all of a sudden. Ryan repeated, "You can do it, bro, punch it when you're ready!" and Brett was gripping the front of the dashboard and shouting, "We're going to make it, we're going to get out of here, I just know it!" When Mia shouted, "Go for it!" I closed my eyes and made a beeline for the road I needed to turn on to, cutting off an entire line of traffic. Since my eyes were closed I didn't see any of this, but I could hear all the cars slamming on their brakes. I opened my eyes and saw that I was in the outer lane now, and the turn was upon us, but of course I panicked at the last second and swerved and punched the gas again to pass a slow, bewildered VW Bug in front of me and ended up missing the turn and driving up onto the curb.

There was a really loud crash, big sparks that I could see out my window. It felt like slow motion, this last bit of the odyssey, and I slammed on the brakes and the car slid into a handicapped parking spot in a corner of the gas station on the road we had to turn on to. The guy in the brightly lit cashier booth had headphones on and was facing the other way and didn't notice any of this. All the cars in the rotary honked in unison at me as the traffic started up again, but I didn't care. I jumped out of the car and Mia did, too, and as we ran around the smoking hood to each other I could feel that my entire back was drenched with sweat. We embraced, and by holding each other I realized my entire body was shaking with tension—my legs nearly gave out and she struggled to hold me up for a couple of seconds before I regained my equilibrium.

"You did it!" she said. "You're my hero."

"I'd do anything for you," I said, soaking up my hero status, embracing my eternally thankful Mia under the glowing Mobil sign, as a chorus of passing cars honked their utter disgust with me and collectively flipped me the bird as they drove past.

"You have to be the worst fricking driver on the planet," Ryan said out his window. "But I have to admit, this is easily the most interesting thing to happen to me in days. Now will you please get back in the damn car and take me home?"

"You got it, captain," I said.

Brett got out of the car and pointed at me and then at the passenger seat.

"No, you're riding shotgun rest of the way," he said. "And for the record, you are never driving my car again."

Brett dropped us off in front of Ryan's house. We shook hands, wordlessly, and I was surprised to find that I felt sad he was leaving us. I felt like I had to say something meaningful, but instead I just stammered for a couple of seconds, struggling to think of something. Thankfully, Brett put a finger to his lips and cut me off. "Shhh. You're welcome," he said, and then got back in the car and drove off. We turned toward the house.

The windows were dark, and I was about to ask Mia

where her parents' car was, but remembered that it was a surprise party. I walked alongside Mia as she rolled Ryan up the brick driveway. I could see corners of shades being lifted as people spied on us. Ryan sniffed the air like a dog.

"I don't smell barbecue," he said sadly.

We hoisted him up the three steps to the front stoop, Mia opened the door, and Ryan rolled on his own into the epic entryway. It was two stories tall with a fan swirling at the top, and when I closed the double doors behind us the lights flickered on.

"Surprise!" everyone shouted. From around every doorway dozens of people came out to greet Ryan: his parents, Mia's parents, Ryan's brothers and sister (who all looked exactly like him, except older), all his lax buddies, and Shauna as well. I got pushed back against the door as people reached for Ryan. Mia wheeled him into the center so they could all take turns hugging and kissing him. I stayed in the background and just clapped heartily. Mia rushed over and hugged Shauna, and the room echoed with conversation and the sharp retort of emphatic high fives. I watched Mia talking to her parents and various lacrosse guys, and it was clear they all knew each other pretty well; meanwhile, every now and then I'd make eye contact with a passing adult or classmate, and their eyes would gloss over me. By the time the crowd was making their way through this hallway into the cavernous kitchen, where they'd indeed ordered barbecue (catering from Redbones), I tried to get Mia's attention, but she was pushing Ryan's wheelchair, as if it had been designated that, even with his family and siblings and best friends around, Mia would still be the official handler. As Kool & the Gang's "Celebrate!" started pumping through the built-in ceiling speakers, I felt for the door handle behind me and turned it, because this was easily the most uncomfortable I'd ever felt in my life. I quietly let myself out.

I walked home at a brisk clip, surprised at how content I felt despite having to leave her. I felt . . . different. I realized it was the same feeling I'd had the night of the candlelight vigil, after we'd worked the cold towel assembly line for Ryan. I didn't really try to think about it at first; instead I just walked with a vibrationy buzz coursing through me. Twenty minutes later I reached home and didn't feel like stopping, so I continued past my house. My parents had returned from their date and—because there was still a little light left—were now in the side yard, still in their nice "date clothes," raking. Typically, when they're doing yard work and someone walks by, they wave wildly, having no clue who they're waving at, but this time they were really focused on the leaves, and I passed by unnoticed. I decided to do a mini-tour of the neighborhood—not so much to investigate the nooks that I hadn't walked down in a while, but merely to extend the walk so I could take in this powerful feeling.

For the first time, Mia's stupid time-out started making a little more sense to me. I don't mean I was outright happy for it, but I started to see the benefits. As I walked down side roads I got the idea that maybe Mia and I could do Habitat for Humanity together the following summer. We'd travel down to a back bayou town somewhere and build houses for poor people, and in the afternoons hang out at the local

Waffle House and develop a taste for grits, and then in the winter we'd fly down to some Haitian village and bring the children a real soccer ball to replace the rotten oranges they used, so they could actually eat the stinky bruised oranges instead. After we liberated the Haitian children we'd then go swimming for hours under a pristine waterfall and spend the rest of the night drinking Shirley Temples at a tiki bar. Okay, so my altruism was comingling with my fantasies about Mia, but the point is this: I breathed in deep through my nose as I walked and swore I could smell *life itself*. Being an intentional loser for two years had made me back away from contributing to society in any way, let alone be a part of it, and I now felt like I was a cog in this grand machine making it all hum, and as a result it made me feel more invested in life. I was a good person, and I was helping Ryan, and I was a part of people's lives now, and it felt really amazing. As sad as it was that Ryan had gotten cancer, there was a silver lining to it, and one of the benefits was that it was, in an indirect way, making me a better person.

I finally walked into the garage and slipped inside the house. I stopped in the kitchen to fill up a glass of water from the refrigerator. A tiny thread of ice-cold water soundlessly lined into the glass, and I waited impatiently for the glass to fill. My mind wandered back to my epiphany about how I was one with the universe and helping to make the world a better place and all that crap, when my mom poked her head into the house via the garage.

"You want to help us rake? You could move the wheelbarrow," she suggested.

"I just got home, for chrissakes!" I snapped at her.

"Sorry, sorry," she said, backing out with her hands held up in apology. I sighed.

Rome wasn't built in a day.

I went up to my room and sat down on my bed to think, but all this altruism had overstimulated my typically self-involved brain, and I must have passed out, because next thing I knew the door was rattling and I was facedown in my pillow.

"Go away, Mom," I said drowsily.

"But you haven't done the dishes yet," Mia said in a deep voice.

I rushed over to the door, but since I was coming out of a nap, I ran straight into it, hard, with my forehead. I unlocked the door and rubbed my forehead at the same time, which I don't think monkeys can do.

"Surprise visit," she whispered.

We hugged.

"What about the party?" I asked.

"It's still going strong," she replied. A pause in our conversation. Mia's eyes drifted to the carpet. "I can't get the image of him laying there out of my head. Him wincing. Like a cat. Like something so weak. I never saw him wince before. Or he never showed me. It's like the cancer is forcing him to be honest with me. Show me the tender side of him. He's just a scared little boy still."

I murmured in agreement, not really knowing what to think.

"I know!" she replied, even though I hadn't said anything, and rolled onto her back. "At first I was staring at that needle in his butt, it was so weird."

"Yeah, it was really gross."

"And he looked so white and scrawny. He's lost so much muscle."

Scrawny? This jarred me, because he was still ripped and ten times huger than me, and if we stood side by side, he'd dwarf me.

"And it was just strange to see him so vulnerable and practically naked," she added.

I faked laughter.

"Yeah, he was like posing for a calendar or something," I said, and it was stupid, but she must've wanted an excuse to laugh, because she did. I leaned over onto my side, mimicked his fetal position, and looked up at her demurely.

"What do you think of my butt?" I asked in a British accent.

"Stop it!" she said, giggling.

I swiveled into a different position and looked over my shoulder at her.

"Be honest, I want your honest opinion, darling."

"Albert," she said, coughing she was laughing so hard.

"Seriously, love, what do you think of my butt?"

"Stop it!" she shouted, her face suddenly bright red.

I sat up. A chill in my chest from her shouting at me. I looked at my reflection in the mirror—I looked terrified.

"I have to go to the bathroom," she said abruptly, and she got up and left.

"Well, that didn't work," I said softly, imagining a televised audience laugh track in the background, but even that died out.

31

At school the next morning all the lax guys were walking around with shaved heads. Everyone knew it was a yearly tradition—the lacrosse team gets their heads shaved down at Bassey's Barbershop before the first home game of the season, but this time they were claiming it was to support Ryan's upcoming cancer treatments. Two senior lax guys were standing outside the gym locker room with clippers in their hands, advertising free haircuts all morning, and—never mind the fact that Ryan was slated to begin radiation treatments, not chemotherapy, and that the doctor had said he likely wouldn't lose his hair as a result—male students showed up in droves between classes to get their hair lopped off. At lunch it felt as if I had a big red U (for "Unshaven") branded on my forehead. I actually got shoulder-bumped by students (even freshmen!) as I navigated my way to Brett's table. Everywhere I looked freshly Mon-Chi-Chi'd guys were glaring at me as they ate spoonfuls of orange Jell-O that had dark hairs in it. I'd guesstimate at least seventy-five percent of the male underclassmen at Bern High had gotten their heads shaved by lunchtime—a nation of Mon Chi Chis supporting Ryan's recovery. Thankfully, Brett and his friends had passed on getting their heads shaved, but it was understood that they hadn't because they were seniors. I thought I was blending in nicely with my new senior pals, but a couple of lax guys approached me midway through my iceberg lettuce salad (which literally had flakes of ice glazing the leaves). "It's not fair you guys can get away with it," I whispered to Brett as the lax guys surrounded me.

"How does a haircut sound, Albert?" Lax Guy # 1 said, ruffling the back of my hair. "You're looking pretty shaggy right now."

"Guys, I'm all for supporting Ryan, but I don't see how shaving my head is going to make a difference," I replied. "I'm not sure I get it."

"Actually, you do get it! Not wanting to shave your head is the point. Life isn't fair, Albert," Lax Guy # 2 said, patting me on the shoulder. "And you know who knows that most of all?"

"I think I know the answer to—"

"Ryan," he said. "Ryan motherfucking Stackhouse."

"Give me a break," I said. "That doesn't mean I have to shave my head."

The lax guys glared down at me.

"What the hell is wrong with you?" Lax Guy # 2 asked.

"We're wasting our time, let's go talk to people who care," Lax Guy # 1 said, pulling his teammate away from the table. When they were gone (and merely glaring at me from afar), Mark spoke up.

"Cheer up, Al, at least they didn't all have their spleens removed," he said.

"Don't get me wrong, I get what you're saying," I told him. "But I'm pretty sure you're going to hell for saying it."

"You bring out the best in us," Kelly said, staring at me.

After lunch I went into the small gym to avoid the roving legion of pro-Ryan skinheads patrolling the halls. The bake sale had ended up going strong for two whole days, but that Friday morning it had fizzled out because everyone's attention diverted to talk about Mia's idea for a Walk for Cancer. Already the idea had garnered a ton of support within school administration and the town board, and she'd officially gotten the high school track secured as the venue. Therefore the bake sale was abandoned. The remaining cookies, after being left uncovered for seventy-two hours on long tables under the basketball hoops, had actually evolved into biscotti by day three. I sat down at a table, bit into a hardened cookie, and subsequently cut the roof of my mouth.

The door opened.

"What are you doing here?" Mia asked.

"I'm just having a really painful dessert," I said. "How about you?"

"I left my Tupperware in here," she said. "I was looking for you at lunch."

She sat down next to me.

"People aren't exactly thrilled that I opted to not shave my head," I explained.

"Isn't that crazy that everyone did that?" she asked. "I keep getting surprised by the people here. It's really impressive."

"So are you saying I should shave my head?"

"Of course not!"

"I mean, he's not even getting chemo, so it doesn't even make sense. If they wanted to really support him they'd stick their hands in a microwave or something."

"Well, it's the thought that counts," Mia said.

"Now it sounds like you want me to shave my head again."

"I'm sorry, I don't, I'm just saying I get why others are doing it."

"Uh-huh," I muttered. She was wearing a thigh-length, black peacoat with a thick, triangular hood. I'd never seen it before. It had big wooden buttons that you stuck through thick, felt hoops. "Is that new?"

"Ryan's mom gave it to me the other day," she said. "It was her jacket when she was in high school. I always used to tell her how much I loved it. She gave it to me as thanks for all my help with Ryan. Do you like it?"

"It looks good on you," I admitted.

She suddenly winced.

"I've had this headache off and on all day," she said, rubbing her temples.

"Let's go to the nurse's for some aspirin," I said, standing up.

She grabbed my wrist and pulled me back into my seat.

"No, this is a great opportunity, I've been waiting to get a headache so I can try to *be* with the headache," she said, steeling herself.

"But I like it when you take aspirin," I said. "You have this weird way of taking the water first and then the pills and—"

"Shh, let me concentrate," she said, her eyes already closed, very deliberately breathing through her nose, trying not to move an inch.

I waited a few minutes.

"It really hurts," she said, her face going from wincing to smiling and back again by the second. "But I think I like it. I don't know."

She kept concentrating hard for a minute, and it looked painful. Finally she opened her eyes and smiled at me.

"Let's go call Ryan. I want to describe to him what it feels like."

"Hmm," I said.

"What is it?" she asked.

"Nothing."

"Al?"

I sighed.

"Look, it's no biggie, I'm not complaining, but it's like every time we do hang out it's always focused on Ryan, and I know I just have to deal with it and—"

"No, I know what you mean. I'm sorry," she said. "Is it unfair that I told you that we have to do what I feel like all the time? I swear I did feel bad about that after the fact, but it's been so hectic."

"I agreed with you, though, and—"

"I know you did, but we haven't had a night about 'just us' in a while," she said. "Look, tonight Shauna wanted to go to the movies, but instead why don't you come over for dinner?"

"I guess," I said, all of a sudden feeling nervous about officially meeting her folks.

"Don't wuss out on me; if you want to be with me so bad you have no choice. How does seven sound?"

"Only if you want to," I reiterated.

She took it wrong.

"I'm not hanging out with you for charity," she said. Embarrassed at how that came out, she tried to make me laugh. "Unless you get cancer, that is."

Her face went red.

"I can't believe I just said that," she said. "I'm awful."

"No you're not, you were just trying to make me laugh."

She winced again and touched her forehead.

"Let's go get aspirin," she said. "Maybe I need them after all."

I went over to Mia's house for dinner that night. I wore a collared shirt under my favorite blue sweater. I'd never willingly worn a collared shirt under a sweater since I was like, three, and it felt scratchy and didn't work on me, yet for some reason it felt like the right thing to wear. The collar was a little loose around my neck, and the sweater made it bunch up in weird places. I wanted to turn around and go back and change into something more comfortable, but my watch read a quarter past seven; I was already late. I stood in front of the double red doors for a moment before clicking the heavy brass knocker. The door swung open. Mia dramatically let go of the handle and made a voilà sign with her hands all in one motion as the door hit the rubber stopper hard and bounced back before she caught it.

"Careful with the door," her dad admonished from the kitchen.

"I like your sweater," she said.

Mia kissed her left hand and touched my chest with it, and I followed her into the kitchen. Her mom was setting plates on the dining room table, while her dad was chewing on a baby carrot. There was a simmering pot of soup on the stove top and fancy marbled bread cut into crumbly slices on a dark wood cutting board. I hate soup, but I was interested in the bread.

Mia's parents were not especially warm toward me during dinner, directing most of their questions at Mia, which I was actually kinda grateful for—it took pressure off me to perform, and it made me feel like they were accepting me into the fold. Mia occasionally looked at me as if to silently encourage me to ask them questions, or at least I perceived her looks to say that, and so I tried.

"Mrs. Stone, this soup's fantastic, where did you get the recipe?" I asked.

"TV," she said. "I'm not much of a cook."

"That's not true," Mia said, turning to me. "She doesn't cook every night, but when she does she cooks fancy meals a couple of times a week."

"What do you do the rest of the nights?" I asked Mrs. Stone.

"We eat leftovers, or order pizza, or Abe makes something, or Mia even cooks a little," she said quickly. "What do you do in your family? Does your mom cook dinner for you every night?"

"Oh, I didn't mean to make offense, I was just curious."

"None taken," she said.

"But to answer your question—I didn't really think about it before, but yeah, I guess she does cook every dinner."

"That's nice."

Okay, so that's a pretty good example of how badly the

conversation sucked, so let's cut it short right there. Everything was all so forced. It became painfully obvious as the night wore on that her parents weren't interested in "getting to know the *real* me." I'm being sarcastic, of course, but I'm well aware that if I were in their shoes I would have been just as disinterested. Meanwhile, my efforts to surprise them with my charisma failed miserably because, quite frankly, it was intimidating being around the Stones. Usually I killed with parents. It dawned on me that the reason I'd gotten along so famously with parents prior to that night was because all my "friends" were in the sixth grade; therefore Billy's parents, for example, were used to making small talk at the start and end of sleepovers with Billy's immature eleven-year-old buds. By comparison I was like Shakespeare, Plato, and Bill Murray all rolled into one, and I easily charmed them with my comparatively mature persona. Billy's mom had once said I was an "old soul," and it delighted me to no end. Here at the Stones' house, on the other hand, I was a child surrounded by three adults—even Mia talked differently at the table with them, as if she'd aged ten years. "Oh mother—isn't it that way, though?" she'd say in response to her mom's comments, and her voice even seemed a little lower than normal.

I picked up a piece of bread.

"Did you make this with a bread maker?" I asked Mrs. Stone.

"No, I picked it up in the bakery at Stop & Shop."

"It tastes so fresh, I thought it had to be homemade."

"Well, it isn't, but that's kind of you to say, Albert."

After a while I stopped trying and just mowed down slice

after slice of crumbly buttered bread—the soup was far too salty for my taste; meanwhile Mia's mom watched me with a curious smile on her lips but I didn't care, and I didn't stop. When there was no bread left, we went into the living room.

A line of framed photos sat on the shelf behind the TV. I quickly perused them and was grateful there weren't any of Mia with Ryan. There was, however, a family portrait, which included Mia's older sister, Mary, who I was surprised to find was a little homely looking. Mary had a ruddy complexion that was a natural fit for her transformation in college into a hippy, mountain-climbing, ultrafeminist. I sat down on the blue sectional. Mr. Stone looked at his watch and stood in front of the TV, hiding the screen from us as he scanned through the stations. Mia sat down exactly one cushion apart from me, closer to her mom. "Keep it off, Abe," Mrs. Stone said.

"I'm just checking the score," he said, flipping to the Sox game.

He finally clicked off the TV and collapsed in the La-Z-Boy in the corner. He picked up a magazine, glanced at the cover, then set it back down. He took a sip of his drink, a brown liquor with ice.

"You a bourbon man?" I asked.

He stared at me.

"Scotch whiskey," he replied. "Why, do you drink, Albert?"

"Abe!"

"No, I was just kidding around."

"What's your dad's poison?"

"He drinks half a Miller Lite bottle after tennis on Wednesday nights," I replied, instantly realizing this wouldn't impress a Scotch whiskey man.

"Let's play a game," Mia said, tugging on my sweater, making my collar completely stick out.

I worked it back in so it was held down awkwardly by my sweater, but it stayed that way for only a second. Like a trap—the slightest movement and the collar popped out again. Mia dug out a box of Yahtzee from under the coffee table.

"Are you sure you want me to extend my record?" I asked.

We'd played Yahtzee for an entire afternoon one day at the inn. We'd rolled the dice in our hands onto the bed, so as not to make incriminating dice sounds.

"We'll just see about that," she replied.

When we'd played in the summer she'd brought dice in a Ziploc bag along with a couple of individual scoring sheets she'd torn off the pad. Now she opened the cracked box and took out the old scoring pad and quickly flipped two-thirds of the way in. She wrote AK and MS on separate columns.

"Not so close," Mrs. Stone said, putting her hands together and parting them slowly. "You know the rules."

"But we're playing a game!" Mia said.

"A foot apart keeps us together," Mrs. Stone murmured.

Mia rolled her eyes. "She went to Catholic school," she said.

I nodded. Mia leaned her torso away from me but in the process subtly pressed her left thigh against my right thigh, and I winked at her reflection in the blank TV screen across from us. Mr. Stone sat oblivious to all this, absentmindedly cleaning his eyeglasses and singing softly to himself, "This is the dawning of the Age of Aquarius!"

"Time-out." Mia jumped from her seat. "I'm getting a Coke, you want one?"

"Sure," I said, mentally flinching as I anticipated one of her parents striking it down, but neither said a thing. In the Kim household I'm not allowed to drink anything with caffeine in it after five p.m., and up until age eleven or so I had accidentally merged the legend of the kid whose head exploded when he ate Pop Rocks with this five p.m. caffeine rule, and feared bodily harm if I broke the law. That summer I'd started a new illicit tradition wherein every afternoon when I got home from the inn I'd go upstairs with an unopened can of Coke, then ten minutes later I'd fill a hotel ice bucket that I'd stolen from the inn with ice and keep the can cool in the closet until late night, so I could drink it in bed with the lights off. It's all about quiet victories in the Kim household.

Mia was gone for only twenty seconds, but it was agonizing to be alone in the room with her parents. That's exactly how it felt, actually. Like I was alone. I picked up the scoring pad and flipped to the front. The pages were filled up in pencil and pen, and the initials were always MS and RS. I scanned the pages, there were at least a hundred games, and they were meticulously dated over the course of three years. I thought I heard Mrs. Stone make a sound, but I was embarrassed to look up at her, because I wanted to seem casual and indifferent about the scoring pad, even though seeing Mia and Ryan's shared history in the pages was kinda breaking my heart at the moment. I flipped to our page and wrote the date in the upper right corner with pen.

Mia finally returned with two Cokes on ice in blue-tipped glasses and set them down on round cork coasters that were built into corners of the coffee table. Mrs. Stone was reading the weekend *Boston Magazine* section of the *Globe*, and I guessed she was watching us peripherally. At least I could feel a vague heat coming from her direction.

"Dad, Albert got three Yahtzees the last time we played, scored over five hundred," Mia said.

"A foot apart, sweetie," Mrs. Stone said.

"Let me see the sheet," Mr. Stone said, snapping his fingers at Mia. "I don't believe he has it in him."

"I don't have it, we threw it out at the hotel," she said.

"Then it doesn't count," he replied. He stared at me. He was clearly busting my balls for fun, so I heh-hehed for him, but at the same time his face never broke into a smile.

"Mom, Dad's being grouchy, why don't you let him watch the game?"

"If he really needs the game to survive he can watch it," Mrs. Stone said, glaring at him. He fingered the remote as his eyes narrowed, but he didn't turn on the TV. Mr. and Mrs. Stone locked eyes. A used Kleenex fell off the stand by his La-Z-Boy, and it caught an invisible current from the central air vent by the floorboards and rolled across the carpet between them. I felt like I was caught in an impending cross fire and it made my stomach rumble uncomfortably, but thankfully the phone rang a moment later. Mrs. Stone leaped up, giving away how she really felt about sitting there with us; she paused and very slowly pressed the pleats in her slacks as if she was embarrassed about how overeager she'd appeared. She went into the kitchen and answered the phone on the fourth ring. Mia and I played a round of Yahtzee; it wasn't remotely fun, we were both rolling terribly, and Mia seemed preoccupied with trying to decipher what her mom was laughing about.

A few minutes later Mrs. Stone rushed into the room with a broad smile on her face I hadn't ever seen before.

"Oh, Mia, I have amazing news about Ryan!" she said.

"Really?! What . . . ?" Mia looked over at me, remembering our ongoing Ryan embargo.

"I want to hear too," I said, squeezing her shoulder.

"What is it, Mom?" she asked. She mouthed the word "thanks" to me.

"That was Janice on the line and she said that before the doctors start him on radiation they're going to freeze his sperm, just in case!"

"What does that mean?" Mia asked.

"It means he'll still be able to have children in the future no matter what, isn't that wonderful?"

"I didn't know they could do that," Mia said to herself.

"You can pretty much freeze anything these days," I said with a straight face.

"Oh yes," Mrs. Stone jumped in, "these days they have the technology so that you can live a perfectly normal life even after chemotherapy, but hopefully the radiation will be enough."

"It's good news," Mia nodded.

"I knew you'd be happy to hear that! They're freezing his sperm next week."

I pinched Mia's shoulder. She turned around, and I held my arms up and opened my mouth as if in fear.

"What am I?" I asked, doing my best impersonation of a frozen sperm, but she seemed distracted and didn't get it. She turned back to her mom.

"Wait, so hold on, is it like donating sperm?" Mia asked.

"I don't know," Mrs. Stone said. "Abraham?"

"Well, I imagine they keep it frozen at a sperm bank," Mr. Stone said. "And I assume that's at a hospital."

"He'll be making a deposit at the sperm bank," I said, but nobody seemed to hear.

I looked from Mia to her mom to her dad and back to Mia. They kept rattling on about Ryan's sperm, saying the word "sperm" in every sentence until they all started sounding to me like the teacher in Peanuts, but instead of "Wuh wuh wuh" replacing human language, Mia's parents were saying, "Sperm sperm sperm spermity sperm whale sperm sperm."

"Question, Abraham." Mrs. Stone raised her hand. "I wonder what the guarantee is that they can freeze his—"

"Sperm?" I said. "Is that what you were going to say, Mrs. Sperm—I mean, Stone?"

They all stared at me. Mia's mouth dropped open so hard I could actually hear a cash register opening in my head. I blushed, realizing I'd gone too far.

"Just kidding," I added feebly.

Mrs. Stone glared at the sofa.

"A foot apart, children," she said.

33

"I can't believe you just called my mom Mrs. Sperm," Mia whispered to me as we headed up the stairs.

"It was an accident," I explained. "I was riffing."

We went upstairs to her bedroom. I was surprised how girly it was, given her sports background. The walls were a faded pink—similar, actually, to the walls in the Honeymoon Suite at the inn. The stereo in the corner was softly playing "Like the Weather" by 10,000 Maniacs. The floor was messy, with markers and rumpled flannel shirts and CD cases and a fungo bat sprawled out all over the place, along with a stack of books on Eastern philosophy and meditation piled high in one corner. The room smelled like a combination of lilies and old sneakers.

"I like your room," I said.

We tried to engage in a little heavy petting with silent kissing, but it was tricky because she had to keep the door open—house rules. Apparently this wasn't even enough, because a few minutes later Mrs. Stone felt compelled to iron some shirts in the guest room next door.

I went over to her desk and looked at a huge, poster-size frame featuring a collage of photos of Mia and Ryan: the former couple posing midway up an indoor climbing wall, wearing red helmets; Mia and Ryan kayaking on the Charles River; Mia and Ryan having an impromptu water fight after a lacrosse game; Mia when she was in eighth grade with outdated bangs. A couple of the frames were empty; some pictures had been taken out at some point and hadn't been replaced. My eyes adjusted and I saw in the reflection of the glass frame Mia, staring at me.

"The photos help me focus on the good times we had, or rather, the time when he was healthy," she said.

I nodded.

"We can talk about something else," she offered.

"I'm just happy to be here," I said. "I appreciate it, but it's cool, I actually want to talk about him a little. Like, when does he start radiation?"

"In November, right after the Walk."

"Is he scared?"

"You know Ryan. He says no, but who wouldn't be, right? Look at this one," she said, changing the subject. She walked over to the big picture frame and pointed at the corner—a snapshot of Mia and Ryan at the beach. "I'm even pointing at his belly, see? He has a six-pack, but see from this angle it juts way out like he's pregnant! That's his enlarged spleen. Me and Jonesey used to tease him all the time about it."

"I can't believe you can see it in the photo," I said.

"I know," she said. Her eyes were watery and her voice sounded sniffly. "Let me show you what I've been learning. Ryan's the real meditation expert. What we would do is he'd read up on it while I was at school, and then he'd explain it all to me when I got to the hospital every afternoon."

My left ear flickered every time she said "We."

"That's great," I said softly.

She rummaged through the pile of junk in the middle of the room. She pulled out a handful of CDs. Mia had bought a boxed set of nature-sound CDs that were supposed to be relaxing. She popped in disc one, "Mountain Streams," and we listened to it for a few minutes. I don't know if it actually relaxed me, but it did make me want to pee.

"I want you to lie down on the carpet," she whispered.

I did as I was told.

"Now, do you feel anything weird in your stomach, or do you have a headache, or any pain anywhere?" she asked.

"My stomach is a little weird," I said. "Not from the food, but just being downstairs with your folks, it was a little tense."

"Well, we're going to get rid of that tension, okay? Close your eyes."

It didn't feel like she was going to lean down and kiss me, but I prayed for it.

"Focus on the pain in your stomach. Visualize an X-ray of your body, okay, and picture that the pain in your stomach is a cloudy ball of red gas, okay? Let me know when you've done it."

"Is it different from the orange ball of gas I'm seeing?"

"You see an orange ball of gas—where?"

"It's lodged in . . . in . . . my ass!"

She sighed. I opened one eye and saw that she was frowning.

"Don't joke, this is serious," she said. "Now focus on your breathing. Start taking breaths, soft but measured and powerful, in through the mouth and out through the mouth, okay? And each time you breathe in, a silvery blue liquid comes in your mouth and down your throat. Take a deep breath into your lungs, and it coats the red ball, making it pinkish. Then when you slowly exhale, that pinkish liquid comes up and out your mouth. The pinkish ball returns to that original red color, but it's slightly smaller now."

"Okay."

"Focus on doing that, and each time it takes a little of the red away, until the ball disappears completely, okay?"

My stomach did hurt, and it was partly from the crappy soup—the excessive salt was eating away at my stomach lining, but truth be told, it was also from staring at the photos of Mia and Ryan together.

"You're frowning," she said.

I tried to focus on the red ball. The sound of the wind picking up, making the windows lightly rattle, dimmed in my ears. The ball was throbbing inside me. I didn't see it as a cloudy, gassy sphere, but a solid object—a child's or dog's red rubber ball, hard and smooth. The liquid I inhaled was a mimetic polyalloy—that liquid silver the evil Terminator was made from, and it coated the red rubber ball completely. The rubber ball represented my ache—everything that was confusing me about our relationship: her past, Ryan's sickness, Mia's parents, plus that godforsaken salty soup—and was *throbbing*, with each exhale it would stop shuddering for two seconds before resuming.

"It's working, I can tell," Mia said softly, positively. I nodded. "Don't let me disrupt you, keep doing it."

I took deep breaths. I could actually hear my breaths as if I was in an empty school hallway. To be honest, I felt a heaviness and lightness at the same time, and my stomach started feeling better! It was incredible; the ball actually was getting smaller. I kept breathing slowly. The ball was discernibly disappearing, bit by bit, and in my head I was able to actually do two things at once—I could keep breathing and visualizing the liquid-silver Pepto-Bismol taking the throbbing red away, while imagining the scenario from a bird's-eye point of view. I was lying on Mia's floor, in her bedroom, just the two of us, and we were happy. My stomachache disappeared completely. I don't know how long it took. When I opened my eyes to tell her I felt it, I saw that she wasn't focused on me at all; she was staring off at the wall, at the framed pictures of her and Ryan. Eventually she turned around.

"So did it work?" she asked.

"No," I said.

34

The school was dolled up for Ryan's return on Monday. A big banner, hanging ponderously in a V shape under the awning of the school entrance, read, WELCOME BACK, HERO! and there were decorations and streamers taped to the walls and ceilings all over the school. Kids had already torn down most of them before homeroom, and so the floors of the hallways were slippery with streamers. Everything was gussied up in red, white, and blue, and there seemed to be a palpable energy in the air; the only thing missing were those creepy straw hats, and it would have appeared as if the Democratic National Convention was passing through our school or something.

Despite everyone waiting with baited breath for his triumphant (or as Shauna had put it, "triumphal") return, Ryan ended up arriving with virtually no fanfare in the back parking lot, because it was during homeroom and everyone was already in their classrooms, except for me. I happened to be in the caf drinking a cup of tea (the lax guys were no longer there, so it felt safe to drink it) when Ryan's Bronco II pulled into the senior parking lot. I was the only student who happened to witness it. He was hunched over, wincing slightly as he ambled over to the side entrance by the gym, with Mia accompanying him. They weren't even looking at each other. Ryan had on his nylon BHS lacrosse pullover, and he was wearing one of those ski hats that have earflaps, over a white baseball cap. They disappeared a couple of seconds later, and when I ran around the corner to greet them they were nowhere to be found. I stood there for a minute waiting for them, but they never showed up. The bell rang again, signaling the start of first period, so I shuffled off to class.

I tried to find them between classes, but most of Ryan's senior classes were in another wing, and at lunch I watched groups of students shyly approach Ryan's table, as if for autographs. Snippets of conversations from tables around me drifted up to my stinging ears: "Mia totally helped him through this—she brought him his homework every day last week." "Aren't they a cute couple? I mean they're not a couple anymore, but they're still so adorable together . . . and tragic. It's just so perfect, isn't it?" "He looks smaller, don't you think?" "I heard they actually got married in secret, because they were afraid he was going to die. Isn't that so romantic?"

The entire day passed without me getting a chance to see Mia for a couple of minutes, a quick hug, anything, which I'd expected and didn't even bitch about—determined as I was to not turn into a broken record, but what *did* irk me was this: At the end of the day I looked out the bus windows and was stunned to find Mia and Ryan leaned up against the brick wall, talking to Jonesey and the lax guys and Shauna. All the lax guys were wearing the same olive-green J.Crew barn jackets that hung almost down to their knees, and white baseball caps of various New England colleges with the severely curved brims pulled low over their eyes. Mia was laughing hysterically at something Ryan said. To anyone on the buses looking at Ryan and Mia it would appear as if *they* were together. I sighed. I shouldn't have cared that hardly anyone knew the truth about us, but I kinda really did. Frankly, it felt like I was being sequestered in the attic, like some deformed son back in the fifties or whenever families last used to hide deformed children from the general public.

Two freshman guys were semiplayfully shoving each other in the seat directly behind me, and the bus driver was threatening to kick them off if they kept it up. My hands were shaking. My heart was racing, making me feel like a hummingbird with a heart murmur. I faced front and stared at a square of unmatching green duct tape stuck to the back of the seat. I pulled it off, stuck my finger in the foamy hole. The yellow cushioning crumbled at my touch, and I pulled some of it out. Behind the layer of foam I could feel the cold metal frame.

I thought about Mia's little spiel about meditation, about embracing the headache, about not running away from the problem, to instead accept problems and deal with them directly. We all had problems to solve. For me, it was learning to deal with how Ryan's cancer was cutting into my relationship with Mia. He was everywhere, even when he wasn't physically present—he was in our thoughts constantly, and now here he was back at school taking away what little freedom Mia and I had from having to deal with his sickness. Ever since the night of the candlelight vigil, I'd always unconsciously tried to steer our conversations away from the taboo subject of Ryan's sickness when Mia and I were alone, and it occurred to me as I sat on the bus that I'd been going about it all wrong, according to the principles of meditation. The answer was to *accept it*, to stop trying to avoid the subject of Ryan and his cancer. Mia had said she was going to be focused on Ryan until October, and trying to pretend this situation didn't exist would only be postponing my getting past it.

"Accept it," I said softly to myself. I realized I'd been sitting there with my eyes closed. I exhaled slowly, opened my eyes, and was surprised to find that I'd been absentmindedly pulling out yellow cushioning the entire ride home. The overweight girl sitting across from me glared at the pile of inedible yellow crumbs on my lap. When she looked up at my face, her eyes widened and she turned away, which scared the shit out of me, and I refused to look at my reflection in the window the rest of the ride home.

I honestly tried my hardest to accept it, but I only saw Mia *less* with each passing day. People mobbed Ryan (and thereby Mia as well) around every corner of the school, and so I rarely got to see her during the day. She just was never alone, and when I caught a glimpse of her from a distance she was almost always with Ryan. After school it was even harder to get near her. The general routine was that Mia would carry Ryan's backpack and escort him home, where they'd then sit in the living room and do homework for a while, and then they'd go to Blockbuster to pick out a couple of action movies. Apparently Ryan had developed an obsession with sitting on his ass and watching action movies during the two weeks he'd been confined to room 327 at the hospital following the surgery. Despite his enthusiasm, Mia said that he always fell asleep midway through the movie, just when the action was getting good. I was envious; despite the fact that he was falling asleep in the middle of a big-budget popcorn movie (in which the explosions are timed to keep even the most tired annoyingly awake), it was still otherwise kinda like a date, the type of night I wanted to be having with Mia.

Sometimes Brett would call after school, inviting me to come over and hang out with everyone, but I'd explain that I was busy. At lunch during the day I wouldn't pay any attention to the conversation and just stare wistfully at Mia. After a few days they stopped trying to get me to join in on their reindeer games, but I barely noticed the change of heart. Every afternoon that week I'd do my homework and then sit on the floor in the growing dark, desperately waiting for the phone to ring so I could intently listen to her boring, repetitive, unemotional phone summary about her afternoon with The House: hours spent sitting by Ryan's bed watching ESPN all afternoon and listening to him repeatedly play the first three power chords of "Smoke on the Water" and mangling the intro to "Enter Sandman" for hours on end. She usually got home around six, just in time for dinner, and then she'd spend a couple hours doing homework, brush her teeth, change for bed, and then dial my number with the lights already off.

Naturally I had trouble sleeping. I felt perpetually antsy, as if I were quitting cigarettes, which—come to think of it—isn't a bad analogy at all, given that I was withdrawing from being around Mia. Nothing brought me relief until this: One night, I closed my eyes and pictured my body as if I was looking down at sort of an X-ray, the way Mia had taught me. I focused on my torso, which was clear but with a slight blue tint to it. I interpreted that the color signified that my lungs, that every organ in my upper body, were perfectly healthy. I then noticed a tiny red dot, tucked against the wall of my left lung. Just a speck, barely visible—I didn't catch it the first time I looked. I then visualized inhaling red smoke, through my nose, slowly, a thin but steady stream; I inhaled the red smoke down my throat and into my chest. Once the stream of red smoke entered the open cavity of my lungs, it expanded into a little cloud before disappearing in a poof, evaporating as quickly as it had appeared, but for a millisecond it made the tiny red speck glow. I kept inhaling the red smoke into my lungs and watched each breath poof in my lungs before making the speck flare up for an instant. I kept doing this with my eyes closed. It took every ounce of concentration for me to see the red speck. After a dozen breaths I realized the dot had grown, just barely, to the size of a well-worn pencil eraser. I realized that for the first time in days, I felt calm, and even a little sleepy. After twenty minutes of focusing on my breathing there was now a small red rubbery ball attached to my left lung, glowing in time with my breathing. I rubbed under my ribs where the imaginary ball was lodged, and I swear it felt tender to the touch.

35

I was so hard up for face time with Mia that I willingly sat with the lax guys as they ate doughnuts and slugged coffee in the caf Monday morning. It took a lot of willpower on my part to sit behind enemy lines like that, not only because all the lax guys hated my guts, but also because of how excruciatingly boring it was to sit there listening to Mia's pals talk, and I couldn't help but question Mia's character just for being friends with these morons. Like I'd mentioned earlier, all they ever seemed to talk about was memories. For hours they could just contentedly laugh as they retold insipid stories about themselves from the recent past that they'd heard a hundred times before, not to mention having actually lived it the first time. It's annoying enough that the Greatest Generation prattles on about WWII and going to drive-ins and drinking root beer floats every night, but we accept it and we allow the elderly to talk about the "good ol' days" because at least:

a) it was a really long-ass time ago, and
b) the least you can do is let them reminisce about the past, because their present lives must be so boring.

But Shauna and Jonesey and the lax guys didn't have that excuse; they were young and able-bodied, and their "fond memories" were only a couple of years old, tops. Every morning before school I'd swallow having to sit there listening to them ask each other, "Remember when . . . ?" simply for the chance to be around Mia an extra few minutes, but by Friday morning I was at the end of my rope, patience-wise.

"Remember that time Ryan and Jonesey took that dissected frog from bio and put it in my locker?" Shauna asked, and everyone laughed.

"That was crazy," The House said, punching fists with Jonesey. "Coach Turncliff reamed us out when he heard about it."

"That's like that time we ambushed whats-her-name with water balloons and Coach ended up literally giving me a wedgie in front of everyone," another lax guy said.

"Was that last year?" Jonesey asked.

"No, that was the first week of school this year, right after the pep rally."

"Oh, right, that was awesome!"

Everyone chuckled again. I tried to picture the lax guy getting a wedgie from Coach, and it seemed more creepy than funny. I sighed. Everyone was smiling and laughing, and at one point (it could have been a few seconds or several minutes) I had a major epiphany about these people. Given the fact that all they ever talked about was the past, my theory was that they were barreling toward an uncertain future. That is, at some point they were definitely going to run out of memories to reminisce about, at which point the only new memories they'd have to reflect on would be moments like these, sitting around remembering the good old days. If my theory was correct, five years from now they'd have no choice but to start every sentence with, "Remember that time we remembered that time . . . ?" This made me laugh out loud; everyone stared at me.

"What's with this guy?" Jonesey asked, nodding at me as he exchanged looks with The House, who subsequently rolled his eyes at Mia, who blushed! My ears felt like they were reddening.

"Oh, Ryan, you should've seen this one day, Jonesey totally stuffed an entire Nutty Buddy in his mouth and got a major brain freeze!" Shauna said.

For once, an actual memory I was a part of, so I emphatically fake-laughed (I actually uttered "ha ha ha") and said, "That was truly classic, broseph!"

Jonesey's eyes became half-lidded as he stared at the center of the table, and I could hear Shauna sigh and mutter, "Hmm," to herself.

"Remember that time you, me, and Mia stopped at the White Hen and I got a crazy brain freeze slugging down that Italian ice?" Ryan asked Jonesey.

"That was intense, dude," Jonesey replied, and the two punched fists wincingly hard.

I glanced over at Mia; she had this serene grin on her face, and I could tell she was being sucked back into this stupid vortex, and I needed to rescue her before she turned into Shauna.

"Maybe we should teach them how to play the Damnit

Game," I suggested. "Or do you think they won't get it?"

"Are you saying we're stupid?" The House asked.

That's exactly what I'm saying, I thought.

"That's real nice, Albert," he added.

"No, it's just that it's hard to figure out. It's this game Mia and I saw some kids playing one time at the inn." I looked at Mia. She smiled at me, urged me on. "Okay, maybe it's best if we just play a round. Everyone put your right hand in the middle of the table."

Everyone put their right hands in. Jonesey immediately slammed his down on Shauna's really hard.

"Jesus, what the hell, Jonesey?" she cried.

"Sorry, but it was just asking for it. I have no control over that."

"So what now?" The House asked.

"We play."

They all stared at each other, except Mia and me.

"What? Do? We? Do?" The House asked.

"Damnit," Mia said, pulling her hand back. "Jonesey, you didn't tell me you'd played this before!"

"You're a natural," I said to Jonesey. Even though he was utterly perplexed, the genius smiled.

"Just watch us play for a bit, Ry, and try to figure out the rules," Mia said.

"Why don't you just tell me the rules?" he asked.

"Figuring it out on your own IS the game," she answered.

We stood facing each other with our hands out, and after twenty seconds she blurted, "Damnit," and we both giggled.

Ryan glared at us.

"What the hell's going on?" he kept asking until finally Mia threw up her hands.

"It's an abstract game," she said. "It makes so little sense that it makes perfect sense, you know?"

Ryan stared at Mia, and then at me, and then back at Mia.

"Were you two pulling tubes when you made this up?" he asked.

Mia frowned.

"No," she said softly. "It's silly, yeah, but in the right mood—"

"I guess I just don't get it," Ryan said, cutting her off.

I watched Mia's face change, and I could tell the fun of Damnit was lost to her forever. The homeroom bell rang, and everyone shot out of their chairs as if they were escaping. Mia wanly smiled at me in a way that suggested she was annoyed with me.

"I'll see you at study hall," she said, and got up.

Usually during sixth period she had painting class, but the teacher had just given her permission to go to study hall instead for a few weeks so she could work on the Walk.

Lately Ryan had been constantly interrupting us anytime Mia and I got a tiny moment to say hi to each other, and it was clear that he was depending on her like she was his private nurse or something. It was unhealthy, and I gingerly tried to point this out to her through humor—a tactic I assume social workers use with suicidal clients. "Why doesn't he just get you a fucking beeper?" I asked one time, for example, after Ryan requested that she ditch her time with me after lunch so she could help him set up a presentation he was making in history class.

"Good one, I'll pass along the suggestion," she said, giggling, as if we were mutually happy for the interruption. "Bye, Al!"

Sixth period study hall became the only one-on-one time I got with her during school, because Ryan had gym class during that period, and all jocks love gym in the fall because that means it's time for floor hockey. Apparently there's something so satisfying about taking a hockey stick and whacking two chalkboard erasers that have been duct-taped together, and then subsequently chasing the proxy puck around the gym toward a square box with walls made of netting that's commonly referred to as a "goal." And it was unthinkable for someone like Ryan to miss it, even if he couldn't go all out because of his stitches. Even if Ryan *didn't* like floor hockey, he'd have still left us alone during sixth period, because we spent the entire study hall organizing the upcoming Walk for Cancer. Although Ryan loved the idea (because he was locally famous for his exploits on the lacrosse field, he'd already been contacted about feature spots advertising the Walk on all the major network affiliates), he had absolutely no interest in helping set the damn thing up. Neither did I, actually, but it meant hanging out alone with Mia in school for forty-five consecutive minutes.

Mia and I spent that first study hall together checking off a big list of "To Do"s for the Walk. The date for the event was set for October 31, the morning of Halloween. Each day we got closer to making the Walk a reality: we'd worked out all these deals with local vendors to have food on site— the local orchard would donate pumpkins and apples; we'd gotten release forms and insurance clauses filled out so the school wasn't liable in case something bad happened; we'd commissioned Kinko's for a huge plastic banner that read, THE KINKO'S RYAN'S WALK FOR CANCER; we'd advertised everywhere with mailings that Mia and I mailed out ourselves; and finally, we'd ordered thousands of candles that people could buy and place along the track to represent loved ones who'd had cancer. It was constant work, but I didn't care because it was a chance for Mia and me to sit at a round table in the caf for forty-five minutes every day, with nary a lax guy in sight. That was our little oasis, our only private time together.

Just us.

My mom picked me up at school on Thursday afternoon and drove me to the doctor's for my yearly physical. It felt weird to be in a doctor's office for myself. I sat under the fluorescent lights in the waiting room, reading wrinkly issues of *Better Homes and Gardens* that felt like they were covered in invisible germs, regretting that I'd worn a tattered old pair of tighty-whiteys rather than my customary plaid boxers. Because of my visits to the hospital with Mia, the smell of the place felt familiar to me. The doctor took my blood, and I was surprised to find that it didn't scare me like it used to. It felt wimpy compared to the procedures I'd witnessed Ryan going through at the hospital, which in turn kinda felt cool, as if this served as proof that I'd matured since my last physical. Then I was given a shot in my right forearm, and afterward he stuck a children's Band-Aid on it. Then he had me pull my tighty-whiteys down, turn to the left, and cough as he casually rubbed my balls together for a couple of seconds with his cold left hand and asked me how school was going, and when I was done answering him he smiled broadly at me and informed me I was free to go.

On the ride home I took off the Band-Aid and itched the spot where I'd gotten my shot. It was red and puffy, like a mosquito bite, and when my mom noticed me scratching she slapped my hand without taking her eyes off the road.

"Stop that," she said. "You'll give yourself an infection."

36

It wasn't until Friday night when Mia and I finally got a chance for some alone time outside of school. I picked her up at her house and we drove over to the Firemen's Carnival. We parked in the back and I waited for her to kiss me first. I'd quickly learned to let her make the moves during this "time-out," because if I tried to kiss her when she wasn't in the mood, it would sour the rest of our time together.

Every year the Bern Fire Department hosts a fund-raising carnival in the gigantic parking lot behind the now defunct Edward's Grocery Store. I lost a phone bet with Brett that Mia and I were going to show up to the parking lot to find that it had gotten renamed *Ryan's Carnival*.

Apparently, this was the rare event in Bern not affiliated with its favorite son. Brett had called me for the first time in weeks to ask me to go with him.

"Sorry, man, I'm going with Mia," I said.

"She could come with us," Brett replied. "Kelly's picking us up in her mom's Aerostar. You'd love it, it's got the same wood paneling we have in our loft."

"Thanks for the offer, but tonight's pretty important. I haven't had one-on-one time with Mia all week."

"Well, look for us when you get there," he said.

I was psyched to have my first date with Mia a full week after having dinner at her house, and I didn't stop to consider for even a millisecond the prospect that The House and all his buds would be there, so my throat made an audible fizzling sound when almost immediately upon entering the carnival grounds Jonesey hollered for Mia.

"Hey, guys," Mia said cheerfully as they walked over to us.

The House was chowing on a plate full of fried dough, and he had powdered sugar all over his face. He snorted at us and Mia giggled.

"*Say ello to my leetle friend*," I said to him.

"What does that mean?" The House asked. "Are you trying to introduce me to your pecker?"

Jonesey laughed.

"C'mon, brandish it, Kim," he said.

"I'm quoting Pacino," I explained. "You know, *Scarface*? It looks like you have coke all over your cheeks."

"*Scarface* was boring as balls," Jamie, generic senior lax guy, snapped. "Besides that one chain-saw scene, at least. *New Jack City*'s way better. Mario Van Peebles is going to go down as one of the all-time greats some day, mark my word."

"*New Jack* can't be better if it actually references *Scarface*," I countered. I felt like one of the old-timers down at Bassey's Barbershop lamenting the death of eight-tracks or egg creams or whatever.

I felt a hand on my shoulder. It was Brett and Kelly. They were both holding big purple teddy bears. Brett's bear was missing his left eye, while Kelly's bear was missing all four legs. When she turned it upside down a steady stream of sawdust poured out.

"What happened to those things?" I asked.

"They got into a fight," Kelly said, and then pretended she was getting weepy.

Mia held her arms out and hopped up and down like a little kid until Kelly handed her the maimed bear.

"It's still cute, though," Mia said. "Even if it's just a torso."

"His name's Bob," Kelly added, and Mia laughed.

"Do you want me to win you a deformed bear?" I asked Mia.

"I want one with his right front paw missing," she said, pretending to look wistful. "I've always wanted a purple teddy bear with his front right paw missing."

"We could call him Lefty," I added, and we all laughed.

The four of us, that is.

Ryan had been standing with everyone else about five feet away, just staring at us. Now he walked up and grimaced at their bears as if he was just noticing them for the first time. Brett smiled at him.

"You look like Tony Montana," he said.

"Huh?" Ryan said.

"You know, *Scarface*?" Brett clarified. "It looks like you have coke all over your face."

Ryan looked at me and then back at Brett, shaking his head.

"Jesus, you two were made for each other."

"Less talky, more ridey," Shauna said. "They're closing the rides in half an hour."

She pulled Jonesey toward the line for the swings ride. Since it was a rinky small-town carnival, there weren't any coasters, just a half dozen variations on that test module that they make astronauts ride to see if they'll puke in orbit: you sit in a two or three-seater and swing around in a circle for a couple minutes, while the actual seat spins around on its own axis.

"Do you guys want to hit the rides?" I asked Brett.

Kelly shook her head. "Bob's too short," she said.

Brett turned to me. "Yeah, we were going to go get a Charleston Chew and see if we could stretch it out the length of the carnival."

"That sounds like fun," Mia said, squeezing my hand. "We could have a contest. I bet Al and I could beat you guys."

"That sounds like a challenge," Brett said.

"Mia, come on, we're saving you a spot!" Shauna hollered.

Mia sighed. "Maybe later," she said.

Kelly held up her limbless purple bear at Mia.

"I know you can't tell, but Bob's waving good-bye to you right now."

Mia laughed.

We stood in line with the lax crew, and when it was our turn to get on, The House waved Mia to sit with him and Jamie. Mia looked at me. The guy running the gate immediately prodded her forward. "Come on, three to a seat, keep the line going."

She shrugged her shoulders at me and got in with Ryan. I tried to follow Mia into the box, but the gate guy blocked me from getting on.

"Three to a seat," he said. The next three-seater swung forward. "Here you go."

"But I'm with her," I said.

"Are you getting on or not?" the lady standing behind me asked.

I sighed, and got in. The lady and her daughter smushed in next to me. A minute later the ride started up, and we began swinging around in circles. I stared at the back of Mia's head. She laughed the whole time and Jonesey repeatedly howled like a wolf. The House seemed to be staring straight ahead, unmoving.

The ride ended five minutes later, and everyone got out. I noticed for the first time that Ryan was walking around fine—I'd gotten used to him hunching over slightly because of his scar. Mia waved a hand in front of my face and smiled at me.

"It's actually faster than it looks," she said. "I kinda feel dizzy."

We got in line at the next ride, and this time I made sure we were in front of The House and his friends, so that I'd get to ride with Mia, but next thing I knew the guy working the gate was nodding for me to get into a seat with the man who was ahead of me in line.

"No thanks," I said.

The gate guy glared at me.

"You don't have a choice, pal, two to a seat!"

I turned around.

"Is anyone alone who wants to scoot up in line? I have a seat here if anyone wants it," I shouted.

"Okay, get out of line, you're not riding," the gate guy said, pushing me back.

"No," Mia said to the gate guy. "Albert, what's with you? Do you want me to get on before you?"

"No!"

I couldn't believe she was this clueless. Grudgingly I got in the two-seater. Mia and The House sat down in the box behind me, followed by Jonesey and Shauna, and then the gate guy hooked a chain across the entry to stop the line.

"That's it, ride's going up!" he shouted.

This time I craned my neck around to try unsuccessfully to talk to Mia during the ride, and turning around like that made me feel nauseous. When the ride ended I felt like booting.

"We have time for one more," Shauna said, and we dutifully marched across the grounds to the biggest ride, this one a four-seater. The entire time in line I kept redoing my math to see if Mia and I would end up together, and we were looking good until the last second.

"I feel gnarly," Jonesey said, rubbing his belly. "I'm sitting this one out."

"No!" Shauna wailed, but he ignored her.

This meant Mia had to ride with Jamie, Shauna, and The House. She got on without even looking at me. To make matters worse, the gate guy at this ride pulled the chain across once she got on.

"Keep your hands in the cart, ride's going up!" he hollered.

"Oh, Albert—that sucks, you didn't get on!" Mia said as the ride started up.

"It's okay," I replied.

The House slowly waved at me, unsmiling. Behind him I saw Brett and Kelly standing next to a fried dough vendor. They were taking the powdered sugar from a plate and liberally sprinkling it into each other's hair. Then they walked around, shaking their heads furiously, and I smiled to myself, realizing what they were doing—they were trying to gross out adults by pretending they had abnormally serious dandruff. I refocused on Mia and The House.

I stood there at the front of the line for five minutes watching them ride by. On one pass Jamie smacked me in the forehead with an incredibly aimed flick of his hardened gum. I stared at Mia and The House. They weren't talking or even looking at each other, but they were sitting next to each other, pressed up close. The good part is that when the ride ended she smiled at me.

"I'm coming down, hold on," I said.

"No, Al, you have to ride it!" she said. "It's the best one by far!"

"Are you coming or going?" asked the guy in line behind me.

"Go ahead, Al, I'll wait for you," Mia said, not realizing that I had absolutely no interest in riding the Turbo Dumbo ride without her; but I did as I was told because I was holding up the line. The gate guy glared at me as I pushed my way back to the front and got in a modified elephant.

The ride didn't start for another minute. As I was sitting there waiting, The House and all his lax buddies and Mia and Shauna stood there staring at me with pursed expressions on their faces. I felt blushy.

"You don't have to wait for me," I shouted. "I'll meet you guys somewhere."

"Just enjoy the ride, Al," The House said, staring at me.

For the next five minutes I spun around in circles as The House and all his friends watched me. I felt like I was a little boy and they were my bored parents, and it was embarrassing as hell. To top this off, as I rode around in circles I watched approximately ninety percent of the attendees leave the carnival, so by the time the ride ended the place was practically empty. Mia bounded up to me and gave me a big hug when I stepped out of the ride.

"I told you it was sick," she said.

"Stoner," The House shouted, and Mia turned around. "We're bolting."

"Bye, guys," she said. She turned back to me. "I could ride those things all night. What was your favorite?"

I couldn't believe how naïve she was!

"Gee, Mia, it's a toss-up," I said. "I liked the one where I sat behind you the whole time, but then sitting in front of you for that other ride was kind of a thrill, too. But no, no, hands down I'd have to say having to ride that last one, all by myself, with you guys standing around bored off your asses watching me was the highlight of the night."

She looked at her own nose and kind of went, "Hmmmm."

"You didn't have fun?" she asked.

"I'm just saying it would have been nice to ride with you just once," I said.

Mia looked exasperated all of a sudden.

"I don't know what you want from me," she said. "Are you saying I should have been more proactive about sitting with you on the rides?"

"Why are you getting mad at me?"

"You're the one who's so upset."

"Well forget it, then," I said.

She sighed and suddenly looked apologetic, but at the same time she seemed a little annoyed.

"I'm sorry, it's my bad. Let me make it up to you; let's go to the can toss. I'm awesome at that, I'll win you a huge pink panda bear, okay?"

I folded my hands together in mock prayer.

"Promise?" I asked in a dainty voice.

"I'll be back in your good graces before the night is through," she said.

We practically skipped over to the can toss booth. She took out a ticket and slapped it down on the counter.

"I'm here to win my boyfriend a pink panda bear," she announced in a cowboy accent, and the guy working the booth stared blankly at us.

"Sorry, we're closed," he replied.

That night, like the night before, and the night before that, I lay in bed visualizing the growing red rubber ball inside me. It was noticeably bigger. I had the distinct feeling that the ball wasn't a good thing, and that in actuality what I was doing was the exact opposite of what Mia had instructed (it was a reverse form of visualization—I was feeding a menacing red ball inside me rather than whisking it out), but at the same time it felt right for it to be inside me. I closed my eyes and pictured the red smoke entering my lungs, making the ball bigger, but on this particular night the visualization didn't bring me the relief that eventually would lead to sleep; instead it just brought me that sick satisfaction I sometimes get when I do something bad. I lost interest in the red rubber ball, and I started picturing the carnival. I visualized me sitting there, in the seat behind Mia and Ryan on that first ride. I focused on the back of Ryan's head. It was unmoving, and I pictured him staring straight ahead, stone-faced, as the ride catapulted us around in circles. His hair bristled in the wind as the ride whipped us around, but his face and neck stayed motionless.

I don't know when I fell asleep. But when I woke up I found myself sitting up in bed with my arms outstretched, clutching at air. I kept the light off and shadowboxed the blackness in front of me and cursed his name under my breath. I was suddenly graced with a special power that gave me the ability to see everything, and I realized in that instant two things about Ryan: that he was trying to break us up, and, more significantly, that deep down he wanted Mia *back*.

Of course it would have been considered heresy to even insinuate that The House was possibly using his sickness to keep me and Mia from being together, so I didn't say anything to her about it at first. Once I realized this was happening, however, it was as if I was now wearing special glasses, like the ones Rowdy Roddy Piper wore in *They Live*, that allowed me to see what The House was really up to in broad daylight. The more I watched him, the more positive I was that my theory was right. There were basically two things that he would do to keep us apart:

1) Anytime The House saw us together, he'd steal Mia away because he had "important news" he needed to disclose to her. Afterward, I'd ask Mia what the big news was and it would be ridiculously insignificant, like that Shauna had seen a really big hornet in chemistry lab, or that Jonesey had succeeded in sticking a freshman inside the wooden trash can in wood shop and that the trash can had literally exploded into a hundred strips of wood, just like in Tom and Jerry cartoons.

2) The second tactic he used was that each time I hung out with Mia at her house after dinner, The House would call within minutes, and even though I could hear only one side of the conversation, it seemed obvious he was trying to find out if I was with her. The moment she'd disclose that I was there he'd make up some bullshit excuse to get her to come back over to his house immediately, even though she'd spent all afternoon with him. Here's the verbatim transcript of Mia's dialogue in one of the phone calls:

Mia: Hello? Oh hey, Ry-Ry, whatchoo doin'?
The House: ?
Mia: Nothing much, me and Al are just hanging out,
watching the—what's that?
The House: ?
Mia: Oh, really? Um, sure, no problem. Do your
ribs hurt? You probably need to take a nap—
The House: ?
Mia: Oh, right—that would be hard to reach.
The House: ?
Mia: Yeah, yeah, no, nothing important,
I'll be over in ten minutes, no problem, bye.

Mia turned to me.

"Ryan's feeling sharp pains coming from his scar, and it's making it hard for him to reach the textbooks on his upper shelves, and his parents aren't around. So I gotta run; maybe we can hang out tomorrow? Al? Are you okay?"

I realized I was frowning.

"I'm okay," I said. "I just want the guy to get better."

She smiled, and placed a hand on my shoulder.

"You're so sweet," she said. "Don't worry, Al, he's going to be okay. I promise."

But of course the next day we'd be just settling down on her couch in the living room, and The House would call up again. This time he needed help on his homework. Another time he accidentally dropped a CD behind the bed and needed someone with skinny enough arms to reach through and grab it. I'd try to point out how lame his excuses were, but Mia would just throw her hands up in the air and reply, "What can I do, say no?"

I should point out that my revelation about The House worried me mostly because I feared the possibility that he might actually be able to screw up our relationship, but the notion that he could actually win her back felt less plausible, because I kept reminding myself over and over the one fact that trumped all others—that their relationship ended last spring because she didn't want to have sex with him, which the more I thought about it the more it seemed to be the ultimate sign (in high school at least) that a girl wouldn't fall for an ex-boyfriend no matter how hard he tried to win her back. That is, he'd already received the ultimate rejection from her, and there was no going back. But still, the guy was trying to sabotage us, and once I realized this I was on edge, constantly.

Not to brag, but despite my deep-seated desire to point out to Mia just how manipulative her ex was, I somehow managed to keep to the high road and hold off telling Mia my conspiracy theory for all of two full days. It might have been longer, but things came to a head, through no fault of my own, the following Monday, and I had no choice in the matter. I simply *had* to tell her what The House was up to.

Here's what happened.

At this point we were no longer even hanging out together during sixth period study hall anymore; the Walk was coming up on Saturday, so there wasn't any major planning left to do besides make posters advertising it. During sixth period Shauna now regularly hijacked Mia away from me so Mia could watch her smoke cigarettes in the girl's locker room and listen to her prattle on about how slutty the freshmen bitches all were, etc. Now that my little sixth-period oasis had gone underwater too, I was downright rabid for some alone-time with Mia, so at the end of the day I caught up with her in the hallway. "Let's go check out the frogs," I suggested, even though every afternoon she went straight over to Ryan's house, and to my surprise she seemed totally up for it.

"I was actually thinking about them the other day!" she replied.

"Ride home on the bus with me, and we'll head straight there."

She looked up at the ceiling, weighing her options.

"Jonesey's going over to Ryan's house because they don't have lax practice, so Ryan should be able to manage without me. . . . Oh—what the heck, let's go!"

I took her hand and we started jogging for the entrance. Right then, the bell rang, and hundreds of students charged out of every orifice of the school (maybe it was my imagination, but I swear I recall sooty sophomores pulling themselves out of the chimney on the roof of the cafeteria).

"Stonewashed!" Ryan called out from the top of the stairs that we'd just descended. He was holding a big stack of textbooks in his arms. "A little help?"

"One sec, Al," she said, and raced back up the stairs and grabbed his books.

They walked downstairs interminably slowly. I looked out at the buses—my bus was at the front of the queue, already revving the engine.

"I have to catch the bus with Albert," Mia said when they got to the bottom of the stairs.

"Just help me put this in Jonesey's car, his car's parked out back."

I pointed at my watch.

"That's a no-go, Mia," I said. "There's no way you'll make it back in time for the bus."

She looked at Ryan.

"I promised Al I'd—"

"You want me to carry these myself? What is this, a new tough-love program?"

"Are you sure you can't carry them yourself?" I asked, feeling itchy.

Ryan pulled up his shirt to reveal the still-pink scar from his spleen surgery. I had to look away from it.

"I guess I'm a Sally for not wanting to risk opening up this four-incher, huh, Albert?" he said.

"Maybe I can hitch a ride with Jonesey and you guys could drop me off at Al's house?" Mia asked him.

"Of course, we'll drop you off at his house. Just take these books to his car, it's unlocked, and I'll go find Jonesey so we can get you over to Albert's ASAP," he replied. My bus coughed again. He looked at me. "You don't want to miss your bus, pal."

"I'll meet you at your house," Mia called to me as I walked away.

I sat there stewing on the bus. Jonesey was hanging out with a frosh lax guy against the wall of the gym. The House came out a minute later and walked over to them, and what I saw next made me see red.

The House and Jonesey walked over to the flagpole. Jonesey

crossed his beefy arms across his chest as Ryan surveyed the pole for a couple of seconds, then he gripped the pole and effortlessly hoisted himself up and did a Superman for almost ten seconds, at which point he released his grip and landed on both feet. Jonesey started clapping and they high-fived. I looked back at Ryan. He was now slap-boxing with Jonesey, bobbing and weaving, getting the better of Jonesey.

"The son of a bitch was faking it," I muttered to myself.

I stood in my driveway with my backpack on my shoulders for almost an hour after school, waiting for Mia, but she never showed up. By the time I went upstairs my shoulders were sore as hell, and I was so enraged that my hands were curled into involuntary claws.

Mia called after dinner. "I am soooo sorry!" she cried. "We stopped at Jonesey's house, and they ended up ordering a pizza, and so I was stranded there and I was going to call you, but Jonesey's little sister was home sick and I read to her a little, and next thing I knew I was late for dinner. It's supposed to be nice out tomorrow, so we can visit the frogs then."

I didn't say anything.

"Albert?"

I cleared my throat.

"Do you remember how you felt about Ryan this summer?" I asked.

I could actually hear her frown, as if she were made of tin.

"What does that have to do with anything?"

"It has everything to do with everything. Do you remember?"

"Yes," she said carefully.

"Then you must be able to recall the fact that you were

glad to be broken up with him, right? It's like once he got sick you forgot all that, Mia. The truth is he hasn't changed on the inside. That's what I have to tell you. He's still the guy you were unhappy with before he got . . . sick."

It felt really good to get that off my sunken chest, but the good feeling only lasted a second.

"That is so wrong that you would say that," she whispered.

I cringed. I was suddenly at the precipice. It wasn't fair because I didn't even realize it was one until I'd reached it. What if it turned out I was wrong about The House? My vigor evaporated as I realized that, despite my theory, when it came down to brass tacks I was still trashing a guy with cancer. I considered backing off my argument, but then a car honked outside, and it jarred me into proceeding with my little speech.

"Well then you're really not going to like what I have to say next, but it's important that you know the truth. Ryan's been trying to break us up all semester, and he's been using his sickness to do it. I've been noticing this for weeks—the way he always drags you away from me for some bullshit reason, but I let it slide, because the guy's sick, I know, and it's a time-out until he gets better, I know, I know. But after school today I saw him doing a Superman on the flagpole for ten seconds. Ten seconds. I don't think anyone could do that for ten seconds and not be able to carry his own books, do you?"

"You really saw that?" she asked.

"Do you think I'd make that up?" I asked. "It's like you don't want to believe it!"

"I don't! That would be terrible if he lied like that."

"Well he did, so he is terrible," I said quickly.

Silence on the other end of the line, as opposed to my hoped for reaction from Mia: *Why—that dirty, scheming bastard!* I didn't say anything, instead listened for her breaths on the other end, and at some point she simply hung up.

I knew not to call back.

I couldn't believe The House was getting away with this deception without Mia having the slightest clue. It was like I was living in one of those *ABC Afterschool Specials*, those two-hour movies that are always about some teen issue, like abortion, or having an alcoholic daddy, and the titles are always so straightforward, basically telling you exactly what the story's about in a bubbly, cursive font, like, *What if I'm Gay?* and *Backward: The Riddle of Dyslexia*, and *Please Don't Hit Me, Mommy*. If they were to make an afterschool special about what was happening to me, I figured it would probably be called something like, *My Girlfriend's Ex Has Cancer and Is Using His Sickness to Steal Her from Me*.

38

The next morning at school Mia stared straight ahead when we crossed paths before homeroom, refusing to acknowledge me. It was really mature of her. I saw her by herself after second period and decided to approach. She noticed me and frowned. With one hand she pulled her loose, maroon turtleneck open and tucked her mouth into it, and I pretended it wasn't meant to be symbolic. Assuming I looked as desperate and pathetic as I felt, I forced myself to smile as brightly as possible—I think I managed to give off the wattage of a dim basement-stairs bulb.

"Oh, hey, how's it going," I said, distractedly looking up at the ceiling.

"Albert, I think it would be best right now if we didn't talk," she said.

Her voice was measured, clinical.

"I don't see why I'm being punished."

She had the gall to roll her eyes at me!

"I'm mad at you, and you know why."

"I'm sorry. I was insensitive."

"I know you're sorry, but it doesn't matter, I'm too upset to talk to you right now, okay? Consider this one of those time-out moments we'd talked about."

"I didn't know we were timed-in," I countered.

She sighed.

"Look, I need space temporarily. I have to micromanage every little detail of the Walk for the rest of the week, so we don't have time to hang out anyways."

"Okay," I said.

We stood there facing each other for a couple of seconds. She sighed loudly.

"Oh, you mean right now?" I asked.

So I did as she said. I had no say in the matter. For the rest of the week leading up to the Walk I gave Mia her space, which meant watching her and Ryan together constantly, surrounded by Ryan's posse. One day I even saw them hold hands briefly, which is ten times worse than kissing. I thought back to the first time I had doughnuts and tea with Mia and the lax guys. The House had realized we were together, because our hands were touching. He understood what that meant, and so did I.

"If you're going to be a zombie at lunch, at least close your mouth," Brett said. "It's unnerving."

I ignored him and stared at Mia and The House's hands, which were now no longer touching. Had I imagined it? It was in moments like that when I'd steel myself. I reminded myself that once the walk was over on Saturday, Mia and I would get back to focusing on our relationship. I reminded myself that all the time she was spending with Ryan these days was business, not personal.

At night I'd lie in bed visualizing the red rubber ball (from a bird's-eye view it probably looked like I was just lying there, feverishly scratching myself), and one night it suddenly occurred to me that the red rubber ball represented frustration. Every time I thought about how Ryan—or Ryan's sickness, rather—was intruding on my time with Mia, the ball grew. It's like I was containing my frustration by visualizing it in my lungs—I couldn't stop it, but at least I could contain it. It felt better to at least be able to see it, and I willingly fed it more red smoke for a good twenty minutes, and it kept growing. I know it sounds weird, but at that moment it honestly felt like a tangible part of me.

It felt real.

* * *

I came home from school on Friday—the day before the Walk for Cancer—to find my mom waiting for me in the kitchen. She looked really upset. I sat down on a chair gingerly, as if I were a cat surrounded by cop dogs, who on top of that had a serious case of feline hemorrhoids.

"Honey, I have some news to tell you," she said.

"What is it?" I asked, instantly alarmed.

"First, a snack," she said, setting down a red plastic cup full of warm water. "Would you like a piece of cake?"

"Holy crap! What's going on?" I asked. "You're obviously stalling because you have really bad news, so go ahead and spill it."

She exhaled, then smiled wanly at me.

"The doctor called," she said brightly, then corrected herself, remembering that she should be acting somber. "Do you remember when you had to get those shots with your physical?"

I nodded.

"Honey, you've tested positive for TB."

"What?"

"I said you've tested positive for TB," she repeated. "It stands for tuberculosis."

My stomach dropped.

"Tested 'positive'?"

"Yes, you've acquired TB. That's what that shot was for."

I groaned.

"I 'acquired' it?" I repeated.

She laughed hesitantly.

"Sweetie, don't overreact, it's going to be fine, the doctor said you're just going to have to take a pill every morning for six months. Here, you can start now, I already went to the pharmacy and picked up the prescription."

She handed me a wax paper bag with the prescription stapled to the top. I didn't know what tuberculosis was, exactly. I assumed the root word was "tuber," from potato, and I had no clue what the heck that could mean, but it seemed terrible. I couldn't believe I was hearing this.

"How did this happen? Do we have a lot of relatives who died from TB?"

"It won't kill you!" She laughed. "The doctor said it's contagious; people who have it cough in the air and it spreads in enclosed spaces, like in hospitals."

"Which means I got this because of The House," I murmured. "Figures . . ."

"Come again, honey?"

"Nothing. Look, I have to go upstairs and process all of this," I said. "Thank you for being so forward with me."

I went upstairs. She called out to me.

"What about the pill? You should start taking it today."

"What the hell difference does it make?" I muttered. My legs were shaky, and my head felt like one of those helicopter leaf things that spin down from the big tree in our backyard every fall. I was positive my chest was caving in, and I even touched it to make sure it wasn't. I stumbled down the hall to my bedroom, so I could grieve for myself in private. I popped the soundtrack to *Apocalypse Now*—which as of late had become the soundtrack to my life—into my CD player and collapsed onto the bed. I stared at the stucco ceiling as the sound of distant helicopters filled the room, and a minute later "The End" by the Doors started playing softly out of the speakers. Already, only a minute since receiving my death sentence, I was staring fondly at the stucco ceiling, which I'd always felt was so boring to look at every night, but now I felt nostalgic about everything.

I reached back and touched the green shades, caressed them between my fingers, gazing languidly up at them.

"I'm going to miss you, shades," I said. "I know it sounds corny, but I mean it."

My throat closed up, and it felt like I could cry at any moment. I looked over at the bookshelf. Stacks and stacks of notebooks that I'd kept simply because I'm a pack rat.

"All that work," I said, shaking my head. "All that work for nothing. I could have been learning to sail all this time."

I leaned back onto the pillow and felt the waves of energy surging through my torso like the glaring green light of a photocopier. My body was clearly freaking out at the news.

"I can't believe this is happening to me," I said to myself, between fits of uncontrollable laughter. "So I'm the one who's going to die."

The laughter dissipated and was quickly replaced by a shortness of breath. Even though my mom had explained that I just had to take this tiny white pill every day for six months and that I'd be fine, I didn't believe it. Everything about me felt infected. My head ached. My hair, each individual follicle, felt sore, and I looked Grinch-green in the closet mirror. Feeling feverish, I stumbled out of my room and into my parents' bathroom and locked the door. I plugged my dad's electric razor into a socket. I didn't even bother looking in the mirror. I just haphazardly ran the razor over my head, nicking my ear like Van Gogh, and in just a few minutes I'd shaved my entire head. It felt oddly comforting to cut off a part of myself, to cut off a hundred thousand pieces of myself. When I was done I looked at the mirror and gasped. I looked ten times worse than I felt; my head looked *blue*. There were tiny patches, tufts of hair sticking out of random parts of my scalp, spots I'd missed; but I didn't bother cleaning it up. Since this was my first time shaving my head, I regretted that I hadn't at least tried to give myself a Mohawk—I'd always been semicurious what I'd look like with one. The skate rats who I was friends with back in Shitsville had always wanted me to shave my head, but I'd refused; hair was too precious to me back then, back when I wasn't dying of TB. It was still mildly disappointing, however, to discover that a shaved head really didn't suit me; I was more George "The Animal" Steele than Sinead O'Connor.

I drifted back to my room and lay there with the door locked. I lay there picturing my body from a bird's-eye view, an X-ray and it dawned on me that I'd given myself a major illness through visualization—the red rubber ball in my lungs *was* the TB. It actually worked! "The irony," I muttered to myself.

I grabbed the phone and began dialing.

"I'm dying," I said when Mia picked up.

"What?"

"I wasn't going to tell you because I didn't want you to feel cursed that both of the guys in your life are afflicted with major diseases."

"What are you talking about? This isn't even slightly funny."

"I don't think it's funny at all, either." I sighed loudly. "I tested positive for TB. The results came in this afternoon. It's official. I've acquired TB."

"What's that?"

"It stands for tuberculosis," I said. "It's a lung disease."

"Isn't that from like the 1800s?" she asked.

"You're thinking of consumption, I think," I said. "No, tuberculosis, it's the real deal. Usually it's elderly people who die from it; I'm probably like, the youngest case ever."

"Are you being serious, Albert? You're scaring me."

"Yes, I am being serious," I said softly, adding, "If I had more strength I would've yelled that."

The sound of helicopters whirred out of the speakers again as the *Apocalypse Now* soundtrack segued into Wagner's *Ride of the Valkyries*, the orchestral music that blares out of the helicopters in that famous scene when they attack the Vietnamese village.

"I don't know what you want me to say to this. But I'm very sorry you have TB."

"You're sorry? That's it?"

"I don't know how to process this, Albert, I really don't. How serious is it?"

"No, you're right, what the hell is there to say? It's cut and dried: we were just starting to date when your ex got sick, so you spent all your time with him, and eventually called a time-out to our relationship, and now he's getting healthier while it turns out I'm dying of tuberculosis."

"Don't say that!"

"The TB is growing," I said, pressing my chest with my free hand.

"Are you really sick, Albert?"

"I'm dying, Mia."

"Albert, don't—"

"I'm not whining—this is a good thing, don't you see? It's perfect, because our time-out ends tomorrow when Ryan walks out onto that track, you'll finally be done being his nurse, and now you can just become my nurse, because now it's me that's dying. You won't have to morbidly miss helping a sick person all this time, because you've got another gig lined up with me, starting tomorrow. I can't wait for the Walk, Mia."

She didn't say anything. I could hear her breathe. I touched my ribs and looked down at my chest.

"I'm going to hang up now," Mia said.

"It's inside me, Mia," I said.

She hung up.

"I can feel it," I said into the receiver.

39

Weather-wise, the inaugural Bern Walk for Cancer couldn't have been on a better day. At 8:20 a.m. the sun was out and already cutting through the morning chill as I stood in the driveway. It was going to be an unseasonably warm day; the sky was bright blue and cloudless. It was downright eerie how silent the neighborhood was. No lawn mowers. No crashing screen doors. No rhythmic whir of pedals as a group of little kids biked by. A ghost town. You wouldn't guess that it was Halloween, aside from the occasional jack-o'-lanterns in the picture windows of houses. Not to sound morbid, but on mornings like these I like to pretend I'm the sole survivor of a nuclear war and that the reason it's so silent is because everyone's dead. Okay, that came out kinda morbid. The air felt cleansing when I inhaled through my nose; it felt fittingly life-affirming, considering the day. My parents were out at Home Depot and had left me the keys to the Olds—they were lying in a tea saucer on the kitchen table with a little note next to it with the word "keys" written on it with an arrow pointing at the tea saucer. I grabbed them and headed back outside.

Mia had been at the school for at least an hour. The official starting time of the Walk was scheduled for nine, and I was slated to be walking at the very start. This is how the walk was set up: over fifty groups had signed up, and the goal was to have at least one person representing your group on the track at all times for a twenty-four hour period. People would be in the stands or stopping by to offer support, to cheer on the walkers at all times, which Mia had said was just as important as walking. Townsfolk had submitted hundreds and hundreds of pledges already. Shauna and Mia had laughed the day before in the cafeteria sixth period (I watched from a distance) as they ran their hands through the big bowl full of pledge cards.

"It's as good as money!" Shauna had exclaimed, running her fingers through the potentially tens of thousands of dollars worth of donations in the bowl.

My team consisted of Mia, her parents, her sister, Mary, me, Shauna Billingsley, and four members of her family. Our team had ten walkers, and we were scheduled to each take two hour-long shifts walking on the track. I was slated to walk first, from nine to ten that morning, and then I'd walk again from nine to ten that night. I'd strategically chosen that slot as soon as they were made available so I wouldn't have to walk in the middle of the night. The parents were for the most part taking on the dreaded early morning hours, at least in our group. Mia was walking the eight to nine p.m. shift, and the final shift eight to nine Sunday morning to finish the Walk for Cancer. Everyone insisted she be the caboose on our team, since she was the organizer of the whole shebang.

Ryan was scheduled to walk the very first hour and the last hour. The fact that I was walking with him at the start and she was walking with him at the end felt like closure. Things were going to be different after today, finally! Knowing the time-out was coming to an end allowed me to think about the root of all this—that Ryan had gotten sick this fall, and that this was a celebration of his recovery, and for the first time in a long time I could finally feel good about him again. And I was excited to walk. Mia brought out the good in everyone, and she was making me a better person. I was so lucky to have her. I got in the car and backed out.

When I turned onto School Road, I gasped. The stands around the track were packed with well over a thousand people. The parking lot was filled to capacity, with hundreds of cars parked on the lawns of the houses across the street. The track, which surrounded the football field, was bright red with repainted white lines separating the lanes. There were already a dozen tents of varying sizes set up in the center on the football field. Italian-ice vendors, a hamburger and hot dog stand, and a line of Porta Potties were set up behind the food vendors. There was even a Snapple van parked sideways with the back doors open and official Snapple volunteers bringing out crates of new flavors and stacking them on a table.

It was all of such epic proportions that it made me feel immeasurably proud of Mia, as if I weren't her boyfriend but her father or uncle or something. *She made all this*. It was amazing—the entire town had to be there. The sun had burned through the morning haze, and it was warm out. The air smelled like summer.

I walked over to the starting line on the track. Mia was standing there with a few others, with a clipboard in her hand and a green poker visor, and she was pointing at various things. I tapped her on the shoulder.

"Hey, Albert!" She noticed my shaved head, and frowned. "Who did that to you?"

"I did it to myself. I'm showing my support for Ryan," I said. She stared at me. "I'm just kidding. I felt like it was a fitting change, given what's happening today."

"What about your TB thing?" she asked. "Are you okay?"

I blushed a little. "Yeah, it's fine; I just have to take a pill for a while, it's nothing major."

A short blast as someone blew an aerosol horn in the stands.

"So what do you think?" she asked, waving the clipboard around at everybody.

"It's amazing," I said. "It looks like the whole town is here."

"You should stretch out," Mia instructed me. "Maybe I'll walk alongside you at some point and say hi, okay?"

We high-fived, and then she took off. I watched her run toward the announcer's booth and smiled to myself; already the time-out was ending!

The elderly wives of the old-timers were stealing glares at the Snapple van and were carefully, yet quickly, putting out hundreds of Dixie cups full of their home-brewed Lipton iced tea. I walked over to them and tried a cup.

"It's authentic, made in the sun," one of the ladies said. "Not processed in some factory in Rhode Island."

It tasted awful—like regular Lipton tea, bitter and sugar free, but it psychosomatically made me feel alert. I dropped the Dixie cup on the grass and walked back to the starting line.

The old-timers from Bassey's Barbershop were standing in a row at the edge of the football field, smoking their Kent 100s. Brett was set up in a corner with a big camera on a tripod, filming the people in the bleachers. Jonesey and the lax guys were huddled around Ryan, who was casually talking to a couple of frosh mice—the same frosh mice I met in the caf the first week of school. I could tell from their body language that the girls were desperately in love with Ryan.

Over the PA system, a smothered giggle, and then Mia's voice boomed over the loudspeakers: "ATTENTION, FIRST ROUND OF WALKERS. PLEASE MAKE YOUR WAY TO THE STARTING GATE. THE WALK IS STARTING IN TWO MINUTES!"

The noise was deafening with hoots and hollers from the

stands, and loud honking from every car and truck that passed by. The Bern High marching band was playing "Oh, when the saints . . ." as the student body executed just about the crappiest human wave in the history of bleacher entertainment.

As a lifelong nonathlete it felt weird to be wearing sweats in front of such a huge audience, and I kept unconsciously covering my crotch with my hands, as if I were naked. People approached Ryan at the starting line and shook his hand, getting pictures taken with him. He was wearing a tattered white Hanes T-shirt that had written in black marker on the front STATE CHAMPS and in the back, in clunky 2-D lettering, *The House*. I remembered after they won the state championship last spring they all wore those homemade T-shirts around school for like an entire week. I was surprised at how strong Ryan looked. He'd been working out again, and, according to Mia, some of his meds had steroids in them. He looked like he did a year earlier, before he got sick. His skin even seemed bronzed.

"This is something, huh?" I asked, holding out my hand.

He shook it, extremely hard as usual, but I realized he was just a big dude, that's all. Nothing malicious about it at all, so I grinned and bore it.

"Mia worked her tail off on this," Ryan said.

"I know," I said quickly.

"WALKERS, TAKE YOUR MARK. ONE MINUTE!" her voice boomed over the loudspeakers.

He turned to me.

"You really think you guys have something, don't you?"

I gulped as indiscernibly as possible.

"We're right for each other," I said softly.

"You're so naïve, Al. You met her when she was a wreck—we'd been dating for three years and had just broken up."

"I know that already, and she wasn't a wreck."

Al: One point. The House: Zero.

"You're the classic definition of a rebound boyfriend, Al. That she's with you, of all people, speaks volumes as to how messed up she was this summer because of me."

"That's not true."

"Look, I'm trying to help you," The House said. "You're going to get burned by her, and the longer this goes on the more it'll crush you. I honestly don't think you can handle that level of rejection."

"Okey-dokey, have a nice walk, Ryan."

"Practically nobody even knows you guys are dating," he continued. "What do you think that means?"

"That's because all they see is her taking care of you constantly."

"Everyone can see it but you," he went on. "I'm not being malicious, dude, I'm trying to help you out. You're not right for her."

"You just still like her, and you can't stand someone else being with her."

"Bullshit," The House snapped, but I saw his eyes flicker for a moment. "I don't still like her, and I'm cool with someone besides me being with her someday; I'm just not cool with that someone being you."

"You're lying, I can tell you still like her, so that's why you're trying to get between us. That's why you're pretending to need help all the time, like a little baby, just to get her away from me, because it tears you up inside to see her finally happy with the right person."

Ryan's face turned red so abruptly I instinctively cowered a little.

"Okay, you ass, I was being nice just now, trying to give you some advice as a compadre, but if you really want to know the score, the fact is you're a joke, Albert, and even Mia knows it, and every second that goes by with you thinking you have something with her is only making things worse for yourself."

I fake laughed. If you had your eyes closed and heard it, I imagine it would have probably sounded like crying.

"You're so entitled it's made you blind," I said. "You think she should be with you instead?"

"I don't want to be with her anymore, but deep down she'd probably rather be with me than you. It's called basic math."

"You have no idea what Mia needs, or what she wants. You never did. She told me herself."

His eyes flickered again. It was really brief, but I caught it, and this gave me a confidence I'd never felt around the guy before.

"What? No she didn't. I went out with her for three years," he said. "Check yourself before you wreck yourself."

"TAKE YOUR MARKS . . ."

"Yeah, and that would be compelling evidence if I didn't already know the truth behind why you guys broke up in the first place."

"What are you talking about?"

"You broke up because she didn't want to have sex with you, that's how special you were to her," I said. "Face it, The House finally lost, and he can't take it."

His mouth fell.

"She didn't say that."

"Am I making it up?" I asked him.

"GO!"

And the Walk began.

40

Ryan took off at a brisk pace and the audience in the stands erupted. I got shoved in the back by an incredibly old man with liver spots even on his earlobes, wearing a T-shirt that read, I HIKED UP MOUNT WASHINGTON AND ALL I GOT WAS THIS LOUSY T-SHIRT. "Move it, boy," he barked.

I speed walked with my hands in fists and caught up to Ryan. He was shaking hands as he was walking and waving at the bleachers like a future president. He smiled at me. "Stoner doesn't really like you," he said again, but his smile looked pained.

"Mia hates you, but you're too sick for her to admit it to herself!" I growled, and walkers looked at us. "You were using her for three years. She was realizing how self-involved you were last summer, and she was happy to not be with you, but then you got sick, so she had no choice but to baby you."

"Watch it, son," he said. "I dated Mia for three years;

it's like you saw five minutes of a movie and feel like an expert."

"Screw you, Stackhouse!" I told Bern's teenager of the year.

A gasp behind us from some walkers. I noticed people getting out of the tents, standing, looking at us. We were shouting at each other. I looked for Mia and she was staring at both of us. I looked behind and saw that the rest of the walkers had stopped, and it was just me and Ryan at this point, power walking around the track.

"You're pathetic," Ryan said. "You're an emotional rapist, and you don't even know it."

"If you didn't have cancer Mia would hate you, and all these people wouldn't be blindly worshipping you, and you know it!"

I had trouble getting out the last few words because I was a little short of breath. Ryan was sweating already, pumping his fists as he walked, retaking the lead. I sped up my walk and my knees weren't even bending, and I sort of skipped to pass him. He downshifted and hit the gas a second time. We rounded the final turn onto the main straightaway, heading toward the main bleachers, and for the first time I saw that everyone was gaping at us. The walkers shuffled off the track to clear a path for us.

"She didn't love you," I gasped. "That's why she wouldn't do it with you, and now you're trying to keep her from having something special with me because you're jealous!"

"She's only with you because I left her," Ryan replied.

We were at a stalemate and we both knew it, and it's like at that point we unspokenly agreed to focus on beating each other in this walk. There were synapses misfiring and circuits smoking in my brain, and my knees finally bent and I started to . . . run.

And so did Ryan.

It all became so clear to me then. It had come down to this: Me vs. The House.

As we raced side by side I was stunned to find that I was actually keeping up with him, keeping up with the all-American athlete, the king of our school, the senior with the adult bodybuilder's physique. The guy with the legs that had sprinted every day for a decade with heavy shoulder pads on, and I was staying with him!

People in the stands began cheering, breaking the silence.

"Beat his ass, Stack!"

"Take him, House, run the freak into the ground."

"Albert Kim, you loser, get off the track!"

Their insults only fueled me. I was in the race of my life. Their shouts were lumps of coal, and I was mentally shoving them into my chicken quads, which were flaming, only growing stronger; I mentally vowed to die running if it came to it. The field hockey girls were seething in their plaid skirts as I passed by, their hands clenched in fists as they screamed at me. Everybody was moving in slow motion, shouting so aggressively that I could see spit spraying out of their mouths, but I couldn't hear anything because of the white noise roaring in my ears. Cindy Durante was apparently so incensed by my actions that she took her homemade sign (written on the whited-out back of a metal real-estate sign) and tried to smash it in half on her right thigh. There was a loud crack and she crumpled to the ground in obvious pain, but nobody around her noticed.

I spotted Gino sitting on the hood of his green Celica, watching all this unfold through a pair of camouflage binoculars, and he had this deeply befuddled look on his face.

"Go, Arnold!" he shouted, pumping his fist in encouragement, and strangely I felt a flicker of gratefulness for the guy.

And I saw Mia again. She dropped her clipboard, dumbfounded, as we ran past her. She put her hand over her mouth, and Shauna ran up to her and they started talking really fast to each other. We were now on the second lap. As we neared the first turn, Ryan and I brushed shoulders. My lungs were on fire; my throat was on fire too, for that matter, and it suddenly occurred to me that I wasn't going to be able to go on for much longer; my mind was willing but my body wasn't able, and I looked over at Ryan and . . . he wasn't there.

I looked back and saw Ryan hunched over in the center aisle of the track, taking huge lungfuls of air, walking slowly across the lanes. I'd won! I beat his ass! I glared at the people in the stands, who were no longer shouting. The House's parents were running across the football field toward him. "What the hell is wrong with you?" Mr. Stackhouse shouted at me as he ran past.

Mrs. Stackhouse glared at me with tears in her eyes as she put her arm around her son.

"Honey, are you okay? Breathe."

Ryan shook her off. He waved at the crowd and they cheered, but he was grimacing, and it dawned on me, Yes, I'd beaten him, but he clearly wasn't the same guy he was even six months earlier; he was weaker and out of shape. He may have looked like the old Ryan, but he wasn't. I'd defeated a husk of a guy I'd once known as The House.

In a nutshell, I'd just defeated a guy with cancer during a Walk for Cancer in his honor.

"GET THE HELL OFF THE TRACK!" A man's deep voice boomed over the loudspeakers.

"Get off!" everyone chanted at me. "Get off! Get off! Get off!"

I realized that the rest of the walkers were starting to walk toward me now like a lynch mob.

I left the track to derisive jeers and whistles. I was so shaky and frustrated, and it didn't help matters that I wasn't paying attention to where I was going and accidentally stumbled through the line of candles as I walked off the track. Hot white wax hit my shins and singed my shin hairs, but I didn't yelp. I heard the gasp of the crowd and I stomped off like a psycho, past the scoreboard, around the island of woods, to the back soccer field, away from all the shouting. I walked until I was completely out of view, and then I stopped.

It was surprisingly quiet, and I was about to have one of those involuntary giggling fits that abruptly turns into crying once the fight-or-flight adrenalin kicks in, but at that moment Mia appeared around the corner. She ran right up to me and shoved me as hard as she could, grunting with the effort. I reeled backward a few steps but managed to hold my ground.

"What's wrong with you?" she screamed. "Why did you do that?"

"I'm sorry," I said.

"You ruined it. All that work I put into, we put into it. You didn't care at all this whole time, did you? It was all an act."

"I did care, I'm sorry that just happened."

"I can't even show my face there, I don't even know if it's going to continue. This is crazy, I can't believe this is happening. Why did you sabotage the Walk?"

Her shoulders heaved, as if she were about to break down and cry. I put a knowing hand on her shoulder.

"I can't do this anymore, Albert," she said to her shoes, softly.

"Do you want to tell Mrs. Stackhouse you need a break from helping Ryan out? That's totally your right, don't let her peacoat guilt you into spending more time with him, you've already done so much for him."

"I'm not talking about him."

I stepped back as if I could distance myself from her words.

"What do you mean?" I asked.

I watched Mia take a slow breath as she stared at her feet.

"Albert, we have to break up," she said.

She didn't even have any tears in her eyes, which made her misery look manufactured solely for my sake. I was so flabbergasted by her sentence that all I could get out was a meager "No."

"I feel like we're ruining something good. It's not fair to you, to us, that we have to turn it on and off like this in order for me to support Ryan. I don't want what we had to fizzle because of this situation."

301

"But killing it isn't going to help things."

"No, this way we always remember it as a good thing."

I didn't say anything. She then proceeded to use the all-time worst cliché sentence girls say to guys when they dump their asses.

"You will always be so special to me, Albert," she said, as if I was about to die or go to prison for life or move to Ecuador or something. "I know you're going to be okay, you're such a good guy, and—"

"Why are you saying this?" I asked. "Did Ryan tell you to suggest this?"

"No, you have to quit thinking like that, it's not Ryan! He's not the villain you're making him out to be."

"But you were sick of him this summer."

"This whole experience has changed him," Mia said. "If there's one good thing that can come out of this, it's that Ryan's . . . become a better person."

"No, Mia."

"I'm tired of letting you down, and I'm . . . just tired." And then she said something that shocked me. "Sometimes I think I should just marry the guy and get it over with."

"What?"

I wanted to go over that last line, but now she was crying, and it instantly slipped my mind. I reached out to hold her, and surprisingly, she let me.

"We have to break up, Albert. This isn't working. Okay, I don't know about that Superman thing you saw, but . . . I can't do both. I can't."

"Mia, we can get through this, I know we—"

"It's over!" she screamed, shaking me off.

I froze. She turned and started walking back toward the track. I couldn't believe this was really happening—a wail formed in my throat, and I stifled it but it made me feel like crying. I fell to my knees, crumpled in a loud heap, and she didn't even turn around. That eternal question: If a guy falls down in the woods and the girl he's deeply in love with doesn't hear it, did he make a sound—and more importantly, would she have given two shits had she heard him?

The answer?

Apparently not.

"Wait," I said weakly. I stood up but didn't chase after her. A cold breeze passed, rustling the trees. I noticed for the first time that the branches were all completely bare; just a thousand brown-and-gray coat hangers leaning in the wind.

This is that bad ending to the traditional love story that I'd mentioned at the start of all this. According to my version of *Romeo and Juliet*, Romeo has just gotten dumped by Juliet for another man, and all that's left is for him to go crazy and die, completely alone.

Fin.

PART 4

Falling Out of Bed

41 I've been lying in bed for hours since coming home from the Walk, unable to move, caught in an unlabeled circle of hell; the circle where you're rendered immobile in your own bedroom and forced to replay in your head the events of the previous five months that led to you losing the love of your life, over and over, ad infinitum. Try as I might, my desperate attempts to distract myself are in vain, and there's nothing I can do to stop thinking about it: Mia carrying The House's books for him down the hall (I stare at the bookshelf and read the titles out loud as fast as possible); the framed photos of Mia and The House hanging on her bedroom wall, *over her bed* (I recite the Pledge of Allegiance a dozen times in a row); Mia sitting next to The House on a carnival ride, their shoulders pressed against each other (I resort to slapping myself repeatedly in the side of the head). But to no avail. Even the red rubber ball in my left lung can't distract me from thinking about what's happened—visualizing the red smoke entering my lungs doesn't soothe me, instead it makes me feel like someone's raking my chest (with an actual rake), and eventually I realize I'm cursed.

Out the window I can hear trick-or-treaters laughing and shouting. Occasionally I peek out the window and watch dozens of happy little witches, princesses, and robots file by on the sidewalk. I forgot it was Halloween. Every thirty seconds the doorbell rings, and downstairs I can hear my dad say each time, "Are you sure that's a costume? Because you look pretty real to me ha-ha-ha!" Every time it rings it makes me wince; it's like Chinese water torture. My alarm clock is turned away from me, and I don't have the strength to reach over and turn it back. I don't go downstairs to eat, and I can't get out of bed to pee—having to hold it in feels right to me. Hunger pains feel right to me, too. The pain comes and goes in waves. At one point I hear shouts, and I peek out the window and see that the sidewalks are empty and that it's completely dark out by this point. A moment later a kid in a red hooded sweatshirt races by on a bike; I can hear him breathing heavily as he whizzes by. Ten seconds later a handful of guys wearing skeleton costumes roar by on dirt bikes, chasing after him. I lean my head back on the pillow and try to focus on the stucco ceiling, feeling dizzy. A moment later Mia starts riding around my brain in a wheelbarrow with The House in slo-mo, and I groan again in abject pain.

At some point in the evening, long after the trick-or-treaters have stopped torturing me, the doorbell rings again. My mom answers the door. A moment later she knocks softly on my door.

"Honey, your friend Brett is downstairs," she says. "He wants to see you."

"No," I mutter.

"What should I tell him?"

"Tell him Albert's dead," I say, turning my back to the door. For a minute she just stands there outside my room, before shuffling away.

And now the transformation period is finally over. Cue the film projector and close the shades; hear the rhythmic rattle as the tape flaps in the reel. A grainy picture as the screen pulled down over the chalkboard slowly comes into focus. It's the number 5, which starts to flicker like a flip-comic, a countdown on the screen . . . 4 . . . 3 . . . 2 . . . and then the screen darkens. It's one of those old nature movies on super-eight film that we used to see during indoor recesses on rainy days back in Bethesda when I was little. A caterpillar on a bright green leaf appears on the screen. It cocoons itself, the passage of months viewed via time-lapse photography, as the narrator explains how there's magic happening on the inside, but all you can see is this strange cocoon, until finally one afternoon a beautiful butterfly emerges. Prior to this morning, I was on course to emerge as that beautiful butterfly. After refusing to leave my cocoon for two years as an intentional loser, Mia had lured me into reconsidering. She'd changed me, reminded me what it was like to actually live, and the new me was in the process of making a grand entrance. But instead, I've emerged not as a beautiful butterfly, but a half-deformed bloody mess. The film flaps off the end of the reel, the picture on the screen melts into flames. Lights turn back on and twenty classmates collectively gasp as they see a version of me that resembles Jeff Goldblum in *The Fly*, a work in progress, a former intentional loser who tasted happiness but then turned into an unnameable freak, yakking up my morning doughnuts immediately after swallowing them and then vomiting my acids onto them before re-eating them in front of appalled classmates.

Look away, I'm hideous.

The town looks like a winter wonderland as I ride the bus to school on Monday. There was a freak snowstorm; it came out of nowhere and overnight we got twelve inches of snow. It's the earliest "first snow of the year" in several decades, according to the Monday morning news. The plows came out in full force early this morning; I could hear them scraping back and forth on Columbus, the constant thunk of the heavy plow shovels dropping down onto the road and shoving the thick, wet snow into scalable snowbanks at the edge of every driveway in town. The bare trees are now weighed down with snow, and you can tell which roofs have good insulation depending on how much snow is on the roof. I used to love seeing the first blanket of pristine white snow of the season. This time, however, the sight fills me with disgust. The sun emerges midway through the drive to school, and my fellow passengers collectively mutter, "Ooh," as the snow lights up into a crystally white. I wince and shield my eyes and focus on the green strip of duct tape covering one of the dozen man-made rips on the seat in front of me, and breathe slowly.

I have to focus every ounce of my attention on it, or else my mind wanders.

In a demented twist of fate, I arrive at school and see Mia everywhere. Back when we were together it was almost impossible to find her, and now that we're broken up I seem to see her around every corner. Seeing Mia depresses the hell out of me, so much so that every time I catch a glimpse of her the opening strains of "Adagio for Strings" from the *Platoon* soundtrack start playing in my head, making me feel like I'm starring in the teen romantic comedy version of *Platoon* or something. In fact, I soon find that anything triggers it, not just the visage of Mia—the bell rings for the next class and the violins start playing again in my head; I take a sip of water from the drinking fountain, and the opening strain greets me once again. Just about everything feels tragic to me right now.

People bump into me in the halls, muttering things under their breath.

"How's it going, Carl Lewis?!"

"Hey Al, congratulations on winning the race."

"You're reeeeaaaalllly, reeeeaaaallllly fast."

A freshman guy comes up and walks alongside me at one point.

"I'm starting to get a sore throat, does that mean you want to race me?" he asks.

I ignore him. A moment later I see Mia standing in a doorway, talking to her history teacher; the violins start playing again in my head and I almost stagger.

It becomes unbearable at lunch, because I know Mia's going to be sitting there with The House, and I just don't think I can handle seeing them together. Brett waves me over when he sees me. My throat starts closing up, and my feet feel like felled logs as I amble over to the table, or at least nearer to it. At the last second I say, "Hold on, I forgot to get dessert," turn and walk briskly back to the kitchen. When I'm out of view inside the emptyish kitchen, I relax. Now what? I don't want dessert. I don't want to go back out there, though; the solitude of the kitchen feels so warm and safe.

"Can I help you?" the cashier asks me.

I stare blankly at her. Behind the register is the door to the private teacher's cafeteria, and I know that there's a door to the main hallway from that room, so I put my tray down in front of the cashier.

"I didn't eat a lick of it, so you can reuse all of this," I say, and walk past her into the teacher's caf.

"You can't be in here," my homeroom teacher, Mr. Stacy, shouts the instant he sees me. He looks around at the others. "Possible one eight seven in progress, people!"

"Oh, right, sorry, I'll let myself out," I say quickly, heading straight for the exit. I hear voices behind me and maybe even feel a slight pull on the back of my shirt, but I force my way out into the hallway and then break into a sprint, feeling as if I'm in a dream, my feet painfully slow, and I get a distinct feeling that someone's going to tackle me from behind at any moment, but nothing happens.

I head to the library and plop down in a carrel in the back. The sudden halt triggers an image of Mia and me vacuuming hotel rooms in the summer, and "Adagio for Strings" starts playing on my mental soundtrack for the hundredth time this morning; for once I let the sad music sweep me up. It feels like I ought to cry, but no tears come out. For a minute I open my mouth and wait for the tears to come. I then try to expedite the process; what I do is I envision a weepy scenario—I pretend I'm the starting pitcher of game seven in the World Series, and earlier in the day I'd found out that my daughter had been killed by a feral dog. It's a full count with two outs in the final inning, and I wind up my motion, and the opposing crowd is silent, well aware that my daughter was half eaten, part of her left arm was found buried among dried-out bones in the neighbor's backyard, and they know that I'd skipped the pregame interview, and the players out in the field and in the dugout all wear black bands around protein-shaked biceps, and I hurl a devastating cut fastball and the hitter swings and misses, and I almost collapse walking to the dugout, and the catcher embraces me as puffs of confetti explode in the air, but there is no sound from the explosion, like the smoke from gun barrels in old silent westerns, and I start bawling under my cap, and everyone in the stadium stands motionless. In real life I open my eyes and they're as dry as cotton. I try harder to generate authentic tears, but all that comes out is a heavy wheezing sound. I force a low, guttural moan.

Nothing works.

It dawns on me that I'm devolving back into an intentional loser, because this is how I used to be back then. I avoided eye contact with people. I stopped participating in class. I no longer attended school assemblies, dances, homecoming games, and I grew cold on the inside, and I no longer cried. I suppose the former intentional loser inside me never died; at first I have to admit that it feels like putting on an old hat. In the afternoon I stare down at my open notebook during classes and take copious notes. Between classes I walk with my head down, and I carry all my books in my bag so I don't have to stop at my locker. It feels like the right thing to do, but at the same time it's clearly not the same as it was before I met Mia. That is, it doesn't make me feel *better*.

The school day ends, and I exhale into my open locker. Am I really turning back into that creepy mute guy to the general public, I wonder? It's complicated because I have friends now—sort of. I mean, I sit with people at lunch. I've gotten used to not focusing on the floor when I walk, and I have to admit it feels like driving without headlights to not make eye contact with people. But then I see Mia standing at her locker, laughing with friends, and I realize I have no choice. The only way I can deal with losing Mia is to return to the old me. I close my locker, grit my teeth, and walk briskly past her, staring at my watch. I get on the bus and sit down in front. The bus driver's being blasted by heat, but the rest of the bus is cold, and my blue jeans are freezing. A minute later Brett walks on. He sits down across from me. I can feel him staring at me, but I stare straight ahead.

"Are you going crazy?" he asks.

"Why would you even ride the bus?" I ask. "You have your own car."

"To save gas," he says. "Duh."

I have to admit: as nerds, we're fairly evenly matched.

"That's pitiful," I mutter.

"Not as pitiful as you turning into the walking dead," he replies.

"I don't have a choice in the matter."

"Do you want to tell me what happened at the Walk?"

I blush.

"I can't talk right now," I say, and gaze out the window. "I'm busy."

A minute later I hear Brett get up from his seat and move to the back.

And so I've returned to my old ways, shunting all blood distribution away from my loins so I can get to and from classes and take notes without falling over and dying of a broken heart. It feels weird to try to cut off my emotions like this, but it's gotten me by for a week at this point. It's not quite the same as it was the first two years of high school, though, because although I avoid looking at Mia—at people in general—I'm still in love with her, and when I happen to come around a corner and find her standing there with her back to me, I can't help but stare. Once she turns around and sees me my heart gets crushed all over again and I have to look away, but so long as it's the back of her head, no eye contact, I can stare freely. They're moments of weakness. I let

"Adagio for Strings," which has now become my theme song, make me feel heavy, and I just stand there blatantly staring at the back of Mia's head in the caf, in the hallways, in the parking lot behind the school; and I attempt to coerce her with my inefficient mind meld. I stare at her and in my head intensely try to transmit brief messages to her: *You love me. Turn around. Come to me. Return to me*, and even though I know it's stupid, I still feel deeply disappointed when she instead closes her locker and walks away unaware. Mia's getting over me, just like I'd feared. I can see it in the way she smiles at her friends, in the way she no longer notices me peripherally, or even bothers to act differently when she knows I'm watching. The first week of our time-out she would cut off her laughter or try to look serious whenever she saw me passing by. Now she no longer censors her happiness in my presence, and laughs freely. Seeing this normalcy on her face makes me feel the worst of all.

It's as if the summer and fall never even happened.

I'm eating dinner in silence with my parents. The silence is nothing new; what's different is that on this particular night I can feel their eyeballs trained on me. Every time I look up at them, however, they quickly turn away, or pretend they're inspecting a spoon or something. It's unnerving, because it dawns on me that this is what I must look like when people see me in school. I sigh.

"What's up?" I finally ask.

"Huh?" my dad replies, effectively putting the ball back in my court.

"Why are you guys staring at me?"

"I'm sorry if you feel that way, son," my mom says in careful tones like a Stepford wife, and it freaks me out, which I assume is the opposite effect she was going for by talking that way. She pauses. "Do you want to get a haircut tomorrow? I could drive you after school. It's so uneven in the back ever since you shaved it."

My dad snaps his fingers.

"That's it, you need a haircut," he says, and smiles at my mom.

I get the distinct feeling that they're about to admit to me that they're cannibals or brother and sister or something.

"I'm done may I be excused thanks that was great good night you weirdos," I mutter in one breath, sliding my seat back.

"Hold on, son," my dad says. He glances at my mom, then back at me. "Er, why don't the three of us go into the living room for a few minutes?"

"Why?"

"That's a great idea!" my mom says. "I'll put on hot water, you boys go on ahead, I'll join you in a minute."

She shoos us into the living room (she actually says "shoo" to us as she does this) and then says something that's not really intelligible (or meant to be) and escapes back to the kitchen. My dad looks around the room with an expression of amazement.

"Over two years we've lived in this house, and this will be

the first time we've ever spent time in this room as a family. It's purely decorative."

"Well, Mom doesn't like anyone sitting on the new furniture," I say. "Hence the plastic covering over everything and the whole never-inviting-anyone-over-for-anything thing."

"Take it from me, son," my dad continues, not hearing me. "When you get a house someday, make sure you use all the rooms. I basically pay money every month to not use this room."

"I was wondering when I was going to get the ol' father-son speech about mortgages."

He nods dumbly.

"Tea coming through, choo, choo!" my mom says brightly as she enters the living room carrying a silver tray with their fancy china that they never use.

We sit down on the plastic-covered sofa and have tea. I have to admit, it tastes better out of the fine china.

"They only have Lipton at school," I offer.

My mom looks incensed.

"I'll call the school board tomorrow, take it to the PTA if I have to to get Earl Grey in the school system," she says, then pulls back a little. "Do you want me to do that?"

"No thanks," I say. "Um, I've finished my tea."

"Have a refill, these tiny cups are equal to maybe a fifth of a mug," she says, pouring more tea into my cup. Some of it spills onto the saucer. "So how's school going? How are your grades looking?"

"Fine. All A's this semester, don't worry, I'm upholding all the stereotypes," I say.

My dad looks over at me. Previously he'd been staring at something really intriguing on the bare wall.

"You know, son, if you ever need to talk about anything, we're here," he says.

My mom smiles and waves at me from point-blank range.

"Why are you telling me this?"

"No reason," he says too quickly. "It's just that, you just seem a little down lately, that's all."

"Honey, back off," my mom instantly scolds him. "Let's just drink our tea and enjoy this bit of family time. Is that okay, Albert, if we do this a little while longer?"

"I'm having a great time," I say.

"Hey, maybe we'll make this a new tradition—high tea at the Kims!" my dad says, holding up his cup, spilling some tea onto his slacks.

Content that they've tricked me into feeling better, they start babbling to each other about painting the living room maybe, something they have no intention of doing, but I pretend not to notice the bullshit meter blinking red behind them. Instead, I reach under the coffee table and take out the tattered photo album underneath it. The album contains all the photos my parents had taken of their life in America prior to my being born in Bethesda. I've looked at the photos every now and then over the years, and they've never really interested me that much, but this time it feels different. The majority of pictures are of my parents back when my dad was still a student. He'd gotten his PhD in architecture at the University of Maryland, while my mom financially supported them both, albeit barely, as a secretary in some dentist's office. Back then they were young and attractive and thin. They were both learning to speak English at the time, and you can tell in the pictures that they're clearly fish out of water. There's a whole set of pictures of them sitting in convertibles that don't belong to them, my mom wearing a pink scarf around her head, and my dad with his buzz cut pretending to drive the car but laughing too hard, as a bunch of white people in owl-rimmed sunglasses—obviously the owners of the car and their white friends—stand around and laugh, and the photo captures them in joyous midclap.

All the pictures are really weird like that. There's one of my mom and dad at the park, sitting, or posing, rather, in a picnic scene, with a stereotypically red-and-white checkerboard blanket with an actual thatch basket in the middle. My dad is sitting cross-legged and holding an impossibly large hoagie up to his gaping mouth, while my mom is sitting demurely sidesaddle. In the background, of course, there are four or five white people (apparently the owners of the picnic basket) smiling and laughing down at my parents, as if they were cats.

I used to look at these pictures and think nothing of them, but now that I acutely recognize the feeling of outsiderness they must have felt as they posed for these pictures, the sight of them as young adults makes my chest heave. I finally understand what my parents meant all those thousands of times when they'd tell me that I needed to do more just to survive in this country.

What they were trying to explain to me was that I simply don't fit.

"Albie, honey, you okay?" my mom asks, touching my shoulder.

"Of course," I reply.

"But you're crying."

I look at my reflection in the window. It's too dark to tell what my face looks like. I wipe my cheeks and sure enough, they're wet and hot to the touch. My parents stare wide-eyed at me. I try to laugh a little, but my voice is getting shakier by the second.

"I guess I'm just feeling a little stressed about classes," I say.

"I knew it," my dad says to my mom, and she nods wearily. "Son, we want you to do well, but you have to learn to know when to take it easy."

"I'm fine, Dad."

"Are your grades dropping this semester?"

"No, it's just a lot of work."

They look relieved.

"Well, it's really important to maintain your GPA, to not blow what you've accomplished so far, but if you need to find ways to decompress now and then—"

"I'm fine, guys, but thanks," I say.

Normally I get annoyed with how clueless they are about things, or I ignore it because I don't even care to be around them, but this time it feels nice to accept their parenting. They're totally clueless as to why I'm really crying, but it doesn't matter, I realize, because deep down they do care about me, and it feels nice to be cared for, so we just sit there for a while, the three of us, quietly sipping our tea and not looking at each other.

* * *

The next afternoon my dad comes home from work with a big box wrapped in green Christmas gift wrap. He places it on the floor by my feet.

"Well, what are you waiting for, go ahead and open it!" he says.

I look at my mom. She just shrugs.

"You better hurry up, kiddo," she says. "Supper's getting cold."

I tear open the wrapping and it's embarrassing to admit to myself that this is actually happening, that I have parents who would baby me to the point that if they saw me feeling sad, the very next day they'd go out and buy me a big-ass present, but I can't control the actions of my parents, and anyway it turns out that they actually got me something I've wanted for a long time: a telescope.

"I can't accept this," I say.

"Don't be ridiculous! We pay thousands of dollars every year to feed and clothe you to begin with, surely you can accept this trifle token of our appreciation," he says.

I think my mom notices me suddenly feeling guilty as hell for even existing, because she quickly adds, "We were think-ing you could use another constructive hobby, and you've said you wanted one of these things, right?"

"I'll pay you back," I say. "I'd been saving up my summer-job money for this."

"Just be happy, son," my dad replies. "That's all we want, for you to pay us in happiness."

"Don't worry about my boy, he's doing just fine," my

mom reassures him, patting me on the back. "I'm glad you like it."

I give them each an awkward Kim family hug, the kind you see actors do in Broadway musicals—that is, over-demonstrative yet barely touching at the same time, presumably so people in the nosebleed seats can see what's going on.

"The receipt and warranty's in there, in case you break it," he adds.

We eat quickly in silence, and then I take the box upstairs and open it in my room. I put it together—it's a small refractor, which is basically a big version of a gun scope. It's a decent department store model. I'd intended on getting a semiserious reflector telescope, but beggars can't be choosers. I peek out the window—it's a clear night. The telescope comes with a cool red vinyl carrying case with straps, so you can wear it like a backpack. I put on my jacket and sling the telescope over a shoulder and head downstairs.

"I finished my homework before dinner," I say. "Can I go outside and try this thing out?"

My parents are thrilled.

"Do you need me to drive you to a parking lot?" my dad asks.

"No, I'm going to bike to the end of Summit—there's a field there where I can try it out, away from the streetlights."

"Be back by nine thirty," my dad says. "Or else we're going to return the telescope and get you a microscope, so you don't have to leave the house to use it."

My mom laughs, touching my dad's shoulder.

"That was actually really funny," she says.

* * *

I ride my bike down Columbus into the wind. It's dark out and I realize I'm not wearing my watch. No matter, I'm only planning on testing out the telescope for a couple of minutes anyway, and besides, it isn't as clear as I'd thought it was; there's a line of clouds rolling through, and the wind is biting, chipping away at my cheeks. I wish I'd worn a scarf. It feels counterproductive to speed up because it only makes the wind hurt more, but I squint my eyes and lean forward and start pedaling harder. The dim yellow streetlights barely light the road because the moon's full. The small, brown snowbanks that haven't melted look hard and green in the moonlight—the kind of New England permafrost that can pop a tire if you drive over it the wrong way. A minute later I realize I'm pedaling right up to Mia's house, and for a flicker I wonder if this was subconsciously my intention all along? The fact that I might be two people gives me the heebie-jeebies, and I nearly fall off my bike.

I almost turn around, actually, but by this point I can make out through the bare trees Mia's driveway just two houses away, and I see the hulking silhouette of The House's Bronco II parked outside the closed garage doors. "Adagio for Strings" starts playing in my head again, and my legs practically buckle. I hit the brakes, breathe slowly for a minute, then carefully walk the bike up to the tall bushes that border the Stones' yard and set my bike down on the neighbor's side. Despite my deep sadness I spontaneously run up to a big patch of ice in her driveway and slide across it. I then creep around to the back and sneak over unnoticed into the Stones' backyard. Plain as day I can see through the big windows into the dining room. The chandelier is lit up and they're sitting at the dinner table: Mr. and Mrs. Stone, Mia, and The House.

They look so comfortable together, because they are, having had dinner together at least a hundred times before. Mrs. Stone circles the table, doling out big spoonfuls of sugared carrots, rubbing The House's shoulder briefly as she passes by. Everyone has smiles on, and I have to admit they look beautiful. Like a TV commercial. Like a family anyone would want to be a part of. It looks warm in there. The wind is so strong it makes an evergreen branch sway, and it rakes my face.

Mr. Stone talks animatedly to Ryan, using elaborate hand gestures (I can't be sure—maybe they're talking about Thanksgiving Day floats, in which case his gestures would seem somewhat proportional), and Ryan nods enthusiastically. Even from twenty feet away in the dirty snow, I can tell he's being phony, but Mia's dad doesn't seem to notice, and Mia's mom beams at him with her hands folded under her chin.

I unzip the carrying case and take out my new telescope. It's too heavy to hold properly, so I find a low-lying branch to prop it on. I suddenly see a bird's-eye image of myself at this moment, and realize I look like a creepy guy aiming a rocket launcher at an innocent family enjoying a peaceful dinner together. I focus in on Mia. She's thoughtfully chewing on asparagus, not really looking at The House. I'm trying to gauge her interest level in him, and it warms my stomach a little to see that she isn't twitting her eyelids at the guy every second. At least, at first this makes me feel good.

But then there's this moment, ten minutes into standing

here behind the tree. . . . Mia's talking, her mom's nodding absentmindedly, and her dad is focused on scarfing down big bites of cooling steak, and Ryan just stares at his food, nodding to feign interest. He looks so fricking stupid to me as he sits there while Mia's talking passionately about something, and it all looks so unromantic, and I almost want to walk through the sliding glass door and sweep Mia into my arms and kiss her, when she abruptly stops talking and leans her head on Ryan's shoulders.

Whereas I would have flinched, Ryan barely notices her, and in that instant I see the ease they have around each other after years of being together. It makes me wonder if I was fooling myself all along this fall, thinking Mia and I had something special. Their history flashes before my eyes and I feel like an insignificant ant. The fact that they aren't being coy or touchy-feely right now depresses the hell out of me, because I realize they don't need to be.

After lunch the next day I hit the gym bathroom for a ridiculously long pee (the kind that makes me regret not having had the foresight to time it), and as I'm washing my hands afterward I hear Jonesey and a few others enter the locker room. Without thinking about it I slip back into a stall and softly close the door and lean up against it. I guess at this point spying is second nature for me. Jonesey and a couple of frosh lax guys sound like they're rummaging through a locker for something.

"So what's the deal with that Sabrina chick?" Jonesey asks. "She's pretty hot."

"Last year, in eighth grade, she looked five years younger," one of the frosh lax guys says. "She developed everything over the summer, I swear."

"Yeah, but does she put out?" Jonesey asks.

"I kissed her at a church lock-in two years ago," another frosh lax guy says.

Jonesey laughs.

"That's all I needed to hear," he says. "I guarantee you I'll be tapping that ass before playoffs."

A smattering of crisp high fives as my stomach turns over. Hearing how horny and aggressive lax guys are makes me feel stressed, but then I remember that Mia and I aren't even dating anymore. Alas, this factoid doesn't help my stomach feel any better. Jonesey changes subjects and starts talking about lacrosse practice, and I tune him out. Instead of listening to them, I start thinking about how Mia never did it with The House, and it feels way more significant than it did when she first told me in the summer. Hearing Jonesey rattle on about how it's only a matter of time before he does it with recently developed Sabrina the freshman hottie makes me realize just how incredible it is that Mia withstood The House's onslaught of pressure to have sex all that time they were dating. Three whole years of it, and she never broke. It feels like a minor miracle.

I exit the locker rooms and see Mia sitting at a table in the caf with Shauna, making posters for the fall semiformal. If there's just one thing I've learned this fall, it's that high school girls really like to make posters. I watch her draw on a big poster board for maybe twenty seconds before I head down the hall, away from the cafeteria, grinding my teeth, drowning out Charlie Sheen's voice-over from the *Platoon* soundtrack as I make my way over to the library. As I walk away I realize this: for some reason I can barely stand to look at her in school, but it's different at night.

I go back to her house the next night and watch her through the telescope. I go again the night after; in fact, I watch her every night for a week. I watch Mia sit at her desk in her bedroom doing work. I watch her twirl the phone cord as she talks to Shauna. I can tell it's Shauna because she giggles often; she doesn't laugh much with The House, as far as I can tell. Sometimes she watches TV downstairs with her parents. She wears plaid PJs and nestles up against her mom on the sofa. She likes to eat bowls of Cheerios as a late-night snack. It's the same routine every night, and it's cold out, and to be perfectly honest the telescope doesn't even work that well (it fogs up at the slightest hint of humidity), but I barely blink. I just watch her intently, and think about how Ryan hasn't been back to her house since that dinner a week ago. He only half succeeded; that is, he managed to break us up, but he didn't win her back. Which doesn't change my status with Mia, but it's slightly comforting, nonetheless, to know that we *both* don't have her.

After dinner I take my telescope and bike back to Mia's house. My parents are under the impression that for the last two weeks I've been working on a project with classmates at the library, and then rewarding myself with some constellation-watching for ten minutes in the parking lot of the library after it closes before biking home. It's sad to admit this, but I just may have the only parents in the entire country who, upon asking their son where he goes off to every night, feel fully satisfied by the answer, "Library. Then telescope." I creep over to my usual spot in the Stones' backyard and watch Mia do homework. It's boring, and yet I blink on average maybe twice a minute. Eventually Mia stands up and leaves the room. The bathroom light next to her room turns on a couple of seconds later. It stays on, and I focus on it and almost yelp out loud when I hear the sliding glass doors of the kitchen open just fifteen feet away, and see Mia, in slippers and with her lime terry cloth bathrobe tightened around her thin torso, step out onto the back porch, using effort to force the sliding door shut behind her. I look over at the dining room—her parents are sitting at the dinner table, going over a pile of bills. I take a step backward and snap a twig, and in the vacuum of the cold air it makes a piercing cracking sound, and Mia instantly looks over in my direction.

I'm hiding behind a tree, but there aren't any leaves on the branches. She doesn't notice me, though. I realize she isn't really looking, she's in deep thought as she stares off into space. Her hands are stuffed into the big deep pockets of the robe, and I can see in the moonlight that she's rubbing her thighs through the pockets because of the cold. She once told me that she sometimes goes out into the backyard to think, especially in winter, because the cold air sharpens her focus.

She just stands there for a minute, staring right at me without even realizing it, and for some reason it makes my stomach drop, and next thing I know my right foot raises off the ground, and I'm about to step out into the backyard and show myself, when she abruptly turns and heads back inside. I feel a tightness in my throat, but it's not a sad thing; I'm now positive that she misses me and that there's still a chance for us.

I know what I have to do.

I rush home, head up to my bedroom, pick up the phone, and start dialing.

"Hello?" a voice asks. It's Billy, like I'd hoped, as opposed to Brett.

"Hey," I say, unsure he'll recognize my voice.

"Albert?"

"Yeah, it's me. I know it's been a while, but can you get the gang together right now without getting caught?"

"What's going on? I haven't heard from you in months."

"I have a mission for us."

I could hear Billy shuffle in his seat.

"You need Columbus Street's help?" he asks.

Columbus Street is the gang name he'd been trying to get everyone to adopt for two years.

"More than ever," I say. "And Billy, do me a favor and keep this on the down low with your brother. He doesn't need to know about this."

"I won't tell Brett. Don't worry, I'll have everyone here in five minutes. Over and out."

I really ought to stop and think of some sort of excuse

for leaving the house at this hour after just getting back, but I'm antsy to get over to the loft, so I head downstairs and stop at the entrance to the living room. My parents look up at me.

"It's still early out . . . um, more telescope?" I ask stupidly.

My mom looks at my dad and smiles.

"Just for a little while, okay, honey?" she says. "And make sure you wear gloves."

I sneak into Billy's backyard and try the door to the loft. It's unlocked. I slip inside and wait. A few minutes later Billy and his friends show up; their postures straighten when they see me, and it makes me feel like a general, a general of a small squad of child soldiers, like in Burma.

"So what's the mission?" Jeffrey asks. "Dude, what'd you do to your hair?"

"Remember Mia, the girl I brought here that one time in the summer?" I ask.

They all nod. Jeffrey pretends he's holding an imaginary dummy and makes out with it. *Cough* . . . shewashot! . . . *cough* . . . didyoudoher? . . . *cough.*

I frown at him.

"No, I did not do her. I didn't have a chance to, because she got stolen from me."

Billy, trying to seem older, puts his hand on my shoulder.

"Chiquitas," he says, shaking his head. "That sucks, man. We've all been there, brother."

I stare at him.

"No you haven't," I say.

He shrugs.

"Well, someday we'll know what the hell it feels like," he says.

"Me, I can relate because I just pretend someone stole, like, my L.L. Bean fleece pullover," Jeffrey says thoughtfully. "I'd want to hunt down the bastard and kick his ass."

"Okay—stop, just listen for a minute, you guys," I say. "I came here because I need your help."

"Are we going after the guy?" Jeffrey asks.

"Sort of," I say.

"What's the objective?" Billy asks.

"The objective is that I need to prove to Mia that this guy, Ryan, stole her from me. He used her, and then broke us up, and she doesn't even realize it. If I can prove this to her, I know I can get her back."

"So how do we do that?" Billy asks. "Phone taps?"

"Is it even remotely feasible we could do something like that?" I ask.

"I doubt it," he replies. "I'm just throwing out ideas."

"We could film him doing something with my dad's camera," Jeffrey suggests.

"Doing what?"

"I don't know, something illegal."

We aren't getting anywhere, and an hour later I leave the loft feeling more annoyed than satisfied. We agree to meet again tomorrow afternoon to continue brainstorming. Even though I don't have a plan, it feels good to at least be proactive about something.

* * *

The next afternoon I show up in the loft and everyone has squirrelly looks on their faces, glancing at each other a dozen times in the span of a few seconds. "Gangsta's Paradise" by Coolio is blasting out of Jeffrey's headphones, and he nods disinterestedly at me as I collapse onto a beanbag.

"We've come up with an idea," Billy says.

"I'm all ears," I reply, sitting down against the wall. The loft is warm because they've been running the space heater full blast. I press my mittened hands directly against it and thaw out my fingertips.

"We're going to need supplies for it, though."

"What do you need?" I ask.

Jeffrey takes out a list.

"Binoculars, a stepladder, duct tape, a tape recorder, some police batons, quite a bit of fireworks, a couple of butterfly knives, throwing stars—"

"What the hell are you talking about?" I ask.

"We're going to kidnap Ryan," Billy says, getting on his knees, spreading his arms out, and adding a Tom Cruise-ish "Ta-daa" at the end.

I groan.

"Albert, it's a good plan. We'll kidnap him, rough him up a little, and get a confession out of him. Then you can play it for Mia and she'll dump the guy and return to you. Admit it's good."

"We're not kidnapping the guy, and besides, he's huge; you guys wouldn't be able to bring him down."

"That's what the police batons are for," Jeffrey says, slapping his forehead. "Where's your vision?"

"Is this the best you could come up with?" I ask.

"We could smash into their lockers to see if there are any clues inside," Billy says.

I snap my fingers.

"Now that idea may have some merit," I say.

"We'd have to make it look like vandalism so it doesn't point back to us."

"How do we do that?" I ask.

"I dunno," he replies.

Jeffrey raises his hand.

"Ooh, oooh," he moans, thrusting his hand higher.

I sigh. "You don't have to raise your hand to speak, Jeffrey."

"To throw off the scent, we could write 'fag' all over her locker with marker or something."

"That's actually a really good idea," I admit.

"And we could smash the locks on a couple of other lockers so it doesn't look like we targeted hers only."

"That's all well and good, but we still don't know why we're breaking into their lockers," I say.

"Planning's hard," Jeffrey whines.

"Maybe if we got some supplies it would help us think?" Billy suggests.

I can't think of a better idea, and the boys look restless, so I drive us over to the Radio Shack at Alewife to pick up supplies, despite not having a plan yet. I'd suggested getting walkie-talkies at Toys"R"Us next door, but they insist on adult walkie-talkies, which are far more expensive. I have to appease them, so I shell out the dough. We're all excited and at the same time thoroughly not excited—a typical feeling for nonadults shopping at RadioShack. It feels like it should be a fun store to be in, because it's filled with cool electronics, keyboards, and RC cars, but it's clearly a store for adults, and there's something oppressive about the setup, with its boring gray walls full of plugs and hookups for phones. The bill comes to a hundred twenty dollars.

"Well, we still don't have a plan, but at least we got the supplies," I say, shaking my head. Billy pats me on the back.

"Good point," he says, scratching under his chin, not realizing I'm being facetious.

I miss the bus the next day and stupidly decide to walk home rather than wait for the late bus, and it takes me over an hour to get home. I head straight for Billy's loft. Feeling good about being proactive has worn off, and I'm anxious to figure out a plan. I want action, damnit. I turn the corner into Billy's backyard, and I'm in my head, so I only vaguely hear the sharp burst of a whistle and Billy shouting, "Now!" My head is down and when I look up I get pelted with two iceballs; a third "kill shot" sails just to the left of my ear, grazing it. My nose is bleeding, or wet at least, I can feel it. I fall backward onto my butt, shielding my face with raised elbows. The first snowballs are extra hard, because they've been packing them the longest, waiting for me. I'm caught in an ambush.

The three of them surround me in a triangular formation, just as I'd taught them during my introductory tutorial of the game laser tag. Billy's hidden behind the steps leading up to the loft, hurling the heaviest iceballs at me. Jeffrey is to my immediate right, behind an overturned wheelbarrow. The third kid stands in the open, seemingly vulnerable, but I quickly realize he's actually in the most advantageous spot, because he's near the woods and there's a rise in the yard, so he's actually hucking iceballs from a raised position. I get nailed a dozen times all over my body. The glancing blows seem to hurt the worst. My left shoulder, my right shin. Even my left ear feels achy at this point.

"Hold on," I shout over and over, waving my arms.

After a third barrage (they must have been packing iceballs for over an hour), Billy blows the whistle again and holds up his right hand. Jeffrey freezes in midthrow, almost pitches forward, and face-plants because of the abrupt stop in momentum. They look furious. They're gasping and breathing animalistic white clouds of condensation, and their cheeks are bright red; clearly they've been waiting out here in the cold for a long time.

"Is this a joke? Because you tagged my left ear, Billy. I'm probably going to get cauliflower ear because of this."

"You're a loser," Jeffrey snaps, and it makes me wince. Usually I walk through life knowing this information already, but there's something less harmful about the fact that it goes largely unspoken.

"What are you talking about?" I ask. I'd anticipated them losing interest in me or figuring out how much of a loser I was by the time they reached eighth grade—at earliest, end of seventh—so it surprises me that they're already on to me like this. "Let's just go inside and talk about this." I say this slowly, in a deep voice to remind them of my seniority.

"Get the hell off my property," Billy says.

"Just tell me what's going on, man."

"We learned about Ryan in health class," Jeffrey says. "You didn't tell us it's *that* Ryan. You didn't tell us it was The House! He came to class this morning and talked about his sickness, and Mia was with him!"

"The guy's the hero of our town, Albert, and you want us to screw him over?" Billy asks.

"Guy's a legend," Jeffrey adds.

I groan.

"He's not what he seems," I say. "He's used his sickness to steal my girlfriend, he's not a good person, you have to trust me on this."

"He's dying of cancer and you want us to help you fight him?"

"No, yes, no, it's more complicated than that! Why can't anyone get around that one little fact about him?"

"We're not helping you, and you're not hanging out with us anymore."

"Billy, we've been friends for years, you should be backing my shit up right now, sight unseen."

They just glare at me.

"Fine, whatever, you guys play your stupid games together," I say. "I'll just get my gear and be on my way," I say, taking a step toward the stairs.

Billy raises his hand, grasping a dripping iceball. Jeffrey and the third guy run over to join him. Billy shakes his head slowly at me.

"This is crazy. I bought that stuff with my own money,"

I point out. "The walkie-talkies cost a lot of money."

"I said leave," Billy repeats. "And don't let the door hit you on the ass on the way out."

"Do you really think I'm going to let this stand?" I ask.

Billy nods. I feel a shiver—not from being cold but from how old he suddenly seems. It occurs to me that he and I are about the same height these days, and he's noticeably thicker. I think he realizes this, too, because he starts smiling at me.

"It's like that," he says.

"Okay, well, bye," I say, turning as if to walk home, but then I launch myself at the loft stairs, and Jeffrey lets loose with an iceball that hits me square in the chest, knocking my wind out and dropping me to my knees.

"Finish him!" Billy shouts.

I don't even bother shielding my face. A sick part of me actually *wants* to get hit.

"I don't even feel anything," I say as another iceball hits me square in the chest.

It's a lie; it feels like the impact broke my sternum. Still, I let out a mad giggle.

"Again, you cowards!" I shout, and I take off my ski hat, revealing my still-messily shaved head. It weirds the Columbus Street gang out. They look almost scared of me. "I said finish it, goddamnit!"

They each raise their iceballs, and I snap out of my delirium, realizing my life really is in danger, but at the same time I can't move. And just as the Columbus Street boys wind up their iceballs and hurl them as hard as they can at my face, I feel a strange calm wash over me. It must be acceptance, because I don't fear death or pain, and I close my eyes and smile at my would-be assassins. A millisecond later I hear three distinct thwocks and a collective stunned gasp from my predators. I open my eyes.

Brett's lying in front of me, and he's planted a huge metal shield into the snow in front of us.

"You just saved my life," I say, still in a daze.

"We don't have much time. Right now my brother and his friends are packing new iceballs, and they won't make the same mistake twice. They'll reposition themselves, and this shield will be useless. There's too many of them."

"But we're safe right now," I say. "I feel so cold."

"Are you listening to me?" he shouts. An iceball hits the front of the shield. *Thwock.* "The front door's locked, we need to get around them and through the back door into the kitchen."

"I think I'm going to take a nap," I say.

"Wake up over there!" he shouts, and slaps me across the face.

I instantly sit up, enraged.

"Nobody slaps me in the face except me," I growl.

"I'm sorry, but we have to go soon or else—"

"Attack!" Billy shouts.

"Too late," Brett gasps, and he pulls me up to my feet with one hand and hoists the shield up like an umbrella as a barrage of iceballs arc overhead like grenades. It's clear to us that Billy had made sure they had a couple extra snowballs at the ready, following this initial volley, and Brett barely pulls down the shield quickly enough to block a second wave of iceballs.

Thwock, thwock, thwock.

We curl around the big oak in the backyard and bolt for the kitchen door, exposing our backs. I take one in the left calf, while Brett absorbs an iceball with the small of his back.

"Ow, Billy!" Brett screams, and I can hear Billy cackle behind us.

Brett practically rips the back door off its hinges, pulls me inside, and then we race through the downstairs, almost wiping out in our wet shoes on the kitchen linoleum. We rush upstairs and I don't exhale until we're behind his locked bedroom door.

Brett drops the shield on the ground and collapses on the bed. I fall onto all fours and gasp in deep, unthreatened breaths for about a minute. Out the window we can hear shouts from Billy and his friends, and a moment later a snowball explodes against the window. The shield is lying on the carpet next to me. I try to pick it up, but it's surprisingly heavy. I look over at Brett and nod.

"Thanks for saving me with your toy shield," I say.

"Actually, the shield's real," Brett says.

"Oh."

"I should be the one doing the thanking," he says. "This was my first time being able to use it in live combat."

We just sit here for a minute, catching our breaths. Then, "So are you going to explain why my brother and his friends were trying to kill you?" he asks.

I sigh.

"I was planning something with Billy. It backfired. So they turned on me."

"What were you planning?"

"Well, we didn't get that far, but the objective was to prove to Mia that Ryan stole her from me."

"I haven't seen you two together in a while. I had a feeling you broke up," he says. "Of course, I couldn't confirm this because you've been incognito ever since the Walk."

I pretend I'm really interested in his stucco ceiling.

"Is she back together with him?" Brett asks.

"What, have you heard something?" I ask.

"No—you just said he stole her from you."

"He screwed up our relationship, but they're not back together. I'm like eighty percent certain, at least. A couple nights ago I watched Mia standing on her back porch, just looking out at the woods for several minutes, and you could just tell that she had no idea what hit her. She has no clue that Ryan was manipulating her this whole time, and I swear I can tell she still wants to be with me."

"What do you mean you saw her standing on her porch?" I look at him.

"I was sort of spying on her, it's a long story—I didn't mean to, but my parents got me this telescope, and—"

"You were spying on her with a telescope?"

"It sounds creepier than it actually is. The point is—"

"Spying's still spying, Albert. That's just wrong—you have to stop that."

"Don't worry, I don't need to anymore."

"But now you're trying to plot with my brother and his little friends to do what?"

"I told you already, we didn't have a plan, but we

bought walkie-talkies, and shovels—"

"You're out of control, Albert," he says. I scratch under my ribs because they're itchy. "You're acting crazy."

I stand up.

"So this is what you do, you save people with your toy shield and then you rip into them like this?" I ask.

"Let's pretend for a second that you're right—that Ryan stole Mia from you. Do you really think proving this to her would make her want you back, after everything that's happened?"

"You didn't see her in her own backyard the other night," I say. "I'm telling you, she still has feelings for me."

"Do you even hear what you're saying? You sound like a psycho."

"Okay, I'm out of here," I say, making for the door. As I head down the stairs he calls out after me.

"If she still had feelings for you, wouldn't you guys still be together?"

I don't say anything.

I stick to protocol the next few days and avoid Brett and everyone else by keeping my head down and darting around in general, but I do manage to notice that there are now a hundred posters advertising the fall semi-formal hanging up all over the place, and it's worth noting that the theme of the dance this year is: *Ryan's Song*. I assume it's a play on the movie *Brian's Song*, in which case I question the logic, given that at the end of the movie Brian dies. At lunchtime I sit in a carrel in the back of the library wondering what the hell I'm going to do about Mia now that the Columbus Street crew's ditched me, when I feel a tap on my shoulder.

"You know, it's one thing to eat snacks in the library," Brett says, pulling up a chair next to me, "but entire meals? Jesus, do you actually have silverware?"

I shield my metal utensils from him.

"I was in a rush, didn't have time for the caf," I say. "I'm eating on the fly, so could I have a little privacy?"

He just stares at me.

"It's rude to watch people eat," I add.

"But you're not eating," Brett replies. "Start eating and I'll leave you alone."

I stare at my sandwich. I made it myself last night, and the tomato slices have soaked through, making the bread soggy and pink. I peel open the metal top on my can of Beefaroni. It's cold. I need a microwave . . . what the hell was I thinking?

"So . . . are you going to live like this for the rest of high school?" he asks.

"Live like what?"

"Eat your lunches in the library, not talk to anyone, get beaten up by my little brother, and have to have me save your ass each time."

"I've never been known to be much of a 'communicator,' in case you never noticed."

"But you've been different this fall," Brett says. "You came back to school a changed man, and now you're going back to isolating yourself because, what, you're no longer dating Mia? That sucks, but how long is the mourning period supposed to last?"

"I don't have a choice! I don't *want* to sit here by myself, and I'm sorry I've been dissing you guys, but I can't stand seeing the person I should be with, or the guy who made all this happen. I just can't handle it."

"But that doesn't explain this." He picks up my mushy sandwich and waves it in my face. "You lost the girl, or she got stolen from you; okay, that's terrible, but this is your life. What does this have to do with what happened?"

"You don't get it—The House stole my life!" I say. "It's because of him that I'm eating a soggy lunch in the library. Everyone hates me because of him. Mia's not with me because of him. I'm just trying to pick up the pieces, get by as best as I can. This carrel feels like a prison cell, but it works for me."

"Do you really think that?" Brett asks. "That you're miserable because Ryan screwed you? That's why you're turning into this psycho?"

"It's a fact."

"Well, then you need to come with me."

Brett gets up and starts walking down the back aisle. He looks back at me. "It's in the AV room, it'll only take a minute."

The audiovisual lab's tucked into the back corner of the library. I follow him into the dark lair of the AV screening room. The lax coach teaches an Intro to Film class where each semester a dozen of his players, along with a few similarly fire hydrant–shaped Greco-Roman grapplers, can openly nap in the dark for a solid A minus as the coach fondly watches *The Graduate* and *The Pawnbroker* by himself for the twentieth time. There are four rows of chairs in front of a large screen. I blindly kick a half dozen capped Snapple iced-tea bottles half full of dip spit rolling around on the floor. Brett motions that I sit smack in the center of the front row.

He starts messing with a couple of buttons, and a moment later the large screen fills up with a freeze-frame of the football stands, filled to capacity, on a sunny day. Brett presses PLAY and the crowd in the stands erupts in hoots and hollers. The scoreboard behind the stands is blank, and as the camera pans the entire crowd I notice that the marching band isn't playing in the corner, and then the camera focuses in on a pair of white-haired ladies handing out Dixie cups. I realize this is raw footage from the morning of the Walk for Cancer. I turn to Brett.

"What's going on?" I ask.

"I was asked to film as much of the event as possible. Mia and a few others wanted a tape of the day for Ryan to have, as a present."

"He got a tape?"

"He did, but not this—this is my own private movie that I made," he says. "This is a little project I've been working on all morning."

"What is it?"

"Just watch, you're the first person to see this. This is the official premiere."

342

The screen shows the grounds for another thirty seconds—the walkers stretching, tents being set up in the middle of the track, kids screaming, and then . . .

The camera zooms in on The House and me toeing the starting line and clearly having a heated discussion. I'm stunned at how weird I look with my shaved head. There's a square patch I missed in the back that looks like it's a button to shut me down or something in case I go berserk.

"Why are you torturing me with footage from the worst day of my life?"

"Just keep watching."

With the lens zoomed all the way in, the screen shows just me and The House on the screen, and while it's too far away to hear the conversation, it's obvious we're in an argument. I blush as I watch this, seeing myself on the screen, talking angrily at Ryan. At the same time I'm glad this footage exists, because it serves as proof that Ryan was glowering at me, too. I try to read his lips, but can't. The sound of the crowd cuts out, and in the background music starts playing—Brett has edited the theme song from the movie *Chariots of Fire* into the footage.

"Look at how happy you two are," Brett says, pointing at the screen.

"Shut it! You don't know what he was saying. It looked to everyone else like he was being friendly with me and that I was freaking out on him."

The gym teacher, standing at the starting line, fires the starter pistol—I can tell because a puff of smoke shoots out from the barrel, and Ryan and I start walking, ahead of the rest of the walkers. I feel embarrassed that I'm seeing this and feel like Brett's mocking me by showing it to me, by putting the *Chariots of Fire* song into the background. At the same time, I have to admit that the image of me and Ryan power walking in slow motion looks kind of . . . funny.

"This is stupid," I say, and accidentally giggle. I glare at Brett.

"Look at your form," Brett says, pointing back at the screen. He makes chewing sounds; I realize that he's eating popcorn from a plastic cup.

"Where'd you get that?" I ask.

"You want some?" he says, holding the cup out.

I turn back to the screen and watch as, in slow motion, Ryan and I start sprinting, and I feel mortified watching this, because we come around the bend and we're running right at the camera, and I look so ridiculously angry, and I'm expending so much effort, which looks funnier in slow motion. I'm taking in giant lungfuls of air and pumping my arms awkwardly, like I'm doing a 1970s dance, and Ryan and I keep exchanging threatening glances at each other, and at some point while I'm watching this I realize that I'm laughing out loud.

"This movie's fiction, it's not a documentary; you're making it look like we're both being schmucks," I say, shoving Brett. I look back at the screen and realize that the images aren't fiction at all. I hate these moments, like when you're a little kid and you come out of a haze to find that your hands are covered in wet paint, and there are handprints all over the dining room walls, and you mutter to yourself, *What the hell was I thinking*? I sigh, and turn to Brett. "I'm kind of crazy, huh?"

"Kinda?"

"But Ryan screwed me up," I argue halfheartedly. "He stole her from me. . . ."

"That's bull," Brett says.

"How would you know, just because you caught the walk on tape? Okay, I was a bit of a dick that morning, but—"

"You blame everything on Ryan."

"Even if he weren't to blame, his sickness is. It's true, without him and his cancer I'd be with Mia right now, and I'd be normal. It's simple math."

Brett doesn't say anything.

We watch the epic sprint down the final straightaway together, me taking the lead from Ryan. When I take the lead, Brett stands and shouts, "You can do it, Albert!" and I nearly fall out of my seat laughing. And this sounds morbid, I know, as if we're trying to qualify for early entry into hell, but when Ryan stops running and doubles over on the screen, clutching his left side, Brett and I instantly stop laughing. The camera pans to me turning around on the track and shouting profanities at Ryan, and it makes me feel sick to my stomach. I can't believe how different this looks compared to my memory of it.

I have to admit I don't exactly look like a victim in this screen shot.

The race is over. The song fades out. Now it's just raw footage, the sound on mute, showing me looking up with a crazed look on my face, the camera panning the audience;

you can see the looks of hatred and confusion on everybody's faces. The camera zooms in again on me as I trudge off the track. As it pulls back it catches me (I've been wincing in anticipation, praying he didn't get it on tape) stumbling over the line of lit candles and goose stepping with melted wax dripping from my sneakers off the track. It almost . . . doesn't look like an accident. On the big screen it shows me breaking into a run and disappearing around the bend. Despite feeling gross about my actions that morning, seeing me run off like that makes me feel sad for myself, and my throat actually chokes up a little, but then the camera turns back to the track and I catch my breath.

Ryan's hunched over in the center of the track with his parents at his side, and Mia's running over to him with the clipboard waving in her hand. She looks so anguished, her face is bright red, and at this point the camera closes in on her face, and I see that she's crying.

She looks indescribably sad, and it dawns on me that everything she did this fall was just Mia being a good person, trying to support Ryan. I'd forgotten that detail the more frustrated I got with not being able to see her all the time, but it doesn't change how Mia felt about the situation—all that mattered to her was that Ryan was sick, and she was simply trying to care for him.

I realize it doesn't even matter if Ryan was trying to break us up, it's a moot point, because the truth is *neither* of us deserves to be with Mia.

The screen turns bright blue with the word REWIND in the upper right hand corner. The tape starts humming behind us.

The movie's over. I look over at Brett. He's staring at the blue screen—not really focused on it—he's thinking about something, or no, he's politely not looking at me, rather. Like he's embarrassed for me. We sit there in the front row for a few minutes, staring at the blue screen. Eventually, the bell for sixth period rings—a dull sound, through the wall, and I can hear Brett get up and leave the room, but I just sit there for a while longer, staring at the blue screen.

I wake up the next morning five minutes *before* my alarm's set to go off, and I feel like I've been awake for hours. Ever since the Walk I've felt lethargic every morning, not wanting to get out of bed. Out of formality I moan a couple of times and kick at the comforter, but it feels forced, and I stop after a couple of seconds.

I feel different.

During classes in the morning I don't bother taking feverish notes with my head down, solely to keep myself busy, and between every period I stop at my locker and take only what I need for the next class. At lunchtime I pause at the entrance to the cafeteria. Mia and Ryan are in here, and it's muscle memory for my body to feel hesitant to cross the threshold. I take a deep breath and walk toward the kitchen and get in line. It doesn't feel like that big a deal, actually. I get my food, and as I'm walking out of the kitchen, Brett and his friends shout, "Al!" and I nod at them and make my way to their table.

"Hey, guys," I say.

I sit down.

"So you've returned from the dead, huh?" Nate asks.

"Sort of," I say, looking at Brett.

He just nods at me, barely, and then bites into his sandwich.

"Are you gonna hit Newbury Comics with us after school or what, Albert?" Mark asks, punching me in the shoulder.

My eyes drift over to the lax tables. I make eye contact with Mia across the room at precisely this moment, and I'm surprised to find that "Adagio for Strings" doesn't kick in. She seems surprised to see me. We sort of nod at each other.

"Look, he's pretending he's looking off in the distance and can't hear us," Kelly says.

"Don't talk about him in the third person," Brett snaps. "He hates that."

After school we hit Newbury Comics and scan the used racks. The objective, according to Brett, is to see who can buy the lamest used CD. Kelly picks up a scratched copy of a Candlebox album. Nate and Mark combine their resources to purchase the album *Dreamland*, by Black Box. I buy the soundtrack to *Beverly Hills Cop III* for one dollar, while Brett purchases Tiffany's eponymous debut album. We rush back to Nate's house to listen to them and judge the worst. Kelly wins, and the reward is she gets to keep all the CDs, which means that we all win.

For the rest of the week I sit at Brett's table for lunch, and it feels increasingly like the norm and that I'm not merely mimicking the actions of a stable human being, and on Thursday night Brett and I ride our bikes out to this field on the other end of Summit, past Mia's house, where there aren't any streetlights, to try out my telescope. We take turns checking out the constellations (that is, we repeatedly locate Orion's Belt and the Big Dipper). Okay, so collectively we don't know jack about the stars, but it's nice to use the telescope for its intended purpose for once. It feels . . . clean.

I tell this to Brett.

"That's nice, Al," he replies. "Of course, generally you're not supposed to feel skeezy using a telescope, but hey—better late than never."

"You're in for tomorrow night, right?" Mark asks me at lunch on Friday.

"I have no idea what you're talking about, but sure," I reply.

"We're all going to the semiformal on Saturday," he explains. "It's going to be at the Bern Inn."

"Oh, uh, I don't know, I'm not really into those things," I say.

"Neither are we, but it's our senior year, and we're going for purely ironic reasons," Kelly says. "It'll be fun, we'll just make fun of people the entire night, as if we're twenty-six-year-olds trapped in high school bodies, and then when we actually hit our late twenties in real life, we'll realize how we were the lame ones for thinking everyone was so immature back in high school. You know, typical rite of passage stuff like that."

"Do you have a suit to wear?" Mark asks.

I scoff at him.

"Of course I do," I say. "I was in band."

"Touché," Marks says.

"You know, I actually worked all last summer at the Bern Inn," I add.

"Maybe you can get paid to go, then," Nate suggests.

"So are you in or what?" Kelly asks.

"I'll go if you guys quit bugging me about it," I say.

"That's what I'm talkin' about," Mark says, holding out his right hand.

We high-five, barely touching hands and almost slapping each other in the face. Kelly shakes her head at us and I start eating my lunch. I realize that this is what I've always been searching for, back when I lived in Shitsville, back during my first two years here at Bern High. Friends. I'd given up thinking it was possible freshman year and had shut myself off, and then I tried again at the start of this fall before aborting it because of what happened with Mia, and now, seemingly without even trying, I've somehow ended up with actual friends. It's surreal. I'm sitting with my friends at lunch, and it's fun, but it's fun in the way that anything is fun for someone whose recently lost a leg or something.

It's fun, but . . .

Like the ride back home from anywhere when you're a little kid, the rest of the afternoon passes quickly. I just placidly stare out the window during AP history not really paying attention to the lecture. Mr. Gurlick's trick is that anytime a student asks him a question, he answers with a question of his own—the rationale being that eventually the students get leery of asking questions for fear of being forced to abruptly handle a different question—and this is how the teacher creates the impression that he's being challenging. I feel restless for no particular reason, and two or three times I actually stand up in class and stretch. With fifteen minutes left in the final period of the day I feel like taking off a little early, so I ask to be excused for the bathroom. Mr. Gurlick never allows bathroom breaks, but since I've never asked to go to the bathroom in two years at Bern High, he lets me leave. I stop at my locker, grab my bag, and continue walking down the hall. I reach the entrance and decide instead to just go outside and try to get on the bus early. The bus driver ignores me as I tap on the glass, so instead I sit down on the purely decorative bench in the garden outside the windows of the administration offices. I don't care if the vice principal sees me. I just sit there for a few minutes, not really thinking about anything.

"You know, people don't actually sit on that bench," Mia says.

She's wearing a plain brown cotton sweater and jeans, and she has on a blue ski hat that has a little white pom-pom on top. Her hands are stuffed in her pockets, and she looks like she's freezing.

"Hello, Mia," I say, not meaning to sound so much like Hannibal Lecter. I repeat myself in a more normal voice. "Hello, Mia."

Even though I've felt different since watching Brett's documentary, my voice is shaky, because it's my first time talking to her since the Walk.

"What class is this?" she asks.

Mia seems nervous as well, and I'm glad for it. My throat loosens a bit.

"Oh, it's a new class, a seminar that they're testing out with me, since I'm such a goddamned genius."

"Is it related to the academically gifted program?"

"Something like that."

"And what's the class, or—excuse me—seminar, called?"

"Um . . . Benches 101?"

"Yeah, you're a genius," she says, laughing. "A real master of improv."

I shrug. A minute passes without either of us saying anything, which I realize *is* us saying something. I take a quiet breath.

"I'm sorry about what happened at the Walk," I say.

"I'm sorry, too," she replies.

"You have nothing to apologize for, Mia!"

"No, I meant I feel sorry that that all happened."

"Oh." A pause. I look at her. "So . . . I'm a little confused. Did you just accept my apology, or should I keep going with it?"

"I thought I was accepting your apology, but now I'm not so sure anymore."

"Well, a lot has happened in the last few seconds," I say.

She nods at me, and it turns into a smile. We sit there smiling at each other for almost ten seconds, and my face starts to feel plastered, so I change the subject.

"Are you psyched for the semiformal?" I ask.

"Those posters, they're so cheesy," she says.

"They're not that bad," I lie.

"It was Shauna's idea, and since I didn't want to have anything to do with it she designed it herself. I just helped color them in."

"Aren't you on the planning committee?" I ask.

She scoffs.

"Heck no! The Walk was my last major act of volunteerism for a while," she says, and mention of the Walk makes us both blush. She quickly changes the subject. "So are you going?"

"I've never been to a dance in my entire life," I reply.

"You should go, it's going to be awful."

"Sounds enticing."

"But it's at the Bern Inn!"

"That actually does make it kinda intriguing."

"You should go," she says again.

The bell rings, and students flood the walkway as the doors spill open. Mia turns back to me, and she has a serious look on her face, but she doesn't say anything. It feels like we should continue with our earlier conversation (about the important topics), but neither of us makes an attempt. Instead, we just stare at each other's shoes, like shoe thieves, until a wave of students starts to pass between us. I look up and notice her face has reset into a wan smile.

"I should go. It was nice talking to you."

"Good-bye, Mia."

She frowns.

"You sound so dire when you say that."

"What should I say instead?"

"I don't know. Just don't make it sound like you're on a deathbed. Say something more hopeful, like, 'See ya later, Mia,' or 'Take it easy, buddy.'"

"See ya at the semiformal, Mia," I say brightly.

She smiles back.

"We'll see," she says.

46

I ride with Brett over to the Bern Inn for the semiformal Saturday night. Nate, Mark, and Kelly are waiting for us in the parking lot when we pull in. Kelly's wearing a bright blue dress to match her blue hair. Nate and Mark are both wearing regular suits, augmented by their skinny black ties and dirty white Converse All Stars high-tops. "Okay, Al, you said you worked here, so start the tour," Mark says, clapping me on the back.

"Well, right now we're in what's known as the rear parking lot," I say.

They stare blankly at me.

"Oh—wait, was that another one of your funny jokes?" Kelly asks.

"Shut up," I say.

"Hey, I'm not the only one not laughing," she replies.

They follow me inside. The sound of laughter and music filters out from the east-wing ballroom as we approach the dance. "Whoomp! (There It Is)" is pumping out the speakers, and I really want to check out the dance floor because I'm curious as hell as to how people would dance to this song. I look back at my new friends, and they look significantly less enthused about being here than they'd seemed during yesterday's lunch. We peek inside the ballroom, and it looks as expected: streamers hang from the walls and the ceilings; there's a mustached DJ in the corner—his table covered in tacky silver Christmas tinsel; there's a long buffet table with white tablecloths featuring bowls of red punch and enough plastic cups to serve a small battalion, let alone a room full of high schoolers; and trays and trays of cookies and other desserts made by PTA parents, still wrapped in plastic. At the entrance there's a big poster featuring a four-by-six photo of Ryan and Mia holding hands after the pep rally, with the title in bubble letters above the photo, RYAN'S SONG.

The Goth kids are standing in one corner, wearing too-tight black suits with dark shirts and skinny black ties, stewing. Paul Waverly stomps around with a walkie-talkie in his right hand, frantically asking a bored teacher/usher some questions. Jonesey comes out of the bathroom, running a hand through his rewetted hair, but I don't see Ryan, or Mia, for that matter. I turn around. Brett's staring at the dance floor. Nate and Mark seem to be staring at their reflections in the shiny floor.

"This is awesome," I say. "I'm really glad you guys made me come to this."

Kelly playfully shoves me.

"Take us somewhere good, you know this place," she says. "Continue the tour."

"Gladly," I say.

They huddle behind me as we head toward the east wing. I lead them to The Three Ferns restaurant.

"Okay, so do you see how rusted all the brass fixtures are on the walls?" I point at the signs above the doors.

"Is that intentional?" Brett asks.

I shake my head.

"Yeah, man, it's really . . . rustic," Nate says, cackling his head off.

"I should introduce you to my dad," I tell Nate. "You guys could sit around all day and write jokes for *Reader's Digest* together. I swear you'd make a killing."

"I don't even think he knows what 'rustic' means," Mark adds.

"So what's the deal with the brass fixtures?" Brett asks.

"Mia and I accidentally 'cleaned' every brass fixture in this entire inn using 409," I say. "Apparently you're supposed to just wipe them down with a damp cloth. So we ended up ruining all the brass fixtures."

We enter The Three Ferns, which is closed for the night. I point out the huge rectangular windows overlooking the back lawn.

"Mia and I cleaned all of these windows," I say.

"With 409?" Mark asks.

"Windex. Anyway, we cleaned them fine, but then afterward we laid them down on the new sod out back and went on our lunch break," I explain, pushing open the door to the back patio. The rectangles of newer grass are no longer a different color, or if they're still discolored, I can't tell because it's nighttime. "Anyway, the thick glass magnified the sun and it made a dozen dead, yellowed grass rectangles on the lawn two days before the owner's son got married here."

"It's amazing you can even pee by yourself," Mark says.

"Otherwise we spent the entire time vacuuming every single room," I say, ignoring Mark. "There are over a hundred rooms, and we had to move all the furniture and, um, vacuum under the furniture . . . oh, and then put the furniture back."

"No offense, Al," Brett says, putting his hand on my shoulder. "But this has got to be the boringest tour I've ever been on."

"Seriously, please stop telling us stories," Nate says.

"Really?" I ask. "These are like, the best memories of my life."

"I feel so bad for you," Kelly says, laughing.

"I guess you had to be there," I say, shrugging.

"I'm glad we weren't," Brett says, pulling up his tie over his head as if he's hanging himself, and I punch him in the shoulder.

We walk back to the main lobby, the sound of bad dance music greeting us. We stand in the doorway and survey the scene. Our peers are all dirty dancing to "Poison" by Bel Biv DeVoe. Jamie the lacrosse player is walking behind various frosh girls and pretending to slap their butts as he rocks his head back and forth, to the delight of The House and Jonesey, who are standing in the corner. They're surrounded by a group of freshmen mice. One of them has her hand on The House's left wrist. I scan the walls for Mia, but she's nowhere in sight.

"They should just undress and quit pretending it's dancing," Kelly says.

"It's not even in time with the music," Mark says.

"If you think you could do better, let's see it," Brett says.

"DANCE-OFF!" Nate suddenly shouts.

Ironically, of course.

Students look over at us. Mark goes over to the edge of the dance floor and pretends he's really scared to step on it. He keeps reaching with his right foot but pulling away, as if he's a cat sticking his paw under a faucet for the first time.

"Go for it, Mark!" Kelly urges.

Mark vehemently shakes his head.

"No, I can't," he wails.

"You've got to!" Brett shouts.

"It's too cold," Mark cries.

"Just do it," Nate says, and Mark starts doing the grocery-cart dance back to us really exaggerated, as if he's a flamboyantly gay hairdresser buying food for the week, and we all laugh. That is, the five of us laugh—nobody else seems to get it.

"Show us something original, and we'll try to figure it out," Brett shouts.

Mark thinks for a couple of seconds, then starts lurching with hands outstretched, and it's obvious he's pretending to walk through a hurricane or something, struggling against the heavy winds. "Sweet. That should be called 'the Wind Tunnel,'" Kelly says.

"Exactly." Mark nods. "Now you, Nate!"

Nate edges out onto the dance floor. He starts dragging his

leg across, pulling at his slacks with both hands. People grimace at him. A few others laugh, pointing at him.

"Oh, I get it, I think. Is that dance called 'My right leg fell asleep but I still have to catch the bus'?" Brett asks.

"You nailed it," Nate says. He looks over at me. "Your turn, Al!"

I think for a minute. Then I get on the dance floor and put my hands behind my back, lean forward and start doing what I think looks like a rooster feeding. It's kinda simplistic and not remotely funny, but it's all I can come up with at the moment. They stare at me, perplexed. "What the hell is that?" they ask.

"You look like a psycho," Nate shouts.

"What are you, twelve?" Mark asks.

"Please stop doing that," Kelly pleads with me, feverishly looking around as if she's embarrassed by me.

I sigh.

A couple of minutes later we go out into the lobby to get some air.

"Hey, let's try playing the Damnit game. It's this cool game we used to play all summer," I suggest. I maneuver everyone into a circle. "Now hold out your right hand in the center of the circle on top of each other, but don't touch anyone else's hand. Okay, and now we play."

"Whoa, hold on a second," Brett says. "What are the rules?"

"You'll see."

A couple of seconds pass. Nate makes a groaning sound.

"This is frustrating, I don't even know the objective of the game," he whines.

"Relax, you'll figure it out eventually," I say.

"But I'm freaking out," he continues whining.

Suddenly I pull my hand back.

"Damnit!" I shout. "Nice one, Kelly—was that your first time playing?"

She stares at me as if I have a pair of balls protruding from my forehead.

"Okay, Kelly won that round, let's try again," I say, putting my hand back in.

Brett laughs.

"What the hell is going on?" he asks. "You obviously know this makes no sense."

We play again. After only five seconds, I say, "Damnit," and pull my hand back.

"I hate this game," Nate says. "Please, Al, just tell me what happened."

"You'll figure it out," I say. "It took me a while, too."

The third time I say, "Damnit," Brett smiles at me. So do Kelly and Mark.

"This game's addicting," Mark says, smiling at Nate.

"Screw you," Nate says, shoving Mark. "Albert, please."

"You almost have it," I tell him, and Brett snickers. "Just pay attention to what happens."

This time Brett says "Damnit," about twenty seconds in. "Nice one, Kelly, you're the natural," he says.

She high-fives with Mark. Nate groans.

"Oh my God—you're playing the Damnit game!" Mia says from behind. "I'm in this round."

Not to sound like a swashbuckler, but Mia looks really

ravishing. Her dress is bright red with a maroon lacy trim, and she's wearing black leggings and black sandals. Her hair is done up in a bun, with two locks of hair hanging down the sides. Even though we only briefly spoke for the first time yesterday, my throat starts closing up again. Maybe it's for old time's sake, given the setting.

Brett looks at me with a concerned expression. I nod, as if to say, "It's cool," and he begrudgingly makes room for her to join the circle.

"Wait, Mia, you know how to play this game? Explain the rules," Nate says.

I smile at Mia. She winks at me. I subtly notice that her leggings aren't black, but green. "Hands in," I say.

Nate's right hand is shaking, and when Mia shouts, "Damnit!" Nate practically starts crying.

"I just want to know what we're doing," he says softly, and he sounds like a dazed little child.

"Nate, there is no point," Mia says. He looks up at her. "That's the point."

It takes a remarkably long time for understanding to pass across his face. It's like watching ants cross a basketball court, and it takes so long I feel like smashing his face with a basketball. Finally he starts laughing, but it's the kind that sounds like crying.

"You guys suck," he says.

"When did you get here?" Mia asks me.

"We've been here a while," I say.

"Al just gave us a tour of all your crime scenes," Brett says.

"I missed the tour?!" Mia stammers. "What was on it?"

"We saw the brass fixtures, the storm windows," Kelly lists. "I think my favorite part was the brass fixtures."

"Kelly had a very unhappy childhood," I explain to Mia.

"Have you seen Gino?" Mia asks me.

"No, I forgot about him," I say. "Did you say hi?"

"Are you kidding? I never want to talk to him again. Here, follow me, you guys."

We follow Mia around the corner to the ballroom. The lights have dimmed a little, with a greenish light illuminating the dance floor as several couples slow dance to Eric Clapton's "Wonderful Tonight." A crowd of girls in shiny silk dresses gossip loudly in one corner. And beyond them, in the shadows, behind an unused bar, is Gino.

He's just standing there with his hands in his pockets, staring in the dark at the crowd of girls in their formal dresses.

"That's Gino," Mia says, pointing.

Kelly says, "Yuck. He looks scary."

"He called me a skank, once," Mia says.

"You're joking," Nate says.

I shake my head.

"It's true," I say. "He's one or two parking tickets away from becoming a full-blown serial killer."

"Are you messing with us? Look, he's standing next to a mop and bucket," Brett says. "He's just waiting for the dance to end so he can clean up the place."

"No, really, he is that creepy," Mia says to Brett. "He's like in his midthirties and he has *Seventeen* magazine covers taped to the wall in his office, which is actually a tiny little closet."

"I don't believe you," Mark says.

"He used to hit on Mia," I add. "And then when he realized this sixteen-year-old girl wouldn't go for his middle-aged ass, he hated her guts."

"But you're making that up about the *Seventeen* covers, right?" Nate asks.

"Dead serious," Mia says. "The guy's twisted."

Mark and Nate and Kelly and Brett look at each other for a moment, then look at us and say simultaneously:

"Prove it."

We slip back out of the ballroom and try to walk casually until we're safely around the bend. Just as we turn the corner I hear the song "Fire in the Twilight" by Wang Chung start playing in the ballroom. Mia and I start walking faster, and everyone quickens, until eventually we're all sprinting down the hallway with the others following close behind. We cut through the empty kitchen of The Three Ferns (the cooks are smoking cigarettes out by the fire escape), head into the south wing, and backtrack to the rear entrance. Finally we reach the cloffice. There's still a light shining through the crack under the door.

"There's no way he got here before us," I say.

"He could have driven," Mia says.

"We would've heard him screech to a stop."

"Maybe not, go check the door," she says.

I jog over to the door and peek out at the handicapped

spot. It's empty, as is the entire row along the back of the inn.

"The coast's clear," I say, giving a thumbs-up.

Mia grits her teeth, takes a deep breath, and then opens the door to Gino's cloffice. The others gasp. The two Niki Taylor covers are still right where we last saw them, taped up side by side on the far wall.

"That's so gross that a grown man would have that hanging up," Kelly says.

"He really is a serial killer, I bet," Brett says.

"We should get out of here," Mia says. "Before he shows up."

"Wait, let's steal the covers!" Nate says, reaching for them. I grab his arm and pull it back.

"No," I say.

"Why not?" he asks. "The guy's a perv, and you said he hit on Mia last summer. He needs justice."

"Maybe it'll teach him a lesson," Brett suggests.

I look at Mia. She actually looks like she's debating it. I'm surprised at how resolute I feel.

"No," I say again. "Leave them alone."

"But you both said he's a jerk," Nate says. "Why are you defending him all of a sudden?"

"I'm not defending him," I say. "He's still a jerk, but I'm not."

I look over at Mia. She's staring at me, unblinking.

"Yeah," Mia says softly. "Let's just—"

There's a sound of tires screeching to a halt outside the back entrance, and a moment later white light fills up the hallway.

"It's Gino!" Brett shouts.

"Save yourselves!" I holler, and we're all instantly bolting back down the corridor.

Kelly giggles as she runs and I can feel every molecule inside me tingling, and the back entrance opens and I hear Gino shout, "Hey you, stop right now!"

"Don't stop, he'll bury us in his basement," Mark shouts.

"Let's split up," I say, and Nate busts open the stairwell door, and Brett and Mark and Kelly follow him through it. Mia and I are in front. We can hear Gino's footsteps as he charges up the corridor after us, so we make a beeline for the restaurant.

I take the lead, and Mia, holding up her dress as she runs, follows right behind me as we cut back through the empty kitchen and out through the darkened restaurant into the east wing, where we disappear in a crowd of people standing outside the entrance to the ballroom. At this point we look behind us: Gino's nowhere in sight.

"Do you see Brett?" I ask Mia.

She shakes her head.

"I'm sure he's fine. . . . I kinda wish we stole those *Seventeen* magazine covers now," Mia says. "It's so lame he actually chased us."

"Nah, it's enough that he saw the cloffice door open. Knowing that others saw it is embarrassing enough, I bet."

"But he wasn't embarrassed to show us his office this summer, and—wait, did you just say 'cloffice?'"

I nod. "I never said that around you before? It's what I call it—his closet-office . . . cloffice, get it?"

She laughs.

"That's new to me. When did you make it up?"

"During the summer, like the first day of work."

"I can't believe you didn't tell me."

"I didn't mean to keep it a secret."

We lean against the wall where the big banner advertising the semiformal is hanging. It's easier to talk out here—inside the ballroom the music's deafening.

"It's weird to be back at the inn," she says, looking around. "It feels like we worked here ten years ago."

"A lot has happened since then," I say.

Mia nods. It now feels awkward between us, like at the end of our conversation the other day out by the bench. Suddenly she grabs my wrist and squeezes it. "Let's get out of here," she says.

"And go where?" I ask.

"Where do you think?"

The frogs.

"Okay," I say.

"Let me get my jacket and say good-bye to Shauna," she says.

"I'll meet you back out here."

We shake on it.

Mia and I head back inside the darkened ballroom. She briefly touches my shoulder and smiles before heading off for the coat racks in the far corner. I head toward the dessert table. The room has emptied out somewhat by this point. "(Everything I Do) I Do It For You" by Bryan Adams is playing and only a few couples are sort of dancing on the fringe of the dance floor, focusing instead on sucking face and thinking nobody's watching them vigorously fondle each other. Each time the bathroom doors open a shaft of bright light shines into the ballroom and the conjugal dancers glare at the door until it closes again. Out the big windows I see a crowd of underclassmen hanging out by the back entrance to the inn, waiting for rides. Clumps of students stand off in the parking lot in little circles, shielding cigarettes from the ushers, who aren't quite motivated enough to actually walk across the parking lot in order to police them.

The table of desserts has been obliterated for the most part, but there are a handful of green cookies left. I find a napkin, unfold it, and fill it with cookies until closing it up into a makeshift pouch, thinking I could surprise Mia with a little snack while we throw rocks at the frogs. It feels ponderous, and I'm worried the cookies are too heavy for the napkin, but it was the last one. I improvise and stuff the pouch into a used plastic cup. Then I turn around and I'm surprised to find Ryan leaning up against the punch bowl table with his arms crossed. He's not wearing his blazer, just a shirt and loose tie, and I notice how ridiculously V-shaped he is, back to normal, really. He nods at me.

"So you're getting back together with her, huh?" Ryan asks.

"What do you mean?"

"Don't play dumb, I saw you two leave the room almost half an hour ago."

"We were just walking around, we haven't been here since the summer."

"You got me all wrong, Albert," Ryan says. "It's cool, man."

I don't know how to respond to that, so I just say, "Okay," which is what I usually say out loud when I feel uncomfortable. I know a manly high five is impending, so I warn myself not to flinch when it inevitably stings like hell.

"She's a good girl," he continues, staring out at the dance floor.

"She is," I agree.

Are we . . . bonding?

"Things were crazy this fall, and she was there for me," he says. I nod. "But things are different now. I'm doing better, and it's like, now Mia and I finally realize that it's over between us. It took us a while to realize that."

I watch him watch the dancers for almost a minute. One of the freshmen mice is dancing by herself at the edge of the dance floor, curling her finger at Ryan in a desperate attempt to mate him, but he isn't budging. It looks like he's talking with his mouth closed, and frankly it's kinda creepy looking.

"I should probably bolt," I say, stupidly holding up the napkin pouch as an excuse. "You know, the cookies."

"It was a mistake that night," he continues, grimacing at the freshman mouse. She stops dancing abruptly and scurries off. "But what's done is done, and everybody's cool, and anyway I just wanted to say I'm happy if you two get back together, you deserve each other."

We shake hands. He smiles broadly at me.

"Thanks, Ryan, I think that—wait, what are you talking about? What mistake?"

"You know, when Mia and I did it after the Walk," he says quickly.

I feel like I've fallen to my knees, but when I look down it appears I'm still standing. It's a strange sensation, to say the least. I take a step back and have to steady myself against the table.

"What are you talking about?" I ask, barely able to get the words out.

"Wait, she didn't tell you?"

"Mia's a virgin," I whisper.

"Oh, my bad. Yeah man, whatever, forget about it," he says, and turns away from me. I grab his wrist and jerk him back.

"What are you saying?" I ask him again.

"It's all good," he says. "Let go of my wrist, Albert."

"Mia's never done it before," I repeat. "She wouldn't do it with you."

He shakes my hand off, and his eyes beadify.

"Sorry to be the one to tell you this, but she has," he says, shrugging. He claps me on mine. "Don't worry, man, like I said, I'm not into her anymore. It was just an emotional weekend, you know?"

"You're lying," I say, my voice shaking.

A shaft of bright yellow light reverse-eclipses the room, and I look over at the bathroom door. It slowly closes, and Mia's standing there looking at us. Her mouth is open, and she looks . . . crestfallen, and I instantly know that it's true.

"Oh my God," I say softly.

Mia did have sex with The House. She's just standing there looking panic-stricken, and I can tell she knows he just told me, and it kills the one thing that I had over the guy. She'd rejected him, she'd chosen me instead; that's all gone in a millisecond. The House holds his right hand out and casually inspects his ragged nails, and I stumble away from the dessert table, dropping the makeshift pouch of cookies on the dance floor. I stagger out to the lobby, and even though my ski jacket's back inside, I have to get the hell out of here, and I see Brett and Kelly over by the front desk waving at me, but instead of heading over to them I make a beeline for the exit. I push through the glass doors and walk out to the back parking lot.

I run through the aisles of cars and into the line of trees. Branches scratch at my face as I push through to the other side. The snow has completely melted and the field is muddy, and I slip as I run over to the ledge. It occurs to me that the frogs might be gone, hibernating by now or something, and I stop to listen for them, but my ears are filled with white noise. I look back at the inn through the line of trees, and I can see my classmates running around in the rear parking lot like little kids. They're decked out in their dresses and suits, laughing and talking animatedly, but I can't hear a thing; I just see tiny puffs of condensation coming out of their mouths as they shiver in the cold air.

My head is racing with facts and questions and theories. . . . Mia had sex with The House. . . . We weren't dating, technically . . . but we'd just broken up that same weekend! Me ragging on The House at the Walk, telling him that I knew she'd rejected him. . . . Jesus, did I provoke them into doing it . . . ? Who initiated it—Mia or Ryan . . . ? Brett asking me, "If she

still had feelings for you, wouldn't you guys still be together?"
I picture the red rubber ball inside me, and it's tumor-sized . . .
and then I remember the footage of the Walk that Brett
showed me in the AV lab . . . that crazed look on my face, so
angry, out of control . . . Ryan hunched over on the track, the
superjock completely gassed after fewer than two laps . . . and
Mia. She looked so sad and worried, rushing over to his aid,
waving her clipboard. I exhale, and my lungs make a sound
like a death rattle.

I look over the ledge. In the moonlight I can see the little
pond, and the frogs are still there. They're not croaking,
though. They're just sitting there, motionless. I can't even tell
if they're alive or dead. I reach down and feel through the wet
grass and pick up a couple of rocks. I aim one at the nearest
frog and let fly. The rock sails well over the pond and lands
in a thicket. I throw another rock and it lands in the center of
the pond. This makes the frogs dive under the water, except
for one.

"You bastard," I say, and huck the last one at the frog and
miss again, but the ripple the rock creates shakes the frog.
The others stay submerged, and in the moonlight I look for
the flickers on the surface of the water that the tadpoles used
to make in summer, but there aren't any. I bend down and
pick up another stone. This time I throw it at the frog as hard
as I can and miss wildly. I look down at the ground. The
blades of yellowed grass flutter in the light breeze.

There are rocks everywhere.

48

Ten minutes later I hear the sound of branches breaking; I look over at the line of trees just as Mia steps out into the field. She's wearing Mrs. Stackhouse's old coat, her tiny hands stuffed inside the deep pockets, and despite the cold weather it almost feels like an insult that she's wearing it here. She walks over to me, staring at the ground the whole time. We don't say anything for what feels like several minutes, but in reality could be just a few seconds, I can't tell. Then Mia holds out her hand, tentatively.

I just stare at it.

"I wish . . ." She starts, then shudders because she's crying. "I wish it was the summer, Albert."

I wish it was the summer, too.

Before Ryan got cancer.

Before I ruined the Walk.

Before you broke up with me.

Before I spied on you with a telescope.

Before you had sex with him.

I shake my head.

"It'll never be the summer again, Mia."

"Can we pretend it is, just for tonight?" she asks.

I don't say anything at first, too much is going through my head, I'm confused, and it's not until I look up at her when I realize . . .

"Okay," I say. "Hi, Mia."

I try to say it cheerfully, but she frowns at me.

"That's not how you did it when we first met."

"I don't follow."

She raises her right hand, palm out, and stares at me gravely.

"How, Albert," she says.

I raise my hand, too.

"How, Mia."

"Let's play a game," she suggests.

"What do you want to play?"

"You decide," she says, and musters a wan smile. "Entertain me, monkey!"

I hold out my right hand. She places her right hand just above mine. We stand there like that for a while, her hand resting above mine, until she says, "Damnit."

She doesn't pull her hand away. I extend my left hand out and she places hers above mine. From a distance it looks like we're holding hands. After a few seconds I whisper, "Damnit."

Our knees accidentally touch.

"Damnit," she murmurs.

We lean in toward each other and the tips of our noses are less than a millimeter from each other. Her red cheeks are glassy, and I feel like I'm about to fall over.

"Son of a—"

"Shhh," she says, rubbing noses. "The game's over."

And then we kiss.

So here we are again.

Together on the ledge overlooking the frogs.

Just the two of us.

But it's different this time; I realize now that the summer was just the beginning. The real love story is what happens once the honeymoon's over.

Mia all of a sudden gets a serious look on her face, and it throws me into a panic that I'm misreading things completely.

"So wait a sec," she says. "What is this? What are we, Al?"

We look at each other for almost a minute before the answer finally comes to me.

"We're something," I say.